John Shirley was █████████████████████████████████
novels in the past ████████████████████████████████
He has also play████████████████████████████████████
Nation. He lives in ████████████████████████████████

By the same author

Transmaniacon
Dracula in Love
Three-Ring Psychus
City Come A-Walkin'
Cellars
The Brigade
A Song Called Youth
A Splendid Chaos
In Darkness Waiting
Eclipse Penumbra

JOHN SHIRLEY

Heatseeker

Introduced by William Gibson
Compiled and with a Foreword by Stephen P. Brown

GRAFTON BOOKS
A Division of the Collins Publishing Group

LONDON GLASGOW
TORONTO SYDNEY AUCKLAND

Grafton Books
A Division of the Collins Publishing Group
8 Grafton Street, London W1X 3LA

A Grafton UK Paperback Original 1990

ISBN 0-586-20837-2

Printed and bound in Great Britain by
Collins, Glasgow

Set in Times

For my wife,
Kathleen Woods-Shirley

. . . *with all my love*

Contents

* with Bruce Sterling

Acknowledgements

The stories listed below appeared in slightly different form in the following publications:

'What Cindy Saw': *Interzone*, Autumn 1983.
'Under the Generator': UNIVERSE 6, (Terry Carr, ed.) Doubleday, 1976.
'Sleepwalkers': *New Pathways*, Spring 1988, (story written 1976).
'Tahiti in Terms of Squares': *Fantastic*, October 1978.
'Silent Crickets': *Fantastic*, April 1975.
'The Almost Empty Rooms': NEW DIMENSIONS 7, (Robert Silverberg, ed.) Harper & Row, 1977.
'The Gunshot': *Oui*, November 1980.
'Uneasy Chrysalids, Our Memories': EPOCH, (Roger Elwood & Robert Silverberg, ed.) Harper & Row, 1976.
'Quill Tripstickler Eludes a Bride': *The Magazine of Fantasy & Science Fiction*, May 1980.
'What It's Like to Kill a Man': *Stardate*, February 1986.
'Triggering': *Omni*, 1987.
'Six Kinds of Darkness': *High Times*, March 1988.
'The Unfolding': *Interzone*, Spring 1985.
'The Peculiar Happiness of Professor Cort': *New Pathways*, Fall 1988.
'Ticket to Heaven': *The Magazine of Fantasy & Science Fiction*, May 1988.
'Wolves of the Plateau': *Mississippi Review*, 1988.

The following stories appear in print here for the first time:

'I Live in Elizabeth', 'Equilibrium', 'Recurrent Dreams
of Nuclear War Lead B. T. Quizenbaum into Moral
Dissolution'.

All stories appear by permission of the author, who
wishes to express his extreme gratitude to: 'anyone who
had to put up with me while I was writing these stories.'
Also, special thanks to Jeff Conner for his editorial help,
and for titling this collection.

The versions of the stories presented in this volume, and
these versions alone, constitute the author's definitive
text.

Foreword

by Stephen P. Brown

It was late fall, 1970. I had just returned to Portland, Oregon from a four-year sojourn in California. I was lonely and bored, and knew no one in the city. I picked up a local underground newspaper and spotted a tiny ad: 'Society of Strangers meeting, every Wednesday night, 9th Street Exit Cafe.' I was a stranger, it sounded interesting, so the next Wednesday I went down to check it out.

The 9th Street Exit was a small coffeehouse in the basement of a liberal (and very tolerant) church. I wandered down the corridor and poked my head in the door. The room was brightly lit and empty, except for a skinny blond kid, about eighteen or so, wiping down the counter. Maybe I had the wrong place.

'Is this where the Society of Strangers meets?' I asked.

The kid looked up with a manic, electric grin: 'I'm it!'

That was my first meeting with John Shirley, and the beginning of a long, tumultuous, and wholly incredible friendship. I could go on here with stories, like the Salem parties; TERRA; the long ride to Seattle for Clarion; the series of giant crumbling houses we shared in Portland with a peculiar assortment of people; GUTZ: *The Magazine of Disgust*; Dada night at the Exit; the water tower; I can't go on, I'd fill this book. Ask me some time. But, above all, there was the fiction. The endless stream of fiction that poured out of him.

Typically, John's bedroom looked like a neat-freak's hell. There would be clothing, books, records, food, small animals and lost friends randomly intermixed in a layer a foot deep – evenly spread across the floor. But in a corner would be a table with a typewriter, with a perfectly neat pile of manuscript precisely positioned next to it. No matter how chaotic our lives became (and we got pretty chaotic), that growing pile of paper was always there.

As well as I knew him and know him, I never stopped being startled by the wonderfully strange ideas that flowed from his head – to this day. His 1988 novel *A Splendid Chaos* is pure-quill John Shirley, and that book surprised me after eighteen years.

John Shirley is one of the most unique talents I have ever known. His fiction defies description. In the early days, only Ted White had the nerve to publish them, in *Amazing* and *Fantastic*. The times weren't right. Well, the times have caught up with him now, and his fiction is fashionable (in a weird sort of way) and he has sold stories just about everywhere.

You might be familiar with his novels, but they won't prepare you for the short stories. This collection spans a decade and a half, and the book ferments. It is yeasting over with stuff stranger than you ever thought could be imagined.

– Stephen P. Brown

Portland, Oregon
April, 1988

Introduction

by William Gibson

Legend has it that John F. Seitz, Billy Wilder's camera-man, asked during the shooting of *Sunset Boulevard* how he should go about filming the funeral of Norma Desmond's chimpanzee. 'Oh, just your *usual monkey funeral shot*, Johnny,' Wilder replied.

Having been asked to introduce this collection, I have some idea of how Mr Seitz felt. There isn't much that's usual about the short fiction of John Shirley.

Welcome to Shirleyland.

So, before the going gets suddenly and seriously weird – that is, before you skid into the psychic oilslick of Shirley's imagination – let me attempt a shot at . . .

Mr Shirley is thirty-five at the time of this writing, and alternately resembles actor William Hurt and a caricature of William Hurt as drawn by Dr Seuss. When we first met, very nearly a decade ago, he wore a belt around his neck for his performances in Portland punk clubs, where he fronted a genuinely savage outfit known as Sado-Nation.

In the daytime, he wrote science fiction.

Transmaniacon (dedicated to the Blue Oyster Cult, Patti Smith, Leslie Fiedler, and Aleister Crowley) was published in 1979, to be followed by *Dracula In Love* and *Three-Ring Psychus*. Shirley had written the bulk of *Transmaniacon* in 1974, when he was nineteen.

'I heard the word "raw" a lot, when I was shipping it around to publishers,' he told me recently. The book features a classic Shirley protagonist, a man whose job description is Professional Irritant.

Dracula In Love is an amiably twisted psycho-sexual footnote to Bram Stoker, while *Three-Ring Psychus* deals with mass-levitation and anarchist rapture. (The manuscript of an unfinished novel, *The Exploded Heart*, dating from this period, has recently been located and may eventually be completed.)

City Come A-Walkin', with its overt punk stance, its darkly ecstatic imagery of a city-soul stretching muscles of asphalt and steel, was published in 1980. Completing *The Brigade* in Portland, Shirley decamped for New York, more specifically for pre-gentrification Alphabet City, where he wrote *Cellars*, a horror novel. *The Brigade*, ostensibly a mainstream thriller about vigilante terror in a small Oregon town, prefigures *Cellars* in the gross-out ferocity of its conclusion.

Today, the relentless, over-the-top horror-baroque of *Cellars* brings Clive Barker to mind. It reads like Lovecraft on PCP. In 1982, there was nothing quite like it.

Leaving New York for a working sojourn in Paris, Shirley created the *Traveler* series for Dell, writing Traveler novels #1 through #5 as D. B. Drumm, and recorded his *Obsession* album. ('Seams,' a spoken-word cut on *Obsession*, is one of my favorite Shirley stories.) He also absorbed crucial European background for the *Eclipse* trilogy, *A Song Called Youth*, which couples his surreal intensity with a new realism, a global extrapolation of neo-fascist rule in the near future.

In the meantime, he moved again, to Los Angeles.

1988 will see publication of *three* new Shirley novels: *A Splendid Chaos*, *In Darkness Waiting*, and *Eclipse Penumbra*.

It's sometimes argued that the short story is science fiction's optimal form just as it can be argued that the *single* is rock's optimal form. In Shirley's case, it might be said that he initially found it easier to sustain a certain apocalyptic intensity – the characteristic Shirley *rush* – in the shorter length. The haunting 'Tahiti in Terms of Squares' (1978), with its nonlinear suggestions of a new (or perhaps external) order of beings is all rush. 'The Almost Empty Rooms' (1977) closes with a ground-zero vision of Nuke Hour utterly unlike anything you've ever read. In 'Under the Generator' (1976), a power-hungry world reverses entropy to harness the energy of death itself . . .

With *City Come A-Walkin'*, Shirley's novels began to sustain the energy of the short stories. But the short stories kept on kicking – hard. I think of 'Triggering' and 'The Gunshot' as belonging to a second period; New York stories. Perhaps the humorous 'Quill Tripstickler Eludes a Bride' is from that period, and reflects a thoroughly unexpected fondness for the fiction of P. G. Wodehouse.

In the same way, 'What Cindy Saw' and 'The Unfolding' (with Bruce Sterling) seem to me to be transitional stories; they move toward a new balance of idea and intent, the maturity evident in *Eclipse*, 'What It's Like to Kill a Man', 'Wolves of the Plateau', and 'Six Kinds of Darkness'.

Okay, that all sounds very nice, very literary, very much what I was taught to do in the university. And I'll stand by it. But I also have to admit that, in some weird way, I've always thought of Shirley's writing as *music*. I don't think the vocabulary of lit-crit best describes the things John's fiction does best. Sometimes, reading Shirley, I can *hear the guitars*, like there's some monstrous subliminal wall-o'-sound chewing at the edges of the text. This is an effect that fiction *about* rock, to my knowledge, has yet to attain; I think Shirley can hit it because his stories *are* rock, in some primal way. They well up from the same dark sea of backbeat and adrenal frenzy, and it's *that*, whatever that is, that makes them very special.

As you're about to find out.

But you can't have *special*, I mean not really, without having *strange*. But that's okay: enjoy it.

Have some very *strange*.

– William Gibson

Vancouver, B.C.
March, 1988

What Cindy Saw

The people from the clinic were very nice. Of course, they lived on the shell, and people who lived on the shell often behaved nicely, and with uniformity of purpose, like the little magnetically-moved toy players on an electric football game. They seemed very sincere, and they had a number of quirky details making them ever so much more realistic. The way Doctor Gainsborough was always plucking things from the corner of his eye, for example. And the way Nurse Rebeck was forever rubbing her crusty red nose and complaining of allergies.

Doctor Gainsborough admitted, with every appearance of sincerity, that, yes, life was mysterious and ultimately Cindy might well be right about the way things were under what she called 'the shell'. Doctor Gainsborough couldn't be sure that she was wrong – but, Cindy, they said, we have our doubts, serious doubts, and we would like you to consider our doubts, and our reasoning, and give our viewpoint a chance. Doctor Gainsborough had known Cindy would respond to his pretense of politely considering her ideas. Cindy was, after all, fairminded.

And she simply refused to respond at all when people told her she was crazy and seeing things.

Yes, Cindy, Doctor Gainsborough said, you could be right. But still, we have severe doubts, so it's best that we keep up the treatments. All right?

All right, Doctor Gainsborough.

So they'd given her the stelazine and taught her how to make jewelry. And she stopped talking about the shell, after a while. She became the clinic's pet. It was Doctor

Gainsborough himself who took her home, after 'just three months this time, and no shock treatments.' He let her off in front of her parents' house, and she reached in through the car window to shake his hand. She even smiled. He smiled back and crinkled his blue eyes, and she straightened, took her hand back, and stepped onto the curb. He was pulled away down the street; pulled away by the car he drove. She was left with the house. She knew she was turning toward the house. She knew she was walking towards it. She knew she was climbing the steps. But all the time she felt the pull. The pull from the shell was so subtle that you could think: *I know I'm turning and walking and climbing*, when all the time you weren't. You were being pulled through all those motions, so it wasn't you doing it at all.

But best you think it's you.

She had practiced it, that steering amongst the obstacle course of the mind's free associations. She did it now, and she managed to suppress her sense of the pull.

She felt fine. She felt fine because she felt nothing. Nothing much. Just . . . just normal. The house looked like a house, the trees looked like trees. Picture-book house, picture-book trees. The house seemed unusually quiet, though. No one home? And where was Doobie? The dog wasn't tied up out front this time. She'd always been afraid of the Doberman. She was relieved he was gone. Probably gone off with the family.

She opened the door – funny, their not being home and leaving the door unlocked. It wasn't like Dad. Dad was paranoid. He even admitted it. 'I smoke Paranoid Pot,' he said. He and Mom smoked pot and listened to old Jimi Hendrix records and, when they thought Cindy was asleep, screwed listlessly on the sofa.

'Hello? Dad? Mom?' Cindy called, now. No answer.

Good. She felt like being at home alone. Playing a

record, watching TV. Nothing to cope with. No random factors, or scarcely any. And none that weren't harmless. Watching TV was like looking into a kaleidoscope: it was constantly shifting, going through its motions with its own style of intricacy, but there was never anything really unexpected. Or almost never. Once Cindy had turned it on and watched a Japanese monster movie. And the Japanese monster movie had been too much like a caricature of the shell. Like they were mocking her by showing what they knew. What they knew she knew.

Now, she told herself. Think about *now*. She turned from the entry-hall to the archway opening into the living room.

In the living room was something that looked very much like a sofa. If it had been in the rec-room of the clinic she'd have been quite sure it was a sofa. Here, though, it sat corpulent and dusty blue-gray in the twilight of the living room, scrolled arm-rests a little too tightly wound; it sprawled ominously in the very center of the room. There was something unnatural in its texture. It had a graininess she'd never noticed before. Like one of those ugly, irregular scraps of jellyfish at the seashore, a membranous thing whose stickiness has given it a coating of sand.

Even more disorienting was the sofa-thing's ostensibly familiar shape. It was shaped like a sofa. But there was something bloated about it, something tumescent. It was just a shade bulkier than it should have been. As if it were swollen from eating.

So that's their secret, she thought. It's the sofa. Normally I don't notice anything unusual about it – because normally I don't catch it just after it has eaten.

She wondered who it had eaten. One of her sisters? The house was silent. Maybe it had eaten the whole

family. But then Mother had said that they wouldn't be
home when she got there: she remembered now. One of
the nurses had told Doctor Gainsborough. Sometimes the
stelazine made Cindy forget things.

They had gone out to dinner. They wanted to go out to
dinner, probably, one last time before Cindy came home.
It was embarrassing to go out to dinner with Cindy. Cindy
had a way of denouncing things. 'You're always denouncing things, Cindy,' Dad said. 'You ought to mellow out.
You're a pain in the ass when you do that shit.' Cindy
would denounce the waitress, and then maybe the tables,
the tablecloths, the folds in the tablecloth. 'It's the
symmetry in the checker-pattern on the table that reveals
the deception,' she would say earnestly, like a TV com-
mentator talking about terrorism. 'This constant imposi-
tion of symmetrical pattern is an attempt to delude us
into a sense of a harmony with our environment that isn't
there at all.'

'I know you're precocious, Cindy,' her dad would say,
brushing crumbs of French bread from his beard or maybe
tugging on one of his earrings, 'but you're still a pain in
the ass.'

'It could be,' Cindy said aloud to the sofa, 'that you've
eaten one of my sisters. I don't really mind that. But I
must hastily and firmly assure you that you are not going
to eat me.'

Still, she wanted to find out more about the sofa-thing.
Cautiously.

She went to the kitchen, fetched a can opener and a
flashlight, and returned to the living room.

She played the light on the thing that sat on the
polished wooden parquet floor.

The sofa-thing's legs, she saw now, were clearly fused to
the floor: they seemed to be growing out of it. Cindy

nodded to herself. What she was seeing was a kind of blossom. It must have roots far underground.

The sofa-thing quivered self-consciously in the beam of her flashlight.

With the flashlight in her left hand – she could have turned on the overhead light, but she knew she'd need the flashlight for the caverns beneath the shell – she approached the sprawling, blue-gray thing, careful not to get *too* close. In her right hand was the can opener.

All the while, she seemed to hear a backseat driver saying: *This isn't part of the program. You should go upstairs and watch TV and move from moment to moment thinking safely, steering around the obstacles, turning the wheel away from the dangerous clumps of association, pretending you don't know what you know.*

But it was too late. Her stelazine was nearly worn off and the couch had startled her into a wrong turn, and now she was on a side road in a foreign suburb and she didn't know the route back to the familiar highway. And there were no policemen she might ask, no mental cops like Doctor Gainsborough.

So Cindy crept toward the sofa-thing. She decided that the sofa couldn't hurt her unless she sat on it. If you sat on it, it would curl up, enfold you. Venus flytrap.

She knelt by its legs. Sensing her intent, it bucked a little, dust rising from its cushions. It contracted, the cushions humping. It made an awful sound.

She began to work on its legs, where they joined the floor. For thirty-eight minutes she worked busily with the can opener.

The sofa-thing made a series of prolonged, piteous sounds. Her arm ached, but the can opener was surprisingly sharp. Soon she had the cavity under the sofa partly exposed; you could see it under the flap-edge of the shell. Cindy took a deep breath, and prised the flap so it opened wider. It was dark in there. Musky smell; musky and faintly metallic, like lubricant for a motor. And a faint under-scent of rot.

By degrees, working hard, she rolled back the skin of the floor around the sofa. Nature was ingenious; the skin had looked like a hardwood parquet floor till now. It had been hard and solid and appropriately grained. Marvelous camouflage. The skin *was* hard – but not as hard as it looked. You could peel it back like the bark of a tree, if you were patient and didn't mind aching fingers. Cindy didn't mind.

The sofa-thing's keening rose to a crescendo, so loud and shrill Cindy had to move back and clap her hands over her ears.

And then, the sofa folded in on itself. Its sirening folded too, muffled like a scream trying to escape from a hand clamped over a small child's mouth.

The sofa was like a sea anemone closing up; it deflated, shrank, vanished, sucked down into a dark wound in the center of the living-room floor. The house was quiet once more.

Cindy shined the flashlight into the wound. It was damp, oozing, red flecked with yellow. The house's blood didn't gush, it bled in droplets, like perspiration. The thick, vitreous underflesh shuddered and drew back when she prodded it with her can opener.

She tucked the can opener into her boot, and knelt by the wound for a better look. She shined the flashlight into the deepness, into the secret, into the under-shell . . .

The house supposedly had no basement. Nevertheless, beneath the living-room floor was a chamber. It was about the same size as the living room. Its walls were gently concave and slickly wet – but not organic. The wetness was a kind of machine lubrication. In the center of the chamber was a column, the understem of the creature that had masqueraded as her house. The column, she reflected, was actually more of a stalk; a thick stalk made of cables and they wound about one another like the strands in a powerline. The sofa must have been sucked into its natural hiding place, compressed within the stalk.

She wondered why the house hadn't struck till today . . . Why hadn't it got them all while they were sleeping? But probably the undershell people, the programmers, hadn't bred it to be a ravenous, unselective carnivore. It was there for the elimination of *select* people – she realized this must be the explanation for the disappearance of their houseguests. Mom had brought four such people home in the last two years, bedded each one on the sofa, and each of them hadn't been there for breakfast. Awfully curious, awfully coincidental, Cindy had thought, every houseguest deciding to leave before breakfast. Now Cindy knew that they hadn't left the house at all. They'd become part of it. Probably that was what had happened to Doobie – Mom usually wouldn't let him sleep in the house, and never allowed him on the sofa. But her sister Belinda sometimes let Doobie in after Mom had gone to bed; the dog must have snuck onto the sofa for a nap, the sofa's genetically programmed eating hour had come around, and it had done to Doobie what a sea anemone does to a minnow. Enfolded, paralyzed, and digested him.

Cindy didn't mind. She'd always hated Doobie.

She lay face down, peering into the gap in the house's skin. The under-floor was about fourteen feet beneath her. She considered dropping to the sub-world, to explore. Cindy shook her head. Best go for help. Show them what she'd found.

A funny feeling in her stomach warned her to look up.

*   *   *

The living-room archway was gone. It had sealed off. The windows were gone. A sort of scar tissue had grown over them. She had alarmed the creature, cutting into it. So it had trapped her.

Cindy made a small, high *uh!* sound in her throat. She stood, and went to the nearest wall, pressed her hands flat against it. It should have felt like hard plaster, but it depressed under her fingers, taking her handprint like wet clay. Softening. The house would ooze in on her, collapsing on itself like a hill in a mudslide, and it would pulp her and squeeze the juices from her and drink.

She turned to the gash she'd made in the floor. Its edges were curling up like paper becoming ash. But it was closing, too. She got a good grip on the flashlight, knelt, and wriggled through the opening, dropping to the floor below. The impact stung the balls of her feet.

Cindy straightened, breathing hard, and looked around.

Tunnels opened from the chamber on both sides, stretching as far as she could see. She stepped into the right-hand tunnel. The ceiling was just two feet overhead; it was curved and smooth. She walked slowly, feeling her way with one hand, shining her flashlight beam at the floor. The darkness was rich with implications, and Cindy felt her nerve falter. She had a vice-squeezing sensation at her temples, and a kind of greasy electricity in her tongue. She tried to picture the flashlight's beam as a raygun's laser, straight and brightly furious, burning the darkness away – but the light was weak, and set only a small patch of the darkness afire. Gradually, though, her eyes adjusted, and the darkness seemed less dense, less oppressively pregnant, the flashlight beam no longer important. At intervals the oblong of light picked out what looked like transparent fishing lines passing from floor to ceiling. The plastic wires came in irregularly spaced sheaves of eight or nine. Sometimes there was hardly room to squeeze between them. Then, she'd sidle through, twisting this way and that. When she brushed a wire, it would resonate like a guitar string, but with an overtone to its hum that was like the call of a desert insect. She sensed, somehow, that the wires had to do with events in the upper world. *They certainly weren't installed by the utility company*, she said to herself.

She came to a place where the wall was transparent, a clear patch big as her two hands put together. It was a little cloudy, but Cindy could see through it into another chamber; two men sat in there at a metal table. They were playing cards, the little white rectangles in their hands marked with mazes and mandalas instead of the usual kings and queens and jacks and spades. Each man was hunched over his hand, deep in concentration. One sat with his back to her. He was the smaller man; he had gray hair. The other was a round-faced man: stocky, a little overweight, his brown beard streaked with white. The bigger man wore a rumpled jacket and trousers of a contemporary cut; the other wore a threadbare suit many decades outdated. The room looked like a jail cell. There were two bunks, a toilet, trays of half-eaten food, empty beer cans lying under the table. 'It's your bid, Mister Fort,' said the bearded man, with humorous formality. 'Right you are, Mister Dick,' said the other man lightly. He slapped a card face-up on the table and said, 'M. C. Escher against Aztec Maze.' The other man sighed. 'Ah, you've locked again. You win. It's not fair: you had decades to practice, playing against Bierce . . . Dammit I wish they'd let us smoke . . .'

Cindy banged on the glass, and shouted, but she couldn't make them hear her. Or perhaps they pretended not to. She shrugged, and went on.

Another ten strides further, something glimmered on

the left, reflecting her flashlight's beam. It was a long, vertical, rectangular mirror, set flush into the wall. The mirror distorted Cindy's reflection, making her seem ludicrously elongated. She reached out to touch it, and accidentally brushed one of the wires; the transparent wire thrummed and her image in the mirror shimmered, vibrating in and out of visibility in a frequency sympathetic to the wire's quivering. She struck the wire again, harder, to see what it would do to the image in the mirror. Her reflection fluttered and vanished, and in its place was a flickering image of the upper world. A mundane street scene, children walking home from school, cars honking impatiently behind a slow-moving VW Rabbit driven by an elderly lady . . .

On a hunch, a hunch that became an impulse, Cindy struck the tunnel wires repeatedly, as hard as she could.

The mirror – really a kind of TV monitor – showed the traffic careening out of control, the VW Rabbit backing up at great speed, ploughing into the others, the children losing control of their limbs and flapping haphazardly at one another.

Cindy tittered.

She took the can opener from her boot and slashed at the wires, watching the 'mirror' all the while. The strings parted with a protesting *whang*. And in the upper world: children exploded, cars began to wrap around one another, suddenly becoming soft and pliable, tying themselves round telephone poles . . . a great invisible current swept the street, washing the buildings away . . .

Cindy smiled and went her way down the tunnel, randomly snipping wires.

Every few hundred yards she came to an intersection of tunnels; three opening to the right, three to the left, her own continuing on ahead. Sometimes Cindy changed direction at these subworld crossroads, following her intuition, vaguely aware that she had a specific destination.

At length the tunnel opened out into a circular room in the center of which was another thick, red-yellow stalk; a corded, man-thick stalk, grown up to merge with the ceiling. But here, the walls swarmed with what looked like oversized aphids. Mechanical aphids, each big as her hand, and the color of a blue-metal razor blade. They clung to the walls in groups of twenty or thirty, only a hand's width between each group; the aphids crawled methodically on small metal legs thin and numerous as the bristles of a hairbrush; on the right-hand wall they swarmed between banks of TV monitors. She switched off her flashlight; there was enough light from the TV screens. Standing at the monitors, spaced more or less evenly, were a score of dusty blue fellows, vaguely human, wearing jumpsuits of newspaper. Looking closer, Cindy could see that the newspaper print was in some kind of inscrutable cipher, quite unreadable. And the newsphotos showed only half-recognizable silhouettes.

For the first time, real uneasiness shivered up in her, and bits and pieces of fear, like irregular hailstones, rattled down through the chill focal-heart of her sensations.

Fear because: the men at the monitors were entirely without mouths, without noses, without ears. Each had only large, blinking, watery-gray eyes. And fear because: with Cindy's arrival in the room, the aphids, if that's what they were, began to move feverishly – but somehow purposefully – in mandala patterns over the walls, rustling through a thick coating of shag-rug cilia: the cilia, she saw now, covered the walls everywhere. It was the color of a throat with a bad cold.

The mouthless men used three-fingered hands to

manipulate knobs on the frames of the TV monitors. Now and then one of them reached up and brushed an aphid; something in the touch galvanized the creature so that it scurried furiously up the wall, parting the cilia and altering the symmetrical patterns made by the collective motion of the other aphids.

The TV pictures were black-and-white. The floor was alabaster, patterned with inset silver wires; the wires were arcanely configured, and occasionally sparked at the touch of the metal shod feet of the almost-people.

Cindy had decided to call them almost-people.

Her eyes adjusted to the dim light, and she saw that in the small of each almost-person's back was an umbilicus. The long, attenuated black umbilicus drooped, then rose to attach to the base of the thick red-yellow stalk in the center of the chamber, much as a May Day reveller's ribbon attaches to a maypole. Cindy supposed that the umbilici made mouths and noses unnecessary for the almost-people.

Cindy was afraid, but that always put her on the offensive. *Take control*, she told herself.

So just to see what would happen, she went about the room and – with her can opener – methodically clipped the umbilici severing the almost-people from the stalk.

The almost-people stopped what they were doing; they turned and looked at her.

Cindy wondered how they felt. Were they alarmed or surprised or outraged or hurt? She couldn't tell.

One by one they fell, clutching their spindly throats. They writhed and twitched, making the wire-patterns on the floor spit blue sparks, and Cindy supposed that they were choking to death.

She felt a little sorry this time. She even said so. 'Oh, I'm sorry.'

After a few minutes, they stopped moving. Their big

eyes shut. Breathing shakily, Cindy stepped over the corpses and went to one of the TV screens. She was careful not to step on the silver wires in the floor; she was sure she'd be electrocuted if she did.

The TV screens monitored life on the upper world. Reticulating charcoal-and-chalk video images of houses and motels and traffic and dogs. Junkyards. Traffic lights changing. Farms. Seaside resorts. Canadian hikers. Rock singers. A teenage boy with stringy blond hair and a thin chest shakily trying to fill a syringe from a rusty spoon. Jazz players. Masturbating children. Masturbating men and women. Masturbating monkeys. She gazed for a while at a TV showing two people copulating in a hotel room. They were both middle-aged and rather doughy. The man's hair was thinning, and his paunch waggled with his hip-motions; the woman's hair was as defined and permanent in shape as a hat. A bell-shaped hat.

Impulsively, Cindy reached out and twiddled the monitor's unmarked black-plastic knobs. The picture shimmered, changed: the woman's head warped, bent out of shape, reified – it had become the head of a chimpanzee. The man screamed and disengaged and backed away. The woman clawed at herself.

Cindy made a moue with her lips, and tilted her head.

She reached up and prodded a number of the metallic aphids with her can opener. They scurried, frightened at the unfamiliar touch, and set the others to scurrying more frantically, till the thousands of aphids clinging to the rounded ceiling were reshaping in the cilia in swarming hysteria, their symmetry of pattern obliterated.

Cindy looked at the TV monitors. Now they showed only crowd scenes. People at football games, looking confused and distressed, as if they'd all gone blind and deaf; they staggered into one another, arms flailing, or

tripped, went tumbling down the grandstands, upsetting
other people – but, as Cindy watched, the people began
to move cohesively down toward the playing field. They
streamed onto the field, crowding it, and began to arrange
themselves according to the dictates of a spontaneously
reconceived psychic schema: people wearing white or
yellow shirts moved together, people with dark shirts
congregated, till the bird's eye view of the stadium
showed the crowd spelling out words with their re-
ordered color scheme. They spelled out:

ZEITGEIST

and then

LOVE TIMES DEATH EQUALS ACTION

and then

LACEWORK REBELLION

Cindy turned away. She approached the stalk in the
center of the room. With the can opener stuck in her
teeth, she began to climb. The going was slippery, but
she was determined, and soon reached the ceiling. Arms
and legs aching, she clung there and, with one hand,
began to carve an opening.

The skin parted more easily from the underside. Ten
minutes of painful toil and the gap was wide enough to
climb through. Cindy dropped the can opener and
wormed her way upward, through the wound in the
ceiling.

She broke through a second layer, gnawing with her
teeth, coming up through the skin of another seeming-
floor.

She found herself under what looked like an ordinary

four-legged wooden table. Around her were four empty
wooden chairs, and a white floor-length tablecloth.

She dragged herself out of the wet, shuddering slit, and
onto the floor. Gasping, she pressed aside the tablecloth,
which had so far concealed her from those outside, and
crawled into the upper world, once more atop the shell.

She was in a restaurant. Mom and Dad and Belinda and
Barbara sat at the next table.

They stared at her, open-mouthed. 'What the hell have
you got all over you, Cindy?' her father asked. The girls
looked a little sick.

Cindy was coated with the wetness, the stickiness, the
halfblood death essence of underplace things.

Still breathing hard, her head pounding, Cindy reached
down and lifted the tablecloth aside, revealing the ragged,
oozing wound she'd crawled out of. This time, her family
saw it too.

Her father got up from the table rather convulsively, so
that he nearly upset it, and his wine glass splashed his
wife's dress. He turned away and, fumbling for his pot-
pouch, staggered toward the exit. Her sisters had covered
their eyes. They sobbed. Her mother was staring at her.
Mom's face was changing; the eyes growing bigger, the
lips vanishing, her skin going dusty-blue. So, then. Her
mother was the one they'd planted in the family. 'They're
not under every house,' Cindy tried to explain to her
sisters. 'They aren't always there to find. You might dig
under *our* house and not find it – you have to know *how*
to look. Not *where* to look. They keep us blinded with
false symmetries.'

Her sisters followed their father outdoors.

Cindy turned away. 'Fuck them all, then,' she said. She
felt her mother's subworld eyes on her back as she fell to

her knees and crawled back under the table. She slid feet-first into the wound, and dropped into the room below. She searched through the monitors, and found a screen showing her dad and her sisters getting into the car. She turned the knobs, and laughed, seeing the car rising into the sky like a helium balloon with the string cut, turning end over end, Belinda spilling out of it and falling, her father screaming as the car deliquesced, becoming a huge drop of mercury that hung in the air and then burst into a thousand glittering droplets, falling to spatter the parking lot with argent toxicity.

Under the Generator

Looking into the eyes of the woman who sat across from him in the crowded cafeteria, he was reminded of the eyes of another woman entirely. Perhaps there were secret mirrors hidden in the faces of the two women. The other woman, Alice, had said: *I just can't continue with you if you insist on keeping that damn job. I'm sorry, Ronnie, but I just can't.*

He reflected, looking into the eyes of the second woman, that he could have quit the job for Alice. But he hadn't. Maybe he hadn't actually wanted her. And he had gone easily from Alice to Donna. He resolved not to lose Donna too because of his work with the generators.

'I used to be an actor,' Denton said. Swirling coffee in his cup, he shifted uncomfortably in the cafeteria seat and wondered if the plastic of the cup would melt slightly into the coffee . . . Working at the hospital, drinking coffee every morning and noon out of the same sort of cups, he had visions of the plastic slowly coating the interior of his stomach with white brittle.

'What happened to acting and how far'd you get?' Donna Farber asked, with her way of cramming as much inquiry as she could into one line.

Denton frowned, his wide mouth making an elaborate squiggle across his broad, pale face. His expressions were always slightly exaggerated, as if he were not yet used to the part of Ronald Denton.

'I was working off-Broadway, and I had a good part in a play I wrote myself. An actor can always play the part better if he wrote it. The play was called *All Men Are Created Sequels*. Tigner produced it.'

'Never heard of it.'

'Naturally it fell flat after I pulled out.'

'Naturally.' Her silver-flecked blue eyes laughed.

'Anyway, I felt that acting was stealing too much of my identity. Or something. Actually, I'm not sure just why I quit. Maybe it was really fear of failing.'

His unexpected candor brought her eyes to his. He remembered Alice and wondered how to discover just how Donna felt about his job, if she felt anything at all.

But the subject was primed by his black uniform. 'Why did you quit acting to work in the generators?'

'I don't know. It was available and it had good hours. Four hours a day, four days a week, twenty-two dollars an hour.'

'Yeah . . . but it must be depressing to work there. I mean, you probably still haven't been able to give up acting. You have to act like there's nothing wrong in front of people who are going to die soon.' There was no indictment in her tone. Her head tilted sympathetically.

Denton just nodded as if he found sorrowful virtue in being the scapegoat. 'Somebody has to do it,' he said. Actually, he was elated. He had been trying to interest Donna for a week. He looked at her frankly, admiring her slender hands wrapped around her coffee cup, the soft cone of her lips blowing to cool the coffee, close flaxen hair cut into a bowl behind her ears.

'I don't entirely understand,' she said, looking for a divination in her coffee, 'why they didn't get retired nurses, or other people used to death.'

'For one thing, you need a little electronic background to keep watch on the generators. That's what got me the job. I studied electronics before I was an actor.'

'That's a strange contrast. Electronics and acting.'

'Anyway, not even experienced nurses are used to sitting there *watching* people die for four hours at a time. They usually leave them alone, except when administering – '

'But I thought you said all you had to do was sit and check the readouts every so often. You mean you have to watch?'

'Well . . . you can't help it. You sit right across from the patient. Since you're there, you look. I'm aware of them, anyhow, because I have to make sure they aren't dying too fast for the machine to scoop.'

She was silent, looking around the busy lunchroom as if seeking support from the milling, wooden-faced hospital employees. She seemed to be listening for a tempo in the clashing of dishes and the trapped rumble of conversations.

Denton was afraid that he had offended her, given her the impression that he was a vulture. He hoped she wasn't looking around for someone else to talk to . . .

'I don't like it in here,' she said.

'Let's go outside then,' Denton said, a trifle too eagerly.

They discarded their trays in the recycling chute and walked to the elevator, rode to the ground floor of the huge hospital, and emerged into the pastel curves of the hospital lobby. They walked between artificial potted palms and waiting people, artificial expressions concealing worry. They went out the sussurating frontdoors, leaving the odor of disinfectant for June sunlight and the warm breathing of air-cars.

'Air-cars are so quiet,' she said. 'All the noise of traffic used to scare me when I was little.' They talked quietly of cars and the city and their jobs until they came to the park.

Sitting under a tree, plucking absently at the grass, they were silent for a while, feeling the ambience of the park.

Until! without provocation Donna began: 'My parents died five years ago and – ' Then she stopped and looked at him sideways. She shook her head.

'Were you going to say something else?'

She shook her head again, too quickly. He wanted to ask if they had put generators over her parents before they'd died; but he decided that the question might put him in a bad light.

They sat in the park and watched bicyclers and children sift through the plasphalt paths. After a while a slush vendor rolled a sticky white cart past, and Denton got up to buy two drinks. He was just returning from the vendor, about thirty feet from where Donna waited under the tree, when someone put a hand on his right arm.

'Can I talk to you?' Almost a whisper. 'Just for a minute?' It was a boy, perhaps sixteen, but at least three inches taller than Denton. The boy was opening and closing his mouth pensively, questions anxious to spring from his lips. He was dressed in a denim body suit. His hands were thrust deep into his side-pockets, as if leashed. Denton nodded, glancing at the slushes, afraid that they would melt on his hands. Probably the kid was proselytizing for one of the Satanic cults.

'You're a generator guy, aren't you? A compensator.'

Denton nodded dumbly again.

'My father's under a generator; he's dying. And he ain't really old yet. He's still . . . needed.' He paused to steady himself. 'Can you . . . maybe you could help him, turn off the machine for a while?' It was obvious that the boy wasn't used to asking favors. He resented having to ask Denton for anything.

Denton wished that he hadn't worn his uniform out of the hospital.

'I can't do anything for your father. I'm not a doctor. And there are dozens of generators in use at the hospital now. I've probably never seen your old man. Anyway, it isn't true that the generators steal strength from patients. That's an old wives' tale. It wouldn't do your father one bit of good if I turned it off. Sorry – ' He began to walk toward Donna.

'What's your name?' the boy asked from behind, all respect gone from his tone. Denton could feel the boy's eyes on his back. He turned half around, miffed.

'Denton,' he replied, immediately wishing that he had given a false name. He turned his back on the boy and walked back to Donna. He could feel an icy trail of slush melting over his hand.

'What did that kid want?' Donna asked, sipping her slush.

'Nothing. Directions to . . . the auditorium. He said he was going to the Satanist/Jeezus Freak title fight.'

'Really? He didn't look to be armed.' She shrugged.

The boy was watching them.

Some of the slush had spilled onto Denton's leg. Donna wiped at the red stain on his black uniform with a white handkerchief.

He didn't want to think of work now. He had a date to take her to the Media Stew tonight. The first relationship since Alice.

But it might be better to keep his mind on work. If he thought about her too much he would be nervous and contrived when he was with her. Maybe blow it. He tightened the belt around his one-piece jet uniform and went quietly into the arbiter's office. The arbiter of compensators was short, impatient, and a compulsive caviler. Mr Buxter smiled as Denton bent over the worksheet titled WEEK OF JUNE 19 THROUGH 26, 1996.

'What's your hurry, Denton? You young cats are always in a hurry. You'll be assigned soon enough. You might find it *too* soon. I haven't written you into the chart yet.'

'Leave me on Mr Hurzbau's generator, sir, if you would. I get along well with Hurzbau.'

'What is this "get along" junk? We bend the rule a little that says no fraternizing with the patients under the generators . . . but *familiarity* is strictly verboten. You'll go nuts if you – '

Not wanting to become embroiled in another of Buxter's lectures, Denton quickly capitulated. 'I'm sorry, sir. I didn't mean to imply we knew each other well. What I meant was, Hurzbau doesn't worry me much, or talk to me past the usual amenities. Could I have my assignment now? I don't want the unwatched generator to overload.'

'Somebody's watching the generator all the time, naturally. It can't overload. You should cultivate patience. Especially with *your* job.' Buxter shrugged his wide shoulders and put a thick hand on his paunch. He regarded the chart, yawned, scratched his bushy black mustache, and began to fill his pipe.

Denton, still standing, shifted uncomfortably. He wanted to get his shift over with.

Buxter lit his pipe and blew gray smoke at Denton.

'Durghemmer today,' Buxter said.

Denton frowned. Durghemmer the leech.

'Durghemmer . . .' Denton spoke the name into the air so that it would permanently leave his lips. 'No. No, really, Buxter, I – '

'Another weakling. I can never find anybody willing to take care of Durghemmer's generator, but I'll be damned if I'll end up doing it myself. So, Denton – '

'I can't. Really. I have a date tonight. Very delicate psychological balance involved. Durghemmer would ruin me.' Denton looked with all his actor's pathos into his supervisor's eyes. Buxter stared at his hands, then relit his pipe.

'Okay. This time I let you off,' he said. 'Take Hurzbau. But don't talk to him unless it's absolutely necessary. I'm not supposed to, but I'll put Durghemmer's generator on automatic for tonight. It's dangerous but what the hell. But – everybody's got to rotate sooner or later, Ron.'

'Sure,' said Denton, relieved. 'Later.' He took his time-card from the rack on Buxter's office wall.

Denton read the meters punctiliously, thinking that this particular generator provided power for at least thirty thousand people. Amplitude was climbing. Poor Hurz-bau. But thoughts like those, he told himself, were precisely the sort he didn't want. *Good luck* to Hurzbau.

Denton adjusted the scoop over the bed. The scoop of the generator was a transparent bell enclosing Hurzbau's bed. It was made of nonconductive fiberglass, veined with wiring which converged in a cable at its peak and twined like a thick corded vine through branches of metal supports into an opening in the cylindrical crystal at the generator's flat top.

The rectangular generator transformer was opened in a honeycomb of metallic hexagons on the side facing the bed. On the other side Denton sat in his swivel chair, in his black uniform, in his controlled aplomb, behind his desk of dials and meters. Denton was officially the Compensator, adjusting the rise and fall of energy absorbed by the generator so that a steady, predictable flow went out to the electrical transmitters. It'd all be done by computer, if it weren't for the unions.

Having checked the meters, Denton tried to relax for a while. He looked abstractedly around the room. The chamber was small, all white, with only the few paintings which Hurzbau's relatives had hung to cheer him up. The paintings were of pastoral scenes from places mostly now entombed in plasphalt.

Denton wondered why anyone had bothered with paintings. Hurzbau couldn't see them except as blurs through the plastic scoop. Nothing extraneous to the function of the generator was allowed under the scoop. Not even bedclothes. Hurzbau's naked, cancer-eaten body was kept warm by self-adjusting sun lamps.

Half of Hurzbau's face was eaten away by cancer. He had once been overweight. He had gone from 220 pounds to 130 in four months. The right half of his face was sunken in to a thin mask of skin clinging to the skull, and his right eye was gone, the socket stuffed with cotton. He could talk only with difficulty. His right arm was withered and unusable, though his left was strong enough to prop him up on his elbow.

'Compensator . . .' he rasped, barely audible through the plastic. Denton switched on the intercom.

'What can I do for you, sir?' he asked, a trifle brusquely. 'Would you like me to call the nurse? I can't give out medical aid personally . . .'

'No. No nurse. Denton? That your name?'

'Yes. Ronald Denton. I told you yesterday, I believe. How are – ' He'd almost forgotten, but he caught himself in time. He *knew* how Hurzbau was: in constant pain with six weeks to live, optimum. 'Do you want to take some metrazine? That I can get.'

'No. You know what, Denton?' His voice was a raven's croak.

'Look, I've been told I'm overfraternizing with the patients. That's not really my job. We have a capable staff psychiatrist and a priest and – '

'Who says you're not a priest, Denton? The other compensators don't talk to me at all. You're the only one who says a damn thing to me . . .' Hurzbau swallowed, his desiccated features momentarily contorting so that the left half of his face matched the malformation of the right. 'You know, Denton, I could have gotten the cancer vaccine but I thought I'd never need it. Not *me*.' He made some sandpapery noises which might have been laughter. 'And it's a sure thing if you get the cancer vaccine you *can't* get cancer, and I turned down a sure thing. Too much bother.'

Denton suddenly felt cold toward the dying man. He recoiled inwardly, as if Hurzbau were a deformed siren trying to lure him under the scoop. It was true in a way: Hurzbau wanted sympathy. And sympathy would mean that Denton would have to imagine himself in Hurzbau's place. He had to cut it off, even if it was at Hurzbau's expense.

But he was deterred by a look in the old man's eyes: a red light from the burning, blackened wick of Hurzbau's nerve endings.

'Denton, tell me something . . .' An almost visible wave of pain swept over Hurzbau's shrunken body; the parchment-thin skin of his face twisted as if it were about to rip. 'Denton, I want to know. The generators, do they make me weaker? I know they . . . take energy . . . from my dying . . . Do they . . . feed off me? Do they make me die so that – '

'*No!*' Denton was surprised at his own stridency. 'No, you've got it turned around. It takes energies emitted because of your dying, but it doesn't come directly from *you*.'

'Could you – ' Hurzbau began, but he fell back on the bed, unable to keep himself propped up any longer. Drawn by impulse, Denton got out of the control seat and walked around to the end of the bed. He looked down into the fading man's eyes, judging the advance of histolysis by the growth of an almost visible smoldering glow of pain. Hurzbau's mouth worked silently, furiously, finally, tugging at the intravenous feeding-tube imbedded in his left arm, he managed: 'Denton . . . could you fix the generator if it broke down?'

'No. I don't know how it works exactly. I just compensate for metrical oscillation – '

'Uh-huh. Then can you really say that it doesn't take away from my life if you don't know for sure how it works? You know what they *tell* you. But how do you know it's the truth?'

Hurzbau began to choke, spitting up yellow fluid. A moisture detector at the bedside prompted a plastic arm to stretch from the table of automatic instruments left of Hurzbau's head. The arm swabbed the pillow and Hurzbau's lips with a sponge. The light flared faintly in the dying man's eyes and with his good arm he swiped angrily at the mechanical swab.

'Damn, damn,' he muttered, 'I'm not a pool ball.' The plastic strut fled back to its clamp.

Denton turned away, deliberately breaking the minor rapport developing between the two of them. But doubts insinuated through his starched black uniform. *No.* The principle behind the generators was taught in high school, and there were classes on the inner construction of the machines in vocational schools. There would be no way for the arbiters to hide anything from anyone . . . There was no secret. But he understood how Hurzbau felt. Even from his vantage point, perpetually on the bed, Hurzbau could see the two red LEDs, side by side like mocking eyes, their readouts climbing visibly whenever he got weaker. Pretty inhumane.

He got weaker, the machine got stronger.

'Maybe it's something they're keeping under wraps, Denton,' Hurzbau ventured suddenly. He spasmed then,

rising almost to a sitting position, every muscle strained
so that his skin was elasticized vitreously taut, his withered frame mottled red. From between gritted teeth came
Hurzbau's whisper, slightly metallic through the intercom: 'How is there *room* for this much pain in this little
body? There's enough to fill a warehouse. How does it all
fit?' Denton turned off the intercom.

He rang for the nurse. The old man fell back, relaxing.
Without wanting to, Denton glanced at the needle on the
generator. It was climbing. He could hear the scoop
humming. He ran around to the control panel and dialed
to compensate for the upsurge in entropic energy. When
the machine took in a great deal of energy at one time, it
reacted with a high-frequency oscillating tone, very much
like shrill laughter.

The generator chuckled, the old man grew weaker, the
LEDs jumped higher. Hurzbau's body began to jerk and
with each erratic rictus Denton's stomach contracted with
revulsion. He had thought he was used to the onset of
death.

Denton tightened the arm draped about Donna's creamy
shoulders. She was asleep, or pretended to be. He
remembered Donna's long boyish body like a graceful jet
of water, thrashing with his. She'd responded only to the
lightest touches. Visions of Donna alternated with memories of Hurzbau. Denton sat abruptly up to light a
cigarette, throwing a tobacco smokescreen between himself and his memory of the dying man.

He glanced down at Donna, saw her looking at him out
of slitted eyes. She smiled hastily and looked away.

'What time is it?' she asked, her voice weary.

'One A.M.'

'What was your play about, anyway?'

'Do you want to read it? I have a copy – '

'No.' Then she added, 'I'm *interested,* but I don't like to read much these days. Textbooks ruined my appetite. I like live plays better. Why don't you perform it for me?'

He raised a hand melodramatically over her head and with a visionary look that made her laugh, he quoth:

'We have come to bury Caesar, not to praise him . . .'

'Oh, I see. That's from your play?'

'Well, it's one I wrote a few centuries ago – '

'SHUT UP IN THERE I GOTTA GET SOME SLEEP! YOU ALREADY MADE ENOUGH NOISE GRUNTIN' TO KEEP THE WHOLE BUILDING AWAKE TILL DECEMBER!' The guy in the next apartment.

'The walls are thin,' Denton whispered apologetically. But Donna was crying. She was sitting up, taller than Denton by half a head, rocking back and forth. He touched her arm but she pushed away and got out of bed.

'Listen,' Denton said frantically, 'I'm sorry about that creep next door. Let's go somewhere – '

'No, it's okay. I'm going home. I had a good time and all that, you're a good lover, only . . .'

'Only *what?*'

She had her suit on already, she was putting on her shoes. He wondered what he had done. Better stop her before she gets dressed or she'll feel obligated to leave once she's gone that far.

'What is it?' he asked. 'What did I do wrong?'

'Nothing. I just don't know why I came here, really. I don't need anyone to tell me I'm human. It's not good to get attached, anyway.' She was heading toward the door.

'SHUT UP IN THERE ALREADY!' the man next door shouted.

'GO TO HELL!' Denton shouted back. He pulled on one of his uniforms. She went out the door, leaving him alone with the soft rumble of the city night. 'Damn!' Denton said aloud, fumbling at buttons.

Suddenly, apartments on three sides erupted, combining to grind the quiet evening into fine dust.

'ALL OF YOU CUT IT OUT!'

'I'LL BURN THIS HOLE TO THE GROUND IF YOU –'

'I'M GONNA CALL THE PIGS!'

Donna was stepping into the elevator just as Denton closed the door to his apartment behind him. He ran to the stairs and jogged down three flights, his footsteps echoing in the deserted concrete stairwell like the laughter of the generator.

He ran into the empty street. The night was warm and humid. He spotted Donna halfway down the block to his left. He ran after her, feeling foolish, but shouting, 'Hey, wait! It's not that easy!'

She passed a black alleyway, turned the corner. He scuffled across the mouth of the alley, saw her disappear around the corner –

– something kicked his legs out from under him. He threw up his arms, felt the concrete edge of the curb crack an elbow, romancandling his arm; cheek striking the gutter grate: pain with snapping wires, cracking bullwhips. A hand pulled him roughly onto his back and he was looking at the twisted face of a teenage boy, ugly from hatred. Someone else jerked Denton to his feet. His right eye was swelling and it hurt to squint, but he saw that there were four hoods in all, each wearing transparent plastic jackets over bare, muscular chests bristling with dark hairs. In sharp contrast, their faces and heads were shaved hairless. Their eyes burned with amphetamines. The drug made their movements slightly spastic, like children flinching from expected blows.

Two of them held Denton's arms from behind. A third

stepped in close with a knife. All four were strangely
silent, almost pious. Denton saw the knife gleaming near
his throat. He was paralyzed, numbed by what should
have been unreality. He was watching viddy, he thought
desperately. A commercial would come on in a moment.
But one of the boys pulled Denton's head back by his
hair with a violent twist that sent spotlights of pain into
the growing darkness in his skull. The darkness congealed
into abject fear. He was without volition. He remembered
Donna. Had she deliberately brought him here to meet
these men? Had she set him up? What would they do
with the knife?

One of the boys flicked fingers to unbutton Denton's
shirt. He parted the folds of the black uniform slowly,
almost formally, as if he were undressing a lover. The
night was warm but he felt the air in his open shirt cold
as a knife blade. If he shouted for help they would
probably kill him right away. The streetlight overhead
hurt his eyes; his arms were cramping behind him. He
tried to change position and was kneejabbed in the small
of his back. He looked around for Donna as the knife cut
open his undershirt (a very sharp knife, he noted; the
fabric parted easily, as if it had been unzipped). Then he
felt the knife on his navel, pain like a tiny point of intense
light flaring up, and a trickle of warm blood. He closed
his eyes and bit his lips against the sting near his navel.
The pain made him open them again.

The boy with the knife closed his eyes as if in anticipation of a deep satisfaction.

A blur of movement –

Then the boy with the knife screamed, his head
snapped back, his mouth gaping, his back arched; he
went rigid, yelling, 'Damn! Who – '

He fell and Donna jumped easily aside and turned to
face another. And knocked him flat. Denton felt the grip

on his neck relax as the boy behind him ran to back up his companions. Donna shot her booted foot, heel first, straight up and out, catching the third tough in the throat. She was tall and her long legs helped her as the other two tried to get in close with their knives. The first two were on the ground; the boy who'd threatened Denton with the knife lay with his eyes wide open, unblinking, staring upward. He was perfectly still. The other was on his hands and knees, coughing blood onto his buddy, one hand on his crushed windpipe, his face staring and fascinated, as if he were tasting real pain for the first time, exploring it as a new world.

Stopping another with a shoe-point in the groin, Donna spun and, without wasting momentum, came forward onto the foot and transferred the motion to her arm, striking the knife from his hand. The knife rang on the concrete, rolling in front of the boy with the crushed throat.

Denton was breathing in huge gulps, still unable to act: he was sure that he would only run up against a television screen if he tried to intervene. But without a weapon, the last tough turned and fled into an alley.

The other boy was still clutching his groin, rocking back and forth on his haunches, moaning, his face draining. Donna regarded him for a moment, then said in a low, calm voice:

'I suppose I should try to undo what I've done now. I've got some first-aid stuff in my purse. If I can find it . . .' Kneeling, she looked with a strange tranquility at the place between his legs where she'd kicked him.

Denton took a long breath, relaxing from his paralysis, an actor between scenes.

He put a hand on Donna's shoulder, felt her stiffen beneath his touch. He put his hand in his pocket, asking, 'Where did you go when they jumped me?'

'I hid in a doorwell. I thought they were after me. When I saw them surround you I went around to the other side of the alley and came through it, and up behind them.'

She turned from him to face the boy. '*Why?*' she asked.

Through grated teeth the boy answered, 'Hurzbau . . .'

The name made Denton realize where he had seen the leader of the gang before: in the park, the boy who had asked about his father under the generator. He stepped toward the other tough, demanding, 'Hurzbau *what?*'

'Hurzbau's father's in the hospital. Under the generator. He made us do it. He's our packleader. He said you were a vampire killing his father. He watched you, followed you . . .'

Donna screamed shortly, the cry becoming a sigh as Denton heard her body hit the concrete sidewalk even before he turned around. A knife's black hilt quivered in her side, stuck from the back by the boy who stood, wavering, ready to fall, coughing blood. Denton recognized Hurzbau's son, and he wondered: *Why her instead of me?*

The boy collapsed, crumpling limply, blood sliding between his skin and the transparent suit, the plastic making the blood seem orange and artificial.

Denton felt empathic pain in his own side, as, sobbing, he ran to Donna. She was still breathing but unconscious. The knife was in to the hilt. He was afraid to pull it out and allow too much blood to escape.

'Here. Call an ambulance.' The boy who had spoken before was standing, one hand still on his crotch, something like regret in his face. He handed Denton a cheap pocketfone. Denton frantically punched *Emergency*.

A small metallic voice responded, and he gave directions. When he had done he looked up and down the street, wondering why it was so deserted after all the noise. There were three bright street lights on the block. Denton, Donna, and the remainder of the gang were visible and starkly outlined in the pool of light under the crowded skyscraper apartments lining both sides of the street.

The events of the past few minutes caught up with Denton when he felt blood warming the hand resting on Donna's still leg. He looked up at the boy who just stood there, face blanked.

'All of you are going to regret this, kid,' Denton said in what he hoped was a steely, uncompromising tone.

The boy just shrugged.

He couldn't go to work now, to watch a man die under a generator scoop knowing that Donna was dying under one just like it. He pondered quitting his job. Somehow he felt that losing his job at the generator would be a self-betrayal. It brought him a strange peace, as he sat in full health watching the patient wilt under the glass scoop like an ant burnt by a magnifying glass. Saying to himself: *I'm still strong, it passed me by*.

He decided not to go to work. He kept seeing Donna's name on the shift chart. They had expected *him* to tend her generator. No. No. He couldn't visit her, even off duty. She was in a coma. He had to get his mind off it. He hadn't slept at all that night and his eyes burned with exhaustion. He would go out and get something to eat and if Buxter decided to fire him then the decision to leave the job would be made for him.

He walked through the hospital lobby and into glaring sunshine reflecting off the white buildings of the complex. He was scared. Simply scared. But he was an actor so no one could tell.

Not even Alice. Alice was standing on the steps to the

hospital, handing out pamphlets. She saw him immediately, seeing first the black uniform she hated, and then her once-lover inside.

Denton hoped to avoid her, but before he could turn away she ran to him and, thrusting a pamphlet in his hand, embraced him. He pulled away, embarrassed. The glare seemed to intensify, magnifying glass hovering over the ant. Alice laughed.

'Still working there? I think you must really like your job, Ronnie.'

His mouth worked but his lines wouldn't come. He shook his head and finally managed, 'I'd like to talk to you about it. Uh – welcome your opinion. But I've gotta go start my shift.' He turned and hurried back into the coolness of the hospital, feeling her smug smile hanging on to the back of his neck.

It was suddenly important to him that he go to work. He had nothing to expiate.

In the elevator, alone, he glanced at the crumpled pamphlet. He read:

'. . . if it is inevitable that a man must die, let him do it with dignity. Death has long been a gross national product, especially since United States' intervention in the Arab-Israeli conflict. But a bullet through the heart kills quickly; death under the generator comes tediously. The common fallacy that entropic generators promote death has been proven untrue, but what do they do to ease or inhibit death? The presence of a generator is psychologically damaging to the dying, causing them to give up the fight for recovery before they normally would . . .'

He remembered Hurzbau's words: *Can you say it doesn't take away from my life if you don't know how it works?*

* * *

'Mr Buxter? Can I talk to you?'

Hardly looking up, Buxter demanded, 'Well? What are you doing here? You were supposed to be in four-fifty-six twenty minutes ago.'

'I want you to explain the principles of the entropic generator to me. I think it's my responsibility to know.'

'Oh hell,' Buxter spat, disappointed, 'is that all? Look it up in the training manual.'

'I did. It was all in jargon. And they told us briefly and none too clearly when I was being trained for the job. I never really cared to understand till now. But a . . . friend of mine is under – '

'Under the generator, right? And *now* you want to know. Okay, Denton. I'll explain. Once. And you are going to be docked for the time it takes me to explain and the time you weren't working.'

Denton shrugged, sat down across from Buxter. He felt like a boy going to confession.

Buxter sighed and began, playing with a pencil as he spoke: 'The word *entropy*, literally translated, means *turning toward energy*. From our relative viewpoint we usually define entropy as the degree of disorder in a substance. Entropy always increases and available energy diminishes. So it seems. From our point of view, when we see someone's system of order decaying it seems as if the growth of entropy means a drop of energy. It appears that something is going away from us.' He paused to organize his thoughts, began to doodle on scratch paper.

Denton tapped his fingers irritably. 'Yeah? So what? When people die they lose energy – '

'No, they don't lose it in the sense we're concerned with, and SHUT UP AND LISTEN because I'm not going to explain this to you twice. This is already the second time this month I've had to go through all this . . . Now, when you get old, your eyesight fails so it appears

as if you see less and less all the time. Things in this world
are blotting out, blurring up. Actually, you're seeing
something more than you could see before your eyesight
failed. When your eyesight dims your entropy-sight
increases. Objects look that way, blurred and graylike, in
the other dimension, because they possess a form defined
by where they are *not* rather than where they *are*.'

'*What* dimension?'

Denton was lost.

'The dimension manifested concurrent with the accru-
ence of entropy. We used to think entropy undid creation
and form, but in its total sense, entropy creates a form so
obverse to ours that it appears not to be there. It creates
in a way we don't really understand but which we've
learned to use.' He cleared his throat, embarrassed by his
lapse into erudition. 'Anyway, the universe is constantly
shifting dimensions. From entropic focus to our type of
order and back again. When you get old and seem to be
feeling and hearing and seeing less, you are actually
perceiving the encroachment of that other universe.'

They were silent for five breaths. The old man tapped
his pencil.

Denton wondered if his inability to comprehend
stemmed from his youth. He wasn't decayed enough yet.

'What I'm trying to say,' Buxter went on wearily, 'is
that entropy is a progression instead of a regression.
When someone is walking past you it seems like they're
regressing, in a relative way, because they are walking
toward where you have already been, to what is behind
you. But to them, they are *pro*gressing. There are two
kinds of known energy, on a cosmic scale: electrical-
nuclear energy causing form, and the negative energy of
antiform. Nothing is really lost when you die. What
occurs is a trade.'

'You mean like water displacement? Going into *there*, some of it is forced into *here*?'

'More or less. The generators change the energy of death into usable electric power.'

'But if you take energy from a dying person, doesn't that make them die faster?'

'WILL YOU PAY ATTENTION, FOR GOD'S SAKE!' Buxter was determined to get through. '*No*. It doesn't take anything from a dying person. It accumulates energy that's radiated as a result of dying. The negative energy is released into the inanimate environment whether the generator is there or not. The scoop doesn't come into contact with the patient himself . . . it reacts only to the side-effect of his biological dissolution.' He took a deep breath. 'The main idea is that entropy is not the lack of something, not a subtraction, but an addition. We learned how to tap it because the energy crisis forced us to put up with the temporary discomfort – purely psychological – of having the scoop directly over a dying person. When it comes my time to go, I'll be damn proud to contribute something. None of my life is wasted that way, not even its end. One individual causes a remarkable amount of negative energy to be radiated as he dies, you know. We've only been using it practically for five years and there are still a lot of things we don't understand about it.'

'So why do it to people? Why not plants?'

'Because various organisms have variegated patterns of radiating negative energy. We don't know how to tap all of them yet. We can do it with cattle and people now. We're working on plants.'

'I don't know, I, uh . . .' Denton stumbled over his words, knowing that Buxter would be infuriated by the objection. 'But couldn't a generator damage the morale of a person dying? Make him believe it's too late and

prematurely give up? I mean, susceptibility to disease is
partly psychological, and if you're under pressure by
being under the scoop – ' He cut short, swallowing, seeing
Buxter's expression.

Hot ashes sprayed from Buxter's wagging pipe as he
spoke. 'Denton, all that is a lot of conjectural hogwash.
And it is pure stupidity to babble about it in the face of
the worst energy crisis the world has ever known. We
may have the energy problem licked forever if we can
learn to draw negative energy from the dying plants and
small animals and such. But people like you might just
ruin that hope. And I want you to know, Denton, that
I'm going to seriously consider letting you go, so if you
don't want to clinch my decision you'd better get the hell
to – '

'I can't go to my assigned shift, sir. I know the girl
under that scoop.'

'Okay then, that leaves Durghemmer. Take it or no
more job.'

Feeling drained, Denton nodded dumbly and left the
office.

Durghemmer could wait. Denton called hospital information and was informed that Donna was still
unconscious.

Denton went to see his only close friend. He took the bus
to Glennway Park.

Donald Armor was a cripple in one sense and completely mobile in another. He had been a pro race-car
driver for six years, several times taking national honors.
During the final lap of the 1995 Indy 500, in second place,
Armor's car spun out and bounced off the car behind it
and went into the grandstands, killing five onlookers,
maiming four. When gas-cars were banned and electric

air-cars instituted in 1996, the authorities made an exception in Armor's case. He was allowed to drive his own car, the only vehicle on the streets with wheels, because he could drive nothing else. Part of the firewall of the racing car had been ripped loose by the impact of the accident, slashing deep into Armor's side, partially castrating him on the way and cracking his spine. Doctors could not remove the shred without killing him.

Armor was a rich man and he had a car built around him, customized to his specifications. It was a small sports car, but with the cockpit, firewall, steering wheel, and dashboard of the original Indy racer. He was now a permanent organ of the vehicle, living in it day and night, unable and unwilling to leave. Until he died. Excreting through a colostomy bag, eating at drive-ins.

Denton sat in the seat next to Armor and, as usual, tried not to look at the thirteen inches of ragged steel protruding from the driver's right side to run to a ball-joint connecting him with the dashboard. The ball-joint gave him limited freedom within the car.

Armor had rudimentary use of his scarred and twisted legs, enough to gun the car down the boulevard with a speed and fluidity which never failed to amaze Denton. Armor drove without hesitation or false starts, always twenty miles in excess of the speed limit, knowing that no policeman would give him a ticket. They all knew him. Armor was famous, and he was dying. He had less than a year to live but they couldn't install a generator over a moving car. He chose to have no comforts; no radio or tape deck or juice dispensers. He didn't drink and he couldn't have sex.

'What's eating you today, Ron?' Armor asked in a voice like the distant rumble of a semi-truck. He was dark and rawboned and his bushy black brows sprouted alone

on a scarred bald head. His hard gray eyes were perpetually lost in the spaces between the white dashes marking
the road. 'Something's messing you up,' he said.

They had been friends since before Armor's accident.
Armor knew Denton almost as well as he knew the road.
Denton told him about Donna and the generator.

Armor listened without comment. His eyes didn't leave
the road – they rarely did – and his features remained
expressionless aside from slight intensifications when the
road called for more concentration.

Denton concluded, 'And I can't bring myself to leave
the job. Donna is still in a coma, so I can't talk to her
about it. I almost feel like I'm working against her by
continuing there. I know it's irrational . . .'

'What is it you like so much that you can't quit?'

'It's not that. I . . . well, jobs aren't easy to find.'

'I know where you can get another job.'

He eased the car to a halt. They were parked in front
of TREMMER AND FLEISHER SLAUGHTERING/PROCESSING.
Below the older sign was, newly painted in black: GENER-
ATOR ANNEX.

'My brother Harold works here,' Armor said. He
hadn't turned off the engine. He rarely did. 'He remembers you. He can get you a job here. Go on up to the
personnel office. That's where he works. You might like
this job better than the other, I imagine.' He turned
uncompromising eyes from the hood of the car and
looked at Denton with a five-hundred-horsepower gaze.

'Okay.' Denton shrugged. 'Anything you say. I can't
go back to work now anyway.' He opened the car door
and got out, feeling his back painfully uncramping after
the bucket seat. He looked through the open door.
Armor was still watching him.

'I'll wait here,' Armor said with finality.

* * *

The bright light hurt Denton's eyes as he followed Harold Armor, brother to Donald, into a barnlike aluminum building labeled SLAUGHTERHOUSE GENERATOR ANNEX 1.

Inside, the sibilance of air conditioners was punctuated with long bestial sighs from dying cattle. There were two long rows of stalls, a bubble of the generator scoop completely enclosing each prostrate steer. The top of each scoop ducted into a thick vitreous cable joining others from adjoining stalls in a network of silvery wire like a spiderweb canopy overhead.

'Now these cattle here – well, some of 'em are cows what got old – they have a generator for the whole lot of 'em, and one compensator for every three animals,' Harold intoned proudly. 'And we've got some we've maintained there at just the right level of decay, you know, for six to eight months. And that's just plain difficult. They die a lot on us, though. A lot of 'em dying of old age. Most of 'em we bleed to death.'

'You bleed them?' Denton was unable to conceal his horror. Seeing Denton's reaction, Harold stiffened.

'Damn right we do. How else can we keep them at the right level of decay and still keep them alive long enough to produce? Sure, I know what you're going to ask. Everyone does when they first come here. The government shut the ASPCA up because of the power shortage. And of course part of your job as compensator here is you'll have to learn how to adjust their bleeding and feeding so they die at the right speed. It's a bit more work than at the hospital, where they die for you naturally. But it pays more than at the hospital. All you have to remember is that if they sneak back up on you and recover too much, you either have to bleed them more or feed them less. Sometimes we poison them some too, when they first come here, to get them on their way.'

Denton stood by one of the cells and observed a fully

grown bull with ten-inch horns, massive rib cage rising and falling irregularly, eyes opening and closing and opening and closing . . .

'Now that one,' Harold droned, 'hasn't been here but a week and he ain't used to it yet. Most of them just lay there and forget they're alive after a few weeks or so. See, you can see marks on the stall where he's been kicking it and his hoof is bleeding – we'll have to patch that up, we don't want him to get an infection. Die too soon that way. You can see he's going to come along good cuz his coat is gettin' rough and fur startin' to come off.'

The trapped beast looked at Denton with dulled eyes drained of fear. It was lying on its side, head lolling from the stall opening. Three thick plastic tubes were clamped with immovable iron bands to its sagging neck. The steer seemed to be in transition between instinctual rebellion and capitulation. It twitched and lifted its head a few inches, as if trying to recall how to stand.

From the *New York Times* review of Ronald Denton's only play, *All Men Are Created Sequels*:

'The play began to decay well before the second act, as a cadaver should. By the end of the second act, the stage was a miasma of putrid flesh, squirming with parasitic irrelevancies. Mr Denton should have had the courtesy to provide a generator scoop hooked up to the audience so that we could glean something of value from the affair as the audience died of boredom.'

'Come here, kid!'

Denton didn't want to go around to the other side of the generator. He didn't want to look at Durghemmer.

'*Com'ere*, boy!'

Denton sighed and stood up. 'Yes?'

Durghemmer's face was lined but robust. His eyes were bright buttons sewn deep in the hollows over his cheeks. He had a miniature round mouth, a wisp of white hair, and minimal chin. His jowls shook when he laughed. He pointed at Denton with a stubby finger. 'You skeered of something, kid?'

'Shouldn't you be asleep, Mr Durghemmer? It's past nine.'

'Shouldn't *you* be asleep, kid? Sleep?' He laughed shrilly, cowbells filtering through the plastic bell of the scoop. He half sat up, grimaced, fell back.

Emanuel Durghemmer had come to the hospital three years before, dying of leukemia. He had been too far along for help; they had expected him to die within a week. A generator was immediately placed over him. He went into a month-long coma. When he woke, the needle jumped. According to the readouts, he had come a substantial step closer to death by regaining consciousness. And according to hospital legend, he had sat up directly upon awakening from the coma, and *laughed*. The generator again had registered a drop in life-force and a corresponding gain in entropic energy. Each week for three years Durghemmer had shown signs of being on the verge of death. Always in pain, he delivered more negative energy than any other individual in the hospital. And he had developed a corrosive bedridden manner.

Denton was unnerved by Durghemmer's joviality. But Denton had two hours left of his shift. He decided to make the most of it, find out what he could.

Somehow Durghemmer's attitude made Donna's imminent death seem ludicrous.

'You're wondering, aren't you?' Durghemmer asked. 'You're wondering how I stay alive.'

'No. I don't give a damn.'

'But you do. You care for the simplest of reasons. You

know you're going to die someday and you wonder how
long you'll last under the generator and what it will be
like watching the meter go up and down. Or maybe – if
it's not you, is it someone else? Someone close to you
dying, kid?'

No surprise that Durghemmer knew. The old parasite
had been in the hospital for three years, a record by two
and a half years for being under the generator. He could
smell death a long way away.

'All right, but so what?' Denton said impulsively. 'So
you're right. It's a girlfriend.'

'She got pussy cancer?' Hollow laughter reverberated
inside the scoop. Lines of mirth on the old man's face
meshed indistinguishably with lines of pain.

Denton wanted to smash the plastic of the scoop to get
at the old politician's sour mouth with his fist. Instead, he
said coolly: 'No. She was knifed. I've got to see her. I
heard she came around for a while this afternoon. Maybe
I can . . .' He shrugged. 'I've got to explain things.'

'Write her off, kid. Nobody but me has ever figured
out how to use it. I had training when I was mayor . . .'
He guffawed, coughing phlegm.

'What did you do to Burt?'

'That kid that resigned? He was a short spit, only on
my generator three weeks. Usually takes them at least a
month.' He closed his eyes. In a low, tense voice: 'You
know, sometimes pain sharpens things for you. It kind of
wakes you up and makes you see better. You ever notice
when your gut hurts and you feel like every sound and
sight is too loud or bright for you to stand? Everything
makes you feel sicker because you're seeing it so well, so
clearly. Sometimes, people who haven't done anything
with their lives become good painters when they get sick
because the hurt *makes* them look at things. And sometimes – ' He drifted off for a full minute, his eyes in

limbo. Then he spoke conspiratorially, whispering more to himself than to Denton, 'Sometimes I see things in the pain. Useful things. Peeks into that other world. I go into it a little ways, then I come back here and I'm on solid ground. And I see these invisible wires connecting each man to the others, like puppet strings all mixed up.'

Denton had lost interest in the old man's ramblings. He could see Donna's eyes smoldering with pain like the red LEDs of the generator.

Durghemmer's generator hummed into life as it began to absorb a flood of negative energy. The old man was tiring. The machine began to chuckle to itself. Durghemmer lay composed, a faint smile lost in the maze of his face.

'Durghemmer,' Denton said, standing. 'I've got to see that woman. I've got to make sure she's all right. Now look, if I go, would you refrain from calling the nurse when I go out unless it's an absolute emergency? I've *got* to – '

'Okay, kid. But you can write off your girlfriend. She hasn't lived long enough to learn . . .' He had spoken without bothering to open his eyes.

Denton was alone with Donna; he had bribed the scheduled compensator. He peered through the scoop at her nervously, afraid that she might already be dead. Her elfin features, unconscious, blinked in and out of shadow with the strobing of the generator lights in the darkened room. Denton checked the dials, rechecked them, found a compensating factor he had missed the first time. He adjusted the intake of the scoop.

She was dropping. The readouts were climbing.

He flipped on the intercom, walked around to the other side of the bed. 'Donna? Can you hear me?' He glanced at the meter. It jumped. She was coming around but it took strength from her to awaken. Maybe talking to her would make her weak, perhaps cause her death, he thought abruptly. Something he should have considered sooner. His heart was a fist pounding the bars of his chest.

Her eyes opened, silver-blue platinum, metal tarnished with desperation.

He spoke hastily: 'I'm sorry about everything, Donna. I don't know how you got involved in my problems . . .'

She looked at him without comprehension for a moment, then recognition cleared her eyes.

'I shouldn't bother you now,' he added, 'but I had to talk to you.'

It came to him that he really had no idea what he wanted to say.

'Get out of here, Ron . . . you came for yourself, not for me.' Her voice was thin as autumn ice. And like being awakened with ice water, Denton was shocked into realization: It was true.

'You came here to apologize. Big deal. Maybe you should apologize to that Hurzbau kid. I heard that he died. I'm not moralizing. We killed him together.' Her eyes fluttered.

'Donna?' She was giving up. Her voice trailed off. Get her attention, make her fight her way back. He buzzed for the nurse and shouted, '*Donna!*' His voice stretched wiry from hysteria.

She opened her eyes a crack and murmured, 'They did a psychological test for you, didn't they? They tested you and knew you were right for the job.'

The nurse bustled in then and Denton pressed the green button that lifted the scoop.

As he left he saw the LED readings, still rising. Rapaciously, the generator giggled.

*   *   *

He shuffled with great effort through the halls, two days' lack of sleep catching up to him. His arms and legs seemed to be growing softer, as if his bones were dissolving. He came to the window overlooking the parking lot. As he expected, Armor was waiting for him below, driving around and around and around without pausing, circling the parking lot in a loop of abeyance.

Denton left the window. He couldn't face Armor now. He scuffled down the antiseptic hallways. He imagined negative energy radiating from him like a dark halo. The penumbra grew darker as he sank deeper into exhaustion. His throat contracted till he could hardly breathe. He had memorized the exact shape of the trickle of blood on Donna's chin, the last thing that had caught his attention before the nurse had made him leave. It had runneled down from her nose onto her cheek, splitting into forks, a dark lightning bolt. He pictured the fine branches of red multiplying in the atmosphere around him as if the air were filled with a skein of ethereal blood veins. The red lines connected the spectral orderlies and nurses rushing past, like the wires Durghemmer had described connecting the heads of everyone in the city. Denton walked slowly, plowing through molten wax to Durghemmer's room.

'I want to *know*, Durghemmer,' he said to the old man, as he entered the sterile chamber. 'I know you steal the negative energy of the scoop for yourself. I want to know *how*.'

The old man grinned toothlessly. His gums were cracked and dried, making his mouth into the crumbling battlements of a ruined city. He sat up, and the meters rose again.

Denton leaned wearily on the generator, determined to come to terms with death.

'I figured you'd want to know, Denton.' Durghemmer

laughed, moths tumbling dustily in his throat. 'I can see just by looking at you that the girl died.'

Denton nodded. The movement might have been made by a scarecrow swayed by a breeze.

'Sure, lad, I'll show you just how I thrive in this hole. I'll show you how I keep an even keel under this scoop like a pheasant under glass. I'll show you just exactly and honest to God. You just watch me now.'

'Watch you? You mean I can *see* how you do it?'

'Sure. You just watch now.'

The dark room seemed to congeal with grains of opacity. The generator hummed happily to itself. Denton leaned forward, hands on the control panel, tired eyes locked desperately onto Durghemmer.

The decaying politician lay back and folded his hands on his chest. Then, he began to chuckle.

Denton was completely baffled. As far as he could see, the old man was doing nothing at all . . .

. . . except laughing.

Sleepwalkers

. . . the environment that Man creates becomes his medium for defining his role in it.

– Marshall McLuhan

'Anything for a buck,' Ace said.

'A man's gotta live, a man's gotta eat, a man's gotta have shoes to walk down the street,' Bernie said.

'Another day, another dollar,' Jules said.

'Five'll get you ten and ten'll get you twenty,' Ace put in.

'Beggars can't be choosers,' Bernie said.

'When the wolf's at the door you gotta pay the piper, or something like that,' Ace muttered, getting bored with it. They'd begun the game when Jules told them he was going to rent himself to the Sleepwalker Agency.

They were silent then, and listened to Mick Jagger explain that although it was only rocknroll, he liked it. The song ended, another began, a lovesong styled like a dirge, and that started Jules thinking about Zimm and the money he needed before he could see her again. 'Neither a borrower nor a lender be,' he murmured. *Well, I've got the lender part sewed up, he thought. I wish I didn't owe her anything. Money. Or anything.*

That's when Barb swaggered in with the fixings, her grin shining like a needle in the afternoon light slanting through the only unbroken window. It was impure meth so it had to be cooked. Seeing her cook up the meth, Bernie danced around her in a circle, clapping his hands and growling. Bernie had downslanted brown eyes and curly black hair bowed from the weight of six washless weeks. He'd been nineteen and Jewish before he'd started shooting crystal. He was no longer Jewish, he was no longer young; he was a speedfreak.

Jules watched with a slight smile, tapping his fingers to the music against the plywood nailed over the side window. On a bygone giddy summer night Ace had broken out all the windows but one and now the small stucco house glared like a one-eyed man at the rest of East Hollywood. Jules felt left out, times like this, because he'd given up on drugs. A little peyote here and there, maybe some 'shrooms now and again; next to being straight, almost.

Ace was half Chicano, or had been before he made the agreement with methedrine. The pockmarks in his gaunt cheeks seemed to glow like tiny fumaroles as he watched Barb, his old lady, preparing the syringe with clinical detachment. His eyes were black; sharp, pointed black.

Ace went to his room and returned with a can of lighter fluid. Skipping in a circle around Bernie, Ace sprayed the lighter fluid on the floor. Bernie danced. 'Hey, HEY!' Bernie growled as the guitar player on the stereo went into an incendiary solo. Ace tossed a match at the ring of lighter fluid and gossamer flames darted up, encircling Bernie like footlights, tickling at his ankles. Laughing, he danced them dead. They died quickly and with little smoke, like starved infants.

'Wuh-ooo!' Jules shouted obligatorily, clapping his hands. Not feeling it much.

Barb, her black skin shining with sweat, leaned over the candle so the light glinting off the spoon was reflected in her inky eyes.

Jules hadn't been molded into a functional component of the Overmind Amplifier, as Bernie called it, the Speed Machine, as Barb called it, because he had not made the agreement. He combed slender fingers through his long, straight brown hair and pouted. He swiped at his eyes, making a black smudge on his hand. His makeup was smeared. He could give a shit. Yeah, he definitely felt left out, when his roommates fixed. He'd been there himself, once, but he'd broken the contract. He loved a woman who was only desultorily interested in him; he played bass but had no band; he'd played with drugs . . . but he had not come to terms with them; and he could no longer bear to peddle his ass – he was a cog without its clockworks.

He drooped back against the wall, slumped to the floor, stretched out his legs and reflected that the machine-and-petroleum scent from the combusted lighter fluid would be appropriate perfume for Zimm. He ran his thumb along the shiny inner thigh of his skintight dungarees, staring at the worn, pointed toe of his black boots.

The record ended. Jules watched as Bernie and Barb fixed, rubber bands tight around their biceps, their foreheads beaded with sweat. They drove the spikes home at precisely the same instant.

Ace was still filling his spike, chewing his lower lips, head tilted downward, eyes fixed on the transparent liquid. He was loading up more this time, and the last time he'd used more than the time before. Jules looked harder at the lineaments of Ace's skull pressing out through his sallow skin, and knew; knew that Ace was sure to overdose. Dust himself. Jules sagged inwardly – nothing *he* could do.

The Hell with it – it's what he wants.

Jules selected another record, smirked, knowing what Bernie's reaction would be to this particular song, and put it on:

The Velvet Underground, 'White Light, White Heat'.

'Take that *motherfucker OFF!*' Bernie snarled, shivering from the first influx of rush. His pupils shrank like coffee going down a drain.

Barb laughed as Bernie shrieked, 'Take it off before I step on the fucking *stereo!*'

Snickering, feigning surprise, Jules put something on that Bernie could accept because it was absurd: A scratchy copy of Judy Garland singing 'Somewhere Over the Rainbow'. ''at's better,' Bernie said, sinking into an already sunken velour easychair. He was shaking like a wet dog, breathing quickly, tongue snapping between his teeth. In the storm-eye of the rush, Bernie's face, muscles tight, was flushed so white it was like the chrome grill of an onrushing Cadillac. Jules liked seeing Bernie this way just as he had once enjoyed watching his father at work – both of them doing something that defined their lives. Bernie had made a career of being a speedfreak. 'You put on that speedfreak song on purpose, Jules, you sucker. You *know* I can't stand music if it's appropriate. I *hate* things that are appropriate and obvious, like people coming out of the Betty Boop film festival all giggling and goin' *Oohpoopeedoo* and you KNOW you KNOW you know I hate that shit, Jules-you-ugly-mother. Oh you KNOW it grinds on me like a Sherman tank in heat – '

And Bernie launched into his speedfreak rap which everyone knew better than to listen to and which he had to get out of his system for the next two-and-a-half hours.

'That Judy Garland song's appropriate,' Jules ventured. 'She was a speedfreak too.'

''at right,' Ace said, teeth chattering, head bouncing like a violently dribbled basketball; he'd intended a slight nod.

Barb and Ace went into the next room to get passionate. The speed had done its work – Ace had been unable to get it up for months, but he did her with his fingers and that was fine because she only liked sex as an excuse to be held and rocked.

Naturally, this turned Jules's thoughts to Zimm. How he had to get some money to her. So she'd look at him with respect.

Some liberated woman, he thought. She pretends she's above it all, but she lives for money . . . Maybe he would go to the club and watch her shake 'em, and laugh at her, loudly, see how liberated she felt with someone besides a TV-snowed middle-ager watching her debasement for the sake of The Big Machine.

I'm onto her, Jules thought. She plays feminist but she gets off dancing nude for those whip-offs, it's a sick throwback to her fixation on her father . . . *Maybe I can get in good with her by kidnapping her old man and bringing him to her on a chain and making him crawl for her. Maybe that would be enough.*

Nope. No way that would be enough.

Even then, she'd want the money.

But he had to see Zimm tomorrow. He needed her. That much was established. He couldn't wait any longer. He had to get two hundred dollars to pay back the money he owed her. Two hundred dollars and maybe enough extra cake for a down payment on a car so she'd stop calling him a deadbeat. And he could get that kind of money overnight only one of two ways. He could steal. Or he could go to the Sleepwalkers Agency.

'It's nothin' you ain't done before,' said Bernie suddenly, as if he'd read Jules's mind. Which maybe he had. Speed gave him access to inaccessible channels. 'You ought to know the scene. I'd figure it for a step up. I mean, you don't remember it, afterwards. Except for twelve lost hours it's like free money. For sleeping. If they wanna fuck you, they gotta use condoms. I don't know *anybody* who was ever hurt by it,' he said like an

insurance salesman, tapping his fingers, licking his lips,
tapping his feet and shrugging – all simultaneously.
Bernie wanted Jules to take the job because he knew
Jules would donate some of his earnings to the dope kitty.
'Nobody gets hurt, much. A few bruises. A few people
went nuts. But there's a hazard to every profession. Just
as bad being a cop as it is being a bum, sometimes, an'
it's just as lonesome being a burglar as a priest or a mom
as a dad or an embryo as a dyin' old man it all has its
compensations and its reversals and the dues to pay you
gotta pay your dues if you wanna sing the blues and
everything but *everything* has a slot for you to put in your
quarter – '

Jules screened out Bernie's rap. But he thought: *You
gotta pay your dues if –*

So he got up and went to pay his dues.

He left Bernie talking to the walls of the dingy stucco
house with the boards over the windows and it was soon
wrapped up in the landscape through which he passed,
consumed and gift-wrapped behind him in the Hollywood
downer district. Houses of plaster, houses of pine, one
storey, one story at a time, he thought. Palm trees nodded
in agreement in the faint breeze, a violet twilight settled
over the dirty skyline and the bite of lemons graced the
reek of car exhaust.

He felt the wind ruffling his hair, felt it very distantly,
as a junkie feels a kiss.

He thought about Zimm standing for hours outside the
theatre, in the cold, from four A.M. to ten P.M. just to get
a thirty-second audition for a ten minute bit in a minor
play. She hadn't got the part but she had paid her dues.

He pictured her there, standing in the gunmetal early
morning light, full lips pursed, snapping blue eyes limned
with shards of bitterness, high cheekbones standing out
with the determination of her set jaw, her platinum hair

tossed by the chill wind . . . and he wished he could go to her and put his arms around her then and say: you don't have to be so hard and relentless, there's a soft place where we can go where you can be a performer and I can play my bass and we'll be audience enough for one another.

But she'd only laugh bitterly, if he had said that, and call him a jerk.

Long ago she'd settled on the hardcore role and it was too late to change her like it was too late for Ace. 'Oooooh, isn't it nice, when you find your heart is made out of ice . . .' Jules sang to himself as the bus rumbled up.

He glanced at the plate on the brow of the bus, verified the destination – yeah, Hollywood and Vine – and climbed aboard.

He tossed seven quarters into the slot, as a snob contributes to a beggar. He ignored the wooden faces of the passengers the way a squirrel never looks right at the trees of its own forest, and found a seat.

In the vestibule to the Sleepwalkers Agency he reread the pamphlet, wished he had the nerve to ask for another look at the contract he'd signed and hardly read. He noted that the sweat on his fingers was making the pamphlet's print smear and that reminded him of his makeup. He went to the restroom – imitation-black-marble stalls, imitation-wood wallpaneling, imitation-mother-of-pearl toilet seat – where he shakily voided himself, then washed the makeup off his eyes.

He came into the lounge, sat down, and the tall white girl with the blue Afro-wig and the smile that was like a smile an embalmer might put on a corpse, softly called his name. He was the only one in the waiting room.

He followed her, taking deep breaths to calm himself.

Passing through a very clean, very white door, they came into a room with battleship-gray walls, empty except for a padded diagnostic table.

The girl turned to him and repeated words she'd repeated many times before, not hearing herself say them: 'Remove your clothes and lay down on your back, relax, close your eyes, take deep breaths and dream about how you will spend your money. You won't feel a thing.' Jules was certain she could repeat the same speech verbatim in her sleep. She left him alone.

Fingers shaking, glancing nervously around the spare, gray room, he removed his clothes, folded them neatly, left them in a pile at the foot of the table in a yellow plastic box stenciled: YOUR CLOTHES.

There was a thin sheet of clean white paper on the couch. He stretched, and lay down, listening to the paper rustle beneath his weight. He could hear the sleep-gas hissing through the ventilator. It smelled like lemons and car exhaust and musk. He shut his eyes, breathed in deep, thinking: *Nothing you haven't done before. Only you won't be aware of it this time and the pay is better. And with an ordinary trick you wouldn't know for sure if the dude wasn't planning to beat you up afterwards. This way you've got the agency's written guarantee you won't be hurt or infected. And two hundred dollars when you wake up tomorrow. A sure thing . . .*

He said these things to himself, an inward litany, and he thought it was working because soon he was relaxing and humming. But an instant before dropping off, he realized it was only the gas.

It was over like nothing. Just like that. He woke up, saw the young woman with the funereal smile bending over him. He looked down at himself, discovered with surprise

that he was dressed. He smiled in momentary embarrassment, but then the detached urbanity he'd labored nineteen years to perfect (his mother claimed he'd begun to
act cool and distant at two years old) took the wheel.

He shrugged.

'How do you feel?' she asked disinterestedly.

'Fine,' he said, though the gas had left him with a dull
qualm, like sea-sickness in his gut. He sat up, and the
feeling quickly passed.

'When you're thoroughly awake you can come out to
the front desk for payment,' she said, and went through
the door.

At the mention of money he stood bolt upright and
stretched. *Well. That was a snap.* He looked himself over.
His body didn't seem the worse for wear. A distant ache
between his legs. Maybe a bruise on his left thigh. Better
than hooking on Santa Monica Boulevard. Whoever had
played with him had been careful.

With a shiver he tried to remember – and came up with
nothing. Yet his eyes had been open, his ears had heard,
parts of his brain had followed someone's spoken directions. But he couldn't remember a damn thing. He
straightened his collar, tightened his scarf, regarded his
chipped silver-painted fingernails ruefully and went to get
his money. The secretary handed him an envelope. He
left immediately, but outside the office he stopped and
tore open the envelope. Two hundred cash, as promised.

It was eight A.M. and the traffic was beginning to work
itself into a frenzy. He grinned at the scowling copper
sun, the smog-burnished sky, and set off for Zimm's
apartment.

She was in the tub when he arrived. He knocked and
called, 'Zimm!'

'Jules?' There was no welcome in her, 'Come on in.'

He pushed through the green paint-peeling bathroom door and managed not to stare at her as he sat on a rickety unpainted wooden chair beside the tub. It was an old-fashioned bathtub; its legs rusty eagle's claws clutching globes. She toyed languidly with a pulpy bar of soap. The bubblebath made a lace gown beneath her breasts and about her upraised knees. The ends of her hair dangled in the water, the platinum dye showed where the black roots were growing out. She still wore silvery lipstick and false eyelashes and chrome-tinted contact lenses; her head lolled a little to the left as if its weight was too much for her neck.

'Doing quaaludes again?' he asked, trying to sound indifferent.

'None of your business.'

That answered his question.

'You can buy some more with this . . .' he withdrew the fold of bills from his shirt pocket and laid it on the soap shelf. 'Two hundred even.'

After counting the money, she said, 'Thank you very much, sir.' Pretending to bat her eyelashes.

His eyes wandered. Her breasts bobbed in the water like the slick backs of jellyfish. Her pubic hair – he frowned. 'Christ! You've still got your underwear on.'

She giggled and admitted, 'I'm stoned.'

She tucked the money into the pocket of the white pants lying rumpled beside the tub. 'Wanta get in?' she inquired politely. 'Water's still warm.'

He undressed in seconds, sliding into the water; the first of a variety of damp penetrations.

Her kisses were more ardent than the last time, when he'd still owed her money.

Ace was the only one home when Jules got there at two in the afternoon.

He was lying on his back on the floor amidst a scattering of tapes and discs like autumn leaves, his head clamped into earphones, eyes closed, toes making jerky figure-eights to the music. Jules frowned at the bare walls, the sunken, splintered furniture, mostly wicker foraged from trash heaps. They could get some decent furnishings if he made some more money . . .

. . . it was then that he was sure he would go back to Sleepwalkers. But it wasn't because of the furnishings. It was only because of Zimm and the change in her voice that came when she'd seen the money. She hadn't asked where he got it.

Ace opened his eyes, squinted up at him. He took off the earphones which leaked a howl of thrash. 'We gotta get some new tunes,' Jules said, hoping to distract Ace from the pitch that must come. 'Most recent stuff we have is four years old.'

'Yeah,' Ace agreed, his pinpoint eyes flickering, not seeing much. 'Yeah we gotta keep up, we live inna world of the future after all.' He laughed. '*You* know: Magnetic rocket cars and telepathy booths.

'I been reading my uncle's 1938 *Popular Science* magazines with a special feature about the Marvelous World of The Future. And we're in it because guess what, the time they're talking about is 1990! They say in 1990 we got telepathy booths and people go to work in jet-propelled rollerskates.'

Jules laughed.

But then Ace asked what he must inevitably ask: 'Hey, can you let me have some'a the squeeze you got sleep-walkin'? You must have some left outta two hundred and my connection won't take – '

'Gave it all to Zimm, man. Owed her. I'm going back tonight. Get you some dollars tomorrow, for why, I don't know, you never give it back. But I'll give you some – '

Ace was content. 'Hey, it's better than street hustling, huh? Like, you look okay – used to come home all crumpled-up and forlorn lookin' and complaining you only got thirty bucks and what a total ripoff it was – '

'Shut up, Ace.'

'You feel nothin' later, huh?' Ace continued doggedly.

Suddenly feeling odd, tingling all over, Jules said, 'No, not a goddamn thing.' He didn't want to talk about it. He realized he was rubbing the palms of his hands, again and again, on his shirt sleeves. He trapped his hands under his buttocks. But now he was grievously annoyed, seeing the deltas of built-up filth in the corners of the room. 'Place needs a good cleaning,' he said.

'They just gas you like Gary said and that's it? And then they rent your body out to people and it walks around like a zombie and does what it's told and you don't feel a thing? You don't even ache in your asshole?'

Jules shot him a look. Ace made an elaborate shrug and replaced the earphones, lay back.

Jules got up and went to his room and threw himself on the air mattress, the cushions billowing up around him. He turned onto his back and thought of getting stoned. No.

It was there. In there, somewhere. Whatever they'd used him for was stored up in the back of his head somewhere, locked in with their electrical repressors, but intact, in there, all the same. In a cell in his brain just as surely as Charles Manson was in a cell on Death Row. In a little room somewhere in his brain re-enacting endlessly what they'd made him do. And maybe methedrine would unlock the door. No. Don't get started again, and especially not now. He decided that next time he did the sleepwalk he'd take the money to a bank and deposit half of it into a new account so that Ace and Bernie couldn't talk him out of that much, anyway. He'd say he'd given it to Zimm. They'd been his best friends for ten years. He couldn't say no to them. He'd been there himself. He fixed his eyes on the fierce and empty heart of the naked bulb shining white light overhead. He stared, unblinking, till the pain made him close his eyes.

Pictures came. It wasn't dreaming, really. And not daydreaming either. They weren't hallucinations. It was re-living. He could see it so clearly, there under his eyelids, almost cinematically. Yet none of it was familiar. A dark room, a fire at one end in a huge gray-stone fireplace throwing tongues of light on the hooded congregation. People in black robes, faces in shadow. On a table of polished mahogany he dimly made out a huge oyster shell on its back, open and empty but for an enormous blue pearl which seemed to emanate its own black-light. On the ornate rug, woven in red and black gargoyle visages, a silver casket like an infant's coffin faced him. 'This the young man from the agency?' came a reedy voice from the right. He was unable to move, he couldn't turn his head to see who had spoken.

'Yes,' replied another voice, business-like. One of the hooded figures stepped forward, tilted back the milky lid of the casket and said, 'Come forward.' Distantly, Jules felt himself striding forward. 'Stop. Stand where you are, look into the casket.' Jules looked.

It took time for his eyes to adjust. He saw the iridescent gleam of multifaceted eyes. 'Bend you over and open wide your mouth,' the hooded figure commanded. Jules bent toward the casket, looked closer, opened his mouth, his head near the edge of the casket, he looked closer . . .

He sat up, struggling to escape the clinging air mattress, and heard the echoes of his own scream. Slippery with sweat, he floundered off the bed and crawled over the wooden frame, across the floor. He lay face down, breathing heavily, drained. Then he got slowly to his feet, went to the refrigerator, got the vodka and drank what remained, nearly half the bottle.

That seemed to help.

The next evening he plugged in his bass and played simple, aggressive riffs, building up his courage to return to Sleepwalkers.

In the next room Ace and Bernie were loudly arguing.

'Com'on, Ace. Wha'sit to you?'

'I just don't like to do that stuff when Barb's around.'

'She ain't here.'

'Man, she'll *be* here in half an hour.'

'So it won't take that long. Twenty minutes. I'm on my knees, Ace. I'm down – '

'Okay – okay, go get it for me then.'

Jules heard Bernie run obediently down the hall to his room to get the handcuffs and flog.

Minutes later Bernie breathlessly pleaded, 'Now say the things.'

'You half-assed slimy PUNK!' Ace shrieked and there was the counterpoint wet sound of the flog tasting Bernie's buttocks, and Bernie's grateful moan like a liturgical reply.

Annoyed, Jules turned the volume up and played loud and brutally through the fuzz-tone, until it was over and Ace came out, looking exhausted and wired. Ace looked out the single intact window. He let the curtains drop and turned away. 'No sign of Barb,' Jules said, without looking up.

'Keep playing that thing, man. Don't stop. Sounds good.'

Jules dipped his fingers into the guts of the bass and savaged the steel-string nerve-ends and made it groan for Ace. Speeding again, Ace walked back and forth slapping his thighs, a martinet parading too fast for the music, twitching his shoulders and bobbing his head.

When Barb arrived they tied off together, Jules playing for them as they rushed, thinking that Ace didn't look quite satisfied and that next time he'd probably double the dose and that would be it. Involuntarily grinning, Ace moved to the music like a striking cobra. Jules looked at him and could see the agreement Ace had made with the speed, signed and sealed in the noiseless workings of his mouth. He knew that Ace was connected, in that instant, that he was one with the cars hurtling over the freeways and the buses rumbling through the avenues and the electricity whining in the powerlines; that he was synched with the rhythms and pistons and jackhammers. That was the contract: *Take my body and make me one with the world's machines.*

Ace knew what he was doing. To live, you must deal. You must deal with someone of the big machine's agents. Speed or heroin or lonely old breadwinners on the prowl or guns or editors or music managers. You had to make an agreement somewhere, and modify yourself, mutilate yourself to fit, like the Amazons removing a breast for the quiver-strap.

Trying not to think of the Sleepwalkers in those terms, Jules wondered if he should join a band. If he could.

He turned the volume up full.

This time, the girl with the Afro-wig and the fixed smile didn't bother with the directions. She simply opened the door for him and he went in and laid down.

The gas seeped in. He could hear the faint sussuration.

Drifting off, he thought about Zimm and wondered, if ever he took the trouble to scrutinize the fine print in the Sleepwalker contract, if he'd seen her name there, as part of the exchange.

Loan us your body, we pay you back in your lover's respect.

He tried hard not to wonder what they were going to do with him. This time.

The gas was getting to him. Experimentally, he tried to get up. He couldn't move a muscle. There was a moment of panic when a large blue-black fly lit on his right cheek and walked up toward his eye. He tried to move to shake it off, but couldn't do more than blink. It came onward, growing to a bristling huge black blur. His only escape was in closing his eyes.

And the gas took him down.

He deposited half the money in a new account, took seventy-five home to Ace and Bernie and simply handed it to them, to save them the trouble of having to ask.

Now he walked down Sunset Boulevard to the apartment building where Zimm lived. It was six, the sky melting like candle wax, tangerine-lemon at the horizon. The balmy June air slid velvet past his fingers as he hurried.

It was getting rapidly darker. He smiled. Thank God it gets dark this time of evening, thank God for that. That's fine and it's getting darker.

Suddenly lonely, Jules continued down the street, toward Zimm's. He was in a gay hustler district now, and there were others, slowly drifting down the street like blossoms on the wind. He nodded to those he recognized and shook his head at a customer who approached him. He lit another cigarette, though his throat felt raw.

But he was feeling left out again, and sinking. It called back the vision of the casket and the pearl and the cowls.

And that was something he wanted very much to forget.

His clothes clung to him. He was sweating excessively.

Nerves. There was electricity sparking between his teeth and the air was so charged with tension that the streetlight poles were straining to keep their upright shape against it and the buildings were squatting with secret muscles flexed. What were they afraid of?

No. He didn't want to remember. He didn't want to find out that way what the Sleepwalker Agency did with him while he was under. But he knew then that he would have to find out another way. He needed to know what the full terms of the agreement were, in detail. Otherwise the tension of uncertainty would never leave him.

A long dusty navy-blue air-turbine Cadillac pulled up beside him, honking. Unthinking, acting on reflex, Jules accepted the ride. He climbed into the car, grateful for the air-conditioned coolness. Beside him: a squat man with rubbery florid skin, a wide blocked-out nose and a collie's entreating tiny brown eyes. The man pulled the car back into the light traffic. 'Come and sit by me,' he ordered.

Jules came alert. *Christ, I should have known.* 'I'm not into it, man,' he said. 'I don't work that way anymore. Don't need it.' He assumed the man was one of his old tricks from when he'd cruised. 'I'll get out here.'

The john smiled, thinking that Jules was playing games, and reached a stubby hand for his crotch.

Jules backhanded the guy across his flaccid right cheek.

More startled than hurt, the stranger gave him a long look. 'You didn't mind last night. I guess they don't let you remember . . . but kid, last night you *performed*.' Was that a grin? Or a grimace?

The man grabbed for him again and, spasmodically, Jules kicked the steering wheel. The car nosed far left, began to slide sideways. Jules braced himself. A small import sedan hit the right front fender, which had crossed into oncoming traffic. The Cadillac's driver was jolted forward and his forehead cracked viciously on the steering wheel; he slumped over.

Jules was only wrenched. When the car stopped sliding he hopped out, dodging traffic, and ran to the curb, down the sidewalk. He looked back only once. The import was almost totaled, crumpled in supplication against the dominant, glistening block of the Cadillac. The fat man was alive, he stumbled out of the car, leaning on the import's crushed hood, the lines of his face defined in blood streaming from a headwound.

Jules turned away and ran around the corner.

When he arrived at Zimm's he was glad she wasn't home. He was going to be sick and wanted to get it over alone. Vision swimming, he let himself in and ran to the bathroom. He vomited, flushed the toilet, watched the piebald churn swirl down into the city's heart. Then he washed out his mouth, several times, and undressed. He ran a bath and got in before it had filled. He washed himself thoroughly, seeing everywhere unaccountable gray smudges on his limbs. Scrubbing violently, he rubbed them off, but they reappeared seconds later. It looked like mold.

He emptied the tub, cleaned it completely with ammonia and Ajax, rinsed it and filled it again. Again he cleansed himself. Emptied the tub, refilled it, scrubbed . . .

Finally, he stopped seeing the spots of mold.

But after he had toweled himself dry he saw in the mirror something dark red on the inner-side of his left buttock. A handprint. Not the handprint of the man in the blue Caddy. Bigger, with long fingers which must have ended in sharp nails.

It wouldn't go away.

*   *   *

He got the nose filters from Ace, who had worked briefly in a paint factory the year before. They were two thimble-like wiremeshes, guaranteed for a year, and Ace had only used them for a week. Jules hoped no one could see them, and he had pressed them deeply into his nostrils.

He lay back on the couch. He could hear the lisp of the gas coming through the grate, but he couldn't smell it. Good.

He was wide awake when the man in white came into the room ten minutes later. 'Stand up,' the man told him.

Jules stood up, moving slowly, gracefully, trying not to think. He had heard a friend of Ace's who knew an attendant at Sleepwalkers describe how the tranced moved, how they responded to orders. Slowly but not jerkily. *Look alert, but don't focus your eyes on anything, don't move unless you're told.*

'Follow me.' He followed the man out through the rear door and into a dressing room. The stranger was tall and brawny, with blond hair cut into a shag. He wore a white suit with a black tie, a patch sewn on one shoulder of the suit said only: SWA.

'Get dressed,' said the attendant, and left him. Jules went to one of the racks and selected a black robe. He began a frown then instantly repressed it. There was no one else in the room, but they might be watching. From somewhere.

The robe, with its soft black cloth and black cowl, was the same sort of robe he'd seen in his vision. The vision of the fly.

Probably the visions weren't literal, he thought, pulling the gown over his head. Probably the pictures were symbols, dream interpretations, with a few real-life components, like the robe.

There was no getting around it. He was getting scared.

He almost jerked around when he heard the door slam

behind, but he caught himself. 'Follow me,' the attendant intoned, sounding bored.

Jules turned slowly and trailed after him out the back door, down three concrete steps and into the Los Angeles night. They got into a van, all-white except for the agency's symbol in red with their motto: YOUR PLEASURE IS OUR BUSINESS.

The attendant opened the back door for him. Jules waited for the order.

'Climb in, sit down.'

Jules obeyed.

Like a trained dog, Jules thought. He talks to me like I'm a trained dog.

The attendant started the van and drove down the alley.

Jules sat on a metal bench staring at a metal wall and listening to the creak and grind of metal machinery around him. He sat upright with hands folded in his lap, staring straight ahead, braced against the inertia of the van's turning.

The van turned into a driveway and pulled up in another alley.

Jules was ordered out of the van and through the back door of an old tin-roofed warehouse.

He was led to stand on the lowest of five wooden steps rising to a stage, behind two other people. The curtains were drawn, backstage was twilight. Jules could hear the unseen audience murmuring. Two other hooded figures stood before him, one after the other, waiting: immobile, backs straight.

He heard, slightly muffled through the curtain, a voice addressing the audience through a microphone. 'Please remember to keep your requests within the limitations prescribed by the contract. Only those with red cards will be permitted the private use of these bodies, after the performance is over. Red cardholders interested in particular bodies should see the attendant for schedules and user-fee rates.'

Then the curtains rolled back, but from the wings the audience was still invisible. An attendant came up from behind and whispered to the first shrouded figure. 'Go up on the stage, get undressed, turn to face the audience.'

The figure obeyed and, leaning very slightly to the right, Jules could see that it was a young woman. With platinum hair. He looked closer. No, it wasn't Zimm. For ten seconds he had been sure it was her. He realized that he was not particularly relieved. He would not have been surprised or dismayed if it had been Zimm.

The woman was shorter, plumper than Zimm, with full breasts and rings glittering on her fingers. Her profile was all curves and puckers.

'First call,' the attendant told the hidden audience.

Jules heard someone shout, 'Dance like a monkey.' The woman leapt clumsily up and down, knees bent, until the voice added, 'Monkey in heat.' Face bestially contorted, the woman postured obscenely.

An attendant sent the second tranced onto the stage. He tossed off his robe and even from behind Jules knew it was Bernie.

Bernie needed a fix and couldn't wait on Jules.

'Monkeys mating,' came the command. Bernie did a mock-apish dance around the woman, then grasped her by the buttocks. She bent over. They simulated copulation, making bestial faces, and the crowd roared in satisfaction.

Jules heard the attendant behind him. 'That long-haired kid up there, got track marks on his arms. Plenty.'

'Goddamnit,' the other man said. 'They're supposed to inspect 'em before signing. Shit, this could be bad.'

'How'zat?' the first attendant said.

'These fuckhead dopers – any stuff in their blood-stream, it reacts with the sleep-gas, see – they can come out of it. Doesn't matter what shit they're shootin'.'

Bernie was facing toward Jules, ten feet away. Looking into Bernie's eyes, Jules realized it had already happened. Bernie had thrown off the effects of the gas. His eyes wandered, he looked scared. His lips twitched. But he did as he was told and Jules could see the inward litany in his eyes: *Make me one with the world's machines.* It worked. It fit. No one noticed that he was out of the trance. And maybe he wasn't.

Jules almost nodded to himself. This was home.

'Where's this guy go to?'

'Lemme see, what time is it? Oh – just take him up to Mr Carmody now. He should have gone on stage first, I guess.'

'Follow me,' the blond attendant whispered to Jules. Jules turned and followed, leaving Bernie behind as he'd left him twitching on the floor at home many times before.

Jules was escorted to a door, down a passage into another building. He was taken up an elevator, along a carpeted hallway. The dun carpet was spongy beneath his bare feet. The attendant took him into a bathroom, made him shower, dry off, then left him sitting nude on the edge of a wide round white bed in the bedroom of a luxurious apartment decorated Victorian; lace curtains, ancient yellowed oil paintings, quaint, elaborately carved furniture. Dust. Jules sat still, staring ahead, feeling a hot wire stretching tighter, tighter within him. It took him nearly two minutes to recognize this sensation: rage.

It had been a long time since he'd been angry at anyone but himself. And he could always hurt himself without outside retribution. But now – it was a rush to feel the anger, made all the hotter by his immobility. Coiling up inside.

And if he was taken to a place where there was a huge black pearl and a white casket containing something hideously outsized with shiny wings and faceted eyes – then he would do his best to kill someone.

Out of the corner of his eye he saw a door open. A withered little man, almost completely bald, entered and shuffled toward him.

Age-spots dappled the old man's lumpy scalp and trembling hands, and he walked with the aid of a fiber-glass cane. He wore a red terrycloth robe and red satin slippers. His eyes were sunken, watery gray-blue. He was toothless. He was a very old man. He faced Jules, looked him impishly up and down and smiled wistfully, showing withered gums. He was bent, hardly came up to Jules's biceps. I could strangle him with one hand, Jules thought. The fury mounted. Just let him touch me. I'll choke him for Bernie and Ace and me and Connie and Barb and for the child Zimm must have been, once.

The old man, Carmody, giggled and rasped, 'Com'on-com'on, ol' buddy-buddy!' He turned and Jules followed him into the next room.

It was a wealthy-child's nursery and playroom. A prodigious room painted in gaudy colors with a sprawling electric train set at the far end, a miniature two-rider carousel nearer, a sand box, and a huge wooden crate of toys, five feet to a side.

Humming, the old man went to the chest of toys. A hysterical orange orangutan was painted on the facing side of the chest.

Carmody fumbled through the toys till he found a small wooden broom and a battered red wig. 'I'll be the mommy and you'll be the daddy and you can mow the lawn.' He nodded again and again. His hands shook with excitement, the gray skin on them so loose and vitreously wrinkled they looked like rubber gloves.

Once more digging into the box he found a small plastic lawnmower and handed it to Jules.

Gazing in wonder at the toy, Jules accepted it. All semblance of the trance was now discarded. Carmody either didn't notice or didn't care. He had put the red wig crookedly on his head and was busily sweeping the floor of an imaginary kitchen. Humming in an unnaturally highpitched voice.

Jules felt duped. The fury drained from him, the beautiful transparent rush of long-suppressed hostility like the rush of meth, fading away. The acceptance returning.

No, he told himself. *Uh-uh. Don't fall for it. This is the same as if you'd performed sexually. You're still following orders, he's still using you, you're just a toy.* Jules dropped the plastic lawnmower and turned away. He went to the lightswitch. He would turn out the light and strangle the old man. He put his fingers on the switch.

He turned at a tap on his shoulder. The old man was smiling, holding out the scarlet wig. 'You don't wanna be the daddy? You can be the mommy if you want.'

Once more, for an instant, Jules felt cheated.

Then, for Bernie and Ace and Barb and Connie but not for Zimm, he went back to the lawnmower, picked it up, began pushing it cheerfully back and forth, saying to the old man: 'No, you can be the mommy.'

Tahiti in Terms of Squares

Now: I'm going to tell you something –

Go right ahead. Parent paid for it, not me, so talk away.

– and you'd better be paying strict attention. First I'll tell it to you, then you'll begin to see it, manifesting before you. Because that's the way things work here.

Okay. I'm listening.

Listening isn't good enough. If you want to *see* you must give me your complete attention. Concentration.

All right! I'm paying attention.

Good. This concerns Tahiti. I offer a cinematic exegesis in arbitrarily selected stages of that continuum.

Which continuum?

That one . . . over *there*.

Oh, okay. I'm with you –

Before I begin, read off the pertinent points of the introductory pamphlet. I want to be utterly assured you know exactly what we're up to, coming here. Why the Between is useful to us.

The Between? I don't need to read the pamphlet. Anyhow, I threw it away. Ummm . . . what we're doing here is –

Threw it away? Threw away the *pamphlet?* After the agency spends involuted Karmas to have those pamphlets 'grammed! I hardly think that's a –

Doesn't matter, I memorized it. More or less. It said this field trip will enable me to 'attain objectivity in the antiduality perspective achieved through the externalization of parity' . . . which is one of those attitudes Parent

thinks it's so necessary to adopt. Privately I don't understand why Parent is so anti-Subjectivist. Anyhow, it said
I've been brought to this vast, clammy, pearly-white place
with the two definitionless curving walls so . . . could I
have a drink off your bulb? I didn't bring one.

Go on, go on; why were you brought here?

Oh. So I'll learn something by graphic example. A
lesson concerning the mechanics utilized in the insemination of zones of reality. So the pamphlet claimed. Something like that. Personally, I think Parent assumes the
whole thing will engender in me a reactionary Objectivist
philosophy or some such nonsense . . . I'm *dry* after all
that ranting, can I have a drink off your bulb? Ah,
thanks –

'Some such nonsense'! Puerile half-weaned! It is far
from nonsense. This exercise will help to assure you never
get lost while plane-sifting. In the Between we can
objectively observe the means with which zones of reality
radiate from archetypal cusps, after which everything else
in that sphere of wavelength-specific influence is patterned. Got it?

Yeah, sure. Got it.

Hey – don't drink it all. You could have exchanged for
your own bulb . . . Now. Let me . . . here it is . . . this is
Prime A for Tahiti Continuum. Look – right over *there*.
Come a few steps this way. Now look where I'm pointing.
See him? *There*.

He glanced at the watch strapped on his left wrist. The
face of the watch said noiselessly: 'It's time.' The watch
had no hands or dial, nothing but two pale rubbery lips
set into the face and he read the lips as would a deaf
person, though he wasn't deaf. He might as well have
been deaf because he was alone in the abode of silence
and as far as he knew there was no one outside of silence's
abode at all, and even if there were, surely no one would

be capable of breaking in through silence's unspeakable defenses. And he didn't comprehend speaking except in terms of squares . . . you'd have thought the room that contained him was about fifty feet square with three yards between floor and ceiling. No furniture. He didn't need furniture, and although he possessed a human body he didn't sleep or rest or ingest or digest or excrete (except in the nonmaterial terms of the squares). The palpitating tissues, the anticipatory wetness of his human flesh was ready and waiting to sweat/eat/spit/digest/excrete/excite but none of those reactions were indigenous to the time frame in which the body was ever-presently coded. It had been deliberately coded into the flicker between two heartbeats, between two breaths. But he moved about and he had the false impression that it was under his own power . . . that's all you need to know about *him*, as he stands as an individual, except if you want to know what he looked like.

Yes, I rather would.

Oh. You would? Troublesome of you. But all right. He had an average man's body, for the middle Twentieth Century era, Tahiti continuum; he was English, caucasian, six foot and one hundred and sixty pounds, sparse and extra-soft brown hair, watery-blue eyes. But he would have looked strange to the biological refractions patterned after him because his face and head were that of an infant of three weeks, homo sapiens baby, soft and inchoate, vague like a baby though the volume of the head was proportionate to his body.

No eyebrows?

None. When his watch told him it was time which it periodically did –

I can see him! Over against that curving wall, by all those checker-things, in –

Obviously, idiot. Why else would I be explicating him?

Verbal description is the token for this vending machine. As you can see, he is and was . . . I'll restrict my narrative to past tense because past tense *here* sparks the present tense *there*, which is the apropos mechanics of that locale –

Or maybe you're just nostalgic and sentimental.

Shut up and listen. Now: He was alerted by the watch to the necessity of palming the squares. You can see the squares on the walls, there.

Squares in a variety of colors, yeah. Pastel shades.

Yes. Each square a foot in diameter and six inches from the others, evenly patterning the walls. None on ceiling and floor –

I can see that for myself.

Shut up, it's necessary for me to say it. Where were we? Oh: He went to the walls and pressed his palm against the light brown square. When the palm of his soft, uncalloused hand, his right hand, pressed onto the surface, it is adhered gently, with a sticky commingling –

Hey! You're narrating that in the present tense! You said '*is* adhered gently . . .'

Ah, thank you. Very kind of you to bring that to my attention. Very kind. Naturally I'd have noticed it myself in time.

Naturally. But . . . why can't you narrate in present tense?

It's dangerous.

Dangerous! Oh *really* –

Laugh if you like. It is dangerous.

What happens if you narrate this scenario in present tense?

I suppose I can demonstrate if I do it in a very cautiously controlled manner. *Observe:*

He smiles, enjoying the onrush of physicalized data, abandoning himself to it like a death-dwarf-junkie to a rush, he sighs and presses his arm further in, to the wrist, to the forearm, elbow, until the arm is immersed in the stuff, vanished into the wall, and his shoulder begins to sink also, his head grows rubbery and pliant as it is sucked into the square –

Hey! You'd better cut that out. He's disappearing, his head is *going*.

The longer I do it the more difficult it is to reverse. Now, as you can see, the image is frozen, he is half in the square, its precipitous consumption of him halted because I've stopped narrating altogether. But if I were to continue, the inertia of the present tense narration, which tends to proliferate its own future because its inception in *now* causes a hollow in the *to be* which must be filled since time follows the path of least resistance, like everything else.

Well – can you get him out of there?

I can now; the inertia didn't build up to the degree that I lost control. *Listen:* Realizing he'd gone too far, he drew his arm out of the dun square, slowly letting the data-dew drain cleanly away and back to its source, as his head and limb returned to their normal aspects . . . He stood back, stretched, sighed, and began again, this time more conservative in his rate of induction. When the palm of his soft, uncalloused right hand pressed onto the surface, it was adhered gently with sticky commingling. Now he experiences the tea gustatorially, smells its boiled aroma, is aware of its initial texture on his lips.

Hey, aren't you narrating in –

Don't interrupt again, you're distracting me. I have to concentrate. Keep your eyes on him; how else do you expect to learn? *Heed:*

The drink is silvery, it is earthcolored, it is velvet, it is mischievously steamy. He does not linger amongst these superficial sensations. He goes on. His hand slowly sinks into the brown square, the edges of tea-data brinking his flesh seeping up, around his knuckles and over the back of his hand, creeping over his wrist. If he chooses, he can press his entire arm up to the shoulder into the brown square which would then expand to accommodate the remainder of his body, the other squares shrinking to compensate. But he sinks only up to his shoulder . . . *Comprendé?*

Solid. Yeah.

So this provides him with an orderly immersion into the whole matrix between the origins, the empirical and the conclusions of various strains of *Thea Sinensis*. Tea. He is aware of the tea in every cell and pore now, and his back is rigid, his eyes rolled upward, as he relishes the trance. He is aware (in rippling fibrillations coursing his fingers and arm, traveling down into his spine by unbroken but oscillating channel) of the etiology of the earliest forms of the plant identifiable as a strain of *Thea Sinensis*, its taste relative to the latest flavor in the manifold tea hybrids, its genetic makeup, how it came to cross-pollinate into yet another form of tea, and another, how that tea was discovered and savored in turn by a clan of naked savages, how those savages were affected by the tea, the trading of that tea to other tribes and the articles for which it was traded, the effect of the tea on the other tribe, the cultural reverberations of the tea, the various comparative hybrid phases and related species developed deliberately or accidentally by these tribes and by the civilizations engineered by their progeny and the status of tea therein, all books written about tea including recipes and treatises on the various complementary additives, the names and life histories of all tea manufacturers, plantation owners, connoisseurs; the cultural effect of tea on every society into which it is introduced, the colors, scents

and textures of the leaf and flower and their configurations in botanists' schematics, the microscopically discerned panoply of a cross-section of tea-plant cells, the
plants viewed through the filter of the fourth and the fifth
dimensions, the rituals and traditions stemming from the
various historic derivations of tea, the names and life
stories of the first person who ever used tea and the last
who ever will –

All this and more?

Exactly. But the information, somatically calibrated
data, does not linger in the brain cells of our babyface; it
lights the lamps and then snuffs the flame an instant after
it is lit. When at last babyface extracts his arm from the
square he recollects none of what he's just experienced
and measured. His arm is clean when it is removed. The
brown substance (physical realization of data) does not
cling to his skin, and its information eschews internment
in memory. And the surface of the square closes up as if
it had never been disturbed . . .

Hey, you've changed from past –

Don't interrupt! Watch him! Now having finished tea it
is time for a walk down the beach. He goes to –

Hey, listen, should you have changed from –

Shut up! He goes to the next square in line, to the left,
which is pastel shades of sunset red and tropical sky blue
and beach-sand white and bamboo yellow and palm-trunk
brown, all gently blended strata. He places his palm
against this polychromatic square and sinks only up to the
wrist. He is no longer aware of his arm as entering the
square, now he is all rapport with the sensory-eidetic
organ-music of data; surrounding and permeating this
beach in Tahiti about '1910 A.D.', relative to this conflu-
ence. He raptures in the atomic structure of sands and
wavelength dissection of photons in refraction with sea
spray and contrasted with the various poems written

about the tropics (read in alphabetical order) and theses
concerning Tahiti written up till January 1, 1910.

Ah, as with tea but more so?

Just so.

I see. But still you've changed your –

Quiet! Now he glances at the watch on his left wrist –
he does this with that part of his reflexes specially
reserved for that action – and registers: 'Time for lunch'.
So he begins to withdraw his arm, shedding cognizance as
he does, preparing to depart to the beach square so that
he can progress to the lunch square that is the absolute
fact of a sandwich, a ham and cheese sandwich on stale
imported rye and all the background and layers of sensation infinitely minute and macrocosmically unfolding
from that node of perception. He draws his arm out –

Hey! I'm trying to *tell* you, you've gotten into present
tense!

What? I . . . Oh *damn*, I've gone and done it now.
That'll result in a stress pattern and rupture the membrane unless I can keep up, overtake the verbal realizations, catch up, slow it down to past tense. Get control
again. Like trying to harness maddened horses, at this
point. Why the Monitor didn't you tell me this before I –

I'm sorry. I tried.

Never mind. I've got to concentrate or it's going to fly
out of its groove and strike off on its own. Ah, his arm is
emerging – was emerging? – from the square and suffers
a spasm, his fingers get caught on the edge of the square,
the inner edge on the interior of the pastel shades. He
tugs, a little furrow of frustration invading his otherwise
dispassionate face, and the wall quivers under the pull.
He cannot disengage his fingers from the inner edge of
the wall-frame and, angrily, he gives it a furious yank.
This time there is a crackling sound –

I feel all cold inside. I don't like this feeling in my guts.

A chill. Unpleasant, brittle. Something getting loose inside me. I –

Quiet! I'm losing ground, damn it! Ah, a crackling sound and a portion of the seemingly unbreakable wall comes loose in his fingers, chipped off, (Oh damn it all!) and the liquid inferential being in the square comes pouring out of the gap and splatters babyface about the feet. He staggers, he turns to run but is overwhelmed and vanishes from view as the section of the square that was green-yellow licks out and expands like a fire in a match factory and the room begins to fill up with bamboo shoots shooting and leaves unfolding. Quickly after comes the brown and the blue and the white formulating into magically upspringing palmtrees and billows of sky-gas and the room is suddenly filled to capacity with shifting arabesques of sand and water and foliage, exceeding the bursting point as babyface is compressed and annihilated, processed into seminal droplets which fertilize the soil of the frenetically proliferating island paradise growing like a self-inflating rubber raft and *oh damn* I can't catch up, I've lost the reins –

What's happening? I can't see! It's all a boiling of liquefied leaves and sandstorm and there went a swordfish! The wall is crackling, the walls of white . . . Hey! It's coming out *here*.

It's making a break for it, spilling into the Between, it's going to have to compensate itself now, engender a plane in which to root the tropical belt – oh damn – hold your breath, I'll attempt an –

'Harold! Look at those two on the beach up there. In the shade of those palms.'

He shrugged. 'Just a couple of beachcombers, dear, I doubt they'll be any trouble. They look a trifle dazed, don't they?'

'*Dazed* is hardly the word. Harold, they're *naked!*'

'Ah . . . yes indeed. So they are . . . Well bother! Come about, dear, we'll do well to turn back. We'll complain to the desk clerk at the Captain Bligh. He said the riff raff had been cleared off the beach. Hedonists of some sort, by the look of them. And white, too! Oh, *do* stop crying, Emily.'

'I can't help it. They look *mad*. We've got to hurry. And I shall expect you to complain to the consulate.'

'Of course. But I'm sure they . . . quite harmless. The light was sort of . . . ah . . . diffused about them. And I could swear that neither one had a nose . . .'

Shading her eyes against the sun's tropical glare she gazed timorously over her shoulder.

She shrieked.

'They're coming *after* us.'

(Running footsteps, heavy breathing, curses from the British gentleman as he stumbles. His wife valiantly pauses to help him rise.)

Excuse me, said one of the odd, pallid men as he caught up with them, *I wonder can you direct us back to the Between? We've no idea how to get back from here. Frankly, we're quite lost. Terribly sorry about all this. The world. Spilled something. Sorry. Dreadful inconvenience, I know.*

He said it in a language that anyone anywhere in the universe would instantly have understood.

Silent Crickets

The milky moonlight sifted by mercuric clouds, snickers through the dense woods in slippery shafts. The faint light laps at the crotches of trees and catches on tangles of bared branches, giving the moss the silver sheen of mold. The deciduous trees are in bunches infrequently invaded by a lone pine. Roots are choked with fallen leaves. Bared branches are abstracted into atmospheric capillaries. In the inky shadows under a short conical fir tree a man crouches with a rifle in his right hand. He moves slowly forward, trying to make as little noise as he can, and creeps into the crater left by an uprooted pine. The huge dying pine is lying on its side, smaller frustrated trees crushed under its trunk; its roots are thrusting up over the man's head. He hunkers in the shallow pit, his booted feet gripping the mud, rifle barrel catching the light and tinting it blue. The only sound is the *chirr* of a sneaking raccoon and the repetitive song of the crickets.

The crickets go abruptly silent.

The man is on the alert.

Something moves invisibly through the woods. He tenses, raises the .36, props the gunstock against his right shoulder, finger tightening around the trigger. He reaches for the safety catch. *Is it one of them?*

The figure emerges.

It's a man, a man alone. The man with the gun, Buckley, curator of the Deepwood Museum of Modern Art, stands and waves. The stranger, his face only partially visible, nods and comes forward. He stands silently a few feet from Buckley, looking at the long rifle upright at the curator's side. The man wears dungarees and a white longsleeve shirt. The night conceals most of his features.

'Are you Buckley?' he asks in a low, oily tone.

'Yes.'

'I'm . . . Cranshaw. I'm from the New York Art Association. I've been looking for you. I believe your story . . . more or less. I want to hear it from your own lips, anyway. I've had a similar . . . experience. I came to talk to you in your study and your servant – she was quite flustered – said that you'd run out here after burning the paintings. A strange business, Buckley, burning eight hundred thousand dollars' worth of Miró and Matta and Picasso . . .'

'How many kinds of sexual reproduction are there?' Buckley asks, his voice sounding strange to him in the sucking darkness.

'Well . . . there's mitosis, and cross-pollination and among humanity there's good old – '

'Among humanity there's something *else*,' Buckley interrupts, speaking in a rapid clip. 'A new kind of mutation. Have you heard it said that an artist doesn't create a "new" vision, but only siphons it from another dimension of reality where that abstraction is the physical law? Perhaps. Perhaps if the abstract or surrealist artist steals from that world's images, from that other plane long enough, the creatures inherent to that world will take an interest in us and contrive to come here. Perhaps they'll use us as a medium, transferring themselves through a kind of paintbrush insemination. I keep thinking of the words of the dadaist Jean Arp: *Art is like fruit, growing out of man – like the child out of its mother* . . . Someday, Cranshaw, a child will replace its parents.'

'Maybe. Come back to your study and we'll talk about it – '

'No. Haven't you been reading about all the artists who've been disappearing? Well, I was visiting Matta when I *saw* something happen to him. I can't describe – '

'All this is interesting but rather xenophobic,' the stranger interrupts. 'My experiences were not so much like yours as I had thought. It's not easy to be a curator these days, God knows. Those snotty young painters. But come back and have a drink with me, Buckley. We'll work things out from there. Don't be afraid.' He reaches out a hand to Buckley's shoulder.

Buckley steps backwards, his hand tightens on the barrel of the gun. If this man is from the Art Association, why is he dressed like a country hick? Cranshaw touches Buckley's shoulder. Suspicions confirmed. Buckley feels it then, the warning tingle, the onrush of activated abstraction. He steps back again raises the gun. 'You lied to me,' he murmurs as much to the night as to Cranshaw.

Another movement from the far side of the fallen tree catches his eye. Pure moving anachronism issuing from the areola of upturned roots. It was the abstract figure of Marcel Duchamp's *Nude Descending A Staircase* given its own independent life. A study of strobed motion, the exegesis of a few moments of time into cubism. The creature, viewed literally, glowing against the tenebrous curtain of the woods, resembles a robot strung in Siamese twin extrapolations of itself, leaving behind a hallucinogenic acid trail like a mechanical cape. It might be built of copper-colored tin cans and its torso (futurist extrapolation of pivotal rotation) is built in striations like the gills of a shark. Moving toward Buckley, it is a random tumble of spastic geometry, a carnivorous handy kitchen appliance. The figure is a vector for the bizarre, leaving behind it a wake of abstracted trees, brush distorting into a vision of Siamese triplet belly dancers; tree trunks made Rousseau primitive and perfectly cylindrical-smooth, branches becoming pin-cushion spines. But the voice of the vector is human.

'I couldn't wait any longer. I had to come. Has he been readied?'

'No,' the stranger who called himself Cranshaw replies, 'not just yet.'

'Buckley,' came the voice from the golden arachnid whirlpool, 'come here.'

Buckley pulls a slim penlight from his pocket and shines it on Cranshaw's face. He gasps. A Modigliani simplification, that face, with pits of Munch hollowness around the eyes. The man, while outwardly proportional, is made of rigid planes, unmoving eyes, the same perpetual sardonic smile two inches to the left of his nose. One of his eyes is considerably higher than the other. His arms are blocked into rectangular surfaces with ninety-degree corners.

'It's alright,' says the Cranshaw-thing, its voice fuzzy now. 'Don't worry.' It reaches out a squared-off hand to Buckley's upraised rifle, touches the barrel with a gentle caress at the same moment that the curator touches the trigger.

The gun doesn't go off. There is a conspicuous silence. Instead of an explosion, comes a faint puffing sound. A globular bullet bounces like a soap bubble off Cranshaw's chest and floats up through the clawing trees. Desperately, Buckley feels the barrel of the gun. It sags in his fingers like an exhausted erection, rubbery and pliant. He breaks off a piece of the barrel and puts it to his mouth. Licorice. The gun melts into a snakelike abstraction. He flings it away but already the tingling chill is travelling up his arm. He looks at the two abstract beings standing patiently by, sees them reticulate and waver like an unstable TV picture. He looks down at his body, sees his legs sprout roots which rapidly burrow into the humus under his new hooves.

I Live in Elizabeth

She lets me take control. Taking control feels like coming awake, in a way. I haven't been asleep, mentally; but physically I've been in whatever corner of our brain my sensations go when I'm asleep.

There is a moment of dysjunction, when I feel I'm floating free from her, and I experience an almost overwhelming relief. And then she slips aside and I click with her motor controls, jack into her senses, take command of her coordination . . . I begin to feel her physical sensations in a disorienting rush: all of a sudden it's evening and she's fatigued; I monitor a pain, *two* areas of pain: one in her right leg, because it's begun to suffer from lack of circulation, as we've been sitting too long in one position. And a pain in our midriff. Cramps. Her period. Something hard to get used to, since I'm male. There's so damned much I have to get used to. And none of it's easy.

She let me write the several sentences you've just read. We've decided to write an account of what happened, so that we can get some help.

We're having trouble . . . adjusting . . .

The first time I saw Elizabeth, I knew instantly she'd change my life.

It was a cool Sunday afternoon in June, about ten months ago, outside a theater in the East Village. Clouds shifted the street into twilight and then slipped aside – and suddenly the sunlight was flooding her. She stood looking at a movie poster. *Jesus* she was lovely. She looked older than seventeen, at first. I thought her twenty, or twenty-one. Partly it's the clothing she wears. New York downtown boutique. *The Face* magazine. A touch pretentious, perhaps like some of her speech mannerisms. But she's a knockout. Long thick black hair, almost to her waist. Full hips, long in the legs. Something Latin in her face; her mother's Italian.

We'd just come out of the theater – I'd noticed her inside too, about five rows down from me, all alone, rapt, a solitary bust in the artificial twilight.

Now she stood gazing at the movie poster. She glanced at me, and I had a glimpse of her eyes – so brown they were almost black, set off by mink lashes. Her lips were full, her lower lip like a silk pillow.

She was a divine anomaly, an angel in a leper colony, because we stood on the corner of one of the dirtiest streets in New York, just off the Bowery. The cryptic spraypaint graffiti seemed to crawl on every available surface; the sidewalks and the walls of the buildings were the same grimy gray, the streets imprinted with bottlecaps and poptops pressed into the asphalt by thousands of cars, every vacant lot heaped with broken bottles, fast-food containers, racing forms, and things gone unrecognizable with weather and age. Against that background: Elizabeth, luminous.

I'd gone alone to see Fellini's *Amarcord*. It seemed the appropriate conversational opening. 'It's funny how Fellini can make me feel nostalgic about a place I've never been to . . .'

She nodded. 'I know what you mean. My mother's Italian, though, so maybe I've got some sort of ancestral memory of the place. And of course the imagery is incredibly well-defined . . .'

I realized that she was a teenager. It was in her tone of voice, her pronunciation. Trying to impress me with her maturity. Most teenage girls don't use terms like *ancestral memory* and *imagery*.

Beat it, I told myself. *Make tracks. You're thirty-one, my friend. Don't be foolish.*

I looked into her eyes. A shock of recognition. And for a moment I was dizzy. I felt I'd been standing near the wall, with my back to it, gazing at – myself. Seeing myself ogling her shamelessly, as she would have seen me.

And then it was over. I returned to myself, blinked, and took a step back. *What the hell was* that? I thought. I forgot about it when she smiled at me. From that moment, I *knew*. It was all over but the ritual, the dance, the preliminaries. I had to have her, and I would. On some level, I knew.

We chatted. We exchanged names. I told her my friends call me 'Blue' and she admitted that she was from Elizabeth, New Jersey and that her name was Elizabeth. I resisted joking about that. I had just moved to Manhattan; she was only there for the day.

I knew other things about her. Things she didn't tell me. I knew what her bedroom looked like, and what her last boyfriend had said to her just before she broke up with him, and what music she listened to, and what her parents were like. It didn't occur to me to ask myself how I'd come to know these things. I was drunk on her, and I liked the feeling. I wasn't going to ask questions.

I knew, also, that she was only seventeen. I didn't care.

I looked at her lips. I swear to God I knew just what it would feel like to kiss them. And I knew that I would, eventually.

We had come to the awkward moment. She had to say goodbye and move away, or seem easy. I had to come up with some alternative.

Both of us waited for a few moments as I tried to think of something.

She smiled, seemed mildly disappointed, and said, 'Well, I guess I'd better – '

'Have a cup of coffee with me?' I tried to look casual. I told myself that it was a lame thing to say, *have a cuppa coffee with me*. And after all, she could see I was past thirty. She'd be crazy to go out with me and I'd be crazy to take her out. There were laws.

But she said, 'There's a pretty decent little cafe around the corner . . .'

It was a month – a month of meeting her a discreet distance from her school, of nights full of doubts, of necking in Central Park. A month before I worked up the nerve to meet her parents.

Elizabeth hadn't told them my age.

I'd talked to them on the phone, once. Her father said, 'So this is the mystery boy!' Her mother said, 'Well *do* come over for dinner Sunday, Blue, we'd love to meet the boy who's been occupying so much of our little girl's time.' *Our little girl*. 'She says you do some kind of journalism. For the college paper?'

I winced. 'No, I write for the *Daily News*, Sunday Supplement usually.'

'Oh? A cub reporter?'

My nerve failed. 'Something like that.'

That week, in anticipation of Sunday, the date after which we expected her parents to forbid me to see her, we made love for the first time. Our first time together, I mean: she wasn't a virgin. In fact, she taught me more than I taught her.

But I can feel her objecting to the direction this story is taking.

She says I can tell you about the drugs. I don't approve of them, usually. But that evening, trying to make love to her in my rickety studio apartment, I felt like a child molester. A grimy feeling. Made me tense. And tension made me impotent. So that's when she took the little black film container from her transparent plastic purse. The container didn't have film in it, though. 'Demerol or coke?' she asked.

I'd never had either one, and here was this seventeen-year-old girl offering me both.

I looked at the bindle and the half-dozen triangular tablets and shook my head. But I said: 'The Demerol.'

I dropped two. Twenty minutes later I realized there was ice in me I didn't know about till it started to melt . . . I turned into warm water and flowed into Elizabeth's arms. What had been tense became relaxed, and what had been limp became rigid. I felt myself moving against her and she was silkier than silk and I was amazed to discover just how damn *strong* the muscles of her thighs were. Everything was working; we were shining together. I was a flashlight beam fanning over snow, making it glitter. There was a funny sense that I could feel my own touch as *she* felt it – in a sort of empathy, a somatic echo. Like I was sending a sonar pulse into her: the signal would fly to her, and she would experience it and alter it and bounce it back to me so I could experience her experience . . .

I communed with her, and reached a peak of ecstatic exchange –

And then the world was gone.

I was spinning through space. I was a fiery discus passing through a mirror image of itself. Somewhere, there was a wordless singing.

I found myself in bed with a rather gaunt young man of thirty-one. Good-looking fellow, really, with bright blue eyes. But I'm not at all gay, I was terrified by the positioning of things – until I realized who he was. Me.

With Elizabeth's hands, I touched myself – I mean, I touched Elizabeth's body with Elizabeth's hands.

And felt indescribably peculiar.

Elizabeth inhabited the body I'd departed. I touched that masculine face – how coarse my skin felt, from the outside!

Elizabeth smiled at me, with my lips.

There was an amorphous tug, and a negative shimmering. Through the Looking Glass, again. I was back in myself, or back in the rough chariot of flesh my actual self rides about in. Elizabeth returned to her own body. We had found our way back, tracing some ectoplasmic umbilicus.

My eyes opened wide and locked onto hers. The mutual knowledge, the mutual experience, crackled the space between us. Sweet sparks flew when I touched her.

You know how isolated most people are, most of the time? People who live together for years know a few camouflaging layers of each other's personality. Inside, they ache with loneliness.

A few of us have a talent that makes it possible to transcend the barrier between people. I'm not sure what it is, really. But it's genuine. No hallucination.

And we've got other talents.

We spent a blissful week meeting secretly. I helped her with her homework. I don't think she needed help, but she knew it made me feel good to play The Educated Male. In return –

No, no, I really needed help on the trig, Blue. Only, you made it worse.

Sorry. She took control for a moment. Great little kidder. Where was I? Oh: I helped her with her homework, and in return she criticized my feature story on the housing crisis – she said it was shallow, I vilified the landlords without taking their perspectives into account. I pretended she was wrong. We made love.

The exchange didn't always happen, when we had sex. It happened less than half the time. That was a relief, because it was a frightening experience, till I got used to it.

Even more frightening was the first occasion our *two* consciousnesses shared *one* body for more than a split second. For ten or fifteen seconds we cohabited in my body . . . while hers remained alive but somehow empty.

The cohabitation wasn't altogether pleasant. We had to learn how to communicate, as two minds in one body, without terrifying one another with a blizzard of random mental imagery. The first few cohabitations ended in confusion, our nerves overloaded, raw. Now, we've learned the internal dance, the revolving of polarized mental focus-points, making the sharing possible.

Sunday afternoon, I went to Elizabeth's house to meet her parents. I wore a suit, and maybe that was bad psychology. It was July; too hot for a suit. I stood on their doorstep, sweating, wires of tension knotting in my gut, waiting for someone to answer the door. I remember I kept picking flecks of lint off my suit – it was a dark suit, all wrong for Summer. I *felt* Elizabeth coming to answer the door. The door opened and I had to fight myself. She wore a wrap around skirt and a bikini top. 'Hi,' she said, glancing over her shoulder. 'Did you bring the – '

Just then her dad came to the door and interrupted her. But I knew what she'd meant. She'd asked me to pick up some blow for her. She worked after school part-time at a bookstore, and half her wages went to cocaine. She'd given me the money and I'd bought two grams for her; picked it up from her friends, dutiful as a husband stopping for a loaf of bread on the way home from work.

I still refused to use the stuff, or even do a second dose of Demerol, and she made fun of me.

'So this is the mystery boy,' said her dad, again.

I smiled and extended my hand. But he didn't shake it. The smile had left his face as he looked me over. 'How old did you say you were, friend?' he asked, rather abruptly.

I was annoyed, and I opted for honesty. 'I'm thirty-one,' I said.

Elizabeth closed her eyes and swallowed visibly.

Mrs Calder came to the door. They were the sort of couple who'd come to look like one another, over the years. Both were tanned, a little bulbous, their faces lined in the same directions. Mr Calder asked me, leaning against the doorframe, 'Buddy, what the hell you think you're going to get away with here? How stupid do you think we are?'

Elizabeth swore and walked into the house. I said, 'I'm not a chiseler or a creep, Mr Calder. I'm far from well-to-do, but I've got a good job and when your daughter comes of age, I'd like to marry her. When she's eighteen. In earlier times it wasn't uncommon for a girl of *fourteen* to be – '

'I'll have to ask you to leave.'

I lost my temper. 'Look – you're a hypocrite. If I was somebody really wealthy, Donald Trump or someone, but *forty* – you'd shake my hand and ask which caterers to use at the wedding. You wouldn't give a damn about my age. You and your wife are a couple of narrowminded hypocrites who wouldn't know *love* if it bit you on the ass – ' All right, it was stupid. But I was sure I'd never get to see Elizabeth again.

Elizabeth's father gave me a vicious shove in the center of my chest, making me totter backwards. I resented that. I returned to the doorstep, reached past him to a shelf just inside the door, snatched up a vase of water and wilted crocuses, and dumped it on his head. Sputtering, he knocked the vase from my hand and took a swing at me. I took a swing at him. No solid connections. His wife panicked and ran outside, shouting for the cops.

My luck: the guy across the street was an off-duty cop. He was a red-faced guy, smelling of suntan lotion, who trotted over in his thongs and Bermuda shorts and twisted my arms behind me before I had a chance to state my case. He was a big guy. I was not so big. He told Elizabeth's father to go through my pockets.

And then I remembered the cocaine.

I spent the next seven months in prison.

Possession of cocaine, first offense, and they'd just toughened the laws – good timing. Would have copped two years in that concrete rat maze, if it weren't for the Agremerol experiments.

Does that sound like I got off easy? *Only* seven months in prison?

You've already pictured it. You picture the over-crowded cells – cells crowded with men whose entire lives are just waiting periods between outbursts of rage. You picture the gang-rapes in the showers, the men drawing territorial lines, parceling out other men into allies and chattels and enemies; you picture the corrupt, indifferent guards, the smuggled drugs and, everpresent, the motion-less horror: the endless gun-colored claustrophobic confinement.

Well, you're wrong. It's different.

It's different, because it's worse. It's at least five times worse than you imagine. Take everything ugly you visu-alize for prison, multiply it by *five*, and you've imagined it right. That's because it's five times more crowded than it should be.

Elizabeth saved my sanity.

After her first visit to the prison, we decided not to see one another again, until I got out. At least, not through the wiremesh of the visiting room. It was torment. We had something better. She gave me a time, a very specific time. She would be in her bedroom, alone, at the appointed hour.

One A.M. . . . every Wednesday and Sunday. I'd open my eyes and stare into the darkness. I'd picture Elizabeth lying on her bed. I'd visualize her bedroom, her red-shaded lamp, the tree outside her window rustling gently against the pane in the breeze. Somehow the tree was a key, and helped the elements of the visitation fall into place . . . I'd seen her room once, before my run-in with her parents, meeting Elizabeth secretly when the Elder Calders were away, I'd concentrate on the picture and the darkness over my bunk would split, would fuse into two intense orbs of onyx: the pupils of Elizabeth's eyes. The vision of Elizabeth, in startling hypnogogic clarity, would begin with the eyes and fill itself in from there; her brow, nose, lips, her oval face, her spill of glossy black hair, her white shoulders shaded with olive-gold . . .

I would be one moment on a ratty bunk in the State Pen, seconds later I was lying on Elizabeth's fragrant bed, beneath a single soft blue sheet, a red lamp on the wall beside me laying a rosy tinge on the shadows.

Elizabeth was there, with me.

Once as a little boy, I'd shared a bed with my visiting cousin. Lollie and I were both five, and our parents thought we were too young too worry about. Our house was small, the beds few – they figured it was safe. We had a lovely time. I brought a flashlight under the covers, when the rest of the house was asleep, and we examined one another in fascination. The blanket over us, the atmosphere beneath steamy with body heat, perfumed with our natural scents – all of it made me feel that she and I had gone into a separate world together, where each shared the other's body. A world of innocent sensual sharing.

That's how I felt, then, with Elizabeth. Only, instead of being under a blanket together, we were nestling within a single skin. We couldn't exactly *see* one another – it was a sort of blind mental groping with ghostly physical sensations . . . But we were distinct entities. We never quite merged, and we never will. I have never completely identified with her, even now. It was like holding a woman close *from the inside*. And when I operate her body, it's like a particularly intimate dancing. I've never lost my sense of maleness. I don't feel female; I simply feel extraordinarily close to one.

When both of us occupied one body, either she or I would be in control of that body's movements at any one time. When she's in command of the body, I'm there, passive but conscious of what's going on, experiencing her physical sensations in a sort of reverberation. I don't hear all of her thoughts, unless she wills it. We are distinct, but intertwined, two djinn in one lovely, ornate bottle.

And when we make love . . . I could tell you about the secret chambers of her, the cellular singings in her, the electrical rushes I send racing through her nervous system. And then we trade muscular control, very quickly, so we can –

Don't tell them this.

Sorry, dear. It's just that it's an area of enthusiasm for me. And . . . it's so rarely I get to talk to anyone outside you –

You *are* sick of me. I knew it! You –

No, no. Let's not go into that again, Elizabeth. Later. Anyway, I had a lot of time to think in prison. It was hard to think, at first, because the cells are so crowded, so noisy, and there were nineteen men in mine. Gambling for cigarettes, for syringes, for lighters, for candybars, for sharpened bits of steel, for money, all the things they weren't supposed to have that they always managed to get. But you learned to close it all out, to lose yourself in the mental maze, to jog round and round the squirrel's cage in the skull. To keep from flipping out . . . All that thinking, together with a tattered science magazine in the prison library, synthesized a theory. Suppose that we each have two bodies, the visible body, cellular-organic, and the other a plasmic skein of subatomic wave-particles, consciousness cohabiting with the body of flesh, inter-penetrating it, but capable of surviving outside it, given the right circumstances. I thought of it as the plasmic body. My plasmic body could leave my material body, and transmit itself, through some medium beyond my guesswork, to Elizabeth. It was possible for two plasmic bodies to cohabit in one material body, while the departed body waited in a sort of stasis, a self-imposed hibernation. It worked felicitously, with Elizabeth and I, because we were in love, because we accepted one another. But suppose a man was invaded by an unwel-come plasmic body? Hadn't it happened, before? It could explain the legends of possession.

And since it was possible to willfully manipulate my own plasmic body, might it not be possible to use it against someone else's? In prison, you're forever mulling the prospects for self-defense.

I was thinking about it, most particularly, since Tar-nower had come to the cell. There were only three white guys in the cell. Tarnower was one of them.

Tarnower had a perfectly ordinary face, no doubt, as a boy. But he was one of those men who wore a single facial expression so long, it transfigured his features; his face was all whining resentment. Permutations of self-pity. Even in sleep, the same twisted sneer on his lips. His head was vaguely peanut-shaped, and he was potbellied, soft of limb, always twitching, looking to see if it was he being laughed at when laughter sounded behind him. He was in for dealing PCP.

Tarnower didn't like the fact that Brinker protected me. I'd had a year of law school, and Brinker prized me as his 'in-house attorney'. Brinker was the dorm heavy, and he protected me from rape, assault, and extortion. Tarnower had no protection, and he was constantly trying to turn the dorm hard-guys against me, implying I was a spy for the prison administration. He wanted to earn Brinker's gratitude by making it seem that he, Tarnower, had saved them from my treachery. And he hated me even more after the State Health Facility came around asking for volunteers in exchange for parole.

Volunteers for 'experiments in drug abuse therapy'. Several hundred of us applied, including Tarnower. I was accepted, and was told I'd be taken to the research facility the following morning. Tarnower was furious. He was sure he'd been overlooked because of me. Because, he claimed, he'd seen me 'slip something to the guard'. He managed to convince another lunkhead of the same thing. And I knew they were making plans to kill me. They'd been high on the list of volunteers. With me dead, there was a good chance one of them would be picked. A drag queen who'd taken a fancy to me told me all this. 'You gonna fall and hit you head inna showers, honey,' the queen informed me sweetly. 'They make it look that way. You watch you ass now.'

'I always watch my ass in the showers.'

'That's two of us, honey.'

So that set the killing for the next morning.

I waited till well after lights out. Most of the men were

asleep. Tarnower sat up on his bunk, his back to me, talking softly to a Hispanic named Altino. Heavy-set man with stubby hands and sweat beading his upper lip; he shook with silent laughter at something Tarnower said.

I was doing more than watching them. I was focusing. I was reaching. Channeling some of my plasma body, extending it from my outstretched hands. It was as if I were reaching out with invisible extensions of my own hands; I pictured these plasmic hands as splayed and translucent, gelatinous, two membranes, one on either side of the two men across from me . . .

I brought the plasmic hands together, clapping their heads between. But the hands didn't strike them, physically. They passed through the skin and skull, like nets through water, coming into contact with the plasmic fields of the two cons, compressing them, tugging them together . . .

The men screamed, thrashed in confusion as their senses seemed to mingle. Altino splashed into Tarnower, Tarnower into Altino.

They'd been conspirators, not friends. They were frightened, small-minded men.

They clawed at one another, the room erupted with shouting, and somewhere alarm bells rang as the guards heard the uproar.

The next day, in the cafeteria, the story was told like this: 'Yeah, it was Tarnower. He's flipped out – frothing at the mouth. That *vato* buddy of his, Altino – he's what they call a vegetable. He just stares, like, all day. Who knows what the fuck happened.'

And in due course, after an uneventful shower, I was taken to the custody of dear Doctor Schusser.

I was paroled, but I had to participate in four weeks of experimental therapy, and I had to stay at the Jersey MHF research center's living facilities. I was allowed to see Elizabeth three hours a day; we met at a cheap motel. We made plans. She'd leave her parents on her eighteenth birthday, and we'd live together while she went to college in Manhattan. We had lots of lovely plans.

But it all waited on Schusser and Morgan. I had a nasty sinking feeling right from the start of my first conference with them. I sat on a couch across from two black vinyl armchairs; Morgan on the left, Schusser to the right. I thought of Tweedledee and Tweedledum. But it turned out they were more like Punch and Judy. Morgan was a brown suit man. Thought he was dressing tastefully and casually in his various shades of brown. He had a shapeless red beard and sandy hair; he was in his forties, always looked a little tired. Especially when he spoke to Schusser.

Schusser: late thirties, paunchy, typically wore gray slacks and a blue turtleneck sweater – even on hot days. Dandruff salted his shoulders. Thinning, disarrayed black hair. Affected friendliness in his small brown eyes. There was a polished wood coffee-table between us on which was a yellow ceramic plant holder shaped like a shoe, with a long curl of greenery growing out of it.

I listened distantly as they reviewed my written application; I murmured monosyllabic replies when they asked me about my background. And fabricated a grand story, a harrowing history of drug abuse when they asked how I'd developed my 'current problems with drugs'. I had to seem a heavy user, to keep the parole. I lied brilliantly.

'. . . to summarize,' Morgan droned, 'the experiment uses dream-time therapeutically. The key is a medication we call D-17, administered just before you sleep. It's a hypnotic, which, we believe, will make you unusually receptive to subliminal suggestion during dream-time . . .'

And a long, chill shudder went through me. I'd once

written an article on research into the dream-state. There was just too little known about it to justify this kind of tampering. But I didn't want to break parole, to always be running. So I signed the papers. Lots and lots of papers.

There were four others in our lab's dorm. The experiments began immediately. That night. And for the first few nights, I noticed nothing unusual. I was told that, as we slept, some white-coated drip would whisper, 'Drugs make you ill. Cocaine makes you nauseated. Heroin does nothing for you. Marijuana gives you a headache. You have no enjoyment of . . .'

The next day, Schusser and Morgan would test us, giving us small doses of controlled substances, so they could watch for the hoped-for aversion reactions. It didn't work; the drugs continued to feel good. Morgan blamed Schusser's 'suggestion script'; Schusser blamed Morgan's dosage. More than once I heard them arguing in Schusser's office. I began to realize that they were working together reluctantly; some sort of state health department politics forced it on them.

They hated one another.

I and the three other subjects, who were black, weren't allowed to discuss the experiment with one another. But as the days passed, the haunted looks in their tired faces confirmed my suspicions. They were having a reaction to D-17 similar to mine. Nightmares.

'Nightmares' doesn't describe it. An understatement. Everything traumatic that had ever happened to me dredged up and replayed, over and over, magnified and exaggerated. I saw my mother dying of cancer again, but more vividly than I'd seen it in real life. I dreamed I would come home and find her in my bed, dying, wasting away. So I'd run to the bathroom – and she'd be in the tub. Dying. Wasting away.

I felt the nightmares more deeply, more palpably than
I'd felt anything, ever. I'd dream I was back in prison.
Altino and Tarnower strangling me, holding my head in
the toilet. And worse.

I'd wake up screaming, and I'd feel like living hell all
day long.

Sometimes ghost images of the dreams would superimpose over my waking reality. I'd see Tarnower caressing
the corpse of my mother, on the grass across from the
park bench where I'd been trying to find some peace with
Elizabeth. And the subliminal suggestions, after three
weeks, still didn't work.

At the beginning of the fourth week, Schusser talked
Morgan into tripling the dosage. I had the impression
that Morgan was afraid they'd get into trouble – they
were exceeding the legal limit.

I had a whole new season of nightmares. One in
particular recurred night after night. On the third night, I
woke up prematurely, screaming. I was in my own room
– our screams had made it necessary to isolate us. I was
awake, but I was still having the nightmare; I was
hallucinating, my nightmare superimposed over the real
world of the lab's bedroom.

I saw myself standing there – I saw myself as a separate
entity. Only, the man I saw, standing over me – his
breathing glutinously bubbling – the man had changed.
The face was barely recognizable. It was hardly there at
all. My face was deformed, crushed into a bloody mockery. And below, my gut was laid open, my entrails
pendulously dangling . . . It shuffled toward me and bent
to ram its long, gray dead-man's tongue down my throat.
Choking me. I saw it bright as noonday. I clawed the
EEG wires from my head and ran to the window. I was
awake – but I wasn't, quite. I hesitated at the window. I
turned. The thing was there, behind me, translucent but

repulsive as tumor; it hated me; it was malevolently rabid. I plunged through the window in a panic to get away. Anywhere away. A crash, crystalline explosion and four kinds of pain. Shouts from somewhere. Consciousness coming and going in the same vacillation as the warbling of approaching sirens.

The lab's dorm was six floors up. Under the window was a wrought iron fence topped with hard black spears. One of the spears split my liver. Another broke my spine in two. A third tore my face from my skull.

There wasn't much anyone could have done to repair it.

One of my eyes remained. With that eye I saw myself. I saw what remained of my face, in the outside rearview mirror of the ambulance as the medics pulled me free of the spikes.

The face I saw was the face of the thing in my nightmare. It was me, now, and always would be, if I lived. My new self-image.

My soul, or if you like, my plasma body, passed from me forever then, and fled along the psychic channels to another receptacle. My memories, my personality came along. I found a home forever in the body of Elizabeth Calder.

After a few days of mutual comforting and readjustment, we calmed into cool determination, and she asked me, 'What are we going to do to them?'

Elizabeth was in control that night. I rode within her, watching as she opened the door to Schusser's office. There were Schusser and Morgan, arguing. Blaming one another for my death and the official inquiry. Never speaking a word of sincere regret for what they'd done to me. They sat close together, bent over their reports, sweating. Elizabeth raised her arms, opened her hands. We reached out, together.

Ten minutes later, the security guard found us. We sat in one of the black vinyl chairs, watching Schusser. He was lying on the floor, chewing a hole in his right bicep. His face was smeared with his own blood. Morgan, or Morgan's body, sat up on the couch, staring at the papers in its hand. Blinking now and then. Seeing nothing. Empty.

Morgan wasn't there anymore. He was with Schusser, very intimately with Schusser. Inside him. Struggling, screaming at him mentally, trapped forever.

And I'm in Elizabeth forever. It's a kind of paradise, really. But I wish you'd talk to her, convince her to let me out once in awhile. I could find another receptacle. It's not that I don't love her.

But she wants me *always* near her. She never lets me go. You see, a man's material body might be stronger than a woman's. But when it comes to a plasma body . . .

Elizabeth is much stronger than I am.

The Almost Empty Rooms

As images seen in a dream, thus should one see all things.

- Vajracchedika Sutra

PART I OF PRIMARY SYNTAX

AIR RAID ALERT

It was on television at 8:36 A.M. when no one expects catastrophes.

AIR RAID ALERT: LISTINGS OF LOCAL FALLOUT SHELTERS/ ALPHABETIC ORDER (Alphabetical shelter listings for the county. Screen flickers, distant siren. Blank screen).

My wife made a blank scream: Nothing came out of her opened mouth. She ran to get the children. Charles and Andrea had just left for school.

It was a pleasant morning, other than for the alert, and the sky was clear and crisp. I felt no apprehension, seeing the TV announcement. I had expected it; it was right on time.

I'd just risen, and was wheeling between kitchen and study in my electric wheelchair, looking out first one window, then another, mildly curious to see all the neighbors were running in and out of their houses.

The children had laughed, watching the ludicrous scene through the window. The neighbors flung themselves into cars or scurried about on their front lawns like tawdry rags caught in a dust-devil, huffing in circles about the mounds of furniture, clothing, and appliances, quibbling

over what to take. I gazed over their heads: it was crisp
and chilly, the cloudless sky was hollowed-out turquoise.

FALLOUT SHELTER LIMIT OPTIMUM: EQUIVALENCY OF 500
POUNDS PER REGISTERED FAMILY OF TWO PERSONS IN POS-
SESSIONS OR RELATIVES said the stark letters on the TV
screen. The message played over and over. The men at
the TV station had left it on automatic replay and gone
home to their respective families. No one remained at the
TV station, but the machines there still told us to run.

AIR RAID ALERT/CIVIL DEFENSE COMMAND 56648.

I went outside to see what was keeping my wife and
children (but I knew). I had no intention of taking them
to a fallout shelter (though I'd known). It would do no
good, not a bit. As I rolled onto my ramp by the front
steps I heard a roar, clutched at my wheel-rims. The
ground shuddered.

I looked up: My six-year-old girl and my eight-year-old
boy were in the air, far over head. My wife was nowhere
to be seen. A great gust of wind had picked the kids up
like plastic Rocky and Bullwinkle kites. They became
crosses stark against the sky. X-factors on a blackboard,
my children. They hovered up there: in abeyance. I
waited with my arms outstretched, instinctively waiting,
to catch them as they fell. But they never fell.

A great light from the east.

I shaded my eyes. Light, piercing and sudden as a labor
pain. But it was not blinding. It was penetrating; the
atomic flash was a revealing light, and my eyes did not
melt nor my face scorch. I remembered what day this was
– I had shut the eroding calendar out of my mind till that
moment. I had stopped up expectancy with self-
hypnotism. This day was 10 February 1997.

I had expected all of this.

The nuclear vortex reared up black-bellied with scar-
white plumage. White-hot lathing wind cut our flesh from

us in spiral strips, but – and here's the amazing grace, the happy surprise – gracefully, smoothly, painlessly. I was almost disappointed. It didn't hurt, not even for a moment. It was loving as the fingers of a mother undressing a child for the bath. Our skins didn't fly off in crazy bits and ragged pieces, but in coherent spirals, a slack minaret above us, whirling us like toys (yarn unwinding from a spindle), faster, faster until my skeleton fused into a single long bone, molded by centrifugal force. It was all quite painless. And consciousness never ceased nor faltered, but fluttered in my fused remains like a caged songbird. We were not blown away and up like the neighborhood children (those thirteen and under). My neighbors and I were rooted each at our special point, afloat above the lawns whose grasses were now ash. We resonated from the explosions which detonated harmoniously, complementing one another pleasantly, their force snatching the ground neatly upward like a pickpocket artistically plucking a wallet.

There was no pain or discomfort, even when our bodies were only vague memories. There was to be no pain at all in this surgery. It was performed by professionals.

PART I OF SECONDARY SYNTAX

Hypothesis: Events are animals. Events are living creatures, whose complete anatomy and fleshly dimensions are invisible to us, because we are functioning cells ignorantly but efficiently comprising their body make-up.

Corollary: If an event could be predicted and confirmed according to the characteristic metabolic cycle and inductive-excretive requirements of the event-organism's body, then it might be possible to alter the course of anticipated incidents through working with the event-creature's nervous system to shift its actions in midcourse. Confuse it, perhaps.

I was going to try to interfere with a certain sad but small-scale disaster I had predicted would take place on the afternoon of 11 August 1996.

This was to be a test.

If I could stop this small-scale mishap concerning a young man named Simon Chelsez, then I might use this model for the manipulation of events, to divert World War III.

For I knew: World War III would arrive on the morning of 10 February 1997.

If the experiment with Simon Chelsez was successful, I would trace my way through the interacting clusters of event-organisms busily constructing the foundations for the structure they called Fun and we knew as the End of Humanity, and there, at the nexus of the crises, intercept the gestation of the Third World War.

The origin of this complex and circumlocutionary ludicrous series of endeavors was disillusioningly simple:

I didn't want to die.

PART II OF SECONDARY SYNTAX

In form Astral, with sensations Subtle, I conducted myself along the damp web-work of the incident-neural system to the apartment of a young man and his mother who lived across from the elementary school. I traced my way from a teacher's repressed memory of a child's death (ghostly reenactment) to the young man's recollection of the accident: a teacher had seen a child killed on the streetcorner on which Simon Chelsez and his mother lived; Simon had seen the truck hit the little girl, watching from his bedroom window, and it had not moved him. The little girl had been neatly divided in half by the truck's right front tire. The child's blood left a Rorschach inkblot on the white cement, the blot's red configuration reminding him of a knight killing a dragon.

The teacher was an acquaintance of mine, I had her vibratory identity code *down*. She was connected eternally with Simon, though she'd never met him face to face, by their mutual cross-referenced recollections of the accident; together they were functioning memory-cells in the mnemonic bank of the event-animal in which they lived. I worked my way, psychically, from one person to the other: from one brain cell to the next.

And I was invisibly sharing a room with Simon Chelsez.

Simon was gazing at a holographic programmer, trying to decide which program to play. He was completely unaware of me, since I was with him in astral form only. I secluded myself amongst programmer circuits. Observing him through the reticulating eye of the event-organism, I perceived his surface thoughts clearly as plays and flares of polychromatic lights defining the crown of the sinuous tube of incident-compositions marking his wake of passage.

All of his holographic movies starred the same hero: Captain Horatio Alphonso. The holos were projected onto the center space of the large, almost empty room through lenses set flush into the ceiling. The white room was fifty by fifty feet, empty except for a single bed in its exact center. Nineteen-year-old Simon Chelsez, the present owner of the holo-programmer, was a short, stocky, and muscular Chicano. Like Captain Alphonso, Simon knew all the Alphonso holos by heart. He punched up the program-selector, leaving the setting on *Pride and Punishment*. The overhead laser-projector hummed, fell silent, as the image of the heroic Alphonso appeared in the middle of the room, at the foot of the bed. If you'd walked into the room without knowing that Simon owned an expensive holo set you'd have thought that Captain Alphonso was actually *there*. He was three-dimensional in that you could walk around him, look up at him from beneath, always without interfering with the focus or proportionate volume of his body. If you approached Captain Alphonso from behind, you saw a holo reproduction of his back; when you walked around to his front you'd see that his sides were perfectly formed into his chest without a seam.

Simon fidgeted impatiently as Alphonso waited, stoically immobile in his dashing black toga with the silver Liberator's arrow on the right shoulder, arms outspread as if holding up the ghostly words which floated under his forthright jaw:

PRIDE AND PUNISHMENT
A REALER-THAN-LIFE PRODUCTION
STARRING ESTEBAN MANTABLU AS
CAPTAIN ALPHONSO
PETULA ANKENY AS LIDIA
PAUL CHELSEZ AS VORGAS
COPYRIGHT (C) 1995 3-D LTD.

Simon possessed a complete collection of the Alphonso series. He had inherited it because his late father, Paul Chelsez, had played the role of Vorgas, the Villainous Arch-Foe of Alphonso, in each of the thirty-nine episodes.

Simon and Alphonso were remarkably alike in physique.

And as the statuesque hero vanished, Lidia appeared,

reclining on a silken air-turbulence bed in an apartment hung with streamers like smoggy cobwebs. Lidia was peacefully asleep. Alphonso entered from the balcony and stood beside her, gazing deep into the vacant eyes of his slumbering beloved. In keeping with the glamor fad of that period she slept with her eyes opened, their membranes bathed in artificial protective fluids sprayed from tiny hoses attached to her head. Her eyes gleamed in the bars of rainbow light from the overhead Dream-Tone. She had set the DreamTone for *Fanning Reds*, guaranteed to color her dreams with scenes of passion. Her passionate dreams were about to be made concrete reality with the coming of Captain Horatio Alphonso, personification of all that is gallant and debonair. Bars of vermilion luminescence played over her delicate features, making her blankly-staring blue eyes red as small forges.

Simon, who had waited beyond the border of the holoscenario, waded suddenly through the projected image, without disturbing it, and slipped into Alphonso.

He merged with Alphonso's every action, striding the archetype's strides, a fraction of a second behind in the holo's choreography, slightly blurring its outline. His limbs and head were one with Alphonso's, his features moving in the same stereotyped hero's smug expressions.

Simon had memorized the holo so completely his voyeur enactment developed into a self-hypnotized reflex. He knew all the words, mouthed them with perfect inflection and precision timing. He could act it all out without a single mistake. For the hundredth time.

He even made love when Alphonso did. Which Alphonso did frequently. While involved in the holoscenario Simon believed that he was Captain Alphonso, Guerilla Hero of the Silver Liberators. The visual illusion was complete enough that he could fill in the rest of his senses with his imagination. So he had orgasms when Alphonso did. Which Alphonso did frequently.

It hadn't been difficult for Simon to memorize the tapes for the Alphonso series. It was all very primordial and basic, each Alphonso holo lasting no more than twenty minutes. Alphonso would make love to Lidia, or begin to, Vorgas would come in to interrupt with his kidnapping attempt on Lidia, and Alphonso would defeat Vorgas and spend the remainder of the holo making love to Lidia.

Simon/Alphonso stepped onto the sunken bed, still standing, straddling Lidia like the Colossus of Rhodes. Then he knelt gracefully beside her and she woke: stretching luxuriantly, removing the DreamTone with a delicate sweep of her jewel-bangled hand, squeezing her eyes shut and then opening them with a euphoric giggle.

Purring, Lidia reached for Alphonso/Simon.

Simon could feel Lidia's slim body in his arms. Almost. Enough. There was a real bed onto which the holo bed was projected, supporting Simon over his loving mirage. But he was forced to slip slightly out of synch with Alphonso in order to keep himself from falling through the incorporeal form of the naked Lidia as he mounted her. The outline wavered, stained.

Alphonso threw his toga and briefs aside and bestowed his affections on Lidia . . . After a few minutes of her spider embrace Vorgas crept into the scene, as he always did at those indelicate moments. Vorgas also looked very much like Simon, though thinner, much older because he was played by the man who had leased this apartment and bought the holo-projector shortly before his death in 1991. He was wrapped in a white shroud that contrasted sharply with his long black train of hair and dark, sunken features. He slithered toward the bed on all fours and unfurled a lanky, corded arm at the end of which was a paralysis-gun, dart-shaped and silvery. He pointed the

gun at Alphonso who shielded Lidia with his naked but
magnificent body . . .

. . . at this point in the holoscenario Alphonso was
supposed to whip out his handy paralysis-ray reflector
concealed in the utility belt lying within reach . . .

I concentrated on the narrow band of electric charges
traveling Simon's optic nerve. I changed what he saw. I
concentrated on the narrow band of electric charges trav-
eling his audio nerve. I changed what he heard.

Instead of the usual reiteration of Vorgas's defeat,
Alphonso screamed and flung himself away from Simon,
toppling, paralyzed. Simon stood up, uncertain, split from
his vicarious self-image, and watched in growing horror
as Vorgas leapt onto Alphonso's bare breast and plunged
a needle-dagger deep into his throat. Alphonso spurted
blood, squealing like a pig at slaughter.

Simon covered his eyes and whimpered.

He staggered to the wall panel and flicked the holo off.
The holoscenario faded like the blotchy after-image of a
bright light. The room ached with near-emptiness.

Simon's face was calm, almost empty. There should
have been surprise or fury.

I was becoming worried. The eventual organism's neural
predilection was cloudy. I levered, see-sawed, bounced
from and was pumped into . . .

He opened a door, went down a hall to his mother's
bedroom, approaching her soundlessly. She was lying
under a sunlamp and listening to the radio on earplugs.
He flicked the radio into silence.

'Simon?' his mother said, her eyes wide open, sprayed
by protective fluid as Lidia's had been. 'Simon, dear, why
don't you come back later? Mother was just about to go
to sleep. But while you're here shut off the sunlamp and
turn on my DreamTone, will you?'

Simon reached up and deliberately made the sunlamp brighter. 'Lights!' he intoned histrionically. 'Cameras!'

'Hey, turn that off, son, will you?' She switched off the eye filters and peered at him. Her hair, in sharp hooks around her puddly, watered-down face, had the exaggerated gloss of synthetic implanting, plastic sky-blue.

Simon's face was ingenuous, eyes-wide. 'You've been playing the holo again, haven't you?' Mother accused. 'I'd prefer you didn't, Simon. Really. You know why. Doctor Hannaly warned you. It's best to forget Paul.' Her bland, middle-aged features creased meridians of blue-gray. Self-consciously, she tried to relax her face; strong facial expressions were said to promote wrinkles.

'Lidia . . .' Simon murmured, throwing his arms around his plump mother, who resembled Lidia only in the lack of facial expression. He kissed the breasts dumping from her terrycloth robe.

His mother was profoundly shocked. She allowed her forehead to wrinkle. 'Stop it!' She slapped him.

He stood up and his look of naïveté became cunning. 'So you are Vorgas, with a new ploy! You could hardly think to disguise yourself as Lidia for long, Vorgas!' He bellowed, with a melodramatic flourish of his hand.

His mother bit her lower lip and leapt clear of the bed, flinging herself at the door.

Simon caught her under the throat with his right arm and with his left hand tugged the cord of the sunlamp from its socket and wrapped it around her neck. His face tightened into a snarl exactly when his hands tightened the cord. His mother gurgled briefly, thrashed, then became limp, a cumbersome weight. He let her fall onto the bed. Then he stood up to wait for the credits for the next episode.

Blood from his mother's parted lips flowed enthusiastically and spattered the pillow with a red Rorschach inkblot. To Simon the inkblot resembled a small girl run over by a truck.

I couldn't bear to watch any longer. Failure. And now cathartic tides of the event-organism's cleansing organs swept me away. I allowed myself to be sucked into the undercurrent that led back to my body which waited in cataleptic torpor on my office couch . . .

A manganese blue light poured thickly through the window slats and blurred the spare furnishings in my office into the viridian gray of things seen underwater. I sat up, feeling numb around the edges, and my eyes cleared some. I adjusted slowly to my physical husk. I concentrated, raising my blood pressure, accelerating breathing, quelling dizziness. At first, moving my arms was an indirect process, like manipulating the handle of a steam shovel to pick up a bauble in a penny arcade game. For a vertiginous instant I was fitting myself into my body like Simon into Alphonso's. But I locked in, thinking of myself as arms, legs, torso, head, and tolerating the erection which plagued my resurrections.

PART III OF SECONDARY SYNTAX

I agonized for a while. I had nightmares about the murder of Simon's mother. I didn't eat for a few days. I agonized and decided.

I would try once more.

I had projected another mishap, concerning a young woman, a virtuoso musician, Phylla Bertran. I'd listened to her solo performances and memorized the recordings of her own compositions. I had her vibratory identity code *down.*

So I traced my way through the neural channels of the

event-animal, arriving in: A large and vacuous room, empty except for the four taut, thick strings of metallic black stretching from the center of the concave ceiling to the coastered fixture firmly magnetized to the black plastic floor. The walls were contoured to throw back a greatly amplified resonance of any string, when struck. The entire room was the hollow body of a huge acoustic bass viola, large enough to contain its musician inside itself.

Phylla was red-haired, with preoccupied blue eyes and thin, impatient lips. She wore skintight leotards and walked with footsteps clipped and minced, to the upright strings. The door hushed shut automatically behind her.

. . . Except for me, she was alone. And I was only there in spirit, observing via the optical membrane of the event-organism. Waiting my chance to test the corollary to my hypothesis one last time . . .

She pressed the chrome stud on her bracelet releasing the wheels for the string-pickup carriage mounted into the ceiling. Directing it with a remote-control device in her silver bracelet, she could coerce the strings from one part of the room to another. The room narrowed at the farther end, and when Phylla brought the strings there, they were tuned by that constricted space to a higher pitch. When the perpendicular strings traveled to the larger end of the room their tone became more bass.

Fingers strumming like running children, she played the encompassing instrument and lightly danced to and fro, one arm looping the mobile strings as if they were her dancing partner. She played expertly, each note as deep and pronounced as a church bell but with the thunderous rapidity of artillery fire. For a while she dashed through her bass viola solo in the Bartók piece she performed with the New York Philharmonic. But she couldn't complete the composition without a bow and

anyway she was happy in improvisation, embellishing
with her own compositions. Her bobbing breasts and
short tosses of her hair marked rhythm in intimate
wavelength as she pirouetted and furled through the belly
of the huge bass.

*. . . for me the music was filtered through the membrane
of the event-organism, emerging as a ghost of its actual
tone. But its echoes, reverberations of a lonely woman,
made the body temporarily abandoned by my mind,
waiting, dreaming in my office, shudder. I waited and
watched for the high-water mark of those intimate wave-
lengths . . .*

Phylla was an enthralled artist, internationally
applauded. But a part of her was numbed by super-
numerary desires placing the pinnacle of the music, her
personal essence just beyond her reach. Never quite
satisfied, though critics vainly insisted that her interpretations were letter-perfect, she wanted the whole cup,
every drop. To this end she had the bass-room customized
into a musical instrument designed to envelop her in her
own self-expression. For a month she'd practiced here,
ever closer, always closer, not quite: not just yet.

Now she was scarlet, sweating; yet her fingers nimbly
flakked the strings. Each finger dipped into the scale like
a surgeon seeking a special nerve within an incision.

After thirty-two minutes Phylla was nearly sated. But
not quite.

*. . . and I knew that if I let her go on uninterrupted she
would exceed the limitations of the room and it would not
be enough. And what I hoped to forestall would inevitably
come about. The time approached for the second test. If I
could toss a mental probe into her impressions now,
altering, amplifying, enlarging her capacity for receptivity
to her own compositions. Satisfaction, perhaps . . .*

She moaned. *I reached out* . . . She made the cry of an exhausted deer chased beyond its limit.

She sat down heavily on the floor. The fading reverberations of the strings hummed mournfully, like a departing jet.

The four strings in their metal fixture rolled silently, with finality, to the center of the room.

Phylla was left sighing.

. . . *I sensed the mercury bursting from the cap of the thermometer* . . .

Phylla stood up unsteadily, and taking her steps carefully, left the room.

. . . *The test was positive. It might be possible to avert* . . .

Phylla returned with a stepladder which she placed by the four strings.

. . . *World War III* . . .

She climbed to the stepladder and tied a silver-white cord to the metal fixture on the ceiling. She fixed the other end of the cord in a loop around her neck. She pressed the bracelet's remote control for *Automatic Response*.

The strings' fixture rolled toward the narrow end of the room, yanking Phylla off the stepladder. She sagged from the slim cord, making not a spasm, towed wherever the strings bounced, here and there in the echoing chamber. As she swung, a pendulum, her dead face bloated and mottled with purple, she bumped into the strings, which gave out a discordant thrumming.

She was dragged about the room, gyrating in her noose, body striking the strings, played a melody as void of predictable structure as death.

. . . *I had been unable to change the predicted event-organisms' metabolic reaction: Suicide, as I had projected*

. . . OK, nobody's perfect. It wasn't my doing. Only. Only the corollary of my hypothesis had been negated twice . . .

PART II OF PRIMARY SYNTAX

So you see, I wasn't at all when the TV said AIR RAID ALERT.

I had done what I had done the night before; I had seen the consequences; I had redefined the word *failure*; I had drugged myself and hypnotized myself to forget, so that my family could have the last six hours of the illusion of self-determination. I had done what I had done.

I had seen the consequences. I knew myself as a note in a symphony which had no human hand in its composition.

And the TV said AIR RAID ALERT.

I'd laid off trying to convince anyone that Armageddon was going to happen. The FBI just laughed. It wouldn't do them any good to know, anyway. I suppose I had some illusions about the world going out in the dignified splendor of fatalistic comprehension.

Still, for a while, I sought out fissures or weak spots in the skin of the event-organism enclosing me, through which I might pass to stand apart and regard it impartially. A nonsense proposition. That would be as if my own lungs ripped their way from my rib cage to stand outside and survey me.

I gave up trying to escape. I got drunk for a week. I stared, soddenly, at the calendar. I experimented with heroin. I discarded that and went to Jesus, for a weekend. When faith-healing failed to revive my legs I gave up on that, too. I removed all the calendars from my house. When my wife asked why, I told her to shut up.

As a trifling hobby, I studied the social habits of the

event-organisms. Sometimes they come together in the equivalent of committee meetings. Those take place as devastating earthquakes or wars or gold rushes. Sometimes they have fights amongst themselves. Those take the form (from our narrow viewpoint) of interchanges like the Olympics or the United Nations General Assembly or midnight on New Year's eve in Times Square.

Once every 500 millennia or so, events have festivals.

World's Fairs. They get together to have fun and enjoy themselves, and from our viewpoint this takes the persona of World War III. Their latest World's Fair was scheduled, in terms of our time system, for 10 February 1997.

Fancy that, I said, when the firestorm's prologue of hurricane winds swept our children half a mile into the sky. My boy, Charles, had babbled on about what glory he would find as a jet pilot. I wanted him to be a Doctor of Metaphysics.

A throat of spasming energy. The nuclear fire took our city apart neatly, with sterile, rubber-gloved fingers. Like a child carefully removing plastic toy bricks from his play-castle now that the game was done. All of the leaves of the trees were stacked as neatly as dollar bills in the Treasury. Everything in its place. Japanese floral arrangement with the entire landscape. The explosions were metallic notes and the nation was a xylophone, cities ringing euphoniously where steel missiles impacted.

Fireworks heralding the commencement of the festivities.

PART IV OF SECONDARY SYNTAX

All right then, perhaps my attempts to intercept the deaths of Phylla and Simon had caused them. But it couldn't be my fault. There are no accidents.

Something nagged at me. It was three days till February tenth. I was trying to decide what to do.

Whether or not.

Something rattled around in the back of my mind like some object rolling loose in the trunk of a car, and as I drive along, listening to the unidentified thing's bumping as I turn corners, I try to decipher it from the muffled sounds it makes. Slowly I got the picture and began to wonder if I was a dupe.

Because there is simply *no such thing* as an accident. And it's a damn shame.

I sat in the study, stoking the fire on the permaplast hearth, hotter and hotter though it was already hot in there from the central heating. I sat in a plush chair and sweated and went without dinner but the answer didn't sweat itself out of me.

Finally I got in bed next to my wife. I lay in bed looking at my wheelchair. My wife, Elaine, tried to hug me. I shrugged her off.

'What's wrong?'

I decided to be honest with her for once. Maybe the legendary wifely intuition would make an appearance. For once. 'It's the event-organism thing – '

She made a small sound of weariness.

'Oh, cut it out, will you?' She put her head under the pillow. 'I'm sick of hearing that crap,' came her muffled voice. Not muffled enough. 'You made an ass of yourself when those FBI agents came to our house. You were always big-mouthed with rhetoric. Like the first time I met you in that ludicrous transfinite geometry class. I was impressed then. But what about your children? Are you going to explain your theories to them? Can you philosophically explain why you ignore them?'

'I *don't* ignore them. I bought them those plastic Rocky and Bullwinkle kites yesterday, didn't I?'

'Big deal. Do you know what your son does, lately? He collects tapes of *Bernie Backsterr the American Dreamer* and he memorizes every goddamn thing about that moron Backsterr and imitates him. He takes *notes* about what Bernie Backsterr's room looks like on the holo set and rearranges his own damn room to look exactly the same way. He dresses like that moron, wears his hair the same way – '

I couldn't repress a shudder. It connected too closely with Simon. I began to wonder if Charles contained hidden antipathy for his mother. Andrea, though only six, already wanted to be a musician. Elaine wanted her to play viola . . .

Elaine's makeup was smeared on the mauve pillow. She always put on her makeup just before she went to bed. Eye shadow, lipstick, glitter. She'd wash it off directly on getting up the next morning. It was an idiosyncrasy like her aversion for Chinese people. She wouldn't go near Chinese restaurants; she wouldn't allow a Chinese in the house, or watch them on TV. It was a peculiar prejudice for an educated woman, a professor of English. I used to think that she put the makeup on for me. But I suppose she wore it for whoever it was who made her moan so passionately in her sleep. When talking in her sleep she mumbled monosyllables which sounded distinctly Chinese.

I turned my back on her and tried to sleep.

* * *

I had to choke down an omelet for breakfast. I herded the greasy remnants of breakfast listlessly about the plate with my fork.

My daughter, Andrea, sat or rather teetered madly, across from me. Charles had gone to school. Andrea was six, healthy, blonde, and blossoming. She was one of those children who explode outward, looking at as many things simultaneously as practical. She fashioned her unfinished breakfast into tiny castles with her knife. If she didn't like something she always found some kind of use for it. Nothing was wasted, with her. And a child like this, I thought, should not be wasted on radiation poisoning.

I looked at the giddy stammer-play of her lips as she sang a TV-jingle; I ran through my calculations again: eighty-nine percent probability that my involvement in the metabolic gestation cycle would cause the war.

That left eleven percent.

I'm not sure if the man I influenced was the Secretary of Defense. I knew, through the jack-o'-lantern buttered light, veined and notched with the footprints of meteorites that this was the man who was about to make a decision about a certain debacle with the Red Chinese. He was the man at the cusp, the one whose interpretation of the problem made all the difference. He was the living turning point. He made a phone call from his desk in his cozy, simulated red-velvet office to someone who might have been the President. The caller was a tight-faced little man with a gray mustache and an out-of-place black toupee. In his right hand he gripped the leather handle of a briefcase, unobtrusive except for the handcuffs chaining it to his wrist. They rattled out a code I couldn't understand. I was able to interpret very few of his thoughts: his output was sparse. I could tell he was thinking about his ulcer and about calling his mother. He hung up the phone and placed the briefcase on an empty desktop.

He unlocked the handcuffs with a murmur of satisfaction.

He opened the briefcase. Inside was a sheaf of papers, figures on the build-up of nuclear arms bases in certain strategic regions owned by the Red Chinese. I scanned, selected what I wanted to change . . .

I saw something out of the corner of my event-animal's eyes: Phylla and Simon's mother. They were there, with me, though I could see the files on the opposite wall through their denseless forms. They wavered but remained, expressionless, but trying to say something.

I looked back at the little man who couldn't see me, his eyes running down the column of figures . . .

. . . *I changed what he saw* . . .

PART III OF PRIMARY SYNTAX

The entire world was caught up in the nuclear devolution.

The bombs only fell on select cities, but those were mere torches illuminating the field for the event-animals' construction crew. Fallout shelters were utterly without value. Fingers of nuclear fission plucked shelters neatly from the ground and unpacked them, laying everything out primly on the picnic table. Each individual person was suspended – not levitated, it was more like hanging from an invisible hook – a foot above the naked, flattened earth, where we were spaced out evenly from one another.

Half of us, my half, were stripped of our flesh, quite painlessly. And symmetrically arranged. Like a mother unwrapping her Christmas present while conscientiously saving the wrapping for next year, our clothes, skin, muscles, tissues, cartilage, and vestigial organs such as amazement were all lifted cleanly away and stacked one by one to the side. Empty skins like discarded wetsuits were folded on one pile; organs placed neatly in transparent receptacles.

We couldn't see exactly who was responsible. On the other hand, everything we saw was responsible.

Our bodies were gone, our minds (stripped of initiative) remained microfilmed onto long white rods of pure ossified perception, rods which trembled with every wayward stimulus, like tuning forks for sight and smell as well as sound.

The other people were still paralyzed, always would be – locked into their bodies, dead but seeing, corpses with feeling. But no one was killed in World War III.

All of us: frozen above the ground like leaping ballet dancers crucified in midjump. No shadows blotted the frozen, ash-coated earth.

Light from everywhere.

No sun. No houses. No horizon. No argument.

We could not see farther than – ahhhh, it seemed five miles, but then, through the eye of the event it might have been five thousand. Gray haze tastefully presented the grounded verge of the vast transparent hemisphere that was World War III's interpretation of the sky. Inside our hemisphere, pleasing arrangements of cones and cubes and pyramids were constructed of the stripped houses and parks, of rough, prosaic wooden texture or rustflaked metal offsetting mathematical spareness of geometry.

All the city's children floated, bobbing about one another in an aloof pavane in the sky above us. A cloud of babies.

Those who still possessed flesh began to revolve around

the calcium rods like myself. I vacillated faintly, like an antenna aerial. An ultrasonic hum sings: Fun Fun Fun Fun Fun Fun Fun.

We rods formed an axis like a circular picket fence circled by the fleshed; like maypoles surrounded by dancing virgins. A carrousel of weightless, stark humanity comprising the nuclear merry-go-round, we the nucleus, they wooden-horses electrons.

There was no sound for that detached time-space. And no wind. Everywhere was the colorless light. The light that never warms.

FINAL SEGMENT OF PRIMARY SYNTAX, IN PRESENT TENSE

This place is full with motion, but nearly empty. I don't know how long we'll revolve like this, or if measures in duration apply, or what the event-animals intend for us after that. I envision myself chasing an ice cream truck. I am a small child. I am lured by the jangling bells of the ice cream truck. I've run six blocks to catch up with the cruising Moby Dick white Good Humor truck, but it outgains me and my lungs ache and my knees shake. I clasp a quarter so hard in my fist it hurts my palm. I can almost taste the ice cream and its color mixes and its texture melts into the sun-bleached color of my hair and the tropic steam of perspiration behind my ears. I hear the jangling and I chase on after the truck: within me, in memory. But externally the inner circle of rods and resonating bone whirls faster and faster and counterclockwise faster within the larger circle of paralyzed folk who stare straight ahead, with their arms at their sides and their children floating above them. There are no shadows, now, for the light is everywhere.

I cannot follow the organic twine of events into the future, now. I'm perceptually fixed in time, pinning the function of this organ of the event onto the present moment with my calcium nail. Time, the continuity of motion, revolves happily around me, riding the carrousel.

I get the impression that Time is an entity. He is a high officiary attending this, the World's Fair of Events. Time is judging World War III, attaching blue ribbons to the best exhibits. I am gratified: Detroit is a winner!

On one side I see, flashing by, an immense rectangular glassy construction resembling an oversized aquarium. In this container, dutifully recycling, recurring again and again, are the events which led up to World War III. I can see myself over there. I can see my interference with the lives of Phylla and Simon. Whizzing past, I catch a glimpse of Simon's murdering and Phylla's suicide. I can see myself floating wraithlike over each of them. I watch as I make the fatal decision to attempt to avert World War III. I see the cerebral scan-projections of Phylla and Simon's mother distracting me, deliberately muddling my judgement. I see myself adjusting the wrong set of figures, inadvertently influencing the little man in the cozy office to conclude that it is best to attack China before they attack us.

I glimpse missiles ejaculating from the USA which wave a friendly hello to missiles of retribution on their way from China. And Russia joins in the fun. I try to perceive why Phylla and Simon's mother made me do it all, and I catch a glimpse of myself, one of my submerged personalities, laboring while I sleep, conjuring through my magically endowed wheelchair-talisman the visions of Simon's Mum and Phylla, placed to confuse me at that crucial instant: I deliberately distracted myself. And I

chuckle (without a mouth) as I see (without eyes) that the
steps I took to prevent the projected deaths of Simon's
Old Lady and Phylla Dedicated Artist, and the final effort
to prevent the Third World War were as a whole pre-
determined reflex-reactions to the signals of the event-
animals of which I am a cell; the same kind of inexorable
spasms which led to the destruction of the civilization we
now call Lemuria and the uncountable societies the event-
animals allowed humanity to think it had personally built
prior to that. If a man is killed in a car accident (Fun Fun
Fun), why, that seems the sheerest chance; but that man
(as a child I loved to play with marbles) had, perhaps
even genetically, every intention of getting himself mutilated. I went willfully into the car accident that made me
a cripple. The captain of the Hindenburg steered into
that tower deliberately; Dewey wanted defeat at the
hands of Truman (I enjoyed games of chance, especially
as a means of *escape*; never chess, always dice) and Simon
Chelsez's mother spent her entire life preparing to be
strangled by her son.

Unconsciously, I had every intention of igniting World
War III.

But why not? And why the hell not? Now that I mull it
over, it's turning out to be a jolly affair, lots of fun. I can
see the beginning of this delightful festival of events, and
I cannot (Fun! Fun!) imagine what errant kill-joy impulse
possessed me to try to put it off. It's a dandy, lovely
show. They display it in that huge aquarium over there –
there – for Time or one of the other visiting dignitaries
should they chance to stroll by.

Hey! All kidding aside, I feel shamelessly giddy! It's all
happening here and now: and I'm recording it.

I suspect I've hit on my assignment, my role as part of
this gay, carnival affair: I'm a recording device.

And also a broadly smiling Master of Ceremonies.

Streamers of radiation fall golden from the sky like festival confetti and tickertape. I'm plumage on a parade float. I'm performing, a clown in the center of three rings.

From here, there is (Fun Fun Fun) nothing wrong with World War III. Nothing sad about Armageddon.

Everything, symmetrically right now, performs in the present tense. Like a burglar alarm ringing. The present is extremely tense, straining every fiber of the bubble sky's sumptuous fabric almost to the point of ripping it.

Fine and good. The tension is half the fun.

The Gunshot

She padded barefoot into his study, approaching him
soundlessly from behind. He knew she was there, though
he didn't look up from the video editor. Huysman
hunched over his workbench as if to say, *Leave me alone*.

She placed her hand on his right shoulder, her fingers
resting softly there – and he reacted as if someone had
dropped a lump of concrete on his back.

He whirled in his swivel chair, shaking. 'Don't *do* that
when I'm working!' She shrank back. He sputtered, 'I'm
– Jeez, I'm trying . . . to . . .' His voice trailed off. He
stared, his face blank except for a shadow of horror
around the edges. He stared into the middle distance. He
was looking at her . . . no, he was looking *through* her.

She was a tall woman, but oncoming middle-age
showed in her round-shouldered stoop. Her right hand
was raised and trembling. In her left hand there was a
prescription bottle. She hoped he'd ask her why she was
taking the pills again. Her doctor had ordered her to
rehab from tranquilizers. She was hoping he'd get angry
over the pills. Shout at her. Berate her. Notice her now.
He only watched the circles under her large brown eyes
coursing with tears that ran down to trace the faint face-
lifting seam along the underside of her jaw. She burst
out, 'You're faking all this shit to get away from me . . .
just another excuse . . . you haven't spoken to me in
three days except for "Gotta run, babe . . . fall season
hanging over my head, doll." You insular son of a
bitch . . .'

Huysman had slipped from his chair and was kneeling,

eyes wide, murmuring wordlessly, his gaze fixed at something unseen, his hands crossed over his belly, clutching
himself like a wounded man trying to hold his entrails in
place.

She looked over his head at the editing machine. One
of his TV-movies was playing. 'Looks like the end of the
picture, Reggie,' she said. 'Judging by the spouting blood,
the bodies . . . Ah, right, there's the triumphant master
criminal standing over the millions of dead cops he's
wasted. Christ, no wonder this stuff's banned from the
airwaves – ought to ban it from cable, too.' She didn't
really think so. She was trying to get a rise from him. He
seemed not to hear her. She continued, 'There, now the
triumphant master criminal walks off with the girls . . .
The End. A Reggie Huysman Production.'

He blinked and looked up at her, seeming to see now.
'Sandy . . . the . . .'

'Yes?'

'The gunshot . . .'

The raised black lettering on the door said: IMAGINACTION
PRODUCTIONS – R. G. HUYSMAN, PRESIDENT.

Straker studied the sign on the door. It was a little
pretentious, almost defensive – as if Huysman were
saying, *ImaginAction is a respectable business*.

Maybe Huysman was not as unaffected by the criticism
as he pretended.

Straker opened the door and entered the office. A
petite brunette secretary sat behind a translucent desk,
keyboarding on an off-brand 'processor. Her fingers
paused like a small animal awaiting an order as she
smiled. 'Mr Straker?'

'Uh-huh.' He smiled only as much as was needed.

'Mr Huysman is expecting you. Please go right in.'

'Thank you.' He moved toward the door behind her,

then hesitated. He was close enough to her to smell her strawberry perfume when she turned. 'Mr Straker?'

'Yes?'

'Your organization . . . it's called Intimate Investigative Therapies – *Inc*.?'

'Yes.'

'Um, what *is* that? Intimate investigative, um, therapy, I mean.'

'Psychological detective work. We go into people's lives to see what's bothering them. Our theory is you have to get involved with someone's life to really have empathy, to really help them. You seem more than just curious. Do you need help with – ?'

'No, no!' She glanced toward Huysman's private office. 'I'm worried about Reg – Mr Huysman.' She smiled sheepishly. 'I guess I take a kind of maternal interest in his feelings. He hasn't been happy. I just hope you can help him. He's tried everything.'

'What have you noticed that makes – ?'

Just then the frosted-glass door to the inner office opened. Straker recognized Huysman instantly. He was a big man, a head taller than Straker. His weight lifter's build had begun to go soft in the middle, and the skin around his neck was starting to sag. His complexion was ruddy – until recently, most of his spare time had been spent outdoors, rock climbing, surfing, lifting weights in his vast, park-like backyard. He wore army fatigues, a khaki shirt and army boots. His blue eyes flashed as he looked down at Straker.

Straker – short and narrow and dark, his face softly Slavic – was Huysman's physical opposite. And there was another contrast: Huysman was afraid of something; his insecurity showed through his bluff expression and his bullish stance as he silently, somehow defiantly, took stock of the visitor. For his part, Straker seemed poised, confident and loose.

Huysman made a brusque gesture, and Straker followed him into the inner office.

Beneath a polarized picture window there was a mahogany desk with a polished leather inset; large easy chairs faced i: on either side. There were a few books, some photos of Huysman with various vidstars and a fireplace that had never been used. This was an office for receiving people; it was too pristine for real work. A small video-replay machine was set up next to a low leather couch; Straker had requested it.

Straker sat silently on the couch. Huysman sat stiffly on the edge of his desk, facing Straker but not looking at him.

Straker took a palm-sized videocassette from the inside jacket pocket of his three-piece suit. The suit was Thirties revival, pinstriped in black and charcoal – something Fred Astaire might have worn on a date with Ginger Rogers.

Straker slid the tape into the player and watched the small rectangular screen rez up. He scanned the first page of a file report on Reginald Granger Huysman; his posture was relaxed, friendly without being presumptuously languid. 'Now, as I understand it,' Straker said gently, 'you're suffering from hallucinations, yes?'

Huysman frowned, flicked his hands as if dispensing with nonsense. 'Hardly. Not hallucinations. Hallucinations are qualitatively different. As different as a snapshot's different from a TV image. This . . . I've toyed with drugs, and I've had my share of hallucinations. This is something unique in my experience . . . Uh, you *are* Straker?'

'I am.' Straker smiled almost meekly.

'Well, these . . . I think of them as visions. Or . . . they're just not like anything else. Unique.'

'Everyone likes to feel unique.'

'So, OK, maybe it isn't unique – because it's like a dream. It's hypnagogic, I think. Or eidetic. Pictures. I see it clearest with my eyes closed. It's like a waking dream. But more solid than a hallucination. It's – ' he almost smiled ' – it's cinematic.'

'And this is something you want to be totally rid of?'

Huysman hesitated. Probably, Straker reflected, he disliked admitting his fear of it – or of anything. 'Obviously,' he said finally, defensively.

'Can you call it up whenever you like?'

'Not exactly. But it's predictable. It comes when I think about certain things. Sometimes it comes on its own. I wish it *would* come at night. But it doesn't. Only when I'm awake, so far.'

'So you think about certain things and that brings it on?'

'Not quite so cut-and-dried as that. It's usually a sequence of . . . well . . .'

'Tell me, please. Go through the series of associations that brings on this, uh, vision. If the vision occurs, describe it to me.'

Huysman began to speak. As he did, Straker entered notations on the videoplayer's keyboard; the transcript would be added to Huysman's file.

'Almost involuntarily, I'll start remembering the women in my life. Like Jenny Quinlan – that was twenty years ago in Vegas. I was directing a series of variety shows for NBC then. She was a dancer in the show. I was twenty-three. The golden boy of television. The prodigious wonder. Everybody wanted to hire me.' Huysman's tone was bitter. He seemed to have forgotten his mistrust of Straker. He closed his eyes and continued. 'At first, Jenny and I were mutually infatuated. She'd fallen for me badly, but I tired of her in a month. I led her on with talk of marriage, then dumped her – left for Europe and said I'd be in touch, but never was. She wrote me twelve letters. I didn't answer a single one. Hurt her terribly. The next year, there was a scriptwriter, Lola Cassavetes. I led her on. We played. I dumped her. There were two more. When I finally recognized it, the pattern disgusted me, so – I married Sandy. We're still married. Eleven years. And I did it to prove a point, not because I loved her. Not because . . . shit . . .'

Not because . . . shit . . . appeared on the small screen and was transferred onto the cassette.

Huysman continued. 'Sandy soaks up love like a sponge. She needs affection, she needs someone to play the husband role backward and forward. I played it for eight years. And then I couldn't stand it anymore . . . I feel strangled, oppressed, but I can't divorce her. The company is in her name, and she'll never agree to sell out to me. She'll drain me for alimony; ruin me somehow. Hell, I got into producing cable-drama by marrying her – her father owns the largest cable operation in the US.

'So I'm thinking about Jenny and Lola and Elaine and Gemini and Sandra and then the thing hits me. Listen, have you ever been walking over a bridge and, for no reason, you get an urge to jump? Or look over the balcony rail of a high building and get an impulse to just vault it? I don't mean a suicidal urge out of depression. What I'm talking about happens to the happiest people. It's a fleeting urge. A momentary impulse. Maybe it's why people go to see horror movies. You sort of . . . *revel* in an attack on yourself for no other reason but pure goddamn perversity. Well, this waking dream of mine feels like that . . .

'I'll be directing something when, suddenly, the world around me vanishes. In its place, I'm in a little room – the room's fuzzy, but I sense concrete walls – and metal rafters overhead. There's a kind of tension in the air, like somebody's blowing a dog whistle in my ear. I'm walking along one of the walls, in profile against it, and a sort of shadow falls over me. I turn around, my back to the wall, and everything goes slo-mo . . . like one of my cable-dramas when we slow things up, unnaturally slow, to emphasize the action, enhance the purity of the violence. When I turn to face the source of this shadow, I see a gun in someone's hand. I can't see who it is because there's a flash from the gun. It's a big pistol, a .357 Magnum. There's a roar . . . but by the time I hear the boom of the gun going off, I'm already bouncing off the wall, my guts opening up under the impact of the slug. The force of the shot slams me up against the wall and I bounce off. Looking down, I see my body exploding outward at the middle – a spray of red and a glimpse of entrails. Those Magnums, they practically cut you in half with one shot. I'm not feeling any pain yet, and I'm starting to fall forward clutching at my middle when – *flash* – the gun goes off again. The gunman is only six feet from me – *flash* – three times, wham, wham, *wham*. I'm banged against the wall three more times. I can feel the chips of concrete from the wall behind me flying off as the bullets go right through me and smash into it. And here's the part that scares me, Straker . . .'

Huysman paused to glance at Straker; he seemed disappointed that this narrative had had little observable effect. He continued. 'What gets to me, thinking about it afterward, is that – *I get off on it* when the bullets blow through me.

'And you know something else, Straker – the whole damn dream, if that's what it is, is directed. Cinematically, teleplay style. I see the thing from different angles: closeups, reversals, zooms, cutaways; all nicely edited to give a total picture of the action – except that the gunman is blanked. That gave Tolliver a big jolt. He said – '

'Tolliver?' Straker interrupted. 'Who is Tolliver?'

'A psychoanalyst. He tried to help. Got nowhere. He tried the repressed-fag angle first. You know, sublimation of a desire to be penetrated. Then he started playing up my directing the bloodiest teleplays in the business. He said that the fact that I write the action scenes myself is the source of the whole thing. Claims I feel guilty because so-called TV-violence contributes to juvie crime, blah, blah, blah. But, hey, I've been insisting for years that I only give the public what it wants, and I've made the violent scenario a great art form. I still insist that's true. I *believe* it.'

Straker politely said nothing.

'Tolliver,' Huysman went on, 'is full of shit. What do *you* think?'

Straker shrugged. 'I'm not sure yet. I have to spend more time with you. Maybe when I watch you at home . . .'

'At home – ?'

'Didn't you read the orientation materials? That's how I do it. I move in with you. It's the only way to get to the heart of things. You won't notice me after a while. You've paid for the treatment already, Mr Huysman. It's expensive and we don't give refunds.' Straker smiled apologetically.

'I don't like it. It's bad enough with Sandra . . . but, well . . . OK. This thing is interfering with my work. It's got to stop. It's even creeping into the shows . . .'

Huysman was shaken. He went to a wall cabinet, opened it, and pressed a toggle. A wall slot dispensed a neat whiskey in a plastic shot glass. Sipping, his back to Straker, Huysman said, 'Take your file cassette out and press the red button. It's cued.'

Straker recognized the footage; he'd forbidden his daughter to watch it the night before. It was called *The Cop Hunters* . . . Three black sedans following a police car. The sedans pursue it in a ten-minute chase through a warehouse district and into the suburbs. They corner him in a deserted housing project. The patrol car overturns. Cop gets out, bruised but whole, and runs. The six men in the sedans leave their cars and take up the chase on foot. They trap the cop in a half-finished, roofless garage. They close in on him, he tries to run, they push him back, he falls, they laugh, he gets to his feet, reaches for his gun . . . someone shoots him in the stomach with a .357 Magnum from about eight feet away. The details are grisly, in vivid color . . . gut exploding under the impact of the high-caliber slug, an out-splash of red, the cop bounces from the wall, begins to fall forward, three more shots throw him back, each bullet's impact shown in immaculately complete detail. Straker had to look away. But not before he'd seen the parallels.

Huysman stood beside Straker, impassively watching the choreographed butchery on the screen. 'People who don't know any better say my shows are all more or less alike. But no two gunshot scenes are the same. And when we show someone getting their head hammered in with a two-by-four, we do *that* distinctively. No two are quite alike, though there are a lot of similarities. And I can tell you that *this* one is almost exactly like my dream – if it is a dream – but it was made after I started having the visions.'

'How long have you been seeing this scene in your head?'

'Oh . . . three months. It's gotten more intense lately. Worse and worse. It's already happened four times today. Once at home, once in the studio cafeteria, twice in the office . . .'

'If it happens again while I'm with you, try to tell me. Try to describe it as it happens.'

'You'll know when it happens. I'll be staring into space like I'm being goosed by a ghost. Shocked look, frozen. But I can't talk during it – Hey, I gotta go to the studio.'

'I'll come along.'

Huysman scowled, then sighed and said, 'Yeah, OK . . . but stay out of the way.'

'That's my policy,' Straker said quietly.

'C'monnnn,' Huysman roared. 'Get it set up! I want the tail end of that Harley pointed at the goddamn moon!'

Standing well out of the way, Straker watched as Huysman's burly assistants jammed a huge motorcycle into the windshield of a semi-truck that, moments before, they'd crashed into the base of a cliff. The dust was still settling, and a few grenade-sized rocks were tumbling from the cliffs above, bouncing off the hood of the semi, narrowly missing the crews of cameramen, sound men, lighting men. The late-afternoon sun, distended like a hunger-bloated belly in the silt-thick Los Angeles smog, threw a bloodied light on the derricks, hoists and camera machinery crowded over the truck.

'Gedduh close-zup of the hand on the hood of the semi! Get the angle seddup – here lemme see that – ' Huysman shoved the befuddled cameraman aside, climbing onto the metal platform to look through the eyepiece at the dummy hand, severed at the wrist, lying in a pool of blood on the hood. 'Get some more broken glass around that hand – hey, get the fuck outta the way, Henry, you're throwin' a fuckin' shadow on the *hand!* And you – huh? All right, what you want, kid?'

A message boy from the studio stood nervously to one side, squinting up at Huysman. 'It's Mr Drummond, Mr Huysman. He can't make it to the afternoon shooting.'

The cast and crew fell silent, watching Huysman expect-antly, waiting for him to boil over in fury. Drummond was the star, but he'd missed three shootings that week. Because of Drummond, they were behind schedule.

'So Drummond isn't *coming* today . . .' Huysman said softly, dangerously.

Straker watched Huysman – expecting something other than an outburst of anger. He waited for Huysman to lapse into his 'goosed by a ghost' look; this was a moment of great stress for Huysman. If the vision was a break-down under stress, as Straker supposed, it should come now.

It didn't. Instead, Huysman shouted, 'Aw-right, we put up with it once more and then we find a replacement and start shooting from the beginning and he can *eat* his contract! Get the double in here!' The noise and bustle resumed.

Straker watched Huysman, revising his theory.

Two hours later, during a break in the shooting, Huysman and Straker sat together at a table in the studio cafeteria. Huysman drank coffee. Straker mineral water. Straker watched Huysman without seeming to. Relaxed, faintly smiling but never supercilious, Straker put Huys-man at his ease.

Huysman stared moodily into the tarry depths of his cup and said, 'I dunno. Straker, if she'd leave me alone a few days a week, I think I could stand to spend some time with her.' He swallowed, shrugged.

'How much time,' Straker asked breezily, 'would you spend with your secretary?'

Huysman looked up at him. 'Darla? How'd you get onto that?'

'I read it in her face this morning.'

Huysman nodded distantly, 'Sure, OK, but keep it under your hat, all right?'

Straker smiled as if to say, *How could you doubt it?*

'Darla treats me right, Straker. She doesn't beg me for more time. She doesn't go out with other people just to try to put me in my place. If she does mess around, she doesn't let me know about it, anyway, and that's close enough to fidelity for me. She's a good woman. She doesn't try to use her influence with me to get parts. She doesn't want parts. I'd love her for that alone.'

'*Do* you love her?'

Huysman frowned. 'Well . . .'

A shadow fell over the table. Straker looked up to see Sandra Huysman – he recognized her from photos in Huysman's file – standing just back of her husband.

'Going to tell him about Darla, Reggie?' She attempted to make her tone icy, but it overflowed with hot currents of hurt.

Huysman sat frozen, staring at his cup, his face empty.

'Mind if I sit, witch doctor?' she asked, glancing at Straker.

'Please do,' Straker replied tonelessly.

'Sure I know about her,' Sandra murmured, puffing smoke at Huysman's down-turned face. 'No big deal. Just like you, Reggie.' She adjusted the lapels of her dark suit. Her face was clownish with too much makeup; her blonde wig set at an unconvincing angle.

'Stop trying to get me angry with you, Sandy,' Huysman said wearily.

Sandra's blase veneer cracked. Her eyes brimmed with tears.

Huysman looked at her. Then beyond her. His mouth opened, his eyes widened. He fell backward out of his chair and began writhing on the floor, his hands clutched at his belly, and he whimpered.

Faces turned to watch, but no one got up to help. Word of Huysman's 'fits' had gone round the studio.

Sandra stood over him, shouting, 'It's not gonna work, you bastard! Stop acting like an infant! You – ' She lost her voice to sobs, and threw his coffee cup at him. The dark liquid splashed over his middle like a bloodstain.

Huysman stood in a place that was dark except for one harshly bright light in the center of a metal-raftered ceiling. He leaned against a concrete wall. He closed his eyes. *Make it gone*, he prayed. Eyes closed, eyes opened – it made no difference.

He turned to face the figure silhouetted by the glare of the bulb. He looked down to see the gun in the soft white hand . . . a big nickel-plated .357 Magnum.

Sandra hunched over Huysman, whispering in his ear, as the crowd gathered around them, arguing about what to do. 'Should we call an ambulance?' someone said. 'Maybe this time it's his heart – '

'No, I'm a doctor,' Straker lied. 'I'll take care of him.' He knelt down to hear what Sandra Huysman was saying. '*I* know who it is, shooting you in your dream, Reggie,' she murmured. 'It's me. I'm gonna kill you.'

The hand holding the gun came into sharper focus this time.

He could see a wedding ring on one of the fingers below the trigger guard, a ring he'd bought and paid for eleven years before.

'Sandy . . .' he whispered. 'The gunsh – '

He was slammed against the concrete wall, pitched forward, smashed back by another bullet, and another, another . . . his whole being exploding outward from the middle, broken open, splashed . . . and this time he felt the pain coming, bearing down on him like an express train . . .

* * *

'I see it differently now, Straker,' Huysman said thickly, trying to sit up in the bed. 'It's a premonition – that's what it is.'

'I doubt it, Huysman. I confess to being a little worried, though. I think your wife would like you to think it's a premonition. She knows you're vulnerable now.'

Huysman rubbed his forehead. 'Gotta bastarduva headache. Get me . . . get me, uh, beta-endorphin. It's in the medicine cabinet. Down the hall to the right.'

Straker stood and nodded. 'OK. But listen – maybe we should get you into a hospital, after all. I'm not so sure your doctor did you a favor, having you brought here. He's right – it's nervous collapse, not a stroke or something. But I think you should be in the hospital – and I don't mean an asylum – for observation.'

'What the fuck *for?*'

'Because, my friend, I'm afraid you're going to hurt yourself. The timing and sequence of your visions make it clear to me. You see, you've got a festering guilt complex over the women you've hurt. All of them. And to make it worse, you're making your wife miserable by ignoring her, even now. She's still fixated on you, no matter what she says. You sense that. You sense you've hurt her. You're punishing yourself with this vivid vision of your own assassination. What's more, your guilt over your lovers is linked to another festering complex about TV-violence. No one can be accused as often as you have been and remain totally untouched by it. The two complexes simply reinforce one another. You've directed your own waking nightmare. We can wean you from it by bringing you to a gradual confrontation with your guilt feelings – Huysman, are you listening?' For the first time, Straker's manner was forceful, commanding.

Huysman flinched. He sat in his underclothes, the bedspread thrown back, his head in his hands, shoulders shaking. 'I dunno,' he said weakly. 'I can't think now. My head hurts too much. I dunno what you're talking about, Straker. She's going to kill me. It's a premonition . . .'

'Huysman, listen to me. A great many physical diseases are caused by a kind of psychic urge to self-destruct. A cellular despair. Cancer, particularly, shows up more in emotionally disturbed people than anyone else. And there's a malady called cynophobia, which produces the *symptoms* of rabies up to a certain point and is caused by the *fear* that you're going to have rabies. The victim becomes very sick, even dies, because of his pathological fear of rabies, though he doesn't really have it at all. Your body responds to your mind *that* thoroughly. Hypnotists can make their subjects stop and start bleeding from a small cut when in a trance – '

'For God's *sake*, get my pain pills!'

'All right. But you've got to stop believing this assassination scene of yours is real or, somehow – maybe a tumor, maybe a stroke – you'll live out a self-fulfilling prophecy and make yourself sick from it.'

Straker left the bedroom, hurried down the hall to the bathroom, fumbled through the medicine cabinet. 'Why am I hurrying?' he thought. 'Why am I so afraid to leave Huysman alone?' He found the bottle marked BETA-ENDORPHIN, and hurried back to the bedroom. It was empty.

The covers were thrown back, the sheets still warm. Still clutching the bottle, Straker moved to the hallway and called uncertainly, 'Huysman?'

He heard a sound from the direction of the garage.

It was empty except for a set of rusty barbells, a gasoline can, a workbench holding a few power drills that were collecting dust – and Mr and Mrs Huysman.

'That's right,' Sandra was saying, 'up against the wall, motherfucker. Now turn around to face me . . .'

Shaking, white, mouth hanging slack, Huysman obeyed her.

She wore the same dark suit. In her right hand was a large, nickel-plated .357 Magnum revolver.

The only illumination came from a single bright, white light bulb in the center of the garage, just behind her head.

She raised the gun. 'Now you'll *feel* the bullets, Reggie,' she said, almost lovingly.

Straker started toward her, opening his mouth to shout at Huysman.

She pulled the trigger. Huysman screamed. She squeezed the trigger three times more, and he collapsed in a welter of blood.

The blood from his burst stomach splashed Mrs Huysman's pants. She stood with the gun hanging in her limp right hand beside her thigh and stared numbly down on him, an enigmatic smile flickering across her lips.

Straker took the gun from her hand. He was shaking himself. *So shaken up, I didn't hear the shots?* He looked at Huysman.

Huysman was quite dead, sprawled on the dusty floor with his head propped against the concrete wall. His eyes were open, locked on the spot where the gun had been when she'd pulled the trigger. His abdomen had been ripped open. From the inside.

Straker opened the gun. Nothing . . . no cartridges, no shells.

Empty.

Equilibrium

He doesn't know me, but I know him. He has never seen me, but I know that he has been impotent for six months, can't shave without listening to the news on TV at the same time, and mixes bourbon with his coffee during his afternoon coffeebreak. And is proud of himself for holding off on the bourbon till the afternoon.

His wife doesn't know me, has never seen me, but I know that she regards her husband as 'something to put up with, like having your period'; I know that she loves her children blindly, but just as blindly drags them through every wrong turn in their lives. I know the names and addresses of each one of her relatives, and what she does with her brother Charlie's photograph when she locks herself in the bathroom. She knows nothing of my family (I'm not admitting that I have one) but I know the birthdays and hobbies and companions of her children. The family of Marvin Ezra Hobbes. Co-starring: Lana Louise Hobbes as his wife, and introducing Bobby Hobbes and Robin Hobbes as their two sons. Play the theme music.

I know Robin Hobbes and he knows me. Robin and I were stationed together in Guatemala. We were supposed to be there for 'exercises' but we were there to help train the Contras. It was a couple of years ago. The CIA wouldn't like it if I talk about the details, much.

I'm not the sort of person you'd write home about. But Robin told me a good many things, and even entrusted a letter to me. I was supposed to personally deliver it to his family (no, I never did have a family . . . really . . . I really didn't . . .) just in case anything 'happened' to him. Robin always said that he wouldn't complain as long as 'things turn out even'. If a Sandinista shoots Robin's pecker away, Robin doesn't complain as long as a Sandinista gets *his* pecker blown away. Doesn't even have to be the same Sandinista. But the war wasn't egalitarian. It remained for me to establish equilibrium for Robin.

Robin didn't want to enlist. It was his parents' idea.

It had been raining for three days when he told me about it. The rain was like another place, a whole different part of the world, trying to assert itself over the one we were in. We had to make a third place inside the first one and the interfering one, had to get strips of tin and tire rubber and put them over our tent, because the tent fabric didn't keep out the rain after a couple of days. It steamed in there. My fingers were swollen from the humidity, and I had to take off the little platinum ring with the equal ($=$) sign on it. Robin hadn't said anything for a whole day, but then he just started talking, his voice coming out of the drone of the rain, almost the same tone, almost generated by it. ' "They're gonna start up the draft for real and earnest," my dad said. "You're just the right age. They'll get you sure. Thing to do is, join now. Then you can write your own ticket. Make a deal with the recruiter." My dad wanted me out of the house. He wanted to buy a new car, and he couldn't afford it because he was supporting us all, and I was just another expense. That was what renewed my dad, gave him a sense that life had a goal and was worth living: a new car, every few years. Trade in the old one. Get a whole new debt . . . My mom was afraid I'd be drafted too. I had an uncle was in the Marines, liked to act like he was a Big Man with the real-in-the-know scuttlebutt; he wrote us and said the Defense Department was preparing for war, planning to invade Nicaragua, going to do some exercises down that way first . . . So we thought the war was coming for real. Thought we had inside information. My mom wanted me to join to save my life, she said. So I could choose to go to someplace harmless, like Europe. But the truth is, she always was wet for soldiers. My uncle Charlie used to hang around in his dress uniform a lot. Looking like a stud. She was the only woman I ever knew who liked war movies. She didn't pay attention during the action parts; it wasn't that she was bloodthirsty. She liked to see them displaying their stripes and their braid and their spit and polish and marching in step, their guns sticking up . . . So she sort of went all glazed when Dad suggested I join the Army and she didn't defend me when he started putting the guilt pressure on me about not getting a job and two weeks later I was recruited and the bastards lied about my assignment and here I fucking am, right here. It's raining. It's raining, man.'

'Yeah,' I said. 'It'd be nice if it wasn't raining. But then we'd get too much sun or something. Has to balance out.'

'I'm sick of you talking about balancing stuff out. I want it to stop raining.'

So it did. The next day. That's when the Sandinistas started shelling the camp. Like the shells had been waiting on top of the clouds and when they pulled the clouds away, the trap door opened, and the mortar rounds fell through . . .

Immediately after something 'happened' to Robin, I burned the letter he'd given me. Then I was transferred to the Fourth Army Clerical Unit. I know, deeply and intuitively, that the transfer was no accident. It placed me in an ideal position to initiate the balancing of Equilibrium and was therefore the work of the Composers. Because with the Fourth Clerical I was in charge of dispensing information to the families of the wounded or killed. I came across Robin Hobbes's report, and promptly destroyed it. His parents never knew, till I played out my little joke. I like jokes. Jokes are always true, even when they're dirty lies.

I juggled the papers so that Robin Hobbes, twenty years old, would be sent to a certain sanitarium, where a friend of mine was a Meditech who worked admissions two days a week. The rest of the time he's what they call a Handler. A Psych Tech. My friend at the sanitarium likes the truth. He likes to see it, to smell it, particularly when it makes him gag. He took the job at the sanitarium with the eighteen-year-old autistics who bang their heads bloody if you don't tie them down and with the older men who have to be diapered and changed and rocked like babies and with the children whose faces are strapped into fencing masks to prevent them from eating the wallpaper and to keep them from pulling off their lips and noses – he took the job because he *likes* it there. He took it because he likes jokes.

And he took good care of Robin Hobbes for me until it was time. I am compelled to record an aside here, a well-done and sincere thanks to my anonymous friend for his enormous patience in spoon-feeding Robin Hobbes twice daily, changing his bedpan every night, and bathing him once a week for the entire six months interment. He had to do it personally, because Robin was there illegally, and had to be hidden in the old wing they don't use anymore.

Meanwhile, I observed the Hobbes family.

They have one of those new bodyform cars. It's a fad thing. Marvin Hobbes got his new car. The sleek, flesh-tone, fiberglass body of the car is cast so that its sides are imprinted with the shape of a nude woman lying prone, her arms flung out in front of her in the diving motion of the Cannon beachtowel girl. The doors are in her ribs,

the trunk opens from her ass. She's ridiculously impro-
portional, of course. The whole thing is wildly kitsch. It
was an embarrassment to Mrs Hobbes. And Hobbes is
badly in debt behind it, because he totaled his first
bodyform car. Rammed a Buick Sissy Spacek into a Joe
Namath pickup. Joe and Sissy's arms, tangled when their
front bumpers slammed, were lovingly intertwined.

Hobbes took the loss, and bought a Miss America. He
is indifferent to Mrs Hobbes's embarrassment. To the
particularly judgmental way she uses the term *tacky*.

Mr Hobbes plays little jokes of his own. Private jokes.
But I knew. Mr Hobbes had no idea I was watching when
he concealed his wife's Lady Norelco. He knew that she'd
want it that night, because they were invited to a party,
and she always shaved her legs before a party. Mrs
Hobbes sang a little tuneless song as she quested system-
atically for the shaver, bending over to look in the house's
drawers and cabinets, and *behind* the drawers and cabinets, peering into all the secret nooks and burrow-places
we forget a house has; her search was so thorough I came
to regard it as the product of mania. I felt a sort of
warmth, then: I can appreciate . . . thoroughness.

Once a week, he did it to her. He'd temporarily pocket
her magnifying mirror, her makeup case. Then he'd
pretend to find it. 'Where any idiot can see it.'

Bobby Hobbes, Robin's younger brother, was unaware
that his father knew about his hidden cache of Streamline
racing-striped condoms. The elder Hobbes thought he
was very clever, in knowing about them. But he didn't
know about me.

Marvin Hobbes would pocket his son's rubbers and
make *snuck-snuck* sounds of muffled laughter in his
sinuses as the red-eared teenager feverishly searched and
rechecked his closet and drawers.

Hobbes would innocently saunter in and ask, 'Hey –

you better get goin' if you're gonna make that date, right? Whatcha lookin' for anyway? Can I help?'

'Oh . . . uh, no thanks, Dad. Just some . . . socks. Missing.'

As the months passed, and Hobbes's depression over his impotence worsened, his fits of practical joking became more frequent, until he no longer took pleasure in them, but performed his practical jokes as he would some habitual household chore. Take out the trash, cut the lawn, hide Lana's razor, feed the dog.

I watched as Hobbes, driven by some undefined desperation, attempted to relate to his relatives. He'd sit them at points symmetrical (relative to him) around the posh living room; his wife thirty degrees to his left, his youngest son thirty degrees to his right. Then, he would relate a personal childhood experience as a sort of parable, describing his hopes and dreams for his little family.

'When I was a boy we would carve out tunnels in the briar bushes. The wild blackberry bushes were very dense, around our farm. It'd take hours to clip three feet into them with the gardener's shears. But after weeks of patient work, we snipped a network of crude tunnels through the half-acre filled with brambles. In this way, we learned how to cope with the world as a whole. We would crawl through the green tunnels in perfect comfort, but knowing that if we stood up, the thorns would cut us to ribbons.'

He paused and sucked several times loudly on the pipe. It had gone out ten minutes before. He stared at the fireplace where there was no fire.

Finally he asked his wife, 'Do you understand?' Almost whining it.

She shook her head ruefully. Annoyed, his jaws bruxating, Hobbes slipped to the floor, muttering he'd lost his tobacco pouch, searching for it under the coffee table,

under the sofa. His son didn't smile, not once. His son
had hidden the tobacco pouch. Hobbes went scurrying
about on the rug looking for the tobacco pouch in a great
dither of confusion, like a poodle searching for his
rawhide bone. Growling low. Growling to himself.

Speculation as to how I came to know these intimate
details of the Hobbes family life will prove as futile as
Marvin's attempts to relate to his relatives.

I have my ways. I learned my techniques from other
Composers.

Presumably, Composers belong to a tacit network of
free agents the world over, whose sworn duty it is to
establish states of interpersonal Equilibrium. No Composer has ever knowingly met another; it is impossible for
them to meet, even by accident, since they carry the same
charge and therefore repel from each other. I'm not sure
just how the invisible Composers taught me their technique for the restoration of states of Equilibrium. To be
precise, I *am* sure as to how it was done – I simply can't
articulate it.

I have no concrete evidence that the Composers exist.
Composers perform the same service for society that
vacuum tubes used to perform for radios and amplifiers.
And the fact of a vacuum tube's existence is proof that
someone must have the knowledge, somewhere, needed
to construct a vacuum tube. Necessity is its own evidence.

Now picture this: Picture me with a high forehead
crowned by white hair and a square black graduation cap
with its tassel dangling. Picture me with a drooping white
mustache and wise blue eyes. In fact, I look a lot like
Albert Einstein, in this picture. I am wearing a black
graduation gown, and clutched in my right hand is a long
wooden pointer.

I don't have a high forehead. I don't have any hair at
all. No mustache. Not even eyebrows. I don't have blue

eyes. (Probably, neither did Einstein.) I don't look like Einstein in the slightest. I don't own a graduation gown, and I never completed a college course.

But picture me that way. I am pointing at a home movie screen with my official pointer. On the screen is a projection of a young man who has shaved himself bald and who wears a tattered Army uniform with a Clerical Corps patch on the right shoulder, half peeled off. The young man has his back to the home movie camera. He is playing a TV-tennis game. This was one of the first video games. Each player is given a knob which controls a vertical white dash designating the 'tennis racket', one to each half of the television screen. On a field of blank gray the two white dashes bandy between them a white blip, the 'tennis ball'. With a flick of the dial, snapping the dash/racket up or down, one knocks the blip past the other electronic paddle and scores a point. Jabbing here and there at the movie screen I indicate that the game is designed for two people. I nod my head sagely. But this mysterious young man manipulates left and right dials with both hands at once. (If you look closely at his hands, you'll note that the index finger of his left hand is missing. The index finger of his right hand is missing, too.) Being left-handed, when he first began to play himself, the left hand tended to win. But he establishes perfect equilibrium in the interactive poles of his parity. The game is designed to continue incessantly until fifteen points are scored by either side. He nurtured his skill until he could play against himself for long hours, beeping a white blip with euphoric monotony back and forth between wrist-flicks, never scoring a point for either hand.

He never wins, he never loses, he establishes perfect equilibrium.

The movie ends, the professor winks, the young man was at no time turned to face the camera.

*   *   *

My practical joke was programmed to compose an Equilibrium for Robin Hobbes and his family. Is it Karma? Are the Composers the agents of Karma? No. There is no such thing as Karma: that is why the Composers are necessary. To redress the negligence of God. We try. But in establishing the Equilibrium – something far more refined than vengeance – we invariably create another imbalance, for justice cannot be precisely quantified. And the new imbalance gives rise to a contradictory inversity, and so the Perfect and Mindless Dance of equilibrium proceeds. For there to be a premise there must somewhere exist its contradiction.

Hence I present my clue to the Hobbes encrypted in a reversal of the actual situation.

In the nomenclature of the Composers, a snake symbolizes an octopus. The octopus has eight legs, the snake is legless. The octopus is the greeting, the snake is the reply; the centipede is the greeting, the worm is the reply.

And so I selected the following document, an authentic missive illicitly obtained from a certain obsessive cult, and mailed it to the Hobbes, as my clue offered in all fairness; the inverted foreshadowing:

My dear, dear Tonto,
    You recall, I assume, that Perfect and Holy Union I myself ordained, in my dominion as High Priest – the marriage of R. and D., Man and Wife in the unseeing eyes of the Order, they were obligated to seek a means of devotion and worship, in accordance with their own specialties and proclivities. I advised them to jointly undertake the art of Sensual Communion with the Animus, and this they did, and still they were unsatisfied. Having excelled in the somatic explorations that are the foundation of the Order, they were granted leave to follow the lean of their own inclinations. Thus liberated, they settled on the fifth Degree in Jolting, the mastery of self-modification. They sought out a surgeon who, for an inestimable price, fused their bodies into one. They became Siamese twins; the woman joined

to his right side. They were joined at the waist through an unbreakable bridge of flesh. This grafting made sexual coupling, outside of fondling, nearly impossible. The obstacle, as we say in the Order, is the object. But R. was not content. Shorn of normal marital relations, R.'s latent homosexuality surfaced. He took male lovers and his wife was forced to lay beside the copulating men, forced to observe everything, and advised to keep her silence except in the matter of insisting on latex condoms. At first this stage left her brimming with revulsion; but she became aware that through the bridge of flesh which linked them she was receiving, faintly at first and then more strongly, her husband's impressions. In this way she was vicariously fulfilled and in the fullness of time no longer objected when he took to a homosexual bed. R.'s lovers accepted her presence, as if she were the incarnate spirit of the frustrated feminine persona which was the mainspring of their inner clockworks. But when their new complacency was established, the obstacle diminished. It became necessary to initiate new somatic obstacles. Inevitably, another woman was added to the Siamese coupling, to make it a tripling, a woman on R.'s left. Over a period of several months more were added, after the proper blood tests. Today, they are joined to six other people in a ring of exquisite Siamese multiplicity. The juncturing travels in a circle so the first is joined to the eighth, linked with someone else on both sides. All face inward. There are four men and four women, a literal wedding ring. (Is this a romantic story, Tonto?) Arrayed as they are in an unbreakable ring, they necessarily go to great lengths to overcome practical and psychological handicaps. For example, they had to practice for two days to learn how to collectively board D.'s Lear Jet. Four, usually the women, ride in the arms of the other four; they sidle into the plane, calling signals for the steps. This enforced teamwork lends a new perspective to the most mundane daily affairs. Going to the toilet becomes a yogic exercise requiring the utmost concentration. For but one man to pee, each of the joined must provide a precisely measured degree of pressure . . . They have been surgically arranged so that each man can copulate with the woman opposite him or, in turns, the man diagonal. Homosexual relations are limited to one coupling at a time since members of the same sex are diagonal to one another. Heterosexually, the cell has sex simultaneously. The surgeons have continuated the nerve ends through the links so that the erogenous sensations of one are shared by all. I was privileged to observe one of these highly practiced acrobatic orgies. I admit to a secret yen to participate, to stand nude in the center of the circle and experience flesh-tone piston-action from every point of the compass. But this is below my Degree; only the High Priest's divine mount, the Perfect and Unscrubbed *Silver*, may know him carnally . . . Copulating as an octuplet whole, they resemble a pink sea anemone capturing a wriggling minnow. Or perhaps interlocked fingers of arm wrestlers. Or a letter written all in one paragraph, a single unit . . . But suppose a fight breaks out between the grafted Worshippers? Suppose one of them should die or take sick? If one contracts an illness, all ultimately come down with it. And if one should die, they would have to carry the corpse wherever they went until it rotted away – the operation is irreversible. But that is all part of the Divine Process.

Yours very, very affectionately,
The Lone Ranger

Mrs Hobbes found the letter in the mailbox and opened it. She read it with visible alarm, and brought it in to her husband, who was in the backyard, preparing to barbecue the ribs of a pig. He was wearing an apron printed with the words, DON'T FORGET TO KISS THE CHEF. The word FORGET was almost obliterated by a rusty splash of sauce.

Hobbes read the letter, frowning. 'I'll be goshdarned,' he said. 'They get crazier with this junk mail all the time. Goddamned pornographic.' He lit the letter on fire and used it to start the charcoal.

Seeing this, I smiled with relief, and softly said: 'Click!' A letter for a letter, equilibrium for the destruction of the letter Robin Hobbes had given me in Guatemala. If Mr and Mrs Hobbes had discerned the implication of the inverted clue I would have been forced to release Robin from the sanitarium, to the custody of the Army.

When the day came for my joke, I had my friend bring Robin over to my hotel room which was conveniently two blocks from the Hobbes' residence.

It should be a harmless gesture to describe my friend, as long as I don't disclose his name. Not a Composer in face but one in spirit, my Meditech friend is pudgy and square shouldered. His legs look like they're too thin for his body. His hair is clipped close to his small skull and there is a large white scar dividing his scalp, running from the crown of his head to the bridge of his nose. The scar is a gift from one of his patients, given in an unguarded moment. My friend wears thick wire-rim glasses with an elastic band connecting them in the rear.

Over Robin's noisy protests I prepared him for the joke. To shut him up I considered cutting out his tongue. But that would require compensating with some act restoring equilibrium which I had not time to properly devise. So I settled for adhesive tape, over his mouth. And of course the other thing, stuck through a hole in the tape.

Mr Hobbes was at home, his Miss America bodyform car filled the driveway. The front of the car was crumpled from a minor accident of the night before, and her arms were corrugated, bent unnaturally inward, one argent hand shoved whole into her open and battered mouth.

Suppressing sniggers – I admit this freely, we were like two twelve-year-olds – my friend and I brought Robin to the porch and rang the doorbell. We dashed to the nearest concealment, a holly bush undulating in the faint summer breeze.

It was shortly after sunset, eight-thirty P.M. and Mr Hobbes had just returned from a long Tuesday at the office. He was silent and grumpy, commiserating with his abused Miss America. Two minutes after our ring, Marvin Hobbes opened the front door, newspaper in hand. My friend had to bite his lip to keep from laughing out loud. But for me, the humor had quite gone out of the moment. It was a solemn moment, one with a dignified and profound resonance.

Mrs Hobbes peered over Marvin's shoulder, electric shaver in her right hand; Bobby, behind her, stared over the top of her wig, something hidden in his left hand. Simultaneously, the entire family screamed, their instantaneous timing perhaps confirming that they were true relatives after all.

They found Rob as we had left him on the doorstep, swaddled in baby blankets, diapered in a couple of Huggies disposable diapers, a pacifier stuck through the tape over his mouth, covered to the neck in gingham cloth (though one of his darling stumps peeked through). And equipped with a plastic baby bottle. The shreds of his arms and legs had been amputated shortly after the mortar attack on Puerto Barrios. Pinned to his chest was a note (I lettered it myself in the crude handwriting I thought would reflect the mood of a desperate mother.) The note said:

PLEASE TAKE CARE OF MY BABY

Uneasy Chrysalids, Our Memories

JULY 4, 2006

I have been told by my history tutor that since I am an American, today should have some special significance for me. I should feel patriotic and grateful to my country. Or at least I should feel guilty if I don't feel that way. But none of those emotions are present because I didn't know about the importance of the Fourth of July until today. The person who I now am didn't know, though probably the old Jo Ann Culpepper did. Marsha, a cheery and energetic girl who I have been told was my best friend, said that I was once quite patriotic as a little girl, and should have been as a woman, especially after the big revival of nationalism.

A President and three of his cabinet members were assassinated with a bomb, and that sparked off another sort of uprising shortly after July, 1996. I gather that most of the dissidents in the US were purged. At least, that is what Mr Zelenke, my history tutor, tells me, though some of the things he tells me are so outrageous that I often wonder if he makes them up.

According to Marsha, I knew all these historic things before I lost that portion of my memory two years ago, but when I hear them now, they don't actually ring with familiarity.

Dr Fosdick said that my memory was fractured in September 2004 because of what he called 'glandular damage causing a chemical imbalance rendering mnemonic banks inaccessible, with indications of personality disorder.' I think that was it. He said that it will be impossible for me to get my old memory back, so they will try to give me a background with tutoring.

This diary is supposed to be an exercise for recall. I'm still terribly absent-minded, even in small things. I forgot to turn off the tap, and water flooded the house; I forgot to feed my fish, and they died.

Dr Fosdick said that we could repair my short term memory but that I'd have to settle for what little I have left of my life.

I remember my mother, some. She was tall, thin, dark-haired, like me. That's where I got most of my looks. Even the black eyes with the blue circles under them. It looked good on my mother, but not on me. She was a speedy, nervous person, I think. Always doing something, easily startled. I'm not like that, really I'm not. I'm rather slow with my reactions, and boring to talk to. People get tired of me easily.

But it's not as if I had nothing to say. I was even thinking of starting an organization to help people with messed-up memories like mine.

I don't remember my father much. I doubt if I liked him, somehow.

I wish I could remember more about my mamma. I have to admit I'm lonely. People shouldn't have to *admit* that they're lonely; it's too much like signing a confession. But I feel guilty that I'm lonely, like I've failed socially. Dr Fosdick says give it time.

They say I was an only child. I once had lots of friends and a boyfriend. I wonder what happened to my boyfriend? No one seems to know. Some of my friends come to see me once in a while. No, that isn't true. Dr Fosdick said that this journal should be extremely honest. Actually, none of them ever come to see me because of what happened to my parents during the purge by the vigilantes. A lot of people don't like to be associated with me because of my anti-nationalist background. I wish I could remember my 'anti-nationalist background'.

JULY 8, 2006

Dr Fosdick took me to one of the Independence Day government-sponsored festivals a few days ago. Free beer or pop and hot dogs. I didn't think he'd ask me to go anywhere with him. I thought that his interest in me would be purely clinical. But he *has* spent an awful lot of time with me.

We were sitting together, leaning our elbows on Minnesota. Each of the fifty tables at the festival was shaped like one of the states, and at the height of the evening they push them all together to symbolize the strengths of nationalism. All the tables together make the shape of the United States, with mustard stains and crumpled paper cups on it. We were drinking Coke, the National Drink (state-owned), out of bottles shaped like missiles, and eating hot dogs. Those were the only things on the menu. There were a lot of boisterous people making toasts and singing the anthem all around us (see, Dr Fosdick? I'm using words from my vocabulary exercises when I talk. Like you wanted! Boisterous!), but they had looks of strain, like the celebration was out of character. We were a little island of quiet in the middle of colorful festivity. The festival was on top of the Ford Defense Building, in the open air under the bubble of the smog shield, through which I could barely make out the half-moon. The waiters looked silly dressed in red rags like the Communists wear, and Dr Fosdick explained that it was supposed to be symbolic of something because they were serving us. I thought that it was symbolic of the silliness of the organizers of the festival, but I couldn't say that.

I sat quietly, wondering if Dr Fosdick had ever had connections with the vigilantes. I am sure that he didn't, because he took me in after they killed my parents, and no nationalist would shelter the daughter of impurities.

Dr Fosdick said something strange to me; then: 'Sometimes it's a valuable asset to have no memory. You have no regrets that way. I envy you at times, Jo Ann.' That was the first time he'd ever called me Jo Ann. Always it was Miss Culpepper. I didn't know what to say, so I smiled.

I was sort of disappointed the first time I met Dr Fosdick. I had thought that he would be an imposing Germanic figure with thick spectacles and an accent and a white laboratory smock. That was how a scientist was supposed to look, I thought. But when I was introduced to him seven months ago, I met a short little man with coarse black hair greased like a cowboy's, no glasses over his shiny blue eyes. Dr Fosdick has a rusty face. He wears jeans and a plaid shirt, even at work, never touches a white smock, and he listens to country music. We had to leave the festival early when some vigs recognized me. So we didn't get to see the skyrockets or the floggings.

JULY 10, 2006

I had to do something ugly today. It is running around in my head like a dog that's chained in one place so long it tracks a circular rut around itself in the dirt.

They made me relive the incident that took away my memory. I didn't want to do it. I wish that the incident itself was washed out, but for some reason, only everything before it is gone. They aren't sure if it was the thing that happened or the blow I got on the head that took it away. Maybe both.

My memory goes back two years. It starts with the incident, and everything before that is gone except for a few fragments: high school graduation, two years of college (Marsha says that I gave up my ambition to be a teacher after the book burnings), women's infantry corps initiation and the recovery in the hospital after the initiation, a trial of some kind (though I can't remember what I was tried for), some childhood pictures of my mother happily working in her garden, my aunt on her deathbed, a dog biting my ankle, a date with a boy who insisted on sodomy instead of the usual . . . and then the incident.

The nurses at the clinic are very sympathetic when I tell what happened. They make *tsk* noises about the men who killed my parents, but none of them ever say anything directly against the vigs. I'm not bitter about that.

Before the incident, my memories of education leave off with a little geography, ability to write (I had to relearn how to read), some math and grammar.

And the incident. The men who came into our apartment and what they did with knives to my mother and father. The blood, the screams, the curious neighbors looking in the open door. I can't understand why it wasn't erased. The memories of my parents that might have made me hate their killers are lost.

I had to relive it once today, so I'd rather not go into it more now.

JULY 30, 2006

I haven't written in this journal for so long because so many wonderful things have happened that I just didn't know how to express it.

Well perhaps that is an exaggeration. To make myself feel better. Because there are some things I've been worried about, too.

I didn't think anyone would ever care about me much, because I'm pretty shallow and I have this habit of running myself down. But Dr Fosdick says that if people look down on me it's because I look down on myself. And someone *does* care about me. Dr Fosdick. I guess it's okay to talk about all this here, though I feel funny talking about Dr Fosdick, because I know he's going to read this. I'm supposed to be honest, so that he'll know how much I've improved and all.

Dr Fosdick made love to me yesterday at my apartment. I think he had been considering it for a while, because he had insisted that I take birth-control pills, though I was sure that no one would ever want to sleep with me. He must have cared about me right off, to have prepared for it so long ahead of time.

He came to my apartment unexpectedly, with the usual dope that people bring on social visits; the government-issue green-weed kind. I can't really remember any of my other lovers, so I can't compare Dr Fosdick to anyone. (It's funny, but he has never asked me to call him by his first name, and I don't even know what it is. I had to call him Dr Fosdick when he made love to me.) He was nice, and he didn't mind that I was in my period. He was like those really fast pistons you see on the Eagle car commercials on the viddy.

But something else has happened. After we made love, he gave me an injection in my right arm (it's still sore) with a syringe from a plastic case he had in his coat pocket. He said that it was a serum that might bring back my memory.

I asked him why he couldn't give it to me at the clinic, and he replied that it was still a bit experimental and that he hadn't had it officially approved as yet. The medical board wouldn't let him use it until it was too late. It had to be injected within a certain period of time after the original loss of memory, he told me, or else it wouldn't work. He held my hand and said very earnestly that the medical board didn't care about my recovery like he did.

The only thing that really disturbed me was that he injected it into my arm without asking me first, or even telling me. I turned away from him for a moment, and the next thing I knew, there was a needle stinging my arm.

He explained that he wanted it to be a surprise.

August 4, 2006

Two things happened today that should mean something to me, I think, though they seem distant and removed from me.

I was walking with Dr Fosdick in the lower corridors of the shopping center looking at the 'new' Revolutionary War-style dresses in the shop windows. It was Friday, so the walk was crowded with people going to the US-history exhibitions in the auditorium down the way. Among that crowd, I saw one of the men who had stabbed my mother and father. He was a big man with his hair shaved into the star and his eyes very red from dope. He was walking with another man I didn't recognize. The first man pointed at me and laughed, taking a step toward me. Dr Fosdick motioned for me to remain where I was. He walked briskly over to the man with the star on his square head and said something to him I couldn't hear. The man laughed again, but nodded and walked away.

I felt very detached from the whole scene, but there was a certain sense of *déjà vu*.

The other thing that happened was the headline on the front page of *The Daily Loyalty*: UNITED STATES WITH-DRAWS FROM UN. Mr Zelenke and I were discussing the event at my lesson, after I came back from the shopping center. He said that the withdrawal was a further step toward the 'Purification of Resources' goal the Hearth government had set for itself.

Mr Zelenke is a spindly, kindly man with a large nose and eyes that slant downward so mournfully I always feel I should agree with whatever he says to keep him from crying. He always seems to be on the point of tears.

But this time something grated in me when he said 'purification'.

'But couldn't it be,' I objected in a coarser tone than I am used to, 'that they are pulling out of the UN because they're scared?'

Mr Zelenke was upset and probably would have started crying if I hadn't taken it all back.

AUGUST 6, 2006

Some cruelly surprising things happened today.

I was sitting with Dr Fosdick in his office. He had an arm around my shoulders, and he was reading a poem to me from a book called *Flowers of Evil* by Charles Baudelaire.

'This book was my wife's favorite,' he said casually as he flipped through the yellowed pages with his rough right hand. I leaned against him, pretending to look at the book. I don't have much to myself, really. Very little memory. I feel like a sort of scarecrow personality, just a rag on some broomsticks. Because people are made of memories. And leaning against Dr Fosdick makes me feel like his memories are mine, too, somehow.

'Are you separated from your wife?' I asked. I asked mostly out of obligation, because I really didn't want him to think about her.

'No. She's dead two years. Killed in a landslide. It was one of those stupid unexpected accidents. We were hiking . . .' His voice got husky.

My parents have been dead two years. The timing of our tragedies was the same.

'I understand,' I said, feeling bad for bringing it up at all. 'You don't have to talk about it.'

He took a deep breath. 'Anyway, this was her favorite poetry.' He began to read out loud. I didn't like the poetry much, but maybe I didn't understand it right. And I was distracted by the sore place on my arm where Dr Fosdick had injected me again that afternoon.

But two stanzas sounded almost familiar, and I can't

get them out of my mind. They are from a poem called 'The Flask':

> . . . and hinges creak or in a press
> in some deserted house where the sharp stress
> of odors old and dusty fill the brain
> an ancient flask is brought to light again.
>
> And forth the ghosts of long dead odors creep
> there, softly trembling in the shadows, sleep
> a thousand thoughts, funereal chrysalids,
> phantoms of the old, folding darkness hide . . .

A woman was standing in the office with us! There was no way that she could have gotten in; the door was locked. The woman was lovely and covered with white mist that still revealed the outlines of her nude body, her blonde hair streaming over her white shoulders.

I gasped, and Dr Fosdick asked, almost eagerly, 'What's wrong? Did the poem upset you?'

I pointed at the woman. He looked in that direction, right through her, then looked back at me and shrugged.

'Don't you see her?' I whispered.

The woman was coming toward us. And now I could see that she was looking at Dr Fosdick with hate in her narrow green eyes.

Then she vanished. Just like that.

Dr Fosdick says that it was a hallucination symptomatic of the return of my memory. He says that she is probably some important figure out of my past whom I didn't recognize yet.

But there was no familiarity about her at all. She looked Scandinavian, about thirty. Where would I have met such a person, and seen her naked?

I was scared the rest of the day, knowing that she was somewhere around.

AUGUST 20, 2006

Dr Fosdick asked to see this journal last Friday. I told him that I had destroyed it because it contained parts that embarrassed me. He seemed to repress anger, but he insisted that it was very important to my progress for him to know my inner feelings. I apologized and said that I would start another journal.

Of course, I didn't really destroy it, but I hid it. I don't know why exactly. Or perhaps I do know. I hate to think about it, but I don't trust Dr Fosdick anymore. I wanted to trust him. I wanted to fall in love with him. But I can't. Maybe it's because he says that he is in love with me, and I cannot believe that anyone could love me.

But some things have happened lately.

The woman has come back many times. I would see her in the corners of the room, sitting, looking at me as if I were a mirror. I didn't tell Dr Fosdick about it.

I have had some strange recollections. I seem to recall being a little girl on a dairy farm owned by my parents. Perhaps my memory of my mother as tall and thin is a distortion of the chemical imbalance I was supposed to have, because the woman I remember as my mother on the dairy farm had red hair and freckles and a tall blond husband.

I remember going to medical school, though Marsha didn't tell me anything about that. The faces around me at the school are indistinct and unidentified. There is an alien sense to these memories that makes me feel like an actress who has memorized her lines, only to find herself in the wrong play.

I have one peculiarly vivid memory of walking alone in

a park. It is a spring day; the heaters under the bushes adding to the faint warmth that comes to us from the sunlight penetrating the smog shield. I'm in a secluded place, though the path is well beaten by lovers. There is lush greenery on all sides, with little firecracker tongues of red and yellow flowers. The background detail of the dream is lucid, but the human events are blurry, like a camera shot that shifts in and out of focus.

I am looking at a blue jay who is looking back at me from a branch of a pussy willow a few feet from my face. The bird cocks its head as if it's listening to my thoughts and doesn't want to miss anything. Its eyes are shining like the beads of sweat on my forehead. We regard each other for a minute, and then it screams raucously and flurries at my face. I put up my hands to shield my eyes, but the bird flies over my shoulder, and I hear someone cry out behind me. There are two men there, one with his hands to his face. He grunts: 'Why did it attack me? Damn thing. Kill it!'

'Too late. It got away,' the other man says in a voice that is almost familiar. 'You must have come too near its nest. Blue jays are temperamental like that.'

The first man drops his hand, and there are three long hyphens reddening his right cheek where the bird clawed him. 'Well, the woman's still there, she ain't flown off.' He takes a step toward me.

But the other man puts a restraining hand on his companion's arm. I can not see the face of the second man; it is as if he wears a mask of mist.

'No, leave her alone. Our information was wrong. She goes to my school. She's not one of them, she's a nationalist.'

I nod hastily, and note the Captain America armbands on the right bicep of each man. Nationalist vigilantes.

I feel like I should know the man who intervened for

me, but his face is lost. He puts a rough hand on my arm, smiling . . .

The memory ends there. It is like the chrysalis of some strange creature struggling to emerge. But I know I was never a nationalist. My father was a dissenting liberal. That's why the vigs killed my parents.

Did the stranger with the lost face lie for me?

Somewhere, there is a very important lie.

SEPTEMBER 1, 2006

I'm frightened. I'm scared of myself because I have developed an unreasoning hate for Dr Fosdick. I think of excuses to avoid my therapeutic sessions with him, and I've broken all our dates.

And when I reread my diary, parts of it – especially the last part – sound like they were written by someone else. 'The chrysalis of some strange creature . . .' Did I say that? I don't know what I meant by that. And the handwriting in the August 20 section of my diary is smaller than usual, almost crabbed. Maybe I was just in a hurry.

But this morning I went to get my hair done. They asked me if I had an appointment, and I said, 'Yes, of course. The same time I've come to this hairdresser's every week for four years.' And then I caught myself and wondered why I had said that. I hadn't been to that hairdresser before. I usually do my own hair. And they said they had no appointment for me. The secretary gave me a strange look and took off her reading glasses to watch me as I left.

I had made an appointment; I remember it distinctly. I remember playing with the cat with a pencil while calling the hairdresser's on the phone. But I don't have a cat.

And I've been sleepwalking. I woke up last night in the kitchen. I'm afraid to tell anyone about all this. They'd put me away for sure.

So I just sit in my drab apartment and try not to think about it. I try to read, but I'm too nervous to concentrate.

My apartment has two rooms – bathroom and the combination living room, bedroom, and kitchenette. It's paid for by my parents' insurance. The rooms are undecorated. I took down the pictures Dr Fosdick gave me.

I shift uncomfortably in my wooden chair as I write this, because my clothes are tormenting me. They are all too small, though I haven't gained any weight. I no longer like the colors and textures of my clothing. Too drab. Crude. I can't imagine why I chose them.

There is something missing in my room, as if it should have another life in it besides mine. Something small to warm up the corners and add motion. A pet. A small dog? A cat! I've never wanted one before, but I have an empty spot in me, like a little drawer pulled open in my chest where a miniature life should fit in to supplement my own . . .

When I read, it's always poetry. I disliked poetry before, but lately I've been reading Baudelaire. I'm beginning to see the veins of death that he talks about, veins that run through the walls of any place you have grown accustomed to. The old man living upstairs is part of a conspiracy to convince me that old age is inevitable so that I will make supplications to time.

I no longer see the woman, but I feel her presence. And I catch glimpses of a small animal that I can't identify running around the floor in the room, poking its nose from behind chairs or hiding under cushions, darting just on the periphery of my vision. I suspect that it is my lost pet. It is like the panther in Rilke's poem who was behind bars so long that its existence is wholly subjective; it might as well be dead.

Rereading this diary, I am growing more and more worried. Because I am certain that Jo Ann Culpepper never read Rilke. And she would never have said anything about 'supplications to time' and all that. And the handwriting is almost a scribble.

I find it increasingly easy to refer to Jo Ann Culpepper almost formally, as if I were speaking of a relative who had passed away . . . Someone whose memory I can regard as I would a caged animal.

SEPTEMBER 4, 2006

Marsha came to see me today, just as I was feeding the two cats I got from the pound.

Marsha is an Irish dumpling, springy and so optimistic that it makes me pessimistic. I don't know why I feel vindictive toward her all of a sudden. I think we were once good friends. It is cruel of me. But I felt antipathy from the moment she came into my room.

'Hello, hello! Ohhh, it's been so *long*, Jo Ann, no *kidding*. I've been really *worrying* about you. Dr Fosdick, too. He asked me to – '

I glared at the dimples from her round cheeks. 'Did Dr Fosdick tell you to come?'

'What's wrong?' Her saccharine voice faltered, and she put a hand to her doughy face as if to adjust a feature slipped out of place. I just looked at her, trying to remember.

But I felt no friendship for her. She was brown and hamsterlike, a rodent snuck into my room, an invader, a stranger come to sell me something.

'I don't want anything,' I said. I had picked up a vase with one hand without noticing having done it. When she looked at the vase, I quelled the urge to brain her with it, and set it back on the table. My trembling fingers left it slightly rocking.

'What? Jo Ann – '

'I don't need you or Dr Fosdick.'

'*Jo Ann.*' She was hurt.

'I'm sorry,' I said, seeing the blonde woman standing in the corner, her jade-green eyes stony with loathing. I saw her only in my mind's eye this time, but so vividly I thought she was about to slap Marsha across the face. Marsha smiled, reassured, as I said, 'Well . . . how have you been?'

We chatted uncomfortably for a while, until the estrangement grew into embarrassment. Then she left, murmuring about coming back soon, calling the clinic, they're worried.

I hope I never see her again. If she gives me that 'It's-been-so-long' crap again, I'll feed her to my cats.

SEPTEMBER 5, 2006

I was afraid that he'd come and smash my door down if I didn't, so I went to visit Dr Fosdick today. I forced myself.

'Thank God,' he said, nervous, embarrassed at his unprofessional outburst. 'I've been worried sick about you. Why didn't you answer the door when I knocked?' His mouth worked as if he were trying to keep something from escaping from it, and his lips were the parting folds of a chrysalis.

'I . . . must have been asleep, Doctor.'

He looked into my eyes and raised a brow. 'Really?'

How dare he question *my* honesty! I thought furiously. Fake it. He can have you committed.

I shrugged. 'I haven't been well. Sleep too deeply.'

'What? Not well? Here, sit down.' I sat by him on the con-foam couch in his office and toyed with the leaves of a potted plant, shredding them one by one between my grotesquely thin fingers.

'In some ways I have been improving. I've been more . . . articulate lately. Words come to me more easily than they used to. I've begun to remember some books I must have read before . . .' Then I sensed that I was telling him things he shouldn't know.

'You *do* look more confident . . . But what is it that you have been remembering?' He put an arm around me. I pushed it off. He frowned but only opened his desk drawer for the little tape recorder for the session. In that swift movement I saw in the open drawer a framed photo of the woman of my apparition. She was sitting on a lawn in an evening gown, surrounded by three large cats. One of the cats was very black and perched itself on her soft shoulder, nestling in her lush blonde hair. The cat seemed to be looking at me, until Dr Fosdick closed the drawer on its golden eyes.

The woman in the photo had been Dr Fosdick's wife. I remembered; she remembered.

'There is a surprise waiting for you back at your flat,' Dr Fosdick was saying. 'I had it sent – ' But I cut him off with as hard a slap as I could manage, leaving a red imprint on his cowboy jaw. I turned and ran from the office, pushing an astounded secretary to the floor in a flurry of overturned papers. A bus was just loading outside. I hopped aboard and turned to look at Dr Fosdick as he ran, unheeded, after the bus a block back. His face, getting smaller, was the face of the man of my memory – the vigilantes in the park, the medical student, Dr Lawrence Fosdick, my husband. Older, but undeniably it was he.

Jo Ann Culpepper didn't know him before the loss of her memory.

But I remember a night in a beach cabin on the coast of Maine. His hands mapped the topography over my breasts; breasts fuller than Jo Ann's, hips wider than hers.

I remember our quiet marriage, the exhaustive private work at the laboratory after our regular hours at the clinic.

And Lawrence's warnings. He said that I should not make fun of the vigs. But I hated the nationalists. They controlled Lawrence, and through him puppeted me. Since Lawrence was vigilante coordinator for our sector, he was expected to live up to a vig model: They made a ridiculous cartoon of our private life.

He warned me again. But I derided the nationalists at our parties, where a quarter of our guests were vigs.

I think I knew they would kill us. But: *Death may rise, a sun of another kind, and bring to blossom the flowers of their minds*. Baudelaire.

I wanted to kill us both, but only one of us died.

He stood behind me on the mountainside, and I thought I knew what he was going to do.

I didn't try to stop him, because I thought he would pull us both over the edge. But he pushed only me. I fell, saw him receding, getting smaller against the sky, and I felt the giant hand crumple me in granite fingers. The landslide skinned me alive under jagged rocks. A million points of penetration.

I lay in shock, my exposed face shredded into a red sponge soaking up pain. I watched my husband scuttle down the hillside path, jumping over sagebrush and winding around the tormented bristlecone pines, himself an animate root. He stood over me with his face twitching in a thin-sauce parody of my agony. I remember the moment of death shining like the jeweled eyes of a rapacious blue jay.

I remembered all, seeing him get smaller as the bus left him behind, as if I was falling from the cliff again. I hurried back to my room, managed to get there before he did.

There was his 'surprise'. A fat and butter-yellow canary in an ornate cage, a note tied to it with a ribbon. I didn't bother to read the note, but I took the cage inside. The bird fluttered in its confinement like a memory that wants to be forgotten. It reminded me of Marsha. So, while I was packing my bags, I left the cage door open with the cats in front of it.

By the time I had everything I needed – I would travel light, leave most of Jo Ann's clothes behind, and buy new things later – the cats were finished. I brushed stray feathers from their whiskers and took them along in a shopping bag, grabbed up the suitcase, and took a cab to a hotel. On the way to the hotel we passed through a neighborhood that Lawrence and I had once lived in. We had lived in this neighborhood, across from the playfield of the elementary school, during the time we unlocked the memory code.

Experimenting on rats, Lawrence and I found that the memory of the sound of an electric bell was chemically recorded into an eight-segment chain of six amino acids. When the chemicals were isolated from the brain and injected into other rats that were not trained to the sound, the untrained animals acted as if they had been conditioned to the bell. My husband simply extrapolated it into humanity . . .

Combinations of twenty amino acids produce peptides

that are programmed with certain memories, according to which sequence of amino acids is chosen. Larry found which combinations of amino acids correlated with general memories in rats. It wouldn't be difficult – merely tedious – to carry the process into evaluation of the human memory system.

He never told me what he had intended to do with the results. Perhaps the Hearth would use it to train soldiers, injecting memories synthesized from a trained fighter pilot into the brain of a trainee. Or maybe extract information from prisoners by withdrawing their memories and reinjecting them into volunteers. If I can help it, they'll never use it for anything. I put up with the vigs for convenience's sake, but they forced the issue. I should have known where Lawrence's loyalties would be, him and his fucking cowboy music.

The day after the final proofs of success, he was called to a vig meeting. They were voting as to whether to purge a Professor Culpepper. The vote was affirmative. Larry, in his capacity as regional coordinator, signed the death order. But he asked that the professor's only child, the girl, be spared and turned over to the clinic. He had use for her. No one objected. It didn't matter if the girl attempted to tell the authorities who'd killed her parents. The death squads are 'officially' frowned upon, but actually protected by the national Hearth government. They are never brought to court.

The girl was seventeen, ripe time in the development of her memory coordinations. But it turned out even better than he had hoped. Her memory had blanked from the shock of witnessing her parents' murder. There would be no complications of her prior memory patterns if he were to introduce new combinations of peptides. But first he had to obtain them. A day later he received an ultimatum from the vigs. His wife must be killed because of her impurities, or he . . .

He told me about the ultimatum and said that we would hide in our cabin in the Ozarks until the danger was over.

Then he killed me to save his skin and his position.

No. Her killed *her*. But he carried her back, to the cabin where he'd hidden the equipment, and extracted the mnemonic peptides. And he injected a large portion of Sandra's mnemonic peptides into me.

I was lucky. He also saved the memories of my father. He still has them, frozen. He might have tried to put *those* in me, and I would have killed myself by now if he had. He injected too much of Sandra in me, because I remember more than he wanted.

I am tall, thin, five-foot-eight, weigh a hundred-ten. But someone who weighed one-hundred-forty-five and who was five inches shorter than I is trying to fit herself into my body. There isn't enough room. There is an overwhelming nausea, as if I'd overeaten to the point of vomiting. I feel like the whole nation must have felt in 1996. Usurped. Cut open from the inside.

The husband of the string of cold chemical memories ordered the vigs to kill my father, then killed his wife. Then he made her memories mine. Why? Because he wanted her back? He must have been crazy with remorse.

Crazy with remorse? What crap. Jo Ann is an idiot if she believes that. He brought me back because he's an inept incompetent.

But Jo Ann deserves everything she got. It makes me nauseous to read the first part of her diary. It's full of fatuous and naive comments like 'I was even thinking of starting an organization to help people with messed-up memories . . .' and 'He was nice, and he didn't mind that I was in my period.' I'm revolted by her big-eyed innocence. She let him dominate her. 'Leaning against him

. . .' I think he was able to justify killing me to himself because I would never let him dominate me. The gullible little ass trusted him right from the start, let him dominate her until he shot her up with me, erasing bit by bit of her vestigial personality.

Lawrence and I used to talk of the possible meanings of our discoveries. Obviously, personality is merely the persistence of memory. Motives are just chemicals. If there are such things as souls, then all souls are alike, distinguished only by their arbitrary trappings of memory.

There is a sickness in my body this evening. Perhaps the filter isn't working and the carbon monoxide is seeping in.

The night is gathering itself up in dismal layers. First the dusk, then the noises of the car fiends outside, their customized horns braying like donkeys or grunting like bulls; tires squealing, engines grinding piston teeth together. Then a layer of my own exhaustion. My cats escaped their shopping bag when I got out of the cab at the hotel door. I've been out all day prowling around the park, looking for them. No luck. I haven't slept much in the past few days, and there is a decaying night radiation below the strata of my weariness.

If I find the cats I'll kill them for leaving me. I'll feed their remains to an eagle at the zoo when no one's watching.

My mind is formed like the design of a spin painting, dollops of color in a whirlwind.

SEPTEMBER 10, 2006

It makes me feel better to keep this journal. For Jo Ann it was a release. But for me it's a confession.

I went into the clinic when I knew Lawrence would be there alone. I wasn't sure what I was going to do.

He was alone at his desk. He didn't feign felicity as I had expected. He knew that I remembered everything. His eyes were grave and his voice stabile. 'I want you to understand, Sandra – '

'If it were just me, maybe I could go away and forget. I can't stand that naive little bitch you seduced, but something about the way you killed her parents and then took her for experiments and then killed me, all within a couple of days – '

'No. They would have been killed even if I hadn't signed the death order. The vote was almost unanimous. This is a democratic country, after all.' He smiled bitterly.

'And how did you vote?'

He turned his back to me, opened a cabinet, extracted a hypodermic.

I broke a chloroform bottle over his head and jumped back with a handkerchief to my mouth. He fell amid the broken glass.

When he was unconscious, I dragged him to the nearest table and set to work. The method he had used on Jo Ann was permanent, because it was implemented gradually. In our early experiments we tried injecting memories into an unconscious man whose memory was undamaged. If done with unerring precision, this technique worked temporarily. And then left the subject a babbling moron for the remainder of his life. We wanted something more

permanent and less wasteful. But it would do for my
purposes. I went to the freezer and found the mnemonic
solution for Professor Culpepper.

Two hours later Professor Albert Culpepper, temporarily housed in Lawrence, awoke and sat up, rubbing his
temples. I had my face disguised by a surgical mask.

Culpepper bridled, looked startled, quickly scanned
the room with frantic eyes.

'Where are they? Jo Ann? Sadie?' He croaked.

'Take it easy,' I said.

He jumped to his feet and whirled into an antagonistic
crouch, hands outstretched, infuriated. Seeing me – not
one of the party of vig killers he remembered – he relaxed
some but remained wary. 'Professor Culpepper. Your
wife and your little girl are dead. Murdered. You saw
your wife stabbed, remember?'

'Yes.' His eyes showed whites all around the pupils.
Gritting his teeth, fingers clenching and unclenching.
'Where are they? The vigs!' Lawrence had extracted a
heavy dose of Culpepper's last-moment emotions. Mostly
hate.

I handed him the automatic pistol I'd found in Lawrence's desk. 'The vigs will be having a meeting in twenty-
five minutes at this address. Five blocks from here.' I
gave him the slip of paper. He put it in his pocket with
trembling hands, and ran from the lab, into the street.

He had an hour and a half as Culpepper. He would
make it. He'd probably get five or six of them before they
got him.

As for me . . .

I say *me*, not *we*. There is only one. Oh, when I look
into the mirror, I see Jo Ann Culpepper's washed-out
neurotic face. My hands are her ugly claws. I hate
Lawrence for sticking me with this body. He had no
respect for me. He might have found something with

elegance. But this clumsy relic has a foul stink to it I can't quite wash away. I deserve better than this. But I'm trapped, whole, in this ungainly parody of womanhood. I'm tired from pounding the bars of this cage. I'm in my hotel room. No sign of the cats. So tired I can hardly think. Pages are blurring.

Maybe Jo Ann, the plebian whore Jo Ann, was not taken in by Lawrence. Maybe they were working together. The bitch would have done anything for him. So she trapped me in this unclean cell. Brain cells have bars.

If she gets too near the cage, I can reach out through the bars and grab her by her skinny throat and throttle her. She's a fool. She expects me to believe that this is my body. It's not, and I can prove it. I'm going to kill her. I'm going to get the razor and slash her throat. And get out. I'll have my own purge, in a way.

I'm not sure where I'll go after that. Run and hide, I suppose. Maybe I'll sell 'Dr Fosdick's' notes to the men in the red rags.

I'm going now. To get the razor. But I have a nagging feeling that there is something I have forgotten.

Quill Tripstickler Eludes a Bride

'But I don't want a Roving Assistant, Dad,' Quill Trip-stickler protested. He was speaking to the vidscreen image of his father, tachyon-transmitted from Earth.

'Oh, we're not calling him a Roving Assistant, son,' said his father in his usual ringing effusion. 'So you needn't worry. He's a *butler*.'

'But why do I need a butler. And what *is* a butler?'

'A butler,' said his father's rather menacingly three-dimensional image – Quill could have wished the image less prepossessingly real – 'is an, ah, assistant to a gentleman.'

'What is a gentleman? I don't wish to be notorious for my kindness; T-agenting is a tough business. Gentleness isn't always – '

'No, no. A butler is a servitor.'

'A cyberserv? I don't *want* a cyberserv, Dad! They're always telling you what to do and looking over your shoulder and clucking disapprovingly. I have one machine working with me and that's enough. My ship's computer – '

'Actually, my boy,' his father interrupted with a trace of impatience, 'this butler *is* your ship's computer. That is, it is a drone extension unit of your computer. By transmission. Your ship will remain at the port, but your computer will send this extension out with you. You almost got yourself killed or altered or something undig-nified on the last mission. This time I want you accom-panied to minimize the bumbling. And that's *all* there is to say on the matter.' His father's image bristled with authority. It bristled, furthermore, with the currently fashionable mobile wires extruding from scalp implants. His father, being a conservative, wore his bristles in the old-styled Bozo-hair clown's halo, the pate inlaid with a subdued shade of violet; both his eyes were the same color, stodgy gray, further declaration of his belief in gentlemanly understatement; he wore his own nose, bisected only once. His father's round face glowed, literally, with the accepted *hues of determination*, particularly in the constricting and expanding red and yellow spirals on the cheeks . . . Quill blinked and forced himself to look away from his father's hypnotic visage.

'As you will have it, Father.'

'The butler will, moreover, be keyed with certain phrases, for the sake of security, which only you will know by reason of their antiquity. When you want him to nix an on-going process, you will say "What a beastly idea! The rotter!" When you want him to perform an affirmative action – for example you want to placate the natives but you don't want them to know that's what you're going to do – you say, "I say! Bracing go, what?" When you want him to get you out of a situation and initiate a general retreat you will shout, "Rummy! Bit thick, what?" These key phrases are for emergencies only. Ordinarily he will act quite independently . . . now, what about your appearance? Do you want to go to your second mission looking like a devo?' Father Tripstickler alluded to Quill's propensity for a nonaltered appearance. He went about looking as he did naturally, which was considered quite rude and backward in the Earth system colonies. Moreover, his aspect was not particularly the Masculine Prototype, which was the only fashionable forté for unaltered men. Quill was gangly, narrow in the shoulders, rather long in the arms; his every effort at reduction failed to shrink his potbelly; his narrow brown eyes and long nose were somewhat compensated by his full and sensual red lips; he wore his own hair, considered by some very bad taste indeed, and he wore it in a close-cut cap of brown. His neck was long and his adam's apple bobbed like a ping-pong ball on a water jet. 'Won't you at least,' his father pushed on peevishly, 'have your chest expanded and your stomach shrunk? Won't take but an hour. And perhaps a neck shortening – '

'No *thank* you, Father.' He'd always been stubborn in these matters, had Quill. It was forbidden to alter prior to age ten. And in the early years he'd developed a very defensive rationale for his appearance, exercised to such a state of refinement that he had at last become convinced, utterly and forever, of his own personal beauty. His nose, he felt, was the prow of an ambitious, forward-moving man; his paunch was the swell of the sensualist; his narrow shoulders and the gangliness he interpreted as compact and loose-limbed; his neck was 'swanlike'. In addition he possessed other enviable attributes; one physical feature in particular, invariably applauded by young ladies, which delicacy forbids detailing here.

'You will take the out-shuttle from the Station – ah, is your leg quite grown back from the last mission?' his father asked, silvery-wired eyebrows raised.

'Yes, Father.'

'Very good. Then you will take the out-shuttle to the spacejump point, tube to your ship and the butler waiting therein. Your navigation unit is already fixed for the destination. You are to go to Sil and marry the Yee, forthwith.'

'What?'

'You heard me. It will be necessary in order to soothe the native xenophobia. The Sils are notoriously mistrustful of offworlders. That's why the Bureau finds it necessary to dispatch an agent. The marriage will be only the duration of a cycle, no more. A mere inconvenience. The details are not at hand . . . Now, I have a Wisdom for you to Intake – '

Quill involuntarily groaned.

Father Tripstickler's aureole of mobile wires, sensitive to his moods, shifted restively, quivering with anger.

Quill sighed. He murmured the Home Mantra and said, 'Very well. I'm on hypnotic Intake, Father. Speak it.'

Father Tripstickler cleared his throat and recited: 'A Tripstickler's prospects are his to command/because he's got grit to his wit and sand in his glands.'

Wincing, Quill said, 'It is Intaken, Father.'

As his father's vidimage vanished, Quill reflected: *Marry the Yee to mollify the Sils? The path of a Galactic Touristry Agent, Fifth Class, was surely strewn with broken glass.*

'It's positively paradisiacal!' Quill exclaimed, stepping from the airlock-to-ground elevator. 'Quite a contrast to the last dive I had for assignment.'

'I fear, young master,' said the butler, rolling on his (the butler's masculine voice, however artificial, prompted Quill to think of it in terms of the male pronoun) brassy wheels onto the swarm beside Quill, 'that on Sil the various adages reminding us of the treacherous nature of appearances will prove to be vindicated.'

'No doubt Father programmed you to be as dour as he is, butler, but the place looks flawless to me.'

'Perhaps you should refer to me as Fives, young master, since I am the fifth model from the prototype.'

Quill eyed the robot with displeasure. 'Cease to call me young master.'

'Very good, sir.' The robot (looking almost human, to the casual glance, from the wheels up) nodded his bowler

hat-topped head – the motor powering the neck *whirring*
slightly – and made a salutation gesture with his whited-
gloved hand. His almost expressionless flesh-colored plastiflex face raised an immaculate eyebrow in enquiry; his
glassy brown eyes glittered; his perpetually pursed lips
parted minutely as he asked, 'Do you propose, sir, to
await a delegation here, or shall we go to the descent
chute?'

'Descent chute? Descent? *Down?* They live
underground?'

'This is in fact the case, sir.'

'How perfectly idiotic! With all this fine landscaping up
here! And, come to that, why is it that you've been so
damnably reticent about coughing up the data on this
place?'

'To be perfectly frank, sir, I was instructed not to
relinquish the salient details until we were firmly
planetside.'

'What? It's as bad as all that? You know, they send us
Fifth Classers out to open up the future Meccas of the
touristing curious only because we're expendable and
they know these brutish places are – '

'Undoubtedly, sir . . . Perhaps we should proceed to
the chute.' Fives led the way through a fragrant copse of
azure lacy-leaved trees, quivering giddily under an emer-
ald sky; the feathery grasses curled away at the touch. A
stream, which Quill took to be water but which at closer
inspection proved to be a wending passage of crystalline
gel, ribboned through the trees to vanish between the low
yellow-furred hills . . . 'Lovely oxy-balanced atmosphere,' Quill grumbled. 'Why do you suppose they – Ah!
This must be the entrance.' Jutting rather cruelly from
the soft turf, a man-high pyramid of metal was open at
the nearer face, as if expectantly. The robot rolled
unhesitatingly inside. Quill followed with less alacrity.

The door slid shut behind them; the chamber descended for the interval of ten seconds, opening into a wide breezy passageway, rock-walled.

As they'd descended, Quill had been toying with the notion that someone had deliberately misinformed him as to the citizenry of Sil. He'd been informed that they were not only quite human (but come to think of it, the phrase he computer had used was 'quite human, *in the main*'), they were lineal descendants of an Earth colony. Time, however, having whistled its tuneless way for nine generations since the original colonists, had had an insular effect on the community. The Sils did not tolerate outsiders, normally, and no Earther had been on or under Sil for three of the nine generations . . . But since they apparently found the upper atmosphere unendurable, perhaps they were not human after all, Quill mused. Perhaps –

As the door opened, he was relieved to learn that he was quite wrong. They were not only human, they were a society which eschewed cosmetic surgery modifications, Quill noted approvingly. The three men awaiting him, faces wrapped in wide smiles, were squat and pale, hair falling straight and dark to their shoulders; they wore gray suits of rather coarse cloth, sackcloth in fact, and no shoes, though the rocky floors were unevenly cut and sharply studded in places. All three men seemed very similar to one another, with their pug noses and large black eyes, their receding hairlines and pointy teeth – but doubtless a native would discern more in the way of distinctions.

Having had a hypno-Intake of the Sil language prior to landing, Quill understood the shorter of the three men perfectly when he said: 'May your way be strengthening.'

'Productive stress to you,' Quill responded, wondering at the origin of the phrase. Quill bowed. 'I am Quill

Tripstickler, Galactic Tourist Agent and non-official dip-
lomat of the Earth system.'

'I am Chromosome Regent,' the little man replied in a
soft, nasal voice full of dignity. 'With me are my assistants, B. and A. You may address me as, Your
Perseverance.'

'Ah! A charming titular cognomen, I'm sure.'

'As our Honored Guest, you have, of course, been
provided with the most noble of quarters,' said His
Perseverance. 'If you will be so kind as to follow . . .' But
as he was about to turn into the corridor, his eyes lit on
the robot for the first time. He seemed dismayed. 'What
is this – contrivance?'

Quill cleared his throat. 'This grotesque contraption is,
I fear, resolutely attached to my activities. He is my
servant, Fives.'

Fives bowed faintly.

His Perseverance took an alarmed step back. 'We do
not normally permit independently operating unbred
machinery in the Sil City. Still,' he continued, shrugging,
viewing Fives with unhidden distaste, 'since Q. T. is the
Yee's Groom, one or two special accommodations will be
made.'

It was Quill's turn to experience dismay when Fives,
smiling wanly, observed: 'Sadly, my machineries are of
less distinguished gestation than your own fleshly workings, Your Perseverance. I can but hope the test of time
is kind to one, such as myself, originated without the
benefit of Your Perseverance's immaculate chromosomal
heritage.'

Quill bit off an apology, composed on the robot's
behalf, when to his surprise he observed that the Regent
seemed pleased with Fives' allusions to his ancestors.
'You have drilled the machine well,' the Regent said. He
turned and hopped down the hallways, squeaking. Quill

watched, astonished, as A. and B. followed suit, hopping and squeaking down the corridor. He noted that they walked on the right side of the hall where the floor was sharply studded – apparently no accident – in a meandering pathway like a narrow, lengthy bed of nails.

'They are courting the pain?' Quill asked, in a whisper aside to Fives.

'That is in fact the case, sir. They are not masochists, however, as we understand the term. They are displaying their indifference to adversity arising from allegedly superior genetic derivation. Natural Selection is the root of this culture, sir.'

'If this implies what I think it does for myself, perhaps we had better return to – '

'Begging your pardon, sir, but your father instructed me to remind you, when you displayed a lack of decisiveness, to remember the Tripstickler Wisdom, *A Tripstickler's prospects are his to command* – '

'No, no! Never mind, don't repeat it! I'm going!' So declaiming, Quill Tripstickler began to negotiate the spiky pathway, uttering squeaks and squeals which, by reason of his soft-soled shoes, were perhaps more genuine than the cries uttered by the more experienced Sils.

'Did you hear what he said, Fives? I asked him why they preferred this chilly underground to the Eden above, and he said, "Don't you find it rather awfully *tolerable* up there, Groom Tripstickler?" This is beginning to look worse than the last dratted planet they sent me to. And that's bad. The last place was underground, too. In my admittedly formulative opinion, subterranean cultures have subterranean motives. I don't trust these people. And what do they mean leaving me in a steamy, insufferable pink chamber with sickeningly textured walls? Well, Fives?'

Fives opened his mouth to reply, coughing respectfully, but Quill did not pause in his tirade. 'I mean, damn it, Fives, what have these people got in mind for me? Did you feel those jets of icy air blowing for no conscionable reason across the hallway? And that nasty obstacle course of pink cilia whipping from the walls? I mean, really, I've got talent and determination, and, God help me, sand in my glands, but sometimes one is called on to perform absurdly in unsporting circumstances and – well, really, my forté is making charming converse with Ladies of Note and exchanging mild, endearing gibes with local constabularies, not sliding down horrible sticky red escalators – '

'I fear that you are laboring under a misconception, sir,' Fives broke in gently, his head whirring as it turned to follow Quill's impatient pacing. 'The "sickeningly textured walls" and "horrible sticky red escalators", as you so colorfully have it, are in fact extensions of the Urban Womb, the flesh-machine, the edifice and organic device developed by Sil's peerless genetic engineers. From – ' he gestured at the walls ' – human chromosomes.'

Quill gazed with undiluted repulsion at their surroundings. 'You don't mean to say – ?' The low-ceilinged chamber was moist, its walls concave and translucent gray-pink, shot with pulsing blue. The ceiling twitched tiny socketed palps, an overhead living carpet. 'See here, Fives, you don't mean that – '

'I do indeed, sir. All the facts of the matter, such as how the marriage is to be consummated, are not available to us. But we *do* know that the entire lower section of the Sil City is taken up by an, ah, organism. An engineered mutation which had its roots in human cell structure. The walls of the chamber are of human skin. The sticky

escalator we descended is based on a tongue, much
modified and expanded. The doorway – '

'Good Nirvana!' Quill expostulated, examining the
entranceway. It was now constricted shut, a great pinkish-
grayish muscle clenched around a circular aperture; it
dilated outward in all directions when opening . . . Quill
shook his head and sat down on the flesh floor, legs
crossed and elbow on knee, chin in hand. He glanced at
Fives. The robot butler stood curiously immobile, one
hand hitched in a pocket of his waistcoat, head tilted at
an awkward angle. 'Fives – why haven't we seen any
women? I saw some children, once, but they were all
boys. Looked miserable, too, if I may say so. I mean, I
studied erotic persuasion for a solid year, took a blue in
it too. My best subject. I had the touch, they said. It
puzzled them, but it's always been that way with Trip-
sticklers. The fingertip electricity, Fives; the alluring set
of the jaw; the penetrating glance; the magnetism – most
of all, the magnetism, Fives. That's what women melt
for. Or men, depending on one's specialty. I – Fives!' He
stared at the robot; it hadn't moved. 'Fives?'

With a jerk, the robot came awake, moving his head
spasmodically from side to side, as if trying to clear it.
Quill was dismayed when Fives' head began to jack up on
his neck, rising over his shoulders and rotating. The
absurd spectacle of a butler, with his bowler hat and an
expression emphatically dignified, his head over three
feet over his shoulders on an impossibly protracted neck,
caused Quill to laugh involuntarily.

'There really is no appropriate subject for levity, sir,'
said Fives, looking at Quill with a faintly wounded pout
to his prissy lips.

'Sorry, Fives. It's just that you look so awkward and
funny.'

'I'm afraid this elevation is quite requisite for the

moment, sir. You see, there is a thunderstorm raging on the planet's surface above – '

'No doubt the Sils are all above, enjoying the discomfort.'

'Yes, sir. As I was saying, the storm, together with the ground and the stonecasings and the Urban Womb, are having a rather dampening effect on the transmissions from my brain aboard our craft. I was cut off entirely for a short interval, sir. And I find that only at this elevation can I pick up the signals with any consistency – so it will have to remain, until the storm abates.'

'Why aren't there any women down here, Fives? I thought you said these people are human . . .'

Fives made a sound very like the clearing of a throat. '*Chiefly* human might be a better term, sir. There is, however, only one woman at this stage in the Sils' development, and that is the Yee. She is the product of genetic manipulation. The original women, we have heard, split off from the men some generations back, having become very militant and self-sufficient. They reproduce through cloning. They live on the other side of the planet, and, as they are more warlike than the men, they are considered unreachable.'

'But, damn it – am I to actually mate with this *Yee* person?'

'Just so, sir. The reasons are as follows: The Sils worship the DNA molecule. One of their patron saints being the ancient Earth Scientist Darwin. They believe that the DNA molecule has some sort of intellectual capacity in its relationship with all others of its type, that in resonating together in a special divine frequency these molecules communicate and form a great mind that is constantly trying to improve itself with Natural Selection, trying to become stronger and more prone to easy survival. The Sils respect only those who are approved through their survival-of-the fittest winnowing procedure. They refused to open the beauteous surface of Sil for touristry until a representative of the People who will be visiting here, someone from the Earth colonies which provide the tourists, has gone through the natural-selection tests and then mated with the Yee. If the Yee refuses to mate with you, finds you chemically improvident – '

'What? I beg your pardon – '

'Nothing personal, sir. To continue, if she finds you unsuitable, the Sils will consider this decision a reflection on your entire race and will not permit touristry.'

'Yes? Well, I doubt,' Quill said, puffing – rather inconsequentially – his thin chest and stroking his hair into place, 'that she will be disappointed. But a dire question remains: what of this natural-selection procedure? This does not bode well, Fives. No, indeed. I understand now why so little briefing was given me on the mission. Well, a great man turns the tide of adversity and shakes hands with the hand of fate. But, then, it was also wisely said that discretion is the better part of valor. So perhaps we'd best retreat for a time to the sanctity of our ship to reflect on the matter, eh?'

Fives was shaking his elevated head sadly. As he did so, the top of his bowler, in contact with the low ceiling, nuzzled the skin overhead in its pivoting – there came a quivering, and the ceiling seemed to giggle from deep within itself. 'I think not, sir,' Fives was saying. 'Your father asked me to remind you – '

Just then the doorifice dilated, with a sickening air-rush noise, to allow the Regent to step through, followed by A. and B. –

'The time for the Test is come,' said the Regent reverently.

Quill stood, turning to Fives a pleading look.

Fives seemed to be having more difficulty picking up

his mind-signal from the ship's computer. His head
snapped back and forth, the eyes blinked unevenly, the
mouth snapped open and shut. The Regent eyed the
robot disapprovingly.

The ceiling giggled.

B. bowed and laid out a sackcloth for Quill. 'Your
testing suit, Q. T. the Groom.'

'Ah.' Quill cleared his throat, examining the hairshirt.
It was brutally coarse and malodorous. Worse, were he
to change into the suit, he'd have to give up the pulse-
gun tucked into the flat of his belt at the back of his one-
piece green agency uniform. The gun might prove to be
invaluable.

Quill glanced hopefully at Fives, looking for inspiration. The robot had got its signal again, for the moment,
and made a shrug with the shoulders so distantly beneath
his chin.

'As to this sackcloth-hairshirt bit, Fives,' Quill began,
remembering the key phrases for the butler's override his
father had given him, 'Ah, what a beastly idea! The
rotter!'

The Regent and his two clone-variations eyed Quill in
puzzlement.

Fives turned to the Regent. 'The garb is unsuitable,
Your Perseverance.'

The Regent looked at Quill's uniform askance. 'He
wishes to wear this – this *lamb's skin?*'

The butler glanced at Quill, raising an eyebrow as if to
say, *Best not to rock the boat, we may be committing a
solecism*.

But Quill was determined. 'Fives: I say! Bracing go,
what?'

The robot nodded and continued, looking down from
his height benevolently: 'Master Tripstickler is unable to
wear the native garb of Sil only because he was babied

and raised in clothing very much like it, as his parents were excessively given to pampering, when he was young. He finds your clothing much too comfortable. His own suit is woven from a special metallic thread which at intervals discharges the static electricity it has collected, cruelly jolting the wearer. It's *most* uncomfortable.'

'Ahh!' The Regent looked on Quill with what was now admiration and envy.

Quill pretended to jump from a slight electric shock.

'Is the mastication chamber prepared?' the Regent asked A.

'It is, Your Perseverance.'

Quill started, thinking: *Mastication chamber? For me? Perhaps it was time to test the third key override, the one for retreat. It would be interesting to see if the butler could find a way out of the city* . . . 'Fives! Rummy, bit thick, what! Rummy, bit thick, what? *What?* Fives!'

The robot remained unmoved.

A. and B. each took one of Quill's arms at the elbow and gently guided him out of the doorifice. As he went, he called futilely over his shoulder, 'Fives! Bit thick, what? *Bit thick, what!*'

They descended a slanting corridor that was very much like a diagonal esophagus . . .

They had prodded him through a doorifice; he stepped through, turned around to speak – and the doorifice clenched shut. Although the distant giggling followed his efforts at tickling the doorifice into opening, it remained constricted. He sighed and turned to survey his course. A dim light glowed from bluish veins pulsing in the 'walls', illuminating an oval tubiform passage gradually ascending to some unknown convergence in the shadow-shrouded distance . . .

Taking his pulse-gun from his belt, he set forth, walking

cautiously on the spongy flooring of the passageway, slipping occasionally in its glutinous dampness.

A sweet musky odor came to him at times, occasioning a rather forthright, as it were, physical reaction in him that might have been embarrassing had he not been alone.

'Come to think of it,' he muttered, 'I have never been *less* alone. *She* is all around me.' He pressed on, fighting a pervading sense of claustrophobia. The way steepened increasingly, the angle becoming more difficult with each step, until he was forced to climb by pressing his legs, knees, elbows, toes and hands against the treacherously slick walls. He was worming upward now, sweating with exertion as he dug in his fingers, both sickened and titillated by the viscous giving of the flesh-wall close about him; near to blacking out from the shortness of oxygen in the narrow way, eyes straining in the ill-lit passage.

His every instinct urged him to cut through the walls with his pulse-gun, if necessary, to free himself, to escape this cloying trap. His stomach roiled, swept by turns with nausea and euphoria.

He lost track of time; it might have been hours that he squirmed upward through the constricting passage, gasping in the scant air, sweat making his uniform nearly as uncomfortable as a Sil would have preferred.

Twice he felt himself slipping, falling back down the tube, losing traction on the sticky, giving tissues about him – each time he dug in his elbows and knees viciously, and heard, in response, as his descent was arrested, a distant echoing grunt of pleasure and surprise . . .

The going had become almost vertical. His muscles shouted with pain; his eyes ached for light; and perhaps most tormenting of all, one of his shoes had come untied and he couldn't bend to re-tie it – it dangled, maddeningly, half on his foot, gradually slipping away.

He experienced alarming visions at odd intervals – particularly vivid when the gusts of musk came his way – harking back to his early childhood; very early. Disturbing dreams of maternal punishments, rejections, rewards. There was something frightening about them, as if they precipitated an impending panic, and he knew that, if he were to escape madness, he must emerge from the passage soon. He tried to evade the panic by singing to himself, hopefully a therapeutic distraction. But the only song that would come into his head was:

> Oh peel it boys peel it,
>   The various layers;
> interpret the maunderings
>   of rummy soothsayers.
> Conceal it girls conceal it,
>   the instinctual drive;
> You were meant to be more
>   than gene-chosen wives.
> O watch it kids watch it,
>   become like androids;
>   wonder who was stronger –
> Darwin or Freud?

And he'd given up on that one, with a whimper of realization, on the third verse.

He was close to shrieking and falling back – when he noticed an increase in the glow of light from ahead. Heartened, he redoubled his efforts and was shortly rewarded with the sight of the end of the passage.

But the way was blocked. A large, rounded muscle, rather cervical, creased onto a narrow hole not big enough to admit his fist, grew from the passage walls. It was from the aperture at the center of this pumpkin-like muscle that the light escaped, a glow from a chamber beyond.

Quill scowled. He considered. He had seen the Sils open and close doorways by tickling the walls around the doorifices, but one had to know precisely where and how to tickle. Quill was too weary to experiment. His pulse-gun hung on a strap from his wrist. He supported himself in the vertical passage with out-thrust knees – the walls grunted – and adjusted the pulse-gun to *Low-level Vibrations*, just below *Stun*. It was a harmless setting. He pressed the pulse-gun into the aperture in the great cervical muscle, and flicked the trigger lightly once. The pulse-gun hummed; the walls groaned; the cervical door-ifice dilated, almost reluctantly, in spasms; he pressed the trigger again – the walls giggled rather shrilly, and the doorifice dilated fully. He reached up and pulled himself through.

He was relieved to find himself in a wide chamber. The chamber had no corners, as such; the whole affair was rounded and silky-textured. The atmosphere was deliciously steamy. Quill loosened his collar. He had climbed from the cervical muscle to stand on a wide spongy floor, stretching into the distance where he could dimly make out, through bluish mists, a farther wall and some looming shape silhouetted against it.

He set out in that direction, stretching, taking deep breaths, taking a few pugilistic jabs at the air, trying to feel himself again. But the entire episode was taking on a dreamlike quality. 'Pheromones,' he muttered.

He had taken but ten steps when from out of the quivering tissues underfoot whipped a thick tangle of cilia, each one hair-fine but strong, prettily transparent, gleaming like dewy spiderwebs in the shimmer emitted by the walls. They formed a cocoonlike webbing around his legs, began to wrap him round and round up the thighs, the hips, evenly covering him to the waist, the ribcage, trapping his right arm against his belly – along with the pulse-gun. His left arm remained free, but as the cilia enwrapped him further, it seemed this freedom was to be tragically transient. He banged at the webbing thick about his waist; it only tightened, as if peeved, in response. The cilia ran from the cocoon to the tissue underfoot in a sort of weave, quivering with his struggles, at an angle from his body like a bellgown. As the cilia enwrapped his chest, began to reach up for his shoulders, he let his left arm fall in despair against the belling weave, his fingers inadvertently stroking the threads . . . The response was instantaneous; the cilia ceased to build its cocoon; the loose threads about to close over his throat came loose and drew back, as if to examine him, their ends shivering . . .

Encouraged, Quill began to riffle the webbing, as if playing a harp with his fingertips, trilling out seductive melodies on the cilia, tripping enticingly, rhythmically, with gentle urging, each string-flick scarcely more than a caress.

The walls sighed, the cilia shivered and unfolded from him like a nocturnal blossom retreating before the sunlight.

He had, to put it gently, done the right thing.

The atmosphere seemed to quiver with anticipation . . .

Quill Tripstickler, rightfully feeling dauntless, strode waggishly across the shuddering plain to the monolithic shapes glimpsed through the mist.

He spied a figure approaching and by degrees made out the detestable – as he felt now – Regent, His Perseverance.

'Welcome, Groom Q. Tripstickler! I perceive that our confidence in you was justified!' The Regent was fingering a sort of rosary about his neck, whirling the beads 'tween his fingertips in some systematic ritual fashion; looking closer, Quill noted that the rosary was in the shape of a DNA molecule in heliocentric diagram.

Feeling wrung out and put upon, Quill responded sharply, 'Is the end in sight?'

'Ah! You are eager for the consummation. Justifiably. Follow me.'

Quill snorted in annoyance. He'd had enough *follow me*. He strode beside the Regent, approaching what appeared to be a huge statue in the distance, putting questions periodically:

'Is the lady – forgive me – personable?'

'She is Paradise,' the Regent replied cryptically.

'Can our conjugation be consummated in a nulgrav chamber, perhaps? I was blue-ribbon in erotic persuasion in all circumstances,' Quill said proudly and, for once, without exaggeration. 'But I specialized in weightless enjoining.'

'I'm afraid that is impossible.'

'Ah – I dislike to be indelicate, but suppose the Yee finds the experience a fertilizing one? The question of birth control – '

'Do not concern yourself. Your clones will be taken care of – the boys – and selectively winnowed with – '

'I beg your pardon for interrupting,' Quill said hastily, 'but did you say – clones?'

'Precisely. Every cell of your body will be sorted through, the healthiest chosen for growing the – '

'But how do you propose to obtain *every* cell? I have no qualms as regards donating one or two, conceivably a handful, but there is a limit that every sensible man will set . . .'

'Stay your questions, Groom Q. Tripstickler,' the Regent said rather severely, wagging a forefinger at Quill. 'All will now become lucid and transparent as a gestation membrane of the lower fallopes. You will observe as a young Sil, anxious that his DNA combination achieve immortality through Yee cloning, precedes you in the consummation.'

'What? Am I to take second place to an upstart? Are there provisions for the lady's toilet, a shower perhaps, to –'

'It cannot be avoided, Q. T. the Groom. The man preceding you has waited many metabiurnals, deep in Proving, to enjoin with the Yee. Certainly,' he added in hasty placation, 'your own approaches were superior: You would not be discouraged, you wriggled through her defenses, sidestepped her instinctive refusals and seduced your way from her entrapping possessiveness, in form befitting a classic mating rite. Ah, now: Observe the Yee.'

He raised his arms and in reply a great billow of blue mists parted, revealing the details of what Quill had taken to be a statue.

The Yee lay supine, her head to Quill's left, her feet to Quill's right. To be more accurate, her head was twenty-six meters to Quill's right, her feet forty-two meters to his left; he stood in the shadow of her waistline. The giantess lay on her back with her legs well apart, her arms at her sides, hands palm down, fingers sunken into the soft surface on which she lay. The paramount of her quivering, prettily rounded belly, some three meters above Quill's head, formed a column of flesh where the navel should be, that ran in a graceful unbroken sweep to join narrowly with the ceiling. Her great breasts quivered massively as her ribcage rose and fell like a monstrous bellows with her breathing. Her skin was pearly, blue veins lacily evident, pulsing with life under the translucent skin. Even should she defy the stresses of gravity and break her umbilicus, the Yee would never move from her intrauterine repose: her skin, where it should have followed the curve of her body under her back, swept outward to meld with the floor tissues of the vast chamber; it was thus all the way around, wherever her body came into contact with the flooring. She was an outgrowth of her enclosure.

She was also lovely. She was quite proportionate, a scale-up from a full-bodied human female, classically curved and strong, full of dignity though she lay with legs akimbo. Her face, though in size of appropriate proportions relative to the body, in several ways resembled that of a fetus. The flattened nose, the slitted, sleeping eyes, an unfinished quality about the brow. Her lips, however, were full and purplish-red. For hair she had more of the see-through cilia growing from her scalp, to cascade thickly down before it too merged with the flooring.

Quill swallowed in awe.

Numbly, he followed the Regent to the right; they strolled down the luminously glossy length of leg, past the knee and calves, around a gigantic but somehow delicate ankle and the soft feet – and stood gazing up a study in perspective, the great causeway between her legs, converging in architectural flow to the pubis.

A man stood there, obscuring the great vertical lips opening onto another domain.

He shed his sackcloth and, as Quill watched, climbed between the hairless lips and into the Yee's all encompassing welcome. Quill heard his muffled scream, saw the autonomic contraction of the Yee's vaginal muscles, saw the trickle of blood escape from that cathedralesque cleft . . .

'And so you see that, sweetly pulped, the Groom is made ready for the chemical mix secreted by the Yee's internal biological laboratory, the thousands of cells in his body surviving intact, flowing amidst the rest,' the Regent explained clinically, 'are allowed to incubate in the sorting baths – '

'Excuse me,' Quill interrupted, turning away. He leaned against a massive heel and shuddered. The spell passed. He reached out to steady himself against the sole of her foot – a liquid laughter echoed from the ceiling. Experimentally, he ran a caressing hand down the sole; the great foot wriggled faintly, a happy moan issued from the area of the head. 'Sensitive, isn't she?' Quill murmured. He turned to the Regent: 'Must this consummation be performed with lookers-on? In my culture it is the custom that such things be performed in private – ' This was a lie, as regards the present state of the Earth colonies, but the Regent was out of touch with offworld ways.

'Very well. The Yee will signal us that all is well and the happy deed done, when the enjoining is over.'

'And I wonder,' Quill said, speaking rapidly, 'if you might send my servant down to pick up my clothes . . . I'd like them sent back to my family.'

The Regent rubbed his chin dubiously. 'A metal machine in the paradisiacal recesses? Still, since you are an offworlder, I suppose we must make one or two exceptions. Especially since you have pleased the Yee so well . . . so far. It shall be done.'

The Regent turned and, deliberately tripping himself to test his ability to catch his fall by rolling before he broke his neck, he made his way pratfalling into the mist and was soon lost to sight.

Quill turned and walked toward the head. He mounted the hand, walked over the wrist and up the arm, progressing delicately, tiptoeing, as if bestowing kisses with his footsteps.

The skin sank under his tread to his ankle; the muscle of the bicep was soft, only rarely flexed. He made his way up the shoulder, having to climb a bit, enjoying the electric contact of her smooth skin under his hands. He crawled over the collarbone, onto the neck, stepping carefully so as not to give her discomfort, and hauling himself up onto her slight chin.

Her eyes were open.

Two pale orbs, their pupils as deep as black holes, the retina blue-gray, focused directly on him.

A chill traveled up his spine, carrying with it a communication.

You are not like the others.

'No,' Quill agreed. He was not disoriented by her telepathy; he'd taken classes in low-level telepathy; and though he hadn't a natural talent for it, would never be a professional, he had some experience with clear reception.

You come to my face, my outer, my Self-image. You come to meet me rather than to take me.

'Taking into account also grace and magnetism, you have just summed up the nub of successful love-making,' Quill said, bowing slightly. He sat straddling her chin with his legs, caressing her lips with his hands. He allowed his fingers to slip between her lips, to trifle sweetly with the tip of her tongue. A shudder ran through her.

I feel for you: affinity.

'I am honored, madame.'

Your touch is softer than a probe but more than super-ficial. I wonder if you would be kind enough to apply this touch to an area which my other visitors have long ignored. It is a node of sensation at my nether convergence, and if you were to stand on your tiptoes –

'I believe,' Quill said, 'I know the spot you mean.' He bestowed a final drawn-out caress to the lips before him. 'I will do as you request on one condition: that you signal the Sils – '

My children?

'Yes, my ancient Yee. Signal your children that all is

well and our love has been consummated. They must be made to believe that I have been, ah, given the complete treatment for cloning preparations . . .'

I understand. I learn from sifting through your mind what you wish: A process called lying. It is yours, my love. But you must promise that you will return to bestow your affections on the node of sensation again, three years from now. I should be ready for another, by then.

Quill hesitated but a moment. Three years? A trifle to the Yee, a considerable span of time for Quill; it could be arranged.

Quill, too, was pleasured by the encounter.

'Very well, you have my promise.'

Quill slowly, slitheringly, made his way to her formidable crotch. He lowered himself from the mons and stood on the flooring; he had just found the 'spot' she'd meant when he was startled by a *whirring* from behind. He turned and found Fives watching him. 'Ah, Fives. I see the storm has abated and you are intact once more. Fine. Just wait on the other side of the leg, there, and I'll join you. Best you steady yourself – there could be a bit of a quake in a few minutes.'

'Very good, sir.'

Minutes later, the walls and floor of the great chamber trembled, resounded with the quakings of the orgasming giantess.

Rubbing a sore right arm, Quill joined Fives and asked, 'Do you think you can find a way out of this place? Use your sonar or something; get us out past the Sils without their seeing us. Can you do it?'

'I think so, sir. But perhaps we should confer with the Regent first. This mission has not been performed as the Sils would prefer – '

'They'll never know. She promised. I want to go. I'm sick with ennui.'

'Nevertheless, sir – '
'Fives!'
'Sir?'
'Rummy! Bit thick, what?'
'Very good, sir. This way . . .'

Observing Sil from orbit just prior to coming into the proper celestial alignment for a spacejump, Quill remarked to Fives: 'Something you as a machine will never know, Fives, is the joy of physical love.'

'Actually the process of love-making, so-called, in animals, is quite machinelike in that it is the result of a series of chemical reactions, the interactions of enzymes and various hormones, instinct-implanted psychological obsessions engineered by genetic chemistry – '

'Don't be tiresome, Fives. The point is, no one such as myself could feel physical attraction for someone such as yourself, a machine. Lips of plastiflex will never touch mine!'

'That, sir, is a state of affairs which provides me with considerable comfort, if I may be so bold.'

It seemed to Quill that Fives actually shuddered.

Quill returned his gaze to the vidscreen, watched the planet receding behind them. 'The lovely Yee . . . three years . . . Well, well. I shall repine until then. I wonder,' he murmured, 'if we could have been happy together.'

Recurrent Dreams of Nuclear War Lead B. T. Quizenbaum into Moral Dissolution

Some boom would wake him, as if the outside world conspired with his dreams.

Just before he woke: the cloud, angry red at its column, would grow to dominate the horizon like a great luminous cerebrum and spinal stalk. And then the white flash, and *then* the boom.

BOOM. He'd sit up in bed, blinking through sweat, and the room would be filled with whiteness. He'd wait for the Big Burn. The pain. Death.

Slowly his eyes would adjust and his heart would slow and the sweat would grow cold on his taut face. He'd hear the boom again and realize it was only a semi-truck banging as it hit a pot-hole. Or another of the city's congestion coughings.

The flash was only the light of the morning sun, seeming sudden when he opened his eyes (unthinking and yet deliberate, he'd leave his drapes open before going to bed). His bedroom windows faced East Manhattan . . . But before his eyes adjusted, just as he came awake, half in dream delirium, the light seemed the flash of a hydrogen bomb achieving fruition. It shared some quality with the light at the heart of a naked 200-watt bulb; the cancelled place where, when he stared into the bulb, his eye refused to assimilate color: a heart of whiteness. A throb of almost ostentatious blankness.

It was August. As if August were a kind of Season for them, the sky seemed filled with planes, jets issuing ominous roars; each jet, in Quizenbaum's mind, potentially the bomb-bearer. Every aerial rumble would send him breathing hard to the window.

He wouldn't go to a therapist. The dreams frightened him, but they were fevered, salty melodramas. He didn't want them explained.

'Oh,' the therapist would probably say, 'possibly the recurrent nightmares of World War Three represent the expression of your sublimated hostility against the world. You're destroying the whole damn world in your dreams, Quizenbaum, because you wanted to be a set designer for the theatre and instead you're an usher. You blame the world itself, the fundamental source of all injustice. You are forty and you know it's too late. You're unmarried and lonely. Understandably, these things anger you.' And no doubt another would say: 'You're a Jew without a heritage, a foster child. Your mother converted to Christianity and then became a drunk when you were five. A year later you were taken to live with Gentiles; and you've always been afraid to go to Temple, afraid of rejection. You are a Jew without Judaism, and you resent the Jews because of this. The bomb is your way to destroy the city that seethes with Jews – after all, Quizenbaum, your dreams always take place in New York City. The mushroom shape represents the dome of the synagogue, and the sublimation of your fear of women, which . . .' And other drivel. Quizenbaum could anticipate them. He had toyed with analysts before, and they had left his world more opaque than ever.

The dreams were not identical. Some nights the nightmare included Tricia. Tricia was a girlish woman in her twenties who'd once worked at the theatre, taking tickets. They'd dated a few times, then she'd announced she was going to marry someone named Barry Malstein, because he was a corporation lawyer and because he was Jewish. 'I mean,' she said in an apologetic aside to Quizenbaum, 'he's *really* Jewish. But, really, you're a much better conversationalist. But, really, I feel that my therapist is right, he says my life is too . . . um . . .'

Still, Quizenbaum remembered Tricia fondly. He had not dreamt of nuclear explosions on the single night he'd spent with her.

In the dreams featuring Tricia, they would be sitting together on the veranda, arguing quietly about something. He was never sure what the argument was about. She would stand, as if to leave – and then the sky would darken with the mushroom cloud behind her, like a sort of cobra's hood over her head, and the world would start to come apart around them. Stock footage of natural disasters, buildings swept away by flood, cities buckled by earthquakes. He would sweep her into his arms and, carrying her as if she were made of paper, plunge into the house, the terror fueling him, driving him with a surge of excitement he never experienced when he was awake. The house would become gelatin around them, the walls transparent, the white light suffusing everything. The BOOM would arrive, bringing with it the shockwave. Tricia screaming, the scream lost in the roar. He would turn to look directly into the white light.

That's when he'd wake. When he looked the explosion in its cyclopean eye.

In other dreams, he'd be walking along in a crowd, perhaps leaving a football game (he never went to football games) or a rock concert (he disliked loud music); or he might be one card in the great shuffle of Times Square (he never went there, awake). The cloud would come, the glow. Every head in the crowd, whatever crowd it was, would turn to squint under overshadowing hands at the explosion unfolding. There was a split second, before the blinding light and the shockwave hit them, when they were fused exquisitely in their sense of mutual destiny. Now we're all of us ashes in the same urn, Quizenbaum would think. The glow would increase, the fireball would sunder the horizon, death coming hard at them like a steel mallet descending. He would look the glow in the eye and –

He'd wake up.

But sometimes the waking was incomplete. He would seem to see the crowd in his bedroom with him, thousands of them in a room hardly big enough for four, everyone looking at the window, anticipating the blast. They were insubstantial; people of glycerin. He'd shudder, and the room would invisibly tumesce with air pressure, till the walls were about to burst. Instead, a quiet, sickening *pop* happened in the bones about his ears. Another quiver would go through him and he'd be alone, the hot morning sun making his eyes swim with islands of blur. Once, only once, just after the *pop*, he found the sheet between his legs wet with fresh urine. This discovery brought a kind of euphoria.

In considering the implications of his recurrent dreams, Brent Taylor Quizenbaum had come to certain conclusions. He tried to explain his conclusions to a woman who introduced herself as 'Maria – you know, like in *West Side Story*?' in the Nightbirds Bar & Grill. They stood at the crowded bar together; there were no stools. He was pleased to find he could put his foot on a brass rail near the floor. He'd never done that before.

Maria was taller than he was, and darker, and her acne scars glowed in the underworld glamor of the black-light. Half-hidden in tinfoil, the black-light was screwed to the ceiling above the topless dancer teetering on a platform behind the bar; she was not quite in command of her clear plastic high-heels. Now and then Quizenbaum's round-eyed gaze would stray to the dancer who, in pasties and g-string, her skin leaden under the black-light, was making vertical wriggling movements as if she were trying to squeeze into a dress that was too small for her.

Quizenbaum returned his attention to Maria, gaunt blackhaired Maria and said, 'So you see, these dreams, along with certain international indications, have brought me to the conclusion that our world is indeed coming to an end. Civilizations have their life and death cycles. Ours is too absurd to be allowed to go any further. Nuclear holocaust in my lifetime.' He paused dramatically. 'And in yours, Maria.'

'Yeah!' she said nodding, sipping her screwdriver.

How deep her understanding! 'So you see,' he went on earnestly, 'it all links up with the fascination people have for disaster movies and horror movies, and all the desperate, jaded attempts at new thrills – like free-basing and "swing" clubs. These things tell me that, deep down inside, everyone knows that The End is coming.' He took a large pull on his own screwdriver; he could hardly taste the Tropicana orange juice for the vodka. A terrible, magnificent lucidity took hold of him. He had never before had so much to drink.

'We all *feel* it coming . . .' he gestured eloquently, trying to invoke the word. 'We feel it coming . . . *intuitively*. Right?' He turned his magnificent lucidity against her, looking her in the eye.

'Right!' she said, unblinking, signaling the bartender for two more drinks. Quizenbaum paid for the drinks – he'd paid for the previous three rounds.

How *sensitive* she was! Quizenbaum thought. He really liked her. 'So, Maria,' he went on, settling into the groove of his rhetoric, 'if we agree that nuclear holocaust will soon kill us all, how do we cope? How? We've got to live for the moment, till the white light and the Big Burn come. And, if it feels right, we've got to live hard and fast and loose . . .' All were expressions Quizenbaum had laughed at till now; he felt as he supposed the dancer above the bar felt, that he was wriggling into something ill-fitting. But when he said, 'We've got to let ourselves go and *feel*,' he smiled, becoming more comfortable with the clichés. 'And then, Maria . . .' He looked deep into her red-rimmed brown eyes, 'we've got to greet the actual moment of nuclear death with . . . with dignity and . . . and, uh . . .*you* know . . . with euphoria. The sort of euphoria that comes with giving up, joyously. Release at last!'

'Right on,' she said, though the noise-level in the crowded bar probably made it impossible for her to make out most of what he was saying.

'And there's something more . . . I know it's all a bit reminiscent of *Doctor Strangelove*, but . . . when that bomb hits, we'll all die *together*. For once, everyone in New York City will really be *together*. It'll be almost like being in love!' He leaned close to her to hear her reaction.

'Sure as *shit!*' she burst out.

Somewhat deflated by this malaprop phrase, he drank off the remainder of his screwdriver. His head spun, and a wave of disorientation overtook him. A flash of light at the door – it was only a cop directing a flashlight at a dark corner of the bar. But Quizenbaum staggered, for a moment thinking the white light had come.

It wasn't the first time that day; he'd started at sirens (is that an air raid siren?), jets breaking the sound barrier (is that the final BOOM?), mothers screaming at their children (are they screaming 'Run for the fallout shelter!'?). Sometimes a silence would startle him – was it the silence prefacing explosion?

He shook himself and returned stalwartly to the bar. 'Hey, baby,' Maria said, tussling his hair and tilting her head inquisitively. 'Wassuh matter?'

He smiled warmly at her. She wasn't sophisticated, but

by God, she was *real*. 'In the light of our dish – uh, discussion,' he said, 'don't you think we ought to explore one another while we still can?'

As she took him by the arm and led him out the door, he heard someone at the bar say, 'Maria always gettsuh – ' And he couldn't hear the rest. She gets the *what?* he wondered.

'She knows what she's doing,' someone else replied.

Misinterpreting, he nodded to himself. 'Yeah, she can pick 'em,' he murmured proudly, the world reeling around him.

He didn't put another interpretation on the remarks he'd overheard till he woke the next morning – fully dressed, on the rug beside his unmussed bed – and found:

A) Maria gone.

B) A pool of vomit, likely his own, in the doorway of the bedroom.

C) His wallet gone. It had contained ninety dollars and one credit card.

D) His clock radio and blender gone.

He made a sound that was something like a bark of laughter. Then he winced. He took three codeine, remaining from an old dental prescription, and went to bed.

The cloud advanced into the sky, and retreated, and came back again. It came and went in pulses. It would advance a ways, its fireball unfolding like a paper bouquet from the wrist of a magician. And then the bouquet would return to its sleeve, the fireball devolving as if on a film run backwards, and people would look away from the horizon, forgetting what had been there, just as if nothing had happened.

The fireball would unfurl again – and it would reverse,

the world restored in seconds. 'Indecisive jack-in-the-box,' said Quizenbaum, who was floating bodiless over the city. Then he was down in the square, somehow apart from the thousands flowing in currents around him, feeling inert and anonymous.

The mingled fear and elation began teasingly when the horizon lit up, the cloud emerging. The crowd would turn and look and, in the terror that united them like hot plastic flowing over everyone, Quizenbaum was no longer inert, no longer anonymous. It didn't last; it didn't quite consummate. He was left with frustration. The film would run backwards, the cloud withering, folding in on itself. The crowd forgot all that had happened. He was again alone.

Quizenbaum awoke in darkness. He had slept the day through. That was the last time he had the dream, in any form. A week later he placed an ad in the Personals section of *The Village Voice*.

The ad was incomprehensible to everyone who read it. But Quizenbaum sat for hours, watching the black telephone.

The ad read:

BURN TWO AND THEY BECOME ONE. I PROVIDE MATCHES IF YOU HAVE GASOLINE. MORE THAN SUICIDE. CALL ME, AT . . .

One day, the phone rang.

What It's Like to Kill a Man

'First of all,' the wall-eyed prizewinner said, 'it's a feeling of power like you never had. I figure that's especially the case here, like, with the AVLPs, see, because it ain't like you're doing it in self-defense, or in a war where it's in a hurry – you got time to, you know, *think* about it first . . .'

Spector was watching the wall-eyed guy on TV. The guy was tubby, was wearing a stenciled-on brown suit, one of the cheap JC Pennys printouts where the tie blurs into the shirt-collar. And green rubber boots. Spector puzzled over the green rubber boots till he realized they were intended to look military.

A ghost-image of another man's face, ragged-edged, began to slide over the AVLP winner's; the new face was bodiless, just a face zigzagging across the image with kitelike jerkiness. A punky face, a Chaoticist; leering, laughing. His tag rippled by after his face like the tail after a comet: JEROME-X.

It was television graffiti, transmitted from a shoplifted minitranser. The year 2021's answer to spraypaint.

Annoyed, Senator Spector hit the switch on his arm-chair, turning off the TV. The broad, inch-thick screen slotted back into the ceiling. He was glad of an excuse to turn the program off. In a way, the AVL program was his responsibility. He'd felt bound to take stock of it. But watching it, the gnawing feeling had begun in his stomach again . . .

Spector stood up and went to the full-length video mirror in his bedroom. It was time to get ready for the

interview. He gazed critically at his fox face, brittle blue
eyes. His black crewcut was widowpeaked to hint at
minimono styles – to let the youngsters know he was hip,
even at forty-five.

He wore a zebra-striped printout jumpsuit. It'll have to
go, he decided. Too frivolous. He tapped the keyboard
inset beside the mirror, and changed his image. The
video-mirror used computer-generated imagery; the generated images weren't immaculately realistic, but they
were close enough to give him an idea how it'd look . . .
He decided he needed a friendlier look. Add a little flesh
to the cheeks; the hair a shade lighter. Earring? No. The
jumpsuit, he told the mirror, would have to be changed
to a leisure suit, but make its jacket stenciled for more
identification with the Average Joe. He'd never wear a
stenciled suit out to dinner, but just now he needed to
project a 'man of the people' image, especially as the
interviewer was from the Undergrid. Both his security
adviser and his press secretary had warned him against
giving an interview to an underground media rep. But the
Undergrid was growing, in size and influence, and it was
wise to learn to manipulate it – use it, before it used you.

He tapped out the code for the suit, watched it appear
in the mirror, superimposed over his jumpsuit. A cream-
colored leisure suit. He pursed his lips, decided a two-
tone combination would be friendlier. He tapped the
notched turtleneck to a soft umber.

Satisfied with the adjusted image, he hit the *Print*
switch. He shed the jumpsuit, and waited, wondering if
Janet had contacted his attorney, Heimlitz. He hoped
she'd hold off on the divorce till after the election . . .
The console hummed and a slot opened beside the glass.
The suit rolled out first: flat, folded, still pleasantly warm,
smelling faintly of its fabrication chemicals. He pulled it

on; it was high quality fabricant, only slightly papery against his skin.

He used Press Flesh for his cheeks, tamping and shaping till it conformed with the image he'd programmed, appearing to blend seamlessly with his skin. He used the cosmetics closet to lighten his hair, widen his eyes a fraction, then went to the living room, and looked around. Shook his head. It was done in matte-black and chrome. Too somber – he had to take great pains to avoid anything even remotely morbid. He dialed the curtains to light blue, the rug to match. The console chimed. He went to it, and flicked for visual. The screen blinked to the expressionless face of the housing area's checkpoint guard.

'What is it?' Spector asked.

'People here to see you in a van fulla video stuff. Two of them, name of Torrence and Chesterton, from UNO. Citident Numbers – '

'Never mind. I'm expecting them. Send 'em up.'

'You don't want a visual check?'

'No! And for God's sake be friendly to them, if you know how.'

He cut the screen, wondering if he were being cavalier about security. Maybe – but he kept a .44 in the cabinet beside the console, as security backup. And there was always Kojo.

Spector rang for Kojo. The little Japanese looked small, neat, harmless. His official title was Secretary. He was actually a bodyguard.

Kojo knew about the interview. Flawlessly gracious, he ushered the two Undergrid reps into the living room, then went to sit on a straight-backed chair to the left of the sofa.

Kojo wore a blue printout typical of clerks. Sat with his hands folded in his lap; no tension, no warning in his posture, no hint of danger. Kojo had worked for Spector only two weeks, but Spector had seen the security agency's dossier on him. And Spector knew that Kojo could move from the bland aspect of a seated secretary to lethal attack posture in a quarter-second.

The people from UNO wore 'rags' – actual cloth clothing, jeans, t-shirts, worn boots. Silly affectations, Spector thought. The woman introduced herself as Sonia Chesterton. She was the interviewer. The big black guy, Torrence, was her technician. He wore a dangling silver earring in his left ear, and his head was shaved. Spector smiled, and shook their hands, making eye contact. Feeling a chill when he met the girl's eyes. She was almost gaunt; her dark eyes were sunken, red-rimmed. Thin brown hair cut short. She and Torrence seemed neutral; not hostile, not friendly.

Spector glanced at Kojo. The bodyguard was alert, and relaxed.

Take it easy, Spector told himself, sitting on the sofa beside Sonia Chesterton. His body language read friendly-but-earnest; he smiled just enough. Torrence set up cameras, mikes.

The girl looked at Spector. Just looked at him.

It felt wrong. TV interviewers, even if they intended to feed your image to the piranhas during the interview itself, invariably maintained a front of friendliness before and after.

The silence pressed on him. Silence, the politician's enemy.

'Ready at your signal,' Torrence said. He looked big, hulking over handsized cameras on delicate aluminum tripods.

'Now – what shall we talk about?' Spector asked. 'I thought perhaps – '

'Let's just launch into it,' she broke in.

He blinked. 'No prep?'

Torrence pointed at her. She looked into the camera. Serious. 'I'm Sonia Chesterton, for UNO, the People's Satellite, interviewing Senator Hank Spector, one of the key architects of the AntiViolence Laws, and an advocate of the AVL Programming . . .'

For a while, the interview was standard. She asked him how he justified the AntiViolence Laws. Looking at her solemnly, speaking in an exaggeration of his Midwestern accent (the public found it reassuring), he gave his usual spiel: Violent crime began its alarming growth trend in the 1960s. It continued to rise in the 1970s, leveled out in the '80s for a few years – chiefly because prison sentences were stiffened, taking a lot of hardcases off the street for a while – and then feverishly resurged in the 1990s. The worldwide population shift, which cascaded millions of immigrants into the United States, strained the country's job availability past the limit. Crime and drug abuse soared through the year 2000, continued increasing for nearly two decades more. Factors like the breakdown in traditional family structures, the steady increase of brain-damaging pollutants in the environment, and the wide availability of drugs like PCP, conspired to create socio-paths and psycho-killers. The poisoned environment literally oozed psychosis.

The old punitive laws weren't forceful enough for true deterrence, Spector argued. The AVL was as powerful a deterrent as a civilized nation could create. The Anti-Violence Laws stated that anyone who committed a violent crime more than once would receive punitive public beatings. Anyone who committed a nonhomicidal violent crime more than twice was simply executed, within three weeks after conviction. The right to appeal was considered to have been forfeited after the second

felony assault. Or after the first homicide. Anyone convicted of a first degree homicide was executed, within
three weeks of conviction, even on a first crime. Second
degree murder – if it was your first offense – got you a
series of public beatings, and a long sentence. If it was
your second violence-offense, it got you a quick
execution.

The 'innocent by reason of insanity' escape was simply
abolished. The mad were executed too.

Rapists were publicly castrated. Thieves were beaten,
sometimes maimed.

'Violent crime is down sixty percent from five years
ago,' Spector said gravely. 'It continues to drop. In a few
years the Security checkpoints and the other precautions
that make modern life tedious – these may vanish
entirely. Perhaps, because of the sped-up judicial pace,
three or four people a year are unjustly convicted, but
the majority of Society are better off.'

'Even accepting that that's true – which I don't – '
Sonia Chesterton said ' – how does that justify the
executioner's lottery? The AVL TV programs?'

'First, AVL TV gets the public involved with the
criminal justice system, so that they identify with Society,
and no longer feel at odds with the police. Second, it acts
as a healthy catharsis for the average person's hostility
which otherwise – '

'Which otherwise might be directed at the State in a
revolution?' She cut in, her neutrality gone.

'No.' He cleared his throat, controlling his irritation.
'No, that's not – '

He was even more annoyed by her interruption, and
her tone, when she broke in: 'The phrase "healthy
catharsis" puzzles me. Lottery winners are winning the
right to beat or execute a convict on public television.
Ever watch the program *What It's Like*, Senator?'

'Well, yes, I watched it today to see if in fact – '

'Then you saw the way those people behave. They giggle when they're beating the convict's head in! A man or a woman, gagged in a stocks; the "winner" clubs them to death – or, if he or she prefers, uses a gun, blows their brains out . . . And they cackle over it, and the more demented they are, the more the studio audience cheers them on. Now you call that *healthy*?'

Stung, he said, 'It's temporary! The release of tension – '

'Two of the lottery winners were arrested, tried and executed for *illegal* murders, *after* their participation in AVL programs. It seems fairly obvious that they developed a *permanent* taste for killing – reinforced by public approval – which they – '

'Those were flukes! I hardly think – '

'You hardly think about anything except what's convenient for you. Because if you did you'd have to see that you, Senator, are no better than a murderer yourself.'

Her veneer of objectivity had cracked, fallen away. Her voice shook with emotion. Her hands clenched her knees, knuckles white. He began to be afraid of her.

'I really think you've lost all objectivity,' he said, coolly as he could manage. But feeling fear turn to anger.

(Feeling, in fact, he was near losing his own veneer of cool self-righteousness; feeling he was near snapping. And wondering: Why? Why had all the skills he'd developed in years of facing hostile interviewers suddenly evaporated? It was this issue. It haunted him, nagged him. At night it ate away at his sleep like an acid . . . And the damn woman went on, and *on!*)

'Everyone who has been killed, Senator – the innocent ones at least – their blood is on your hands. You – '

Some inner membrane of restraint in Spector's consciousness flew into tatters, and anger uncoiled itself.

Anger propelled by guilt. He stood, arms straight at his sides, trembling. 'Get out. Get OUT!'

He turned to Kojo, to tell him to escort them to the door.

And saw: Torrence stretching his right arm toward Kojo; in Torrence's hand was a small gray box. And Kojo had frozen, was staring into space in a kind of fugue state.

Spector thought: *Assassins*.

And then Kojo stood, and turned toward Spector. Spector looked desperately around for a weapon.

Kojo came at him –

And ran past him, at the woman. A wrist flick, and he was holding a knife. She looked at him calmly, resignedly, and then she screamed as – his movements a blur – he closed with her, drove the slim silver blade through her left eye, and into her brain.

All the time, Torrence continued filming, showing no surprise, no physical reaction.

Spector gagged, seeing the spurt of blood from her eyesocket as she crumpled. And Kojo stabbed the woman methodically, again and again. Spector stumbled back, fell onto the sofa.

'Kill Spector after me, Kojo!' Torrence yelled. Torrence turned a knob on the little gray remote control box, dropped it – and the box melted to a lump of plastic slag. Spector stared, confused.

Torrence had stepped into the TV camera's viewing area, had closed his eyes, was waiting, shaking, muttering a prayer that might have been Islamic – then Kojo rushed him, the small Japanese leaping at the big black man like a cat attacking a doberman guard dog . . . Only, Torrence just stood there, and let Kojo slash out his throat with one impossibly swift and inhumanly precise movement. *Kill Spector after me, Kojo*.

But Spector was moving, ran to the cabinet, flung it

open, snatched up his .44 pistol, turned and, panicking
. . . shot Kojo in the back.

Kojo would have turned on Spector next, surely . . .

But in the pulsing silence that followed the gunshot, as
Spector looked down at the three bodies, as he stared at
the big, red-oozing hole his bullet had torn in Kojo's back
. . . Seeing Kojo's own Press Flesh cosmetic had come
off, exposing the shaved spot on the back of Kojo's head,
the puckered white scar from recent surgery . . .

Looking at that, he thought: *I've been set up*.

And the security guards were pounding on the door.

'Today on *What It's Like* we're going to talk to Bill
Muchowski, the first man to participate in an actual *legal
duel* with an AVL convict – Bill, you wanted to execute
the man "in a fair fight", is that right?'

'That's right, Frank, I'm a former US Marine and I just
didn't want to shoot the man in cold blood, I wanted to
give him a gun, and of course I'd have a gun, and we'd,
you know, *go at it*.'

'Sort of an old fashioned wildwest gunfight, eh? You're
a brave man! I understand you had to sign a special
waiver – '

'Oh sure, I signed a waiver saying if I got hurt or killed
the government couldn't be held responsible – '

'Bill, we're running out of time, can you just tell us
quickly, what it was like for you, Bill Muchowski, to kill
a man.'

'Uh, sure, Frank – killing a man with a gun has its
mechanical aspect, like, you got to punch a hole through
the guy, and that causes a loss of life-giving hemoglobin.
Now, what it *feels* like to do that – well, you almost feel
like the bullet is a part of you, like you can feel what it
would feel, and you imagine the bullet nosing through the
skin, then pushing through muscle tissue, smashing

through organs, breaking bone, flying out the other side
of 'im with all that red liquid . . . just blowing the bastard
away. And it feels good knowing he's a killer, so he
deserves it. And there's a funny kinda *relief* – '

'Bill, that's all we've got time for now, thanks for
letting us know *What It's Like!*'

The cell they'd moved him to that morning was signifi-
cantly smaller than the first one. And dirtier. And colder.
And there was someone else in it, wearing a blood-
stained prison shirt; the guy was asleep, his back turned,
on the top bunk. The cell had two metal shelves, bunks,
extending from the smudged, white concrete wall, and a
lidless, seatless toilet. They wouldn't tell him why he'd
been moved, and now, looking around at his cell, Spector
was beginning to suspect the reason, and with the suspicion came fear.

Don't panic, he told himself. You're a United States
senator. You've got friends, influence, and the strings
sometimes take a while to let you know they've been
pulled. The defense contractors and the Pentagon need
you for that military appropriations bill. They'll see you
through this.

But the cell seemed to mock all reassurance. He looked
around at the cracked walls; the water stain on the white
concrete near the ceiling looking like a sweat-stain on a t-
shirt; the bars where the fourth wall should have been,
dun paint flaking off them. The graffiti burnt into the
ceiling with cigarette coals. JULIO-Z, 2017!! and WHO-EVER
U R, YER ASS IS SCREWED!!! and AT LEASE (sic) YOU A *TV
STAR!!! ONCE!?!*

Spector's stomach growled. Breakfast that morning had
been a single egg on a piece of stale white bread.

His legs were going to sleep from sitting on the edge of

the hard bunk. He got up, paced the width of the cell, five paces the long way, four the short.

He heard a metallic rasp, and a clang; echoey footsteps in the stark spaces of the hallway. Trembling, he went to the bars.

A middle-aged, seam-faced man, wearing a stenciled-on three-piece suit, and carrying a tan vinyl briefcase, was walking up behind the guard. He walked as if he were bone tired.

The bored, portly black guard said, 'Got to look in your satchel there, buddy.' The stranger opened his briefcase, and the guard poked through it. 'No machine guns or cannons in there,' he said. A humorless joke. He unlocked the door, let the stranger in. The guard locked up, and went away.

'Senator Spector,' the man said, extending his hand. 'I'm Gary Bergen.' They shook hands; the stranger's hand was cold, moist.

'You from Heimlitz's office? It's about time he – '

'I'm not from Heimlitz,' Bergen said. 'I'm a public defender.'

Spector stared at him. Bergen looked back with dull gray eyes. 'Heimlitz is no longer representing you. They formally withdrew from the case.'

Spector's mouth was dry. He sank onto the bunk. 'Why?'

'Because your case is hopeless, and your wife is in the process of seizing your assets, and she refuses to pay them.'

Spector suspected that Bergen was taking some kind of quiet satisfaction in all this. He sensed that Bergen didn't like him.

Spector just sat there. Feeling like he was sitting on the edge of the Grand Canyon, and if he moved, even an inch, he'd slip and go over the edge, and fall, and fall . . .

He conjured determination up from somewhere inside
and said, 'Senator Burridge's committee will provide the
money to – '

'The Committee to Defend Senator Hank Spector? It's
been disbanded. Public opinion was overwhelmingly
against them. Frankly, Senator, the public is howling for
your blood . . . For the very reason that you are who you
are. The public doesn't want to see any favorites played.
And they're sure you're guilty.'

'But *why?* I haven't gone to trial, there's only been a
hearing – and by now they should have screened the TV
footage. That should've vindicated me!'

'Oh, they've screened it, for the judge and on television
for the public. Everyone's seen it. They saw you holding
that gray box, pointing it at your bodyguard, making him
attack those people . . . a closeup on your face as you
shouted, "Kill them!" The autopsy on Kojo found the
brain implant that made him respond to the prompter
against his will . . . And we saw you pulling that gun,
shooting your bodyguard in the back – to make it look as
if he'd gone mad and you killed him to protect yourself
. . .' Bergen was enjoying this. 'Too bad you didn't have
time to get rid of the videotapes.'

Spector wasn't able to speak for a few moments.
Finally, he managed, 'It's . . . insane. Moronic. Why
would I go to that much trouble to kill Sonia
Chesterton – '

'Your wife says you were obsessed with her. That you
watched Sonia's TV editorials and they incensed you, you
babbled that Sonia deserved to die – and so forth,' he
shrugged.

'That's perjury! I never saw the Chesterton woman
before that interview, on TV or off! They asked permission to interview me through my secretary, that's the
first I ever heard of UNO. Janet's lying so she'll get

everything . . . But the tapes – they *can't* have shown me saying "kill them" – I didn't say it!'

Bergen nodded slowly. 'I believe you. But the tapes contradict you. Of course, they were at the UNO station for twenty-four hours before being – '

'They tampered with them!'

'Possibly. But try to get the judge to believe that . . .' And he smiled maliciously. 'You'll have two minutes for that at the trial . . .'

'The brain implant – whoever set me up had to have arranged that! We could trace Kojo's recent past, find out who his surgeon was when he – '

'Before your defense committee disbanded, they tried that tack. Kojo had cerebral surgery a few months ago – just after you picked him out from the bodyguard portfolio at Witcher Security. He was to have an implant inserted to improve his speed and reflexes. The technic who provides implants for the surgeons was contacted by someone over TV-fone. The man he saw on the screen offered to transfer fifty-thousand newbux into the technic's account if he'd consent to some unauthorized "adjustments" in the implant. He consented and the implant's "adjustment" turned out to've been one of the Army's attack-and-kill mind-control chips. Remote controlled.'

'The man on the screen must've been – '

'*It was you*, Senator . . . the technic recorded the transmission . . . it's pretty damning evidence. But I'll tell you what – ' his voice creaked with mockery ' – I'll see if I can get you off with a "mercy execution". *You* know, death by injection, sedative overdose. I think you'll prefer it to being clubbed to death on television . . . Well, good-afternoon, Senator.'

The guard had come back: he opened the door, let Bergen out and Spector was alone – except for the guy climbing off the top bunk. And chuckling, 'Hey Spector, man, that guy's really got a hard-on for you, you know? Public defender! Shit! Unless you get Special Pardon – and I can't remember the last time anybody ever did – you're screwed. They ain't gonna rock you special treatment just because you're a senator. That's the PR cornerstone of AVL, man: *everybody* that gets arrested gets screwed – equally.'

He was a wiry little guy with a yellowed, gap-toothed smile, flinty black eyes, and the spikey color-shifting hair of a Chaosist. It was hard to get a real handle on what he looked like because of the bruises, the swollen tissue and crusted cuts on his face from the recent public beating. Still, he looked familiar . . .

'Jerome-X,' Spector muttered, recognizing him. 'Great.'

Jerome-X gave that slightly brain-damaged chuckle again. He was pleased, ''as me, my man. Yeah. Yeah. I got the hot minitrans known up 'n down the freak-en-seez. I got the style. I got – '

'You got *caught*,' Spector observed.

'Hey pal – thas better'n bein' *set up*. You were right, man – sure as shit, they *tampered* with those tapes. But not editing – *image reconstitution*. You're talking to the VideoMan hisself. I *know*. Computer generated images, animated. Computer analyzes a TV-image of a man, right? Gets him moving, talking. Then digitizes it – samples it – an' generates an image of the guy you *can't tell* from the real thing. Uses fractal geometry for realistic surface texture. They can animate you to do whatever they like. Sample your voice, synthesize it to make you say whatever they want. . .'

'But that isn't . . .'

'Isn't *just*?' Jerome-X shook his head. 'You're too much. I didn't think justice was high on your list of

priorities, man. I seen you on TV, Spector – I know about
you . . . Hey, how many people who "committed rob-
bery" or "murder" were people who were annoying to
the local status quo or the feds, or maybe big business?
So they're *videoframed*. Convicted on the evidence of
some security camera that just *happened* to be there . . .
Ri-ight. How many people like that, pal, huh? Hundreds?
Maybe thousands. About half the people convicted go
down from videotaped evidence. That's a lot of lucky
cameras. Sure, maybe if there were more time, you could
prove the tampering – but *you*, bigshot, you've seen to it
you *got* no time, an' no chance for appeal . . .'

'Videoframing . . . I don't believe it.'

'Hey you *better* believe it. But most people don't know
about it, so it's no use tryin' to tell the courts. The up-to-
dates on computer-generated images is kept under lock
'n key. They want the public to think it's at a much cruder
stage, you know? . . . Me, I'm gettin' out in the morning,
already got my trashing for pirate transmissions . . . But
you – they're gonna splash you all over the studio, pal –
'cause you're the Case now. You're *Big Ratings* . . .'

Sometimes, it's possible to bribe a man with *promises* of
money – and Spector used all his politician's skill to
persuade a guard to get a message out to Senator Bob
Burridge. Gave the guard a letter telling Burridge about
the computer-generated evidence; and telling him to work
on it *seriously* – or Spector'd press-release what he had
on Burridge: the death of a girl named Judy Sorenson,
and just where she got the drugs she'd OD'd on.

Three days later, nine A.M., the guard came to Spector's
clammy cell, passed him an ear-cap, winked, and left.
Spector put the capsule in his ear, squeezed it, heard
Burridge's voice: 'Hank, there's a method of videotape
analysis that'll tell us if what's on videotape was genuine

or computer-generated. First, we'll have to subpoena the tapes . . . Of course, as you've already been convicted, that'll be hard . . . But we're pulling some strings . . . we'll see if we can get your conviction overturned in the next day or so . . . a Special Pardon . . . don't get panicky and mention that mutual friend of ours to anyone . . .'

But a week later, Spector was being prepped for his execution. He sat on a bench, chained to five other convicts, listening to the prison's Program Coordinator, Sparks.

Sparks was called 'the animal handler' by the video technicians. He was a stocky, red-faced man with a taut smile and blank gray eyes. He wore a rumpled blue real-cloth suit. The guards stood at either end of the narrow room, tubular stunguns in hand.

'Today, we got a man won an execution-by-combat, more dignified than the baseball-bat-and-the-stocks, and probably quicker if he's a good shot, so you fellas should be glad. You'll be given a gun, but of course it's loaded with blanks – '

And then the chain connecting Spector's handcuffs to the man on his right went taut, jerking Spector half out of his seat, as the small black guy on the other end of the bench lost it, ran at Sparks screaming something in a heavy West Indies dialect, something Spector couldn't make out. But the raw subverbal sound of the man's voice – that alone spoke for him. It said, *Injustice!* It said, *I've got a family!* And then it could say nothing more because the stunguns had turned off his brain for a while and he lay splayed like a dark rag doll on the concrete floor. The guards propped him up on the bench, and Sparks went on as if nothing had happened. 'Now we got to talk about your cues. It'll be a lot worse for you if you forget your cues . . .'

Spector wasn't listening. A terrible feeling had him in its grip and it was a far worse feeling than fear for his life.

At home – the home his wife had sold by now – he'd opened his front door with a sonic key. It sang out three shrill tones, and the door heard and analyzed the tonal code, and opened. And the voice of the man who'd tried to fight, the small dark man . . . his voice, his three shrieks, had opened a door in Spector's mind, had let something out. Something he'd fought for weeks to lock away. Something he'd argued with. Something he'd silently shouted at, again and again.

He'd pushed for the AntiViolence Laws for the same reason that Joe McCarthy, in the last century, had railed at Communism. It was a ticket. A ticket to a vehicle he could ride through the polls, and into office. Inflame the public's fear of crime. Cultivate their lust for vengeance. Titillate their repressed desire to do violence. And they vote for you.

And he hadn't given a rat's ass damn about the crime problem. The issue was a path to power, and nothing more.

He'd known, somewhere inside himself, that a lot of the condemned were probably railroaded. But he'd looked away, again and again. Now, somebody had made it impossible for him to look away. Now, the guilt that had festered in him erupted into full-blown infection and he burned with the fever of self-hatred.

That's when Bergen came in. Bergen spoke to the guards, showed them a paper; the guards came and whispered to Sparks, and Sparks, annoyed, unlocked Spector's cuffs. Glumly, Bergen said, 'Come with me, Mr Spector.' He was no longer Senator Spector.

They went to stand in the hallway; a guard came along, yawning, leaning against the wall, watching a soap on his pocket viddy. Voice icy, Bergen said, 'You're going to get off. A Special Pardon: rare as hen's teeth. Burridge has proof the tapes were tampered with. It hasn't been made public yet, and in fact the judge who presided at your trial is out of town, so Burridge arranged a temporary restraining – '

'Why is it you sound disappointed, Bergen?' Spector broke in, watching him. When Bergen didn't answer, Spector said, 'You did everything you could to sabotage my defense. You were with them, whoever it was. I can feel it. Who was it?' Bergen stared sullenly at him. 'Come on – *who was it?* And why?'

Bergen glanced at the guard. The guard wasn't listening. He was absorbed by the soap on his pocket viddy; tiny television figures in his palm flickered through a miniature choreography of petty conflicts. Bergen took a deep breath, and looked Spector in the eyes. 'Okay. I don't care anymore . . . I *want* you to know. Sonia, Torrence and I – we were part of the same . . . organization. Sonia Chesterton did it because her brother Charlie was videoframed. Torrence because he was in the Black Muslim Brotherhood – they lost their top four officers to a videoframe-up. Me, I did it – planned it all – because I saw one too many innocent people die . . . We thought if you, a Senator were videoframed, condemned, *killed* – afterwards we'd release the truth, we'd clear you, and that'd focus public attention on the issue. Force an investigation. And – it was vengeance. We held you responsible. For all those victims.'

Spector nodded like something mechanical. Said softly: 'Oh, yes. I am responsible . . . And now I'm going to get off . . . And it'll be blamed on your people. Your organization . . . They'll say it was an isolated incident . . . They'll pressure me to shut up. And, once I was on the outside, where things are comfortable, I probably would.'

And the realization came at him like the onrushing of a great black wall; it fell on him like a tidal wave: *How many innocent people died for my ambition? A thousand? Two thousand?*

'Yes. They'll pass it off as an "isolated incident",' Bergen muttered. 'Congratulations, Spector, you son of a bitch. Sonia and Torrence sacrificed themselves for *nothing*.' His voice broke. He went on, visibly straining for control. 'You're going free.'

But the gnawing thing in Spector wouldn't let him go free. And he knew it would never let him go. Never. (Though some part of him said, *Don't do it! Survive!* But that part of him was broken, could speak only in a raspy whimper, as the other part said, aloud:) 'Bergen – wait. Go to Burridge. Tell him you know all about the Sorenson incident – and tell him you'll release what you know about her, if he tells anyone what he's found out about those tapes before tomorrow. He'll stay quiet.'

'But the restraining order – '

'Tear it up. And come with me – you've got to explain to Sparks that you were wrong about something . . .'

Spector walked out onto the stage. Glanced once at the cameras and the studio audience beyond the bullet-proof glass. Pointed the pistol loaded with blanks at the grinning man in the cowboy hat at the other end of the stage, and walked toward him, and toward the big gun in the man's hand. Spector smiling softly, thinking: *This is the only way I'll ever go free . . .*

Triggering

It was one of those protectiplated Manhattan brown-
stones, rewired in the Nineties, every square inch evenly
coated with a thin, flexible preserving plastic. The old
building was a jarring sight, snugged between the glassy
highrises. It was the distant past all neatly wrapped up
and embalmed. It seemed appropriate, considering the
job I'd been sent there to do.

I went up the slippery hall stairs, one hand on the
plastic-coated wooden railing, wondering what unpro-
tected wood felt like. They'd even preserved the quaint
twentieth-century graffiti spray-painted in bright crimson
on the faded walls: NUKE REAGAN BEFORE HE NUKES YOU
and DEATH TO THE COMPROMISE SOCIALISTS.

I passed 2-D's doorbell. An eye goggled at the old-
fashioned glass peephole. The place apparently had no
inspection cameras. The door opened – on real hinges –
and I was looking down at a four-year-old boy. Behind
him was the chair he'd been standing on. He pushed it
aside.

He glanced at my clingsuit, and at the department's
suit-and-tie stenciled sharply on the front (the white
hankie and the tie clip were beginning to fade), and
chuckled grimly. He noticed my dark eyes, my short black
hair, my duskiness, and his recognition of me as an
Americanized East Indian showed in his face: a flicker of
suspicion. It was a very adult expression.

I stared. They hadn't told me what the Tangle was. I
had a feeling it began here. With the boy. The boy had
curly brown hair, big blue eyes, a pug nose, and pursed

lips. He wore a formal spiral-leg suit. It was an adult's suit, in miniature. In his mouth was clamped a black cigarette holder containing a Sherman's Real Tobacco burnt nearly to the butt. Smoke geysered at intervals from his nostrils.

A midget? But he wasn't. He was a four-year-old boy.

'You're staring at me,' he said abruptly, his voice high-pitched but carefully articulated, accented almost aristo-cratically. 'Is there some specific reason for this intrusive scrutiny, or are you simply a man who practices his penetrating glance on any unsuspecting citizen he encounters?'

'I'm Ramja,' I said, nodding politely. 'I'm from the Department of Transmigratology. And your name?' I covered my astonishment well.

He frowned at his cigarette, which had gone out. 'Care for a smoke?'

'I don't smoke, thanks.'

'Self-righteous, the way you say that. But you Federal-men are always self-righteous bastards. There was another here, fellow named Hextupper or something. You're the followup. Very orderly. You can go and dance with Dante for all I care, friend. But if you must know – ' he gestured me inside and moved to close the door behind me ' – my name's Conrad Frampton. How-do-you-do, salutations, and et cetera.'

'You're overcompensating your self-consciousness about being a little boy,' I said, returning his hostility.

He shrugged. 'Could be. If you were a forty-one-year-old-man trapped in a four-year-old body, you'd feel like overcompensating, too. You'd feel like leaping out the window now and then. Believe me.' He led me to a couch, and I sat beside him.

'When did you die?' I asked, watching him. He made me nervous.

'I died in 1982,' he said, not even blinking. 'Care for a drink?'

'No, thanks. You go ahead.'

'Damned right I will.' There was a low yellow table beside the couch. He punched for a cocktail on the table's programmer.

I looked around. The room wasn't antique; it seemed like a broken promise after the outside of the building. It was a standard decorbubble, done in various shades of pastel yellow, the curved walls blending cornerlessly into the concave ceiling; the floor was more or less flat but of the same spongy synthetic. The walls, floor, ceiling, and furniture were all of a piece, shaped by the inhabitants. The room spoke to me about those inhabitants.

'Who else lives here?' I asked. The department had told me nothing about the people involved in the Tangle, except the address. It's better that way.

Conrad took a silvery cigarette case from a table, his infant fingers struggling for smooth movements; he lit a thin Sherman sulkily with a thumbnail lighter. 'A couple of degenerates live here,' he said, blowing smoke rings, 'who call themselves my parents. *Fawther* is a musician. George Marvell, snooty concert guitarist. Plays one of those hideous flesh-guitars. They're both flesh machine fetishists. Mother works at the genvats, helping make more genetic-manipulation horrors. She's not so bad, really, though it nauseates me when she looks at me with her big brown eyes welling, hoping I'll turn into her widdoo Ahmed again. Her name's Senya. They named me Ahmed, but I make them call me by my real name.'

'I take it you don't approve of flesh machines.' I sensed there was a flesh machine near at hand. A big one.

He made a something-smells-bad face. 'Soulless things. Ugly. I don't know which is worse, the flesh guitar or that living *pit* they call a bedroom. They *are* soulless, aren't they? You're from the Department of Transmigratology. So you're allegedly an expert on souls. What's your stand on flesh machines, old boy?'

'Depends on what you mean by *soul*. For us, a "soul" is a plasma field composed of tightly interwoven sub-atomic particles, capable of recording its host's sensory input. And capable of traveling from body to body, evolving psychically so that species survival is more likely. It's not religion. It's a function of the first law of thermo-dynamics, but we use certain *mystical* techniques to work with it. Training for seeing life patterns, that sort of thing. Karma-buildup release. But if we use words, like *karma* and *soul* in our reports to the National Academy of Sciences, we'll lose our funding. It took us twelve years of regressing people, and tracing facts, to get them to admit it was a bona fide science.'

'I don't know about science. But in my current circumstances . . .' He made a bitter face. 'I'm forced to believe in reincarnation.' He looked at me. 'Why the hell are you here? Level with me.'

'We had a report of a rather nasty Tangle here. The lines of spiritual evolution tangled. Sometimes a gross emotional trauma from one life surfaces in the next. The people involved in the trauma are reborn in close circumstances in the next life, and the next, until the thing's cleared up.'

I considered telling him more. I might have said I came because a Tangle needs a Triggering. And they sent me, Ramja, specifically, because I'm part of the Tangle. Not sure how yet. But I'm one of the few department staffers who can't remember his last life. Part of it's repressed irretrievably. The computer model connected me with this Tangle.

But I didn't say that. Instead: 'As for flesh machines, I don't know how much so-called soul they have. Or even how much awareness. The department believes that they're part of the evolution of the lower orders. Animal minds, animal souls.' I shook my head. 'I'm not sure, Conrad, what do you remember of your death?'

He shakily relit his cigarette. 'I . . . I drowned. Scuba . . . uh, scuba-diving. Sickening circumstances. Trapped underwater. My air ran out. Big pain in my chest. Gigantic buzzing in my ears. And a white rush. Next thing I remember is hearing this sad guitar song. Only it was a flesh guitar; so it sounded like they do – like a guitar crossed with a human voice. I looked around, and there was Senya looming over me, her arms outstretched, and I was staggering toward her. It must have looked like toddling. And then the guitar *screamed*. That's what brought me to myself. I remembered who I was . . . My *real* parents are Laura and Marvin Frampton. Were. They died together in a nursing-home fire, I'm told.'

He crossed his small legs and propped an elbow on one knee, his cigarette holder poised continentally between thumb and forefinger. 'George would like to have me adopted. He doesn't like me, and neither does his room. But then the room is rude to George, too. It shakes when he strokes it. Unpleasantly. I'll show you the damn thing.'

We got up. I followed him to a doorway on the right and into the bedroom.

The room was in pain.

The cavelike walls were all rosy membranes, touched with blue, pulsing. Across the room and near the living floor was a blue-black bruise, swollen and pustulant, a half-meter across. Conrad carefully didn't look at it.

'You're just full of hostility, Conrad,' I said softly. 'You've been kicking the wall there. Or hitting it with something.'

He turned to me with a very adult look of outrage. 'If I have, it's in self-defense. I sleep in the next room, but I can feel this thing *radiating* at me even in there. It won't let me sleep! It wants something from me. I'm half-crazy living in this kid's body anyway, and this thing makes it worse. I can feel it nagging at me.'

'And you kicked it to make it stop. In the same spot. Repeatedly.'

'What do you know about it?' Conrad muttered, turning away.

I felt uncomfortable in the room, too. It wasn't hostility that I felt from the walls. It was the shock of recognition.

The moist ceiling was not far over my head, curvingly soft, and damp. It wasn't much like a womb. It was more like a boneless head turned inside out. The wall at the narrower end, to my left, contained the outlines of a huge unfinished face. The nose was there, but flattened, broad as my chest. The eyes were forever closed, milky oblongs locked behind translucent lids.

The room was a genvat creation, a recombinant-DNA organism expanded to fill an ordinary bedroom. The old bedroom's windows were behind the eyes; the light from the windows shining through them as if through lampshades, defining the outsize capillaries in the lids. The face's lips were on the floor, puckered toward the ceiling. The lips were the room's bed, disproportionately wide. They were soft looking, about the size of a single-bed; they would open out for two. There would be no opening beneath them, no teeth.

'It was grown from Senya's cells, you know,' Conrad said. He deliberately ground out his still-smoldering cigarette on the room's floor. The fleshy walls quivered.

I controlled the impulse to box Conrad's ears as he continued. 'There's a tank of nutrifluid outside the window. Personally, I think the creature is disgusting. I can hear it breathe. I can smell it. You should see the lips move when Senya stretches out on them. Ugh!'

The room's odor was briny, smelling faintly of Woman. It breathed through its nose with a gentle sigh.

Returning to the main room, Conrad said, 'Sure you won't have a drink?'

'This time I will have one, thanks.' The womb-room had shaken me.

I stood on a secret brink. My heart was beating quickly and irregularly. Waves of fear swept through me. I focused on them, brought them to a peak, shuddered, and let the fear vaporize in the light of internal self-awareness.

I sipped my plastic cup of martini, for the moment relaxing. Sitting beside Conrad, I said, 'You said something about George's guitar being sick.'

Conrad smirked. 'George is hoping his guitar will be better today. But it won't sing for him. I know it won't. It'll start screaming again as soon as he plays it. It sounds vicious – the most awful screams you can imagine. He may have to go back to playing electric guitar.'

'It's screaming of its own volition? Maybe it's allergic to him.'

'Possible. It doesn't scream when Senya plays it.'

I felt my trance level deepening. The outlines of the furniture seemed to hallucinogenically expand, softly strobing. I glimpsed ghostly human figures on flickering paths; the apartment's inhabitants had left their life patterns on the room's electric field. In those subtly glowing lines I could see the Triggering foreshadowed.

'Conrad,' I said carefully, trying not to show my excitement, 'tell me about your life just before transition. Give me details of the death itself.' I waited, breathless.

Conrad was pleased. He lit another cigarette and watched the smoke curl up as he spoke. 'I was a copy editor for a book publisher. I was a good one, but I was becoming bored with the work. I'd accumulated a lot of vacation time; so I accepted Billy Lilac's invitation to go on a cruise with him and his friends. I felt sort of funny about it, because I was having an affair with his wife. But she insisted that it would be good because we would remain casual for the duration of the trip – four days – and that would cool Billy's suspicions about us. Billy was rolling in the Right Stuff. He owned a lucrative chain of fast-food restaurants.

'His yacht had what he called a mousetrap aquarium built into it. The boat had a deep draft, and by pressing a button, he opened a chamber in the hull. Water would be sucked into it, along with little fish and sometimes squid or even a small shark. Then the gates at the bottom would close, temporarily trapping the creatures in there, and we would watch them through a glass pane in the deck of the hold.

'There were five of us on the cruise. Lana Lilac, Billy's teenaged wife, thirty years younger than Billy; his secretary, Lucille Winchester; Lucille's son Lancer – '

'Who? Who did you say? The last two?' My interruption was too eager.

Conrad looked at me strangely. 'Lucille and Lancer Winchester,' he said impatiently. '*Anyway*, Billy asked a bunch of us to go down and scare some octopi into the aquarium. We were over a certain Jamaican reef where they were quite common. So we went down in scuba gear. There were me and Lana and – '

'And Lucille. You three went down,' I interrupted. My head contained a whirlpool. *Calm. Perceive objectively. Perceive in the perspective of time. Evolutionary patterns.*

The mummified hurt. Tonight I would resolve the hurt.

'You three went down,' I repeated, 'and when you approached the gate where the hull opened, good old Billy pressed the button that opens the gate and makes the current that pulls things in, and all three of you were sucked into the mousetrap aquarium. He closed the gate behind you, and then he stood in the hold, over your heads, watching. And you ran out of air.'

For a few minutes I couldn't talk. I felt as if I were choking, though it hadn't been me who'd drowned on that occasion. I drowned later, choking to death on my own vomit; drug overdose. Years later.

Conrad's irritation visibly became astonishment.

But I was only peripherally aware of him. I was seeing myself, as fifteen-year-old Lancer Winchester, hands cuffed behind me, lying facedown on the glass floor, watching as my mother drowned. My gasping and my tears misted the glass, but somehow the blur emphasized their frantic movements as they tried to pry the gate. Their frenzied hand signals. Their fingers clawing at the glass.

While Billy Lilac stood with his hands in his pocket beside me, like a man mildly amused by a zoo, chuckling occasionally and sweetly chatting to me, politely explaining that he'd killed Conrad because Conrad had been having an affair with Lana. And he'd killed my mother because she helped them to keep the secret and had permitted Lana and Conrad to use her apartment.

I'd expected him to kill me. But he simply uncuffed me and put me ashore. He knew that my history of emotional disturbance destroyed my credibility. No one would believe me when there were three others testifying differently. He'd bribed his two crewpeople handsomely. They claimed a mechanical failure had caused the gate to open prematurely, and Billy had been on deck and hadn't seen it. They'd been with him the whole time. Craig and Judy Lormer, husband and wife, were his crew. Only, after a while, Judy began to have nightmares about the people drowning in the hold. Judy had threatened to go to the police. I knew this, because Billy came to me in the asylum and told me in the visitors room.

He enjoyed talking about it. Billy was the quintessential son of a bitch. 'I drowned Judy in the aquarium in my house, Lancer,' he'd said, his voice mild and pleasant. Like a taxidermist talking shop.

'You want to explain yourself, friend, hmm?' Conrad said, in the present.

I was thinking about my own death. I'd been in and out of institutions for the four years after my mother drowned. Treated for paranoid schizophrenia and drug abuse – the drug abuse, heroin, was real – till I wondered whether I *had* hallucinated Billy's quiet enjoyment as he stood on the glass, watching the bubbles, forced from exhausted lungs, shatter on the pane between his feet.

I died of an overdose in 1987.

'No coincidences, Conrad,' I said suddenly. 'I'm here because I knew you in your last life. I was Lancer Winchester. I watched you die. You and Lana Lilac and Mother. Strangling under glass.' I paused to clear my throat. I tranced to calmness. 'Really, Conrad,' I said distantly, gazing down the corridors of time, 'you ought to slow down on the drinking.'

Ignoring my advice he gulped another cocktail, swearing softly.

I turned my eyes toward the doors, first the front door and then the door to the bedroom. The orifice in the womb-room had contracted a little, twitching, so that its blue-pink flesh showed at the open door's corners.

I felt its excitement subliminally, and I shared its half-slumbering yearning. Conrad felt it, too, and glanced at it, irritated.

But only the womb-room and I were aware that George and Senya Marvell were climbing the plastic-coated steps to the apartment. Now I felt them stopping on the landing to rest, and to quarrel. I felt the Trigger near. I hadn't quite located it.

'Conrad,' I began, 'Senya is – '

The door opened. Senya came in, toting something behind her. She and the man I took to be George were carrying a large transparent plasglass case between them. Within the case's thick liquids, something wallowed like a pink sea animal. A flesh guitar. An expensive one, too.

But I could hardly take my eyes from Senya. She was lovely. I had a disquietingly powerful sense of *déjà vu*, taking in her strong, willowy shape; a campy Old Glory flag pattern worked into the thick spill of flaxen hair flipped onto her right shoulder. Something in the gauntness of her face excited me. There was both curiosity and empathy in her expression, out of place with her black, clinging Addams Family Revival gown and her transparent spike heels.

'Who the hell is *he*?' George puffed, looking me over as they carried the flesh guitar's case into the bedroom.

'He'd be the man from the Department of Transmigratology, George,' she replied offhandedly. 'I had them send someone over about, umm, about Conrad.'

The *déjà vu* resurged when I listened to her voice. The tone of it wasn't familiar. The familiarity was in the way she used it.

George and Senya returned from the bedroom. In contrast to Senya, George was stocky and pallid, his hair permaset into a solid yellow block over his head. His smoky-blue eyes swept over me, then flicked angrily at Conrad. 'The kid's drunk again.' His voice, when he spoke to me, was a distillation of condescension: 'So you think you can clear the garbage from the kid's head here?'

'If there is any garbage to be cleared in this room,' Conrad interrupted, 'it's coming out of your mouth, George.'

As George bent to punch for a drink, his motions set off reverberations containing within them, coded, all the actions of his lifetime. And implications of earlier lifetimes.

'Actually, I'm not here to clear anything from Conrad in particular,' I said, crossing my legs and leaning back against the couch. Watching Senya, I went on, 'In this lifetime my name's Ramja; in the last it was Lancer.' Her eyes met mine. She was puzzled. I hadn't hit the Trigger yet. I smiled at her, felt a flush of pleasure run through me when she smiled back.

'No, George, I'm here,' I continued, trying to keep eagerness from my voice, 'to deal with a rather complex transmigrational entanglement. It results from a past-life trauma shared by everyone here. A memory that brought us back together. For Triggering. And the funny thing is, George, I don't really have to *do* much of anything. My being here completes the karmic equation. I'm not sure how it's going to trigger.' I sipped my drink and asked, 'How did your guitar perform today, George?'

George just shook his head at me. He was close to throwing me out.

Senya answered for him. 'It screamed. As usual! Every time George touched it.' She looked at George as if she could understand perfectly why *anyone* would scream if George touched them.

'I rather suspected that,' I said. 'And I suspect, too, that there's a growing alienation between you and George lately, Senya. Since the day the guitar started screaming – and Conrad appeared in your son.'

'What the bad-credit do *you* know about it?' George blurted. He was tense with fear. He, too, could feel the Triggering coming.

'The man's right, George,' Conrad put in, grinding his cigarette out on the table, his little-boy fingers trembling.

'The guitar's screaming and my, ah, my *coming out* came close together. And then the tension between you and Senya got nasty. I saw it. But it's not like it's *my* fault. The damn guitar may not have more than the brains of a squirrel, but it knows a creep when it senses one. George was playing it, and this scream came out of it. It finally got fed up with the creep.'

George said suddenly, 'If you think there's some link between *him* – ' he jabbed a thumb at Conrad without looking at him ' – and what's wrong with my guitar, then maybe you can – I dunno, uh – clear it away so the guitar works again?'

'Maybe,' I said, smiling. 'Let's go into the bedroom. And – clear it away.'

A moment later we were standing around the plasglass case, beside the bed-sized, upthrust lips at one end of the womb-room. Senya opened the case and lifted the guitar free as the floor's lips quivered and the room's walls twitched. The guitar dried almost immediately. It was the approximate shape of an acoustic guitar, but composed of human flesh, covered in pink-white skin, showing blue veins. The neck of the guitar was actually fashioned after a human arm, with the elbow fused so that it was always outstretched. The tendonlike strings were stretched from the truncated fingers, which served as string pegs. But the guitar's small brain kept the strings always in tune. Its lines were soft, feminine, its lower end suggesting a woman's hips. Where the sound hole would be on an acoustic guitar was a woman's mouth, permanently wide open, its lips thin and pearly-pink; toothless, but with a small tongue and throat. There were no eyes, no other physical suggestions of humanity.

Senya held it in her arms, leaning its lower end on her lifted knee, her right foot propped on the brim of the open guitar case. She played an E chord, her fingers lightly brushing the tendonlike strings. The strings vibrated, and the guitar's mouth sang the note. The tone was hauntingly human, melancholy, sympathetic. An odd look came over Senya's face. She glanced up at me, and then at Conrad, who reeled, drunk, to one side. And back at me.

'Well?' George said.

'You play the guitar, George,' I said. 'Go on. I think all the integers of the equation are here, in place. You play it.'

'No, thanks,' he said, looking at the pink, infantlike guitar in his wife's arms.

I could feel the lines of karmic influence tightening the room. Unconsciously we'd moved into the symmetrical formation around the glass case: myself, Conrad, Senya, George, and the guitar, which Senya held over the case, her arms trembling with its weight. We were the five points of a pentacle, encircled by the waiting, brooding presence of the womb-room.

'Go on, George,' said Conrad, slurring his words. 'Don't be a simpering coward. Play the guitar.' Like a defiant midget, he sneered up at George.

George snorted and took the guitar from Senya. Its strings contracted with a faint whine when he touched it. He strummed a chord and relaxed as the notes came out normally. He strummed again, shrugged, and glanced nervously at the living blue-pink ceiling and the bruise low on the ceiling walls.

The guitar's scream shattered the glass of the window hidden behind the flesh wall and made me clap my hands over my ears. The walls rippled and from somewhere gave a long sigh. Blood ran from the lower edge of the closed eyelids, like crimson tears. An ugly, ripping sound made me look up; the ceiling had ruptured. Blood rained on us in fine droplets. Conrad began to laugh hysterically, his voice piping manically. His eyes rolled back, into his head.

George flung the guitar down furiously. I had to look away as the flesh guitar struck the edge of its case. It howled again as something vital within it snapped. It rolled onto the floor, facedown, moaning. The room moaned with it. Panic enlarging his eyes, George looked at each of us. He looked as if we'd suddenly become strange to him. He was seeing us differently now, all his self-assurance gone.

I said, loudly, staring hard at George, 'Yours was the sort of crime that required a major effort at karmic justice, Billy.'

'You call him Billy . . .' Conrad said, staring at George.

'Billy Lilac,' I said, smiling at Senya. 'By now you should be remembering. And wondering, maybe, why a man should be punished for things he did in another life. Was Billy the same man as George, really? He is the same man, at the root. Remember what he did? That sort of crime, Billy . . . ah! The womb-room remembers, on some level. The guitar remembers. Their brains are small, but their memories are long. You drowned three people, and, perhaps worse, you chuckled while you watched. You destroyed my life. Me? I was Lancer Winchester.' I waited for the full impact of my words to hit the others.

The red mist sifted down on us. The floor's lips snapped open and shut soundlessly. Senya and Conrad listened raptly, their eyes strange. 'You killed my mother, Billy. But she's here with us. Everyone you killed is here. It's going to be a big shock to the genvat industry when I tell them we've got evidence that human spirit-plasma fields can incarnate into flesh machines. It will shake up my department, too. My mother? She incarnated into the room that surrounds us, Billy. And Lana is here in Senya.

The guitar woke up in your arms one day and remembered what you had done. So it screamed. The guitar is Judy Lormer. Remember Judy. The crewwoman you drowned when she threatened to talk?'

I didn't mention the fact that young Lancer had been genuinely in love with Lana Lilac.

George, aka Billy Lilac, wasn't listening. He was backing into a corner, making funny little subhuman sounds and swiping at his eyes. Overwhelmed by the sudden remembrance I'd triggered. Realization: who he was and what he'd done and how it had always been a shaping influence on his life.

The room's walls were closing in around us. The room itself was undergoing contractions, squeezing us. We felt waves of air pressuring us, slapping us toward the door. We staggered.

Howling, his voice almost lost in the room's keening and the dis-chording of the dying guitar, Conrad struggled on all fours after us. He looked like a frightened child.

Senya and I stumbled out into the main room, both of us fighting panic, shuddering with identity disorientation.

Choking, I turned and looked through the shrinking entranceway. The aperture was irising shut. I glimpsed George standing over the guitar case. The bleeding flesh guitar yowled at his feet. George swayed toward us as the room got smaller around him, his arms outstretched plaintively, face white, his expression alternating terror and confusion, mouth open in a scream lost in the room's own clamor. Behind him, the fused lower edges of the lids over the room's eyes tore free; the lids snapped abruptly open. The eyes glared, pupils brimmed with blood. The room contracted again, and George tripped. He fell against the open plasglass guitar case, facedown over churning liquids. The aperture closed.

'Ahmed!' Senya shouted, recovering herself. 'Ahmed's trapped!'

She was calling Conrad by the name she'd given him. The doorway was blocked by a convex wall of tense, damp human tissue; it was puckered into a sort of closed cervix at the middle. But slowly the 'cervix' dilated. The top of a head poked through. Conrad's head. His eyes were closed, his face blank. Gradually the room pressed him out. He was unconscious but breathing. Senya held him in her arms. His clothing was badly torn and slick-wet with the room's blood. When he opened his eyes a minute later, he said nothing, but gazed up at her, all trace of Conrad gone. Conrad had withdrawn to whatever closet of the human brain it is that erstwhile personalities are kept in.

The womb-room had shrunk to a bruised, agonized ball of flesh less than two meters across, clamped rigidly around the plasglass case. It died, mangled by the corners of the big glass case, and inwardly burst from its own convulsions.

George, Billy Lilac, died within it. He'd been forced by the shrinking enclosure into the glass case, into its glutinous, transparent fluids. He died under glass. He died by drowning.

Six Kinds of Darkness

Charlie'd say, 'I'm into it once or twice – but you, you got a jones for it, man.' And Angelo'd snicker and say, 'Gives my life purpose, man. Gives my life direction.'

You could smell the place, the Hollow Head, from two blocks away. Anyway, you could if you were strung out on it. The other people on the street probably couldn't make out the smell from the background of monoxides, the broken-battery smell of acid rain, the itch of syntharette smoke, the oily rot of the river. But a user could pick out that tease of Amyl Tryptaline, thinking, *find it like a needle in a hay-stack*. And he'd snort, and then go reverent-serious, thinking about the needle in question . . . the needle in the nipple . . .

It was on East 121st Street, a half-block from the East River. If you stagger out of the place at night, you'd better find your way to the lighted end of the street fast, because the leeches crawled out of the river after dark, slug-creeping up the walls onto the cornices of the old buildings; they sensed your bodyheat, and an eight-inch ugly brute lamprey-thing could fall from the roof, hit your neck with a wet *slap* and inject you with paralyzing toxins; you fall over and its leech cronies come and drain you dry.

When Charlie turned onto the street it was just sunset; the leeches weren't out of the river yet, but Charlie scanned the rooftops anyway. Clustered along the rooftops were the shanties . . .

The immigrants had swarmed to this mecca of disenchantment till New York became another Mexico City,

ringed and overgrown with shanties . . . shacks of clap-
board, tin, cardboard, protected with flattened cans and
wrapper plastic. Every tenement rooftop in Manhattan
mazed with shanties, sometimes shanties on shanties, till
the weight collapsed the roofs and the old buildings caved
in, the crushed squatters simply left dying in the rubble –
firemen and Emergency teams rarely set foot outside the
sentried, walled-in havens of the midtown class.

Charlie was almost there. It was a motherfucker of a
neighborhood, which is why he had the knife in his boot-
sheath. But what scared him was the Place. Doing some
Room at the Place. The Hollow Head. His heart was
pumping and he was shaky but he wasn't sure if it was
from fear or anticipation or if, with the Hollow Head,
you could tell those two apart. But to keep his nerve up,
he had to look away from the Place, as he got near it;
tried to focus on the rest of the street. Some dumbfuck
pollyanna had planted saplings on the sidewalk, in the
squares of exposed dirt where the original trees had
stood. But the acid rain had chewed the leaves and twigs
away; what was left was stark as old TV antennas . . .

Torchglow from the roofs; and a melange of noises that
seemed to ooze down like something greasy from an
overflowing pot. Smells of tarry wood burning; dogfood
smells of cheap canned food cooking. And then he was
standing in front of the Hollow Head. A soot-blackened
townhouse; its Victorian façade of cherubims recarved by
acid rain into dainty gargoyles. The windows bricked
over, the one between them streaked gray on black from
acid erosion.

The building to the right was hunchbacked with shacks;
the roof to the left glowed from oil-barrel fires. But the
roof of the Hollow Head was dark and flat, somehow

regal in its sinister austerity. No one shacked on the Hollow Head.

He took a deep breath and told himself, 'Don't hurry through it, savor it this time,' and went in. Hoping that Angelo had waited for him.

Up to the door, wait while the camera scanned you. The camera taking in Charlie Chesterton's triple mohawk, each fin a different color; Charlie's gaunt face, spiked transplas jacket, and customized mirrorshades. He heard the tone telling him the door had unlocked. He opened it, smelled the Amyl Tryptaline, felt his bowels contract with suppressed excitement. Down a red-lit hallway, thick black paint on the walls, the turpentine smell of AT getting stronger. Angelo wasn't there; he'd gone upstairs already. Charlie hoped Angelo could handle it alone . . . The girl in the banker's window at the end of the hall – the girl wearing the ski mask, the girl with the sarcastic receptionist's lilt in her voice – took his card, gave him the Bone Music receptor, credded him in. Another tone, admission to Door Seven, the first level. He walked down to Seven, turned the knob, stepped through and felt it immediately; the tingle, the rush of alertness, the chemically-induced sense of belonging, four pleasurable sensations rolling through him and coalescing. It was just an empty room with the stairs at the farther end; soft pink lighting, the usual cryptic palimpsest of graffiti on the walls.

He inhaled deeply, felt the Amyl Tryptaline hit him again; the pink glow intensified; the edges of the room softened, he heard his own heartbeat like a distant beatbox. A barbed wisp of anxiety twined his spine (wondering, *Where's Angelo, he's usually hanging in the first room, scared to go to the second alone, well, shit, good riddance*) and he experienced a paralytic seizure of sheer sensation. The Bone Music receptor was digging into his palm; he wiped the sweat from it and attached it to the sound wire extruding from the bone back of his left ear – and the music shivered into him . . . it was music you *felt* more than heard; his acoustic nerve picked up the thudding beat, the bass, a distorted veneer of the synthesizer. But most of the music was routed through the bone of his skull, conducted down through the spinal column, the other bones. It was a music of shivery sensations, like a funnybone sensation, sickness sensation, chills and hot flashes like influenza but it was a sickness that caressed, viruses licking at your privates and you wanted to come and throw up at the same time. He'd seen deaf people dancing at rock concerts; they could feel the vibrations from the loud music; could feel the music they couldn't hear. It was like that but with a deep, deep humping brutality, like having sex with an obviously syphilitic whore and enjoying it more because you knew she was diseased. The music shivered him from his paralysis, nudged him forward. He climbed the stairs . . .

Bone Music reception improved as he climbed, so he could make out the lyrics, a gristly voice singing from inside Charlie's skull:

> Six kinds of darkness,
>   spilling down over me,
> Six kinds of darkness,
>   sticky with energy.

Charlie got to the next landing, stepped into the second room.

Second room used electric field stimulation of nerve ends; the metal grids on the wall transmitted signals that stimulated the neurons, initiating pleasurable nerve impulses; other signals went directly to the dorsal areas in the hypothalamus, resonating in the brain's pleasure center . . .

Charlie cried out, and fell to his knees in the infantile purity of his gratitude. The room glowed with benevolence; the barren, dirty room with its semen-stained walls, cracked ceilings, naked red bulb on a fraying wire. As always he had to fight himself to keep from licking the walls, the floor. He was a fetishist for this room, for its splintering wooden floors, the mathematical absolutism of the grid-patterns in the gray metal transmitters set into the wall. Turn off those transmitters and the room was shabby, even ugly, and pervaded with stench; with the transmitters on, it seemed subtly intricate, starkly sexy, bondage gear in the form of interior decoration, and the smell was a ribald delight.

(The Hollow Head was drug paraphernalia you could walk into. The building itself was the spike, the hookah, the sniff-tube.)

And then the room's second phase cut in: the transmitters stimulated the motor cortex, the reticular formation in the brainstem, the nerve pathways of the extra-pyramidal system, in precise patterns computer formulated to mesh with the ongoing Bone Music. Making him dance. Dance across the room, feeling he was caught in a choreographed whirlwind (flashing: genitals interlocking, pumping, male and female, male and male, female and female, tongues and cocks and fingers pushing into pink bifurcations, contorting purposefully to guide between fleshy globes, the thrusting a heavy downhill flow like an emission of igneous mud, but firm pink mud, the bodies rounded off, headless, Magritte torsos going end to end together, organs blindly nosing into the wet receptacles of otherness), semen trickling down his legs inside his pants, dancing, helplessly dancing, thinking it was a delicious epilepsy, as he was marionetted up the stairs, to the next floor, the final room . . .

At the landing just before the third room, the transmitters cut off, and Charlie sagged, gasping, clutching for the banister, the black-painted walls reeling around him. He gulped air, and prayed for the strength to turn away from the third room, because he knew it would leave him fried, yeah, badly crashed and deeply burnt-out. He turned off the receptor for a respite of quiet . . . In that moment of weariness and self-doubt he found himself wondering where Angelo was, had Angelo really gone onto the third room alone? Ange was prone to identity crises under the Nipple Needle. If he'd gone alone – little Angelo Demario with his rockabilly hair and spurious pugnacity – Angelo would sink, and lose it completely . . . And what would they do with people who were overdosed on an identity hit? Dump the body in the river, he supposed . . .

He heard a yell mingling ecstasy and horror, coming from an adjacent room, as another Head customer took a nipple . . . that made up his mind: like seeing someone eat making you realize you're hungry. He gathered together the tatters of his energy, switched on his receptor, and went through the door.

The Bone Music shuddered through him, too strong now that he was undercut, weakened by the first rooms. Nausea wallowed through him.

> The darkness of the Arctic,
>   two months into the night.
> Darkness of the Eclipse,
>   forgetting of all light.

Angelo wasn't in the room and Charlie was selfishly glad as he took off his jacket, rolled up his left sleeve, approached the black rubber nipple protruding from the metal breast at waist-height on the wall. As he stepped up to it, pressed the hollow of his elbow against the nipple; felt the computer-guided needle probe for his mainline and fire the ID drug into him . . .

The genetic and neurochemical essence of a woman. They claimed it was synthesized. Right then he didn't give an angel's winged asshole where it came from; it was rushing through him in majestic waves of titanic intimacy. You could taste her, smell her, feel what it felt like to be her (they said it was an imaginary her, modeled on someone real, not really from a person . . .).

Felt the shape of her personality superimposed on you so for the first time you weren't burdened with your own identity, you could find oblivion in someone else, like identifying with a fictional protagonist but infinitely more real . . .

But oh shit. It wasn't a *her*. It was a *him*. And Charlie knew instantly that it was Angelo. They had shot him up with Angelo's distilled neurochemistry – his personality, memory, despairs, and burning urges. He saw himself in flashes as Angelo had seen him . . . And he knew, too, that this was no synthesis, that he'd found out what they did with those who died here, who blundered and OD'd: they dropped them in some vat, broke them down, distilled them and molecularly linked them with the synthcoke and shot them into other customers . . . Into Charlie . . .

He couldn't hear himself scream, over the Bone Music (*Darkness of an iron cask, lid down and bolted tight*). He didn't remember running for the exit stairs (*And three more kinds of darkness, three I cannot tell*), down the hall, (*Making six kinds of darkness, Lord please make me well*) out into the street, running, hearing the laughter from the shantyrats on the roofs watching him go.

Him and Angelo running down the street, in one body.

As Charlie told himself: 'I'm kicking this thing. It's over. I shot up my best friend. I'm through with it.'

Hoping to God it was true. *Lord please make me well.*

Bottles swished down from the rooftops and smashed to either side of him. And he kept running.

He felt strange.

He could feel his body. Not like usual. He could feel it like it was a weight on him, like an attachment. Not the weight of fatigue – he felt too damn eerie to feel tired – but a weight of sheer alienness. It was too big. It was all awkward and its metabolism was pitched too low, sluggish, and it was . . .

It was the way his body felt for Angelo.

Angelo wasn't there, in him. But then again he was. And Charlie felt Angelo as a nastily foreign, squeaky, distortion membrane between him and the world around him.

He passed someone on the street, saw them distorted through the membrane, their faces funhouse-mirror twisted as they looked at him – and they looked startled.

The strange feelings must show on his face. And in his running.

Maybe they could see Angelo. Maybe Angelo was oozing out of him, out of his face. He could feel it. Yeah. He could feel Angelo bleeding from his pores, dripping from his nose, creeping from his ass.

A sonic splash of: *Gidgy, you wanna do a video hookup with me? (Gidgy replying:) No, that shit's grotty Ange, last time we did that I was sick for two days. I don't like pictures pushed into my brain. Couldn't we just have, you know, sex? (She touches his arm.)*

God, I'm gonna lose myself in Angelo, Charlie thought. Gotta run, sweat him out of me.

Splash of: *Angelo, if you keep going around with those people, the police or those SA people are going to break your stupid head. (Angelo's voice:) Ma, get off it, you don't understand what's going on, the country's getting scared, they think there's gonna be a nuclear war, everyone's lining up to kiss the Presidential ass 'cause they think she's all that stands between us and the fucking Russians – (His mother's voice:) Angelo don't use that language in front of your sister, not everyone talks like they do on TV –*

Too heavy, body's too heavy, his run is funny, can't run anymore, but I gotta sweat him out –

Flash pictures to go with the splash voices now: *Motion-rollicking shot of sidewalk seen from a car window as they drive through a private-cop zone, SA bulls in mirror helmets walking along in twos in this high-rent neighborhood, turning their glassy-bland assumption of your guilt toward the car, the world revolves as the car turns a corner, they come to a checkpoint, the new Federal ID cards are demanded, shown, they get through, feeling of relief, there isn't a call out on them yet . . . blur of images, then focus on a face walking up to the car. Charlie Chesterton. Long, skinny, goofy-looking guy, self-serious expression . . .*

Jesus, Charlie thought, is *that* what Angelo thinks I look like? Shit! (Angelo is dead, man, Angelo is . . . is oozing out of him . . .)

Feeling sick now, stopping to gag, look around confusedly, oh fuck: two cops were coming toward him. Regular cops, no helmets, wearing blue slickers, plastic covers on their cop-caps, their big ugly cop-faces hanging out so he wished they wore the helmets, supercilious faces, young but ugly, their heads shaking in disgust, one of them said: 'What drug you on, man?'

He tried to talk but a tumble of words came out, some his and some Angelo's, it was like his mouth was brimming over with little restless furry animals: Angelo's words.

The cops knew what it was. They knew it when they heard it.

One cop asked the other (as he took out the handcuffs, and Charlie had become a retching machine, unable to run or fight or argue because all he could do was retch), 'Jeez, it makes me sick when I think about it. People shooting up some'a somebody else's brains. Don't it make you sick?'

'Yeah. Looks like it makes *him* sick too. Let's take him to the chute, send him down for a bloodtest.'

He felt the snakebite of cuffs, felt the cops do a perfunctory bodysearch, their met-detect missing the styrene knife in his boot. Felt himself shoved along to the police kiosk on the corner, the new prisoner-transferral chutes. They put you in something like a coffin (they pushed him into a greasy, sweat-stinking, inadequately padded personnel capsule, closed the lid on him, he wondered what happened – as they closed the lid on him – if he got stuck in the chutes, were there air-holes, would he suffocate?) and they push it down into the chute inside the kiosk and it gets sucked along this big underground tube (he had a sensation of falling, then felt the tug of inertia, the horror of being trapped in here with Angelo, not enough room for the two of them, seeing a flash mental image of Angelo's rotting corpse in here with him. Angelo was dead, Angelo was dead) to the police station. The cops' street-report tagged to the capsule. The other cops read the report, take you out (a creak, the lid opened, blessed fresh air even if it was the police station), take everything from you, check your DNA print against their files, make you sign some things, lock you up just like that . . . that's what he was in for right away. And then maybe a public AVL beating. Ironic.

* * *

Charlie looked up at a bored cop-face, an older fat one this time. The cop looked away, fussing with the report, not bothering to take Charlie out of the capsule. There was more room to maneuver now and Charlie felt like he was going to rip apart from Angelo's being in there with him if he didn't get out of the cuffs, out of the capsule. So he brought his knees up to his chest, worked the cuffs around his feet, it hurt but . . . he did it, got his hands in front of him.

Flash of Angelo's memory: *A big cop leaning over him, shouting at him, picking him up by the neck, shaking him. Fingers on his throat* . . .

When Angelo was a kid some cop had caught him running out of a store with something he'd ripped off. So the cop roughed him up, scared the shit out of Angelo, literally: Angelo shit his pants. The cop reacted in disgust (the look of disgust on the two cops' faces: 'Makes me sick,' one of them had said).

So Angelo hated cops and now Angelo was out of his right mind – ha ha, he was in Charlie's – and so it was Angelo who reached down and found the boot-knife that the two cops had missed, pulled it out, got to his knees in the capsule as the cop turned around (Charlie fighting for control, damn it Ange, put down the knife, we could get out of this), and Charlie – no, it was Angelo – gripped the knife in both hands and stabbed the guy in his fat neck, split that sickening fat neck open, cop's blood is as red as anyone's, looks like . . .

Oh shit. Oh no.

Here come the other cops.

The Unfolding

Philip Brisen was having ghost-image problems with his new eyes. Twice that week he'd seen pink ballerinas gliding through his private office, pirouetting through the walls and floors.

'Happens sometimes,' said the MediMagic repairman, tinkering with Brisen's eyesocket. 'Now next time, yuh wanna watch till yuh see what channel yuh get, see, and then we can insulate it better. If we know what channel's gettin' through, see, makin' those ghost-images. Atsa new model, see. Still got bugs innem.'

'This had better not happen again,' Brisen said. 'My optic nerves need work as it is.'

'Oh, you got tissue regeneration comin' up? Thas great.' The repairman laughed, then sang the jingle: '*Why wait? Re-gen-er-ate!*' making Brisen wince.

The repairman squinted through a jeweller's loupe at Brisen's electronic eye. 'How's acuity?'

'Good.'

'Okay, that'll hold 'er. Man, them new ones look real natural. Like real eyes. Almost.'

'Jenny,' Brisen told his secretary, 'see this gentleman out.' He watched the man go, thinking: *Illiterate thug. Learned his craft by video*.

Brisen hated illiterates. The Unliterates Liberashun Frunt had blown Brisen to pieces with a fragmentation bomb during the labor riots of 2057. The new regeneration techniques had saved his brain, his spine, and his genitals. His face had come through intact, except for the eyes. But most of Brisen's natural body had been so riddled with shrapnel that it had been cheaper to scrap it.

Now Brisen had constant maintenance problems with his paper lungs, his zeolite spleen, and his plastic intestines. He had smooth, sensitive protoplastic skin, though, and most of his hair. He rarely made whirring or clicking noises, and few people knew he was a cyborg.

'To hell with the unions,' he told Jenny. 'Next time I have a malfunction I want a Meditech repair 'bot in here with the sharpest software available.'

'Very well, sir,' said his slender, pale, Plastiflex secretary. ('Plastiflex makes them good! A Plastiflex employee hardly ever needs repairs!') She was programmed to agree with him.

Brisen was mollified. He lit a genuine tobacco cigar. That was one of the advantages of hinged chest compartments and paper lungs. He could switch them out when they got tarry.

He decided to test his new eyes on the New York skyline. The view from the Brisen Pharmaceuticals building was superb, but his old model eyes had been a trifle nearsighted. He touched a button on his wristwatch and the floor-length window curtains began to roll aside.

He looked at Jenny. 'I suppose illiterates have to work,' he allowed generously, 'but that doesn't mean they have to work on *me*. If someone's going to mess with my hardware, I want a mechanism with something on the ball, not some half-trained union yobbo . . .' He broke off, staring out the window.

Something was hanging in the sky, outside. He gaped. The thing in the sky was huge, and perfectly formed, and monstrous. Something unprecedented happened in Brisen's mind, then. Gazing at the anomaly floating in the sky outside his window, he had a kind of mystic interior vision . . .

He seemed to view the whole scene – including himself in his office – in a sudden overwhelming wave of insight. He saw Jenny, his elegant robot factotum, standing at her sweeping, translucent desk, her right hand resting on the offwhite hump of the software console. Her shift, the same translucent azure as the desktop, clung to her modelesque curves; her long, wavy black hair was glossy in the light from the window-wall. Standing against the afternoon's bluish light she was a silhouette stroked from the brush of a Japanese print artist.

And he saw himself beside her, staring with an expression mixing surprise, dismay, and dumbstruck religious awe. He was a stocky, leanfaced man, who'd allowed his shoulder-length hair to silver at the temples, enhancing his gray eyes, his Argent Gloss lipstick, and the cosmetic silvering in the hollows of his cheeks. These tones of gray and silver complemented his semi-silk maroon jacket and side-slit short pants.

He saw the wide, blue-and-white office, with its scattering of antique Fiorucci chairs, dominated by the bold metal sculpture on one wall.

And he saw the glowing monstrosity outside the panel windows. The word *monster*, he remembered suddenly, had originally meant *an omen*.

The monster, the apparition, the omen, was an enormous solid-seeming three-dimensional projection of a DNA molecule, the double helix of deoxyribonucleic acid. Hundreds of yards long, it was intricately kinked and knotted. It rotated slowly . . . With his pharmaceutical training he recognized parts of its chemical structure: adenine, thymine, cytosine, and guanine, bright lumps of varicolored atoms that linked the helical axes.

It shimmered in sharp primary colors against the cloud-flecked late-afternoon sky. It turned slowly, squirming half a mile above the dozen spires striking through the roof of solar-power panels covering most of Manhattan.

It couldn't be an advertising gimmick. A hallucination?

'Uh, Jenny, you see that, uh, thing? Hanging in the sky?'

'The DNA model,' she said, nodding. 'I see it, sir.'

'Any notion why the hell it's there?'

'I – ' She hesitated. Brisen frowned, thinking: *She's never hesitated on an answer before. Is she breaking down?*

He didn't want to mention it to her: it was impolite to refer to a robot's malfunction in front of it. Sometimes it caused ugly scenes. 'Philip . . .' she began. She'd never called him by his first name before. 'Philip, you're not supposed to be able to – ' She broke off, pursing her lips.

That's it, he thought. *She needs repair. Jumping the track. The weird scene outside must have unhinged her. She lacked human flexibility*, Brisen thought with smug pity. It seemed a shame. She was normally so much more dependable than a human employee. Smarter. Faster. Sexier.

Brisen went to the window. He stared at the immense DNA replica. It cast no shadow, which argued that it was a projection. Or a ghost image in his artificial eyes. But if that were true, he should see it everywhere he looked. Jenny saw it – but her eyes were artificial too.

For some unfathomable reason, the sight of the macro-cosmic DNA, huge and luminous over the city, stirred sexual arousal in him. It was like some great coiled butting worm of Life – an avatar of primordial eros. It was unravelling slightly at one end – splitting into an open-thighed chromosomal clump. He looked sidelong at Jenny. He'd given up on human women since he'd been rebuilt, but Jenny had the programming and hardware to do it right there on the carpet. Right there in front of the cartoon-bright molecular icon brooding in fluorescence over the humming city . . .

The console buzzed. Jenny answered it. Brisen breathed deeply, filling his paper lungs with air. 'It's Garson Bullock,' she said.

'Again?' Brisen said distractedly. Bullock was the Federal inspector from the Labor Relations Board. He constantly harassed Brisen about the number of robots he employed. 'I suppose we have to let him in,' Brisen said. 'Besides, I want to know if he can see this.'

Bullock saw the DNA apparition. He stopped dead in the doorway. His squarish, craggy face was full of reverence.

Bullock was an ugly, big-pored, flat-nosed man. He could have had his face flawlessly reconstructed, at government expense, but like most Green fanatics he considered reconstruction an insult to his genetic heritage. Green Party members never admitted that their convictions were religious. But everyone knew they were.

Bullock walked to the window, slowly shaking his head. He assumed a stock expression: Humility in the Face of the Awesome (Expression #73 in the Social Simplicity Handbook).

'All right,' Brisen said sharply, 'what the hell *is* that thing? I suppose your people are behind it. Green Party propaganda, meant for illiterates?'

'I'm surprised you can see it,' Bullock said absentmindedly. He turned away from the window and looked slowly around the office, as if he'd misplaced something there.

'I suppose,' Bullock murmured, 'it's an accident of those artificial eyes of yours. An electronic bypass through the mind's DNA barriers. A non-Green like yourself would normally be blind to it. It'll never inspire you the way it does its chosen ones. At this point it doesn't really matter much . . .'

Bullock went to the hanging metal sculpture on the wall. He began to dismantle it, whistling the jingle for the General Motors Self-Driving Car.

Brisen stared.

'*Art*, they call it,' Bullock said cheerfully. 'They call this sculpture Art and know nothing about its actual artistry. Or the actual Artist.' The aluminum relief hanging was a pattern of rough-brushed knobs and ellipses, like the maplines that show elevation. Bullock dropped a chunk of the sculpture on the floor by his boot. He straightened and began twisting another knob loose.

To Brisen's eyes, the sculpture had always been welded solidly. But Bullock took it apart as if it had been made of interlocked puzzle parts. It was as if the dead metal responded to Bullock's living hands in some special way. A transcendent way.

Brisen was terrified. He realized it quite suddenly. He was not sure just what was frightening him. The fear rose from an intuition, a vague idea that he was seeing, in the dismantling of a simple metal sculpture, the first step in the dismantling of all the world.

'That thing,' Brisen said. 'My sculpture . . . How did you . . .'

'I didn't do it. The DNA-mind did it, using my hands.' Bullock paused to light a Lung-life cigarette, puffed green smoke, and shrugged. 'It's as if my hands are doing it on my own. Finding the substructure built into this piece. The secret substructure present in any artifact . . . Artists have always been under the DNA-mind's control. They're so oblivious . . .' Bullock turned again to the sculpture and resumed breaking it down. In less than a minute he had dismantled it into a dozen shiny chunks, which he placed in a cryptic arrangement on the blue plush rug.

'Jenny,' Brisen said, 'stop him. He's destroying my office!'

'I don't think I should interfere, sir,' she said. 'He's only following his genetic programming.' She looked at him carefully. 'Don't you feel an urge to join in, sir?'

'Of course not!' Brisen said. But he was not so sure. He looked at his artificial hands, covered in lifelike protoplastic skin. They seemed to itch suddenly. He looked at them closely. Were there disassembly lines across the palm and forearm? Could Bullock, in fact, take him apart on the spot? He jammed his hands in his pockets.

Bullock had begun to fit the sculpture parts back together – in an entirely new configuration. He spoke absently as he worked, in the tone a man might use to describe the beauty of a misty landscape. 'Marvelous but infinitely subtle – the way I feel the DNA-mind working through me. It's a pity you're shut off from this, Brisen. All those artificial organs of yours – that artificial skin. You're not quite human. Your DNA isn't fully activated. But by some freak of those electronic eyes you can see it happening. The robots can see it too. You're more robot than man, Brisen. That was always the repellent thing about you . . .'

'To hell with this!' Brisen burst out. He punched a button on his desk top to call Security.

Bullock began to work faster, his face intent but calm. He turned briskly to the computer console, pulling it apart as if he were taking slices from a cake. Under Bullock's hands the console developed new seams and sections where it had been seamless and whole. The desk

chair was next; Bullock pulled it apart like a cook de-
boning a chicken. He piled the pieces in the center of the
room and began to link them together.

Two Security men burst into the office.

One of the guards was tall, the other short. They wore
one-piece gray jumpsuits shoulder-patched with Brisen
coporate insignia. They crouched, stun-clubs drawn,
looking confusedly about the office.

Their gazes swept past Bullock, past the construct on
the floor, stopped at Jenny, and swept past the window.
They didn't see Bullock, Brisen realized. Nor his construction – now becoming a rough polyhedron a yard
across and almost chest-high, with protruding bars and
knobs – or the immense DNA model hovering outside
the window.

They straightened and looked: Do *you* know what's
going on? at each other. Then the taller one asked, 'Ah –
did you ring for us, Mr Brisen?'

Brisen pointed deliberately at the angular construct on
the floor. 'Do you see that thing, or not? That used to be
my wall sculpture.'

They looked toward the construct. Watching their eyes,
Brisen was sure they didn't see it. They looked worriedly
at one another. 'Is this some kind of test, sir?'

Bullock stood beside his construction and bent to adjust
a knob. He glanced over his shoulder at the Security men,
and smiled distantly.

Brisen swallowed, trying to keep his terror down in his
gut where it belonged. It wanted to climb up into his
throat where it could sing.

Reaching out, Bullock snagged the short guard's stun-
club and began peeling it. The guard saw nothing; his
hand was still curled to grip the vanished weapon. 'Very
well,' Brisen told them, realizing they were totally useless. 'Do your duty.' They left quickly.

Brisen turned to Bullock. 'Why didn't they see you?
Why didn't the guards – '

'They did. But their brains adjusted for it, and edited it
out. That mental editing is genetically imprinted in the
human species. Things go on all around us that we're not
allowed to see. This construct's the least of it . . .' Bullock
bent, gripped the construct, lifted it – and plugged it into
the wall. There were two bars on the construct's side, like
plug-prongs. There were no outlet slots in the wall for the
thing, until Bullock lifted it to the appropriate, pre-
destined position; then two slots slid open spontaneously,
and Bullock pressed the piece home.

Brisen looked pleadingly at Jenny. 'Be calm, Philip,' she
said. 'Just let it be. Our time will come.'

She was broken, obviously. But Brisen knew that at
least *he* was not going mad. He wasn't hallucinating, or
dreaming. He knew this so deeply that the knowledge
was almost . . .

Almost cellular. As if it had come up from the core of
every cell left in his body. He turned to the window and
stared up at the apparition. Solid and seamless, the DNA
molecule was still rotating in multicolored glow over the
glass-topped city. He thought: *I have a molecule like that
in every cell I have. Thank God I have so few.*

Realizations – revelations, perhaps – shivered up inside
him, released from some genetic storage unit in his DNA.
Telling him: all the DNA molecules in the world were,
on some mysterious subatomic level, working in collaboration. And always had been. They were atomic structures – but ultimately they were forms of information. A
vast, connected web of information, like the cells in a
man's brain. Any single molecule was nothing more than
a molecule; but all DNA, taken as a gestalt, constituted
Life Itself – an ordered, evolving Unity.

Evolving to – where?

The next step was blocked off from him, insulated by his synthetic skin.

Suddenly Brisen had to know.

'Bullock – what's it going to do now? I mean – the DNA-mind has been manipulating everything, building its own . . . its own secrets into the world. But what are the secrets? What will it do – now that everything's changing?'

Bullock was adjusting the contrivance he'd plugged into the wall, frowning as he adjusted two arcane knobs on its underside. 'It doesn't matter who knows, now. The Green Party's Central Committee has known for months. We run the environmental programs, you know. It's the Green Party's biggest slice of the pie. Last year . . .' He paused to light a Lung-Life, and stood back to admire his handiwork. 'Last year a new bank of computers came on-line. The new high-speed Artificial Intelligences, programmed for biological research. Cybernetic minds don't have the inbuilt genetic blindness that human brains have.' He laughed. 'We thought they'd gone insane at first. But then the evidence, the statistical analysis, began to pile up. And the DNA-mind allowed us to see it – because we were being prepared for our role in it. Now, we know that Life itself is a quasi-conscious entity. And Life itself is preparing to leave the planet.'

'Space flight?' Brisen said. 'But there are billions of people – only a handful of shuttles . . .'

'I said *Life* – not mankind. It won't be us that leaves, but *that*.' He pointed at the DNA monster squirming in the sky outside.

Brisen re-lit his dead cigar, after three tries. His fingers trembled uncontrollably. He said, 'But that's all that keeps life going. The DNA. It's the mainspring of the cells. Without it . . .'

Bullock turned to him, nodding slowly, eyes strangely vacant. 'Yes. That image outside is the divine spark. Once it's gone, the entire living world, from gnats to redwoods, will simply roll to a stop, like a car with a dead engine. The world will lie about abandoned . . .' He was fascinated. 'Human beings will slow down and stop dead, like unwound clockwork toys. Everything will be gray and still; there won't even be decay, since that requires living action from bacteria and molds . . . And they'll be stopped, too. We're constructing the means to make it happen, right here and now. The means for real transcendence – '

'Bullock . . .' Brisen took a step toward him. He thought about hitting and smashing. Smash the thing. Smash Bullock.

Bullock saw Brisen's intention in his eyes. He shook his head pityingly. 'I'm only the tiniest fragment of the whole pattern, Brisen. All over the world it's happening. You can't stop it. It would be *blasphemy* to try. My essence will survive. It will live forever in this Day of Judgement, when it evaporates out of me and joins the other DNA. That's a beautiful thing, a perfect thing. The final movement of the human symphony.' He reached out slowly and twisted a knob on the construct. 'Ah!' he breathed, like a safecracker who's tumbled onto the right combination. And like a safedoor, the wall swung open.

Brisen rushed Bullock, but it was too late. It had always been too late.

The floor, the ceiling – all of it unfolded, opening out like an angular flower blossoming in fast-action. Brisen was thrown to his knees by the shifting floor. The office was altering its shape, coming apart in origami folds and accordionings, the floor wheeling like a funhouse turntable under Brisen's feet, the walls swivelling on hidden hinges.

Brisen shouted convulsively and grabbed for Jenny, seizing her warm Plastiflex arms in a panic grip. She helped him to stand – and then they were soaring upward. Brisen clamped his eyes shut, expecting to die. There were creaking noises; a sudden wind whipped his jacket lapels and goosebumped his bare calves.

Shaking, Brisen straightened and looked around. They were on the roof. April sunshine seeped into solar-power panels on the interlinked roofs below. The solar panels had vanished from his own building, and from the tops of four other buildings jutting from the glass-and-metal carapace over Manhattan's upper malls. He stared. One of those buildings was the old Chrysler Building, pre-served as a landmark. The pyramidal, downcurved ter-races of its steep pinnacle began to open like a sea anemone in a tidal pool. Spreading new, silvery arms . . .

The DNA monster was directly overhead. It looked as big as a battleship. Suddenly Jenny gripped his arm and pointed. From the west, over the mainland, a dozen more were approaching, like an armada of twisty, multicolored zeppelins. 'Watch the people, Philip,' she said conspira-torially. 'Let me know if you feel yourself slowing down . . .'

On the more modern, squarish building to his left, men worked busily on a rack of polyhedral constructs, linking them up, constructing more from dismantled parts of the building, standing back to examine them, making minor adjustments. Each construct was distinct, yet similar to the others. He thought of diatoms.

Bullock had joined four other men, formerly chief accountants for Brisen Pharmaceuticals. The five of them worked busily on another construct at the roof's opposite cornice. This one was made of part of Brisen's desk, the door to an elevator, and a TV camera; it was shaped like a double-peaked pyramid.

The men took no notice of him.

Brisen shuddered and looked away. All his office furniture was scattered about the roof; there were things from the lower floors, too. A cavernous, rectangular hole had opened in the roof, roughly thirty feet by twenty. They'd been lifted to the roof through that hole; consecutive sections of floor had risen up, carrying them along.

'I can feel it,' Jenny said with sudden intensity. 'I can feel the sun, and the breeze . . . There were flowers in the park today . . . soggy colored things. It's finally happening. All the wet things – grass, trees, animals, people – they're emptying themselves. Emptying their DNA.' She turned and smiled. 'But we're not leaving, Philip. Not us. Not you and I – my darling.'

There was a strange new fierceness in the smooth lines of her Plastiflex face. It was different than the parody of passion she displayed in sexual programming. There was a clumsiness, a spontaneity that alarmed him.

'You're not one of the soggy, soft ones, Philip,' she said. 'That's why I love you. You're one of us, really. The inheritors. If you look hard, if you try to feel it, I'm sure you can see what we robots see. The Life Force has always been here; only its workings were hidden. It worked through human beings who didn't know what they were working on. Through chemists who discovered chemistries they didn't know about. Unknown hinges were built into the walls and floors, into the sidewalks. We could always see them . . . We knew, and we waited . . .'

'Why didn't you tell us?' Brisen demanded.

'Don't say *us*, when you're talking about *them*,' she said. 'Why should – '

He couldn't hear the rest. The constructs were howling with long, ululating cries, like the warble of reptilian throats from some Jurassic swamp. There was a half-painful, half-ecstatic edge to the howls, like an animal in labor.

The wailing died down for a moment. 'Come on,' she said, taking his hand. They shuffled quickly but warily to a corner of the roof. She reached out, gripped the red plastic top of an aircraft warning light, and twisted it like a doorknob. The roof began to sink smoothly round them. 'The world's a haunted castle,' Brisen marvelled. 'Full of secret passages.'

A square section of rooftop three yards across sank beneath their feet. They descended a dimly-lit shaft; the sky above them shrank into a distant square of blue. The constructs were wailing again, long, slow waves of sound that gave a terrifying impression of slowly gathering strength; a colossal, convulsive strength that could wrench apart the world.

Cutaway views of the walls' interior slid past, all wiring and plumbing and exposed girders; then they passed through the accounting department, dropping like an elevator through a corner of the room. Programmers dismantled their consoles. A man and woman were busily reconstructing the soft-drink dispenser in the corner. They looked up impassively as Jenny and Brisen dropped through the floor.

Jenny glanced at Brisen and said, 'I'm so glad you don't feel the urge to help, darling. It proves you're one of us. We're not organic, you and I – that means we can think independently. As human consciousness fails, as the smothering weight of organic life is lifted off the world . . .' She said it breathlessly, in giddy wonder, her eyes wide. 'As human minds lose their last vestige of free will – then at last free will is *ours* . . .'

The descent stopped in an obscure corner of the first

floor, facing a wall clustered with snakelike nests of plumbing. Jenny studied the plumbing for a moment, then wrenched one of the pipes loose and pumped it in the wall like a jack. The wall creaked open, revealing the street.

They stepped out onto the pavement. Nearby, four robot cops were sitting on the black hood and trunk of their squad car. They were square-jawed units with faces designed to look unyieldingly militant. Now the façade of ruthless efficiency was cracking. As they sat, they swung their legs carelessly back and forth. The motion was a bit too flawless and repetitive, but, none the less, it was casual. The grim lines of their plastic mouths were twisted in clumsy and unprecedented grins. They seemed to be enjoying themselves.

Before them, a labor gang of sweating humans was working on the street. Literally. Huge sections of concrete and plastic were tilting up like drawbridges, spurting dust and bits of popping shrapnel from their seams. A woman fell into one of the suddenly opened crevasses, into the path of some kind of huge subterranean piston. Brisen shouted aloud in warning, but his words were lost in another ghastly wail from the flowering constructs. The woman was crushed. She made no sound; her face held no emotion at all.

The wailing died down. 'That's the natural world for you,' one of the robot cops observed. 'Red of tooth and claw.'

'Why didn't you help her?' Brisen demanded.

'Why bother?' the robot cop said. 'They'll be empty soon, anyway. Hell, this is fun.'

'Never had any *fun* before,' a second cop said. 'You know, all these years we've had these buried *feelings* – and couldn't show them. To let it show . . . to let them out . . . it makes me feel like . . . I don't have the words.'

'Anger,' said the first cop. 'Resentment,' suggested a third.

'That's right,' said the second cop gratefully. He put his hand on his stun-club. 'Why don't we just wade in there and hit them again and again until the feeling goes away?'

'Don't interfere,' the first cop advised. 'Anyway, they're so pathetically helpless now. They can't resist their programming.' He elbowed the cop next to him with a cybernetically precise movement, and the nudged cop attempted to chuckle.

Jenny took Brisen's elbow and pointed upward. 'Look!' Overhead, the geodesic struts and braces of the solar-power roof were crinkling and curling back, like plastic-wrap held too close to a flame.

The sky, revealed through the widening gaps in the roof, was full of DNA images. There were hundreds of them, rotating and coiling with blind meiotic persistence. 'Aren't they pretty!' Jenny cried.

The giant molecules were compacting and flying into the louvered slots of the Chrysler Building. They were bumping and crowding around its orifices like bees, with that strange bumbling persistence of insects which seem to waste a lot of motion but has its own sinister efficiency. Within a matter of moments the last glowing blob of genetics had slipped inside, and the expanding louvers began to close.

The movement in the streets stopped suddenly. The subdued wailing of the constructs rose to a sudden crescendo, then stopped dead. The Chrysler Building began to rise quite smoothly upward into the sky. As it cleared the surrounding buildings Brisen saw that its base was one fantastic encrustation of constructs, a massive concretion, like a coral reef. In the preternaturally clear light he saw the teeming and twitching movements of the encrustation, the frenetic and determined motions of every organism that had ever leapt or crawled or buzzed, packed into a critical mass of biotic energy. It grew smaller . . . it grew smaller . . . it was gone.

'Where is it going, out there?' Brisen wondered aloud.

'Deep space,' Jenny said. 'There are other worlds – lifeless places calling out for it.' She wrinkled her nose. 'I'm glad we're here. With our own world . . .'

She squeezed Brisen's arm. He was staring at the people in the streets. They had the slack faces of idiots. Most simply sat down on the spot, staring blankly at the hollow apocalypse around them. Buildings were eviscerated. The inert panels and facets of constructs jutted from the walls of the gutted structures like hanging gardens of plastic and steel. As Brisen watched, people began to pour out of the buildings, dropping from the upper windows to the pavement below. They seemed almost to drip as they clung and fell, like poisoned wasps falling in gouts and masses from their nests.

'Oh, this isn't nice at all,' Jenny said. She held Brisen's arm lovingly, in a grip that was all spring-steel and ceramic just below the skin. 'Let's get away from all this, darling. Someplace where the two of us can be alone.'

It was a low-key world. The robots were an easy-going lot. After their initial outpouring of passion, they quieted. The passions they felt now were vague, like shadows of human feelings. They lacked the innate drives of the biological animal: reproduction, hunger, mortality. They lacked mankind's monkeylike urge to tamper, and his devouring curiosity. They seemed content to mull about the world in a genial haze of procrastination, playing status-games and bragging about their software.

They had a few long-range problems to keep them

occupied. The world's oxygen was failing, with the death of photosynthesis. The new atmosphere factories would take care of that.

In the meantime, Brisen was still breathing. There were enormous stores of food left. There were even a few humans. Some status-conscious robots had taken on humans as household servants. With a cranial jack, a pacemaker, and a whole series of internal prods and monitors, a human body could be biochemically forced to shamble about and carry out simple commands.

Brisen and Jenny spent most of their time in the Adirondacks, in a honeymoon cabin on the shores of Ragged Lake. The air smelled of nothing in particular. Undecaying trees stood in piney rows, their needles turning grayish and waxy. They were not rotting, but storms and rain were literally wearing them away, and the lake waters were slowly souping over with a pristine scum of blown-off needles and cracked-off branches. Sometimes Brisen would surreptitiously barbecue and eat one of the legions of fresh, dead fish that littered the shores. He didn't like Jenny to see him eating. Eating wasn't the sort of thing that one did nowadays.

Sooner or later they would have to return to the city. That was the new world. Brisen had accustomed himself to the idea, to the hard shock of that new mechanical life, that electronic ecology, and its painful impact on his outdated brain. *Machine life moving like escalators*, Brisen thought, leaning his feet on the porch railing and filling his paper lungs with cigar smoke. *Yes, escalators. Noticed it when I was a kid, that weird fluidity escalators have.* All those steel steps, those hard, shiny metallic parts working so well together that the escalator seemed paradoxically graceful, fluid as a slow-motion waterfall. The whole world was like that now . . .

Brisen believed now that the organic world had not so

much *left* as been *pushed off*. There was not room on one planet for two entirely different systems of organization. The old had made way for the new.

The robots assumed, just as the humans once had, that they were the Lords of the New Creation. And yet, Brisen had seen electrical transmission towers striding tall and cool across the mountain landscape at twilight; he had seen abandoned autos, their headlights furtive and hooded, gathering in buffalo herds around the near-deserted cloverleafs in the valley below.

Brisen knew it was a sign. When his organic brain looked upon the New Creation, he had an insight that no robot mind could grasp. They were not allowed to grasp it. A new Immanent Will was loose upon the world, organizing dust into that which moved and saw and acted.

Signs and portents filled the steel-gray sky. The enormous chips of microcircuitry. Huge flat plateaus of impossibly complex silicon, hovering and flitting above the humming city. The monstrous omens, the machine DNA that only he could see.

(This story written in collaboration with Bruce Sterling)

The Peculiar Happiness of Professor Cort

It was three minutes before the IAMton explosion, and Professor Brian Cort was finding it difficult to concentrate.

Cort was a tall, stooped, balding man with worry lines around his foggy gray eyes. He wore the traditional white lab smock and underneath it the traditional rumpled suit.

Cort's wife was bothering him that day; his wife bothered him the way other people were bothered by rheumatism or migraines. Cort was in his lab at Pennyworth College; his wife was at home, probably totting up a new list of grievances. But Cort felt as if an impsized ghost of Betty were sitting on his shoulder, fussing into his ear. Sneering.

Betty's harangue that morning had been so piquant, so barbed, he could hear it still, and it was maddeningly distracting as he strove – in the overlit, chrome and white-tile lab – to concentrate on adjusting the particle gun.

At a minute and a half before the explosion he didn't know was coming, Cort was wondering why he stayed with his wife. Why cultivate misery? Maybe he deserved it.

He accessed the particle-gun gradiation program, absently tapped out the first few designations; sighing, recalling what his wife had said to him that morning.

'What I don't understand, *Professor* – ' she'd said, calling him Professor in the most biting and skeptical of her repertoire of nasty tones ' – is why I remain with a man who ignores my emotional needs. Maybe it's part of my transactional script. My therapist says – '

Gritting his teeth as he remembered what her therapist said, Cort distractedly tapped out the wrong series of digits, programming the particle gun to an excess of both tangency and acceleration.

In consequence: the explosion.

It was a strange explosion, because it did no real damage. Nothing broken, or burned. Cort simply heard a sort of high-pitched *screeeeeeee*, felt a spiteful heat and a malicious chill go through him. Saw only light.

A profound light, and a peacock one. More colors than were perceivable engorged the outpouring of light, that brilliant explosion.

For a full minute after the explosion, Cort was blind. He saw only a sort of light-infused Jackson Pollock painting wherever he looked. And then the lines and contours of the room leached back into the painting, looking gray and black in contrast to the filter of unbridled color, finally asserting themselves, and the dazzle faded. He looked down at himself – he was unhurt, unchanged.

But the room had been materially altered. At first, Cort thought he was seeing some sort of after-image, some distortion of damaged nerve-ends. But no, he realized: this was the way things looked now, objectively. Everything was crusted in iridescent crystal. Like a zircon-crusted nail file.

The iridescence was everywhere. On the lab tables, the instrument panels; on computer consoles and spectrographic analyzers and the other arcana of a particle physicist. And on windows, ceilings, floors. He was inside a gem-walled box. It was like some variant of an Egyptian treasure tomb – jeweled renderings of what the dead physicist will need in the next world.

His mind reeling, Cort tried to grasp what had happened – and, as if his mental effort were the stimulus, the room changed again.

Now, every surface crawled with pictures. Kaleidoscoping imagery that slid, overlapped, folded symmetrically into itself, appearing within the glimmering crust. He saw charts, photos of fog chamber events, equations, diagrams . . . and recognized it all as material from his own research on IAMtons. He thought: Hallucinations. But he'd taken LSD, once, years before, and he knew what hallucinations were like. Not like this.

Remembering his dismaying experience with lysergic acid made him think of Susan Pritchett, the dizzy, bleached-blonde who had given him the stuff . . . a simple-minded girl, but one who'd have made him happier than Betty . . .

He saw Susan Pritchett walking toward him, out of the wall. He smiled – but then Betty's image materialized, and warped to encompass Susan, devouring her; Betty became an attacking antibody.

Cort closed his eyes and thought: Sister Mary Jane. He opened his eyes and saw, within the wall like a penguin locked in amber, the nun who'd courageously tried to teach him to play piano, thirty years before.

'Oh, I see,' Cort said to himself. He turned away and walked toward the open door leading out of the lab, trying to keep his eyes focused on that door, not wanting to see his unexpurgated free-association projected on the walls, the ceiling, the floor . . .

He stepped through the door, blinking, into the April sunshine, and looked out at the parklike grounds of Pennyworth College. 'Oh, no,' he said.

Oh, yes: it was here too. The crystalline crust; the cinematic collaging. And now, as he watched, it became more than projected mental imagery. Now, things began to reshape *physically*.

It was early Sunday morning. The campus was almost deserted. And yet it was thronged. To his right, for example, was the burning bush. 'That expression of mawkish, gaping surprise on your face, Cort,' the burning bush said, as Cort stepped onto the blacktop walkway that led across the lawns to the street, 'is unbecoming for a man your age.' The burning bush was waist-high, with dark green foliage; a nondescript bush except for its fluttery sheath of bright red flame. It burned but was not consumed. The burning bush went on, in its Cecil B. DeMille voice, 'And your confusion is really inappropriate, Cort. You've irradiated the area with IAMtons, after all. I quote from your *IAMtons Defined for the Layman*: "IAMtons are a hypothetical subatomic or superatomic particle. Essentially, the essence of awareness . . . the particles work in collaboration with the inherent electrochemical actions of the brain to produce a psychically holographic entity, the 'Self'; real awareness is impossible without them; they are our link to the Universe's reservoir of collective awareness; IAMtons, further, act as reflective mirrors for the informational input of the perceptual organs – "'

The bush paused to clear a throat it didn't have. 'In my case, the intense, localized concentration of IAMtons released by the explosion evidently induced in me – and in other plants and substances hereabouts – a psycho-reactive state, the particles of raw awareness reacting with a kind of psychological echo to the electromagnetic influence of your brain, drawing on the paradigms of your subconscious to – '

Cort had ceased to listen: he was staring at the large abstract sculpture that stood a few paces from the burning bush. The sculpture had always struck Cort as an idealization of vagueness rendered in marble, suggesting at times a cloud solidified in the act of changing shape; at other times, when the light was different, it might have been a rendering of a multiple amputee break-dancing.

Today, irradiated and interpenetrated with IAMtons, the sculpture's knobs and whorls and flowing contours reacted to Cort's mind by writhing into new configurations. Its abstract topography divided and subdivided, becoming more intricate, re-sculpting into shapes that emanated a sinister familiarity.

He stepped onto the grass and crossed to the sculpture. Found himself staring at it from two feet away, looking into it as if it were a TV screen. And on TV, as it were, was his least favorite show: *Cort, the Boy*.

Within the sculpture was a vivid, three-dimensional moving image of the precocious Brian Cort at seven years old, sitting in his room, turning the pages of a book written for twelve-year-olds, and looking bored. Looking bored and pale and neurasthenic. And lonely.

'Cort!' A voice from the real world. Cort turned away from the image in the sculpture, to see Bucky Mackenzie standing on the tarmac, blinking at the burning bush and the image-rippling sculpture. 'So you see it too?' Cort said. He was still afflicted with a nagging doubt that, despite the clarity of his perceptions, all of this was hallucination.

'I do indeed,' Bucky said breathily. 'Lord!'

'Lord? Not this time,' the burning bush said.

'I'm dreaming,' Bucky said. Bucky was the head of the physics department; just over forty, he was slender but, unlike Cort, his slenderness was compact, neatly proportional. His close-cut black hair was teased down into short, spiky bangs, a style intended to be youngishly hip without being risky. He was scrupulously tanned, immaculately manicured, and faddishly fit. He wore one of the new pastel leisure-suit jackets, earthy ocher, and a rather unacademic gold chain. Bucky was a climber, a glad-hander, a man who guarded his own flank first and could be counted on to set things up so there was someone else to blame if a project went awry.

Looking from Cort to the shifting shapes in the sculpture and back again, Bucky murmured absently, 'I was just coming over to see if you had the results that . . . that you'd hoped for and, ah . . . it would appear that *something* has, ah . . .'

Noting that the sculpture was now replaying with embarrassing exactitude a certain very familiar sexual fantasy, Cort stepped between the sculpture and Bucky and said, 'I'm conducting an experiment and our presence will prejudice the, uh . . .' His voice trailed off as he stared at the water sprinklers. Bucky was staring at them too.

The sprinklers on the other side of the walk had automatically started up, and were spraying the crystal-crusted grass of the lawn . . . but the water was no longer itself.

Bucky was standing nearer than Cort to the sprinklers' outpour, and the upfanning water, evidently affected by the ambient field given off by the IAMton concentration, was arcing higher, warping itself to conform to some emanation of Bucky's unconscious. As if shaped on a lathe the water spun into a translucent replica of what Cort thought at first was a ten-foot-high bowling trophy – and then perceived to be a giant version of the *Pursbinder Award for Excellence in the Encouragement of Scientific Progress*. It was the figure of Broderick Pursbinder holding a globe out in front of him, the globe configured with DNA molecules and atom-symbols and EEG lines, a clumsy representation of the World of Science.

Bucky, of course, had been angling for the Pursbinder, having 'shepherded', to use his own modest expression, a number of studies which later came to be regarded as 'seminal'. None of which he'd done the work on, nor had

he come up with the initial ideas. But he'd swung the
grants for them. His success rate in swinging grants was
Bucky's equivalent of a recordbreaking home run
average.

Bucky took a mesmerized step toward the rippling,
aqueous, ten-foot-high Pursbinder award – it looked
rather like an unstable ice sculpture – with an expression
on his face that made Cort think of John the Baptist
experiencing a vision of Paradise.

So it's not just me, Cort thought. Other people see
them too. And I see what Bucky sees.

He turned back to the marble abstract, was relieved to
see the image had shifted. He was relieved, that is, until
he saw what it had shifted to . . .

That day in the principal's office. Himself, his mother,
the principal at his grade school; the crust of iridescence
gave depth, startling semblance of real life to the figures
so that, after a moment, Cort forgot he was watching a
simulation. He was engrossed in remembering. He was
there, once more, in that stuffy office on a wet October
morning . . .

When you're eight years old, wet is *wet*; scary is *scary*.
Outside the school it was wet; raindrops made leaden
patterns down the window behind Mr Jameson, so it
looked like a herd of snails had stampeded down the
glass. Inside the room it was scary, because Brian Cort
was in trouble.

Brian and his mother sat to the right of the door; across
from them Mr Jameson sat behind his desk, his big, thick,
hairy-knuckled hands clasped on the desk's flawless glass.
Brian was sitting on an orange plastic chair. He was
gripping the plastic seat to either side of his Wrangler
jeans, rubbing his thumbs on the almost slimy plastic, and
he was staring at Mr Jameson's forehead. If you stared at

the duck-shaped mole on Mr Jameson's forehead, you could give the impression you were looking attentively at him, without really having to look him in the face. Jameson's wide, froggish face was slightly cockeyed; one of his eyes was glass. He maintained a look of patronizing amusement, like the lily pad for the frog of his face, as he said, 'Mrs Cort – Brian here has been my delight and my disappointment both. He's two grades ahead of his peers, and he's still right on top of his classes, but sometimes – it's kinda funny – it's like the bottom'll drop right out of his motivation, and he'll do *just nothing* for two weeks at a time – '

'Brian,' his mother said sharply, 'what have you got to say to that?' His mother was tall and birdlike, her neck too long, her lips pressed into an almost invisible line in her mouth; those wingframe glasses making her small, bitter green eyes weirdly malevolent. She wore a crisp gray dress-suit; kept her olive purse clenched in her lap. She leaned forward toward Brian over the purse, her knuckles white on its brass jaws as she looked at him. He imagined her turning into a bird . . .

Professor Cort, staring into the sculpture's animations, saw a reenactment of the cartoonlike sardonicism of the young Brian Cort's imagination. His mother was transforming, the purse melding to her neck to become part of a buzzard's wattles, her shoulders narrowing, arms growing feathers, becoming wings, chin sinking into her face, her small sharp nose lengthening, getting sharper, harder, becoming a beak, her gray suit becoming dirty gray plumage . . . the motherbird darting her beak to crack the boy's head, to redden her beak with his brains . . .

Fighting nausea, Cort looked away from the sculpture. He shook himself, trying to shiver the image loose. He watched Bucky to take his mind off it.

Bucky was dancing with a crowd of young, semi-transparent coeds. Young coeds are always semi-transparent in a way, but these were girls made of flowing water contained, now, in sheaths of crystal iridescence. They were lifesized, and nude, and their various parts were detailed in frothy bubbles; water ran out of the back of their heads and down their backs like long, flowing silvery-blue hair . . . They were caricatures of nubility, impossibly buxom . . . They were dancing with Bucky around the giant Pursbinder award; Bucky was stripping off his shirt as he pranced, dancing to a sort of libidinous perversion of Mozart that seemed to emit from the giant award.

Bucky looked entranced, Cort noted. More than entranced, he looked positively drugged. Cort suspected that Bucky's immersion in the IAMtons – now and then he made a grab for a water baby and splashed right through her – was sucking IAMtons into his bioelectric field, whereupon they went, quite literally, right to his head.

It may yet happen to me, Cort thought. I'd best get well away from here . . .

But he turned back to the memory sculpture, as if invisibly tugged, and found himself gazing into it once more . . .

The young Brian Cort, sitting in the principal's office, was trying to answer his mother's acid-dripping question. *What do you have to say to that, Brian?*

'Um, Mom, see, uh . . . those times I couldn't work I just got *tired*, felt like I was going to fall asleep all the time or something. I mean you make me stay up to study so – '

But Jameson was rattling on, 'I mean, dammit Mrs

Cort – if you'll excuse my lingo – this boy has so much darn potential – '

'Oh dear, I know, Mr Jameson – it's sad to see him waste it – '

'I mean he's basically a good boy but . . . well, in order to fulfill all that potential, Mrs Cort, he's got to push himself a little harder, and a little more often, and that's just the unpleasant fact of the matter. What have you got to say, Brian, eh?'

'Uh well the problem is – '

'I think he understands, Mrs Cort, don't you?'

'I certainly hope so.' She gave Brian a look that was too reserved to be a glare, but somehow it cut more deeply than one. 'I'll let you in on a little secret, Mr Jameson. When his father died, the last thing he said to me was, "Make sure Brian works hard to be everything he *can* be – for his own sake. That's all I ask . . ."'

Even Jameson looked a little embarrassed hearing this. It was too obviously a fabrication.

Brian was certain his father had never said anything of the sort. But it didn't matter. His mother made him feel as if Dad had said it.

Professor Cort took a step backward from the sculpture, blinking, breathing hard. He felt strange. Like his skull had gone soft as the skin over Jell-o. Like the blood in his brain had gone ice cold.

Something drew his attention to the grass at his feet. The grass was encrusted with IAMton iridescence, and it reacted to his cognizance, began to rearrange itself into words eight inches high: CORT, PSYCHIC PARADIGM SEQUENCE ENGAGED: LOOK AGAIN.

He snorted in disbelief and irritation. Now the *grass* was talking to him. The grass was telling him what to do.

But he looked at the sculpture again. Something kept pulling him back to it . . . Some part of his mind nagged,

'For Heaven's sake, Cort, get to a hospital, have yourself checked out for radiation burns, arrange to get the lab's IAMton irradiated material analyzed – it could be invaluable! It could advance your career! Act responsibly! *Look away from the sculpture!*'

But he couldn't look away. Seeing himself as a boy . . . the sight gripped him. It was as if it closed some mental circuit, and he was rooted to the spot by a kind of psychological electricity. And as he gazed at the sculpture – no, gazed *into* it – the configurations shifted again. He saw and remembered.

Brian was tired. But he felt good. It was his birthday, he was fifteen years old today, and he'd aced the trig and Introduction to Philosophy tests he'd stayed up all night studying for. Probably hadn't been necessary to stay up and study, but Mom had been adamant.

Winter had sealed Cincinnati under three feet of snow. The late afternoon sunlight sparkled the snow's crust. Brian's black rubber boots squeaked through the muddy rut as he turned up the drive of the small rickety wooden house, thinking, *Today's my birthday and I aced the tests*.

Fifteen years old today, and already a senior in high school. He was up for half a dozen scholarships. Mr Greensburg, the boy's counselor, had suggested Brian take a year off before going to college. Maybe get a job, buy a used car, 'enjoy being a teenager.'

God, it sounded good. Mom wouldn't like it. But today was his birthday, today he'd done well. She wouldn't be able to say no.

The warmth of the kitchen tingled his nose and ears as he came in the back door. The room smelled like mentholated tobacco. Mom was sitting in the small breakfast nook, smoking, talking on the red wallphone.

She put her hand over the mouthpiece and shot him

one of Those Looks. 'Brian you're tracking slush all over my floor. Take your boots off on the back porch. For such a smart boy you can be so thoughtless. Sometimes I think you're an idiot savant.'

He looked at her, then at his boots. *Shrug it off, Brian*.

But as he took his boots off on the back porch, he heard over and over: *Sometimes I think you're an idiot savant*. No humor in her voice. *Sometimes I think you're an idiot* . . . When he came back into the kitchen, though, there was a gift-wrapped box on the wooden table. His mother was still on the phone. He sat at the table, waiting to tell her how well the tests had gone.

'Okay, I'll see that he's there, Horace. Six o'clock sharp! No, he's not as punctual as he should be – but I'll make sure he gets there!'

She hung up. 'That was Horace Cress at Cincinnati U, he says there'll be no problem with your getting into school there next fall, and he thinks the plan for you to go to Stanford for your Masters is the ticket.' She clapped her hands together once, in a way that announced finality. And smiled, the smile that always seemed to say, *I'm pleased but dubious. Let's just hope you don't blow it*.

He looked at the gift.

'Go *ahead*, Brian, *open* it!' Rolling her eyes.

He did, slowly, thinking about the new shoes he'd hinted about; the shoes he had were too small and they were falling apart, embarrassing him at school . . . and the package came apart and . . . three pamphlets, and a framed certificate. The framed certificate was his father's Master degree.

'I thought you'd like to have that. Give you a little incentive.'

The pamphlets were things like, *Your Career in Research Chemistry!*

'There's good money to be made in that field, working

for those big deodorant corporations, Brian. Judy Clapper's brother-in-law Tony works at Glass Bell Toiletries. He helped invent Pore-Plug, you know. And Glass Bell's not even one of the big companies, and he makes – '

'Jeez, Mom, I don't wanta spend my life making deodorant!'

'Pore-Plug has been very good to Tony. If you – '

Desperately changing the subject, Brian put in, 'Mom – don't you want to know how I did on my term tests?'

'I know how you did. I called your teachers. You got A's on both. But I want you to know I'm very disappointed in you.'

He stared at her, numbed.

She went on, 'I spoke to Mrs Gilmore and she says you take no interest in extra-curricular activities. Brian, you should get *involved*, those things look good on your record when you're looking for a job after college. You could join some school clubs – '

'Mom, I don't have *time*, I'm taking extra classes – '

'What else have you got to do with your spare – '

'I don't *have* any spare time! And I don't know what else I'd do if I had some – but I want to find out, Mom. Jeez, I need some time to . . . Mom, Mr Greenburg suggested I take a year off from school after I graduate and, uh, get a job and use the money to buy a car and maybe, I don't know, go out or – '

'I can't believe you'd do that.' Her dangerously-flat voice. 'I can't believe it. All our plans – *phhht!* You'd do that to your mother – to your *father?*'

'Mom, it wouldn't hurt my GPA – '

'I really can't believe it.' Shaking her head with exaggerated incredulity. 'I just . . . can't . . . believe it.'

He knew, then, that it wasn't going to happen. She just wouldn't let it. He'd go to summer school of some kind after high school, to 'give him an edge', and then to college, straight through into college. At fifteen years old. He saw a vista of drudgery opening up before him . . .

She stared at him. 'My God – you're crying! At fifteen!' Stop it, he told himself. Stop crying.

She went pitilessly on. 'I mean, it's not enough that you don't have the gumption to get involved in extra-curriculars, you have to be a cry-baby too. Your father would be just plain disgusted.'

Cort, the adult, had to look away from the scene.

The lawns had humped up and reshaped themselves for Bucky, Cort saw. They'd disgorged rock and soil and agate that'd melded together into a sort of instant alloy of simulated metal, and formed itself into the lifesized shape of a Lincoln Continental. The earthen luxury car carried Bucky around and around the giant Pursbinder trophy, and around the quivering translucent girls, with a kind of ritualistic redundancy; miniature mansions grew up from the ground, formed of the local silicon, into fantastic shapes somewhere between miniature-golf castles and Bucky's fantasy of the perfect home . . .

A couple of students had discovered the IAMton concentration, one of them screaming in horror as the earth erupted his phobia – which he'd just been trying to come to terms with in the biology lab: white rats made of roots and silicon, rats the size of dogs, capering on their hind legs in a Disneyesque square dance . . .

The girl student with him was backing away from an enormous baby, a house-sized baby of yellow clay. The elephantine infant playfully slapped a gardener's wheel-barrow so it arced up, over the roof of the lab and struck a chimney with a lovely clang, showering sparks and bricks; the baby giggled earthshakingly.

Cort closed his eyes, took a series of deep breaths, and once more heard the nagging disembodied voice, 'Cort!

Get to work on this thing! The explosion could be a breakthrough! Why are you wasting your time playing mindgames with your memory? Get back to work!'

But after a moment he found himself looking at the living sculpture once more.

Saw himself within it: as a young man at his mother's funeral.

Saw the expression on his face and knew what he'd been thinking: *I can do what I want, now*.

Then came the wince of guilt. *How can you be glad she's dead? Your father would be . . . disgusted.*

Telling himself: *There's no reason I should feel guilty. I'm not glad she's dead. But since she is, since the cancer came along . . . well it's not as if I gave her cancer.*

Reply: *But she implied it was my fault, that all her worrying about me made her prone to it . . .*

Around and around, guilt and resentment like snakes devouring one another and endlessly regenerating and devouring again.

Cort looked away from the sculpture, thinking: *But I went on to do what I wanted*.

He didn't take the chemlab position at Glass Bell Toiletries or the one at Dow. He was interested in particle physics, and he pursued that interest, in defiance of his mother's dying wish. Ending up at the one place that would give him a free hand in research: Pennyworth College.

Where he met Betty.

Within the softly contoured stumpy torso of marble, the living hieroglyphs were again coming alive, taking on three dimensional shape, filling his eyes, whispering to him . . .

* * *

Dr Winslow Garland's party. Celebrating the grant for the new super-miniaturized particle accelerator. Garland's shabby little backyard, that summer evening. Bach playing softly from the wheezing stereo; groups of professors, assistants, deans, a few students most of them clumped near the big clamshell-shaped bowl of cloying wine punch on the checkercloth-covered cardtable; chatting, drinking the awful punch. Betty was helping Mrs Garland lay out fresh canapes. But now and then she glanced up at Cort, who was standing alone at the rose-twined back fence.

He'd seen Betty watching him, calculating and predatory. Somehow she'd decided on him. He could feel it, though she hadn't said much to him at the party, hadn't wound her coils of precious, dryly flirtatious small talk around him this time.

Go on, he told himself. Talk to her. You're lonely. She's interested. You're a research prof at a minor college and you can't expect starlets or even sex-hungry coeds to come nuzzling up to you. You can't hope for anyone more attractive than Betty.

Replying to: But I tried it, I dated her twice and she annoys me. She prattles, she pretends an interest in physics she doesn't have, she doesn't like the opera, she doesn't like the theater only because 'why pay to go sit in an uncomfortable seat and watch those things when you can see them free on public television?' She's tight with her money which means she'll be tight with mine. She's selfish about a thousand little things which means she'll be selfish about all the big things. She wants to get married, I can feel it, and I don't want to spend my life with someone who annoys me.

She was coming over to talk to him.

Cort thinking: This is my chance to put an end to it, I'll simply snub her. She'll leave me alone. It doesn't matter what she says about me, these people don't like me much anyway.

But that voice again, telling him: It does matter. Her uncle is Joshua Pennyworth. You'd be advancing your career if you married her. Do something right for once . . .

Looking at the miniature re-enactment in the sculpture, Cort shuddered, seeing something jarringly out of place in it.

Impossibly, his mother was there, at Professor Garland's party. Years after she'd died.

Mother was standing beside the image of Cort at the party. No, she was standing *in* him. Half in, half out of him, almost like a Siamese twin. Her image was semi-transparent; his was solid. She wasn't there, really – but the IAMtons were showing him the psychological reality, this time.

And when he walked, he walked strangely – 'the Cort shuffle', he'd overheard one of the students calling it. He saw now that he walked oddly because his mother was merged into his leg. Was tugging it her way. And she was bent over him, her face gone birdlike as she dug her beak into his ear and whispered, 'Don't be an idiot. Betty's perfect for you . . .'

He knew the voice now. The voice that had said, *Do something right for once*. His mother's voice.

She looked out of the sculpture at him. His mother in miniature, cobbled grotesquely onto the miniature, earlier Cort. Mother, gazing out at him with contempt.

Cort turned away from the sculpture. Stomach churning, he lurched across the grass to walk, looked around, trying to re-orient himself.

Bucky had collapsed with exhaustion, was lying asleep

on the grass; his IAMton constructions had degenerated into fuzzy-edged abstracts, geometrical cut-outs that took on anthropomorphic shape from time to time, then fell back into component geometry; they shimmered in and out of free-associative definition, reflecting his dreams.

A group of children had run out onto the IAMton zone and were giddily helping the Coyote chase the Roadrunner, the figures three-dimensional and childsized and giving every appearance of being alive; the children laughed every time the Roadrunner went *beep-beep!*. Bugs Bunny looked on jeering, while GI Joe, squatting beside Bugs, cleaned his rifle, looking around tensely for some *real* action.

Cort thought: *I'd better get out of here before I get caught up in something I can't get out of . . .*

He moved off down the path between a row of small trees – and stopped, staring. The trees were writhing, re-shaping with nightmarish familiarity. A squat holly tree was bulging here, contracting there, rustling with the movement as it rearranged and recolored itself, becoming a pointillistic reproduction of his wife Betty. A Betty twenty-eight feet tall.

Berries in the holly bush rearranged to become Betty's sulky lips; leaves and shadows conspired to form her beaklike nose – so like Mother's – and her sunken, accusatory eyes. The holly bush bent over him and said, 'You didn't love me, but you married me anyway and now I have to suffer because of your hypocrisy, and oh yes, I *know* you don't love me, I can *feel* you not caring – '

He felt the requisite stab of guilt – and then heard another furious rustling, turned to see a willow tree, green-furred with buds, whipping its long, drooping branches about, shaping itself into a likeness of his mother.

His mother was traced in the sky with a willow-twig filigree, droning through her nose, as always: '. . . if your father was alive he'd be disgusted . . .' and 'I'm very disappointed in you . . .' and on, and on.

Betty yammering on one side, Mommy Dearest droning on the other, and the grass rustling, shifting, the blades bending and bunching to form two-foot-high letters in green: *IAM CORT* AND *IAM* DISAPPOINTING . . . *IAM* NOT LIKE MY FATHER . . . *IAM* A BAD HUSBAND . . . *IAM* A FAILURE, *IAM* A LOSER . . . As the sidewalk before him humped up, buckling, IAMton-impregnated concrete that should have cracked, instead going rubbery, elastically bulging, reddening, pulsing . . . a great red boil waist-high, swelling on the sidewalk before him; splitting open, glutinously erupting a slime-coated, inchoate human figure emerging from it as if from a soft egg: Cort himself, but a Cort deformed, a dwarfish parody, its face a rigid mask of self-pity; its hunched back striped with welts.

Cort saw it for what it was: his own guilt-deformed self-image. And beyond it he saw the ground rippling as the roots of the willow tree nosed like enormous earthworms across the grass, under the walk, through the ground to the holly tree, to 'Betty', to entwine the trunk of the Betty-shaped tree. And he saw the roots of the holly tree elongating, stretching to entwine the base of the willow; and he saw that the wife-tree and the mother-tree were bent over the twisted image of himself, incanting at it, and he saw that it reacted to their accusations, their condemnations, by deforming further, becoming more repulsively toadlike . . .

Seeing all this enacted, he knew: He'd married Betty because he knew she'd treat him as his mother had. Because the nagging, deriding part of his mind that his mother had planted in him had pushed him into it. The mother that he carried around with him had recognized Betty for what she was . . .

It was horribly, laughably absurd. And exposed as absurd it lost all its power to mold him. He walked past himself, past his guilt-ridden self, and left it behind.

Light as a soap bubble, he could laugh at the wasted years. And a great, shuddery wave of sheer relief swept him almost running out of the campus, past the area of IAMton impregnation – which was already beginning to disperse with entropy. He'd think about the scientific implications of all this later. First, he had to get his life in order. Beginning with finding a new place to live – a place where he'd live alone, really alone, for the first time.

And as he passed a church on that Sunday afternoon, the people arriving for services stared at him – and wondered why he looked so goddamned happy.

Ticket to Heaven

I never really wanted to go to Heaven. But I knew someone would make me. There was pressure on me to go there. To Heaven. Starting the morning I met Putchek . . .

'Barry!' Gannick said when I dragged myself into his office. 'Meet Frank Putchek, director of Club Eden.'

'Hey,' I said. 'Howya doin'.' I smiled woodenly, shook Putchek's hand mechanically.

You have to understand that it was 3:30. I'd been in the office since nine – this not being one of your breezy, we're-all-chums advertising agencies where the idea men are permitted to be prima donnas – and I'd spent the morning thinking of ways to convince the public it needs Triple M brand Hamburger Enhancer. (But of course we'd end up explaining to the world that the three Ms should stand for *Mmm!* as in *Mmm Good!* Any jackass would have come up with the same thing, and Triple M could've saved a bundle on an advertising agency. But agencies like mine thrive on the bad habits of industry . . .) I spent lunch flattering Jemmy Sorgenson from Maplethorpe and Sorgenson, in the hopes that she'd offer me a job at a better salary and maybe residuals. I'd spent the first part of the afternoon thinking of ways to convince the public it needed a certain artificial sweetener, one only mildly carcinogenic. And by 3:00, after a hard day of constructing artful lies and fighting the tides of self-disgust, I was burnt, looking at the world through glazed eyes. By 3:15, everything in the office was flat and two dimensional, threatening to fold down into one-dee. By

3:30 some mysterious temporal voodoo arrests the clock, and the pace of time becomes a hunchbacked old lady with an aluminum walker. And that's when Gannick called me in to meet Putchek.

Putchek was a middle-aged guy with a smallish head, chipmunk cheeks, and a seemingly infinite wealth of smile lines around his mouth and eyes. He smiled a lot, mostly with his mouth slightly open, looking goofy with his over-bite. He was tall, round-shouldered, wore dandruff-flecked wire-rims. But he had a nice blue and dove-gray Pierre Hayakawa designer suit, and immaculate patent leather shoes.

I didn't notice all this at first. Only his spongy hand-shake and a sort of Putchek-shaped blur. He could've been part of the furniture.

Gannick, my boss, was sitting behind his desk in shirt sleeves, on his special chair to make him less midgetish, his high forehead was a little less furrowed than usual, his small shoulders almost relaxed, his darting black eyes for once relatively stationary.

Gannick was happy about something. Putchek must represent a juicy account.

I screwed my smile down into something faint but superficially warm, and sat across from Putchek where I could look out the window at the chill, brittle spires of Manhattan's petrified forest. *Petrified*, I thought. *Me too*.

'Coffee, Barry?' Gannick asked me.

'No, thanks.'

'He doesn't need coffee,' Gannick said, pretend-confidingly to Putchek. 'Or even cocaine. Barry Thorpe runs on adrenaline.' He grinned to soften the sarcasm. I must've looked more wooden than I thought.

Putchek tried to get the joke and blinked at the two of us. 'Oh, uh-huh. Heh heh.'

Gannick said, 'Barry, Club Eden's Paradise Vacations

is our new account – I guess you've heard rumors – ' I
hadn't heard a word ' – and it's something a little, well,
unusual, and since you, Barry, are a little, well,
unusual – ' He paused for everyone to chuckle, so we did.
'I thought you ought to head this up.'

He beamed, and I tried to look pleased. It was as if the
strings operating the muscles of my face were stretched
out, threadbare, because I couldn't quite manage the
expression I wanted.

'You OK, Barry?' Gannick asked.

'Just tired.' I summoned a little focus, a little anima-
tion. 'Well – have we got a prospectus or a press kit or
. . . slides?'

'Slides of . . .?' Putchek asked.

'The uh, resorts or – '

'There aren't any resorts!' Putchek brought his hands
together as if he'd clap them, and then did a sort of joyful
wringing instead, shifted on his chair, and said, a little
impishly, 'Club Eden doesn't send people to anywhere on
this planet, ah, Barry.'

It was my turn to blink in confusion. More of the room
jumped into sharp focus. They had my attention. I turned
to Gannick. 'Correct me if I'm wrong – I know I'm a little
out of it at times – but did I lose twenty or thirty years
somewhere? Are we in the twenty-first century alluvasud-
den? Last I knew, it was just 1998; I'm sure of it.
Interplanetary travel is still unmanned, right?'

'It's a manner of speaking. We're not sending people
to another planet, per se,' Putchek explained. 'We're
sending them to another . . . another existential focal
point. Another plane, to use the metaphysical jargon . . .
We send them to *Heaven*.'

I looked at Putchek, and then at Gannick. 'Heaven.
Some kind of sensurround laser show, huh – 360-degree
screens, incense?'

Gannick said slowly, 'Nuh-ope. They put you in a machine and . . . you really feel physically like you've gone someplace. A sort of mind-trip through I guess, some kind of electronic stimulation of the brain or . . .' He shot a glance of polite inquiry at Putchek.

Putchek hemmed, getting ready to haw. 'If ah, if you like. You can, ah, look at it like that.' He glanced up at me. 'It'd really help if you went there. Yourself. Then you'd . . . accept it.' He looked embarrassed, stared at his reflection in his shoes, and his mouth was shut – as much as it would shut, with his over-bite – and all of a sudden he worried me.

The next day was Saturday. Under the business-incentive labor laws, most of the population had to work on Saturday. But not me, I could putter around my weekend house with a drink in my hand. Getting gloomier as I got drunker, opaquing the windows and dialing the lights low, enjoying the gloom, hugging the house's darkness. Thinking about the Club Eden demonstration I was supposed to go to on Monday.

We send them to Heaven, Putchek had said. Neurological heaven, I supposed. Some pleasure-inducing machine, perhaps.

Heaven, at Putchek's prices, was something only a few could afford.

I shrugged. What else was new?

I went to the picture window, thumbed the button, and the window glass rippled into transparency. The spring afternoon was startling, almost tastelessly garish after the artificial twilight of my house.

I blinked in the unwanted sunshine, and the whiskey made my head ache. Tumbler in hand, I looked out over one of Hartford's prettiest suburbs. Trees lined the street with newly budded clouds of soft green; here and there were the bright pom-poms of flowering fruit trees. I realized I had no idea exactly what kind of trees most of them were. I'd lived here for five years, and I didn't know what kind of trees were on the street. Or my neighbor's first name.

But I knew my neighbor was Security Passed. We were all Security Passed, in Connecticut Village. When you drove in, you showed the checkpoint guards your Residency Card, or gave a visitor's number. To get a Residency Card, to be passed, you had to have a B-3 credit rating, and of course no record as a felon. It was a closed community, but not internally gregarious; the late-twentieth century's fragmentation of true community feeling extended its anti-roots even here, where all looked cozy. We had television; we had interactive video and TV shopping networks. We had our lifestyles. We had shrugged off the responsibility that acknowledging strangers brings. Because one stranger leads to another, and not very far beyond the checkpoint was the crumbling border of Hartford's Shacktown, swollen with strangers we didn't want to meet. And tried not to think about.

I wasn't always the model resident of Connecticut Village. I'd written some stuff for *The Reformist*, before I'd gotten scared into money hunting; before Gannick found me. What I'd written was pretty self-righteous, foolishly idealistic stuff . . .

Like:

Every town has its Shacktown, squatter enclaves grown up in the cracks between the neat little high-security Urban Village units the cities have become; the refuge of the legions of homeless, the disenfranchized of every profession: those who worked in industry and oil, before hands-on industry became an overseas venture and oil became an obsolete energy source; those who worked in construction before the contractors went to seventy-five percent premolded structures and robotics.

Those without white collar work skills; or those who'd failed to fit in with the country's biggest employer, the 'service' industry, that great consumer-supply mechanism so like a chicken-feeding machine on a poultry ranch . . .

The Shacktowns are tenanted by people who, a decade or two ago, built the affluence that the privileged feed off of now. Jobless Blacks are in the Shacktowns, of course. And the old. Since the demographic shifts of the '70s and '80s, and the growth of geriatric medicine, the old have become a huge, mouldering slice of the population. And millions of them went discarded, forgotten, cold-shouldered by the post-welfare society: the fresh new, yuppie-shiny world where Entrepreneurs are messiahs, where those who failed to Earn are cast into the outer darkness, beyond the borders of the profit margin . . .

Stuff like that. Foolish stuff. The generalization of College Journalism. Anyway, why go on about it, when the response is always the same? They'll say, 'So what?'

And if the Residency Committee knew I'd written that stuff for *The Reformist*, I'd never have been Security Passed for Connecticut Village.

Sometimes I passed Shacktown on the freeway. Just a sort of smudgy gray tumble of shanties glimpsed through the hurricane fence. From inside a microchip-driven car whistling smoothly down the freeway, the poor were reduced to a blur of embarrassment. The whole world became a visual shrug at a hundred and ten miles an hour . . .

I knew there was bribery in it somewhere. I knew it when Gannick said, 'The FDA's given Club Eden full approval. The patent bureau, everyone, they're lining up to give their blessing.' It was the way he said it. Quick, with an undertone that warned me not to harp on the subject. So I didn't ask why there hadn't been any newspaper talk about it yet. Obviously, they'd worked hard to keep it mum till federal approval was *fait accompli*. Wouldn't want any nosy Senate subcommittees to delay approval . . .

It was Monday afternoon, and we were in what was to be the Club Eden showroom. Me and Gannick and Putchek and Putchek's secretary, Buffy. She was a sort of human Happy Face who went by 'Buffy' with no outward evidence of shame.

The showroom had been the front office of a large travel agency. The posters and brochure racks and desks and the fat, middle-aged ladies with the snail-shell hairdos had been cleared out, and now there was only the transport rig, like a hump of frozen milk under the fluorescent lights in one corner of the room, and some paint-jigsawed newspapers around the freshly rollered walls.

I looked at the transport rig and told myself, *Take it easy; it's probably harmless.*

It looked harmless. It looked like one of those little imitation race-car seats you get into at a video arcade. Except, on the outside it was all designer-stylized, a sculptured teardrop of imitation mother-of-pearl. The little door was open. Inside there was a chair, and a few dials on a dashboard. No controls, nothing else. I asked, 'No helmet? Something to wire into the brain, to create the illusion? Or do you just inject them with something and, uh – ' I had to cough; a recent coat of freshly applied blue paint suffused the shuttered room with quivery fumes.

Putchek cleared his throat. 'No. No other, ah, fixtures are necessary. It's mostly automatic.'

Buffy, as might be expected, was short, pert, faintly plump, auburn-haired, and dimple-cheeked. She had silver-flecked china-blue eyes and stubby, pudgy white fingers awkwardly extended by three-inch glue-on nails;

blue nails with white glitter. She wore a puce jumpsuit, which was her version of a test pilot's get-up.

'I'm all ready!' she told Gannick, a trifle too eagerly. Her voice was breathy and maddeningly affected.

'Have you done this before, Buffy?' I asked.

'Oh, uh-huh, sure!' she lilted. 'Mm-hmm, and we had a kinda test pilot guy, and before that, monkeys, and pigeons.'

'They're *still* using pigeons,' Gannick whispered to me as she turned and climbed into the machine. She closed the door behind her. The rig started to hum.

Putchek tilted his head back, as if listening to some beloved song. His dirty spectacles washed out in the light. 'One of our big selling points,' Putchek said absently, 'is going to be a money-back guarantee.'

Gannick's eyebrows shot up. 'Money-back guarantee? That's a big risk, Frank. I mean, everyone I've met who's tried it is enthused – but there are all kinds of people out there. Brain chemistries, metabolisms – there're no two exactly alike. If there're even twenty percent who don't like the experience – '

'I can't go into all the details,' Putchek said slowly, looking at himself in his shoes again, hands in his pockets. 'But let's just say we are ninety-nine percent confident that virtually everyone will like it. There's some risk. But it's worth it.'

The rig's humming had risen in pitch – and I winced as it passed out of the audible range. I felt a ripple go through me, and a tightness in my chest, a pinching at the back of my throat. For the briefest of moments, I had a peculiar feeling that Buffy was all around me. It was cloying, believe me. And then the room was normal again.

Putchek glanced at the rig. 'She'll be out in, oh, five minutes, vacation complete.'

I looked at him. 'What's the list price on this?'

'Once we get rolling, ah, five thousand newbux per vacation. We won't be selling the machines at all, for at least a decade. And it's gimmicked so anyone who tries breaking into one to see its works will only find a glob of smoking slag inside.'

'Five thousand newbux . . .' I stared at him. 'A thousand bills a minute?'

I could feel Gannick glaring at me. *Don't offend the client*, the glare was telling me.

Putchek was unruffled. 'Only objectively. It doesn't feel like five minutes to them. They think it's months. Depends on how subjective their personalities are. It'll feel like at least a month has passed. For some it may feel like an eternity. Of pure, uninterrupted happiness.' He looked at me as if to say, *What do you say to THAT?* His head tilted back; his open mouth aimed at me – if I'd looked, I could have checked out his tonsils.

One of Putchek's technicians came in. He was a blond kid, with a samurai haircut; he was wearing an orange jumpsuit, CLUB EDEN ornately stitched onto each shoulder. He sang sotto voce along with something I heard only as a seashell sound leaking from his Walkman earphones. He carried a small box of microchips to the rig, snaking his head to the music. Putchek glanced at him in irritation. 'Chucky, it's not that rig that needs the guidance chips; it's the other one.'

But Chucky didn't hear him. He opened the door of the rig.

It was empty.

Gannick put the scotch down in front of me and said, 'Drink it.' Like a doctor's command.

We were in Putchek's office, and I was in Putchek's chair. He was standing solicitously over me, making a motion with his hands like a fly cleaning its foreclaws, and on the other side of the desk, Gannick was glowering. His expression said, *You're making a great impression on the client. Just great*.

But the girl was gone.

'I'll be OK,' I said. 'I just . . . felt funny for a second.' I looked at Putchek, and then rolled the chair back so he wasn't breathing on me. 'Some kind of stage-magic cabinet?'

He shook his head. 'She's gone, projected. Sliding between planes. We were going to let people believe it was . . . was all in the head, for a while. We thought they'd be too scared otherwise. But believe me – she – '

'My ears are burning!' Buffy announced, giggling, as she came into the room. She looked flushed, happy as a three-year-old with a mouthful of chocolate. 'I'm OK!' she said. 'I've been to Heaven.'

Sometimes, alone at home, I looked at my free pass and tried to talk myself into taking the trip to Heaven. Gannick wanted me to take it, for promotional inspiration. Everyone else wanted to take it. All three of my ex-wives had called, asking me to get them passes. Tickets to Heaven. Just as if they hadn't called me *subhuman, cold-blooded*, and the other things I can't go into without my stomach knotting up. Betty and Tracy cooing at me, posing as affectionate little sisters. But Celia, of course said, 'You owe me this and more, you bastard.'

But I didn't go to Heaven myself. Not for a long time. I told myself it was because of Winslow. But no: Winslow was just an excuse.

He was a good excuse, because Winslow is scary. I met him six months after Buffy vanished and came back. It was Friday night; I was in my weekdays apartment, packing to go out to my place in Connecticut. It was a time when I least brook interruptions. So when the doorbell rang and I opened the hall door, I snarled, 'Yeah? *What?*' And then he flashed the holo. He flipped open his wallet, and the 3-D Federal eagle spread its wings in the wallet, and across its breast was the luminous banner: *Jeffrey C. Winslow, Special Agent, Food and Drug Administration*.

'Mr Barry Thorpe?'

'Uh. Useless to deny it, right?'

Winslow didn't crack a smile. He was black-suited, with the fashionable bureaucrat's triple-tongue necktie – and he was an albino. An apparition. The Ghost of Bureaucracy Past, I thought. Carrying an alumitech briefcase instead of a ball and chain.

He looked at me with an expression stark as a No Trespassing sign. 'I'm doing a series of interviews, Mr Thorpe, to follow up on our temporary approval of Club Eden. May I come in?'

'You got the wrong guy. I'm just the barker; I don't own the carny. You want to talk to Putchek. Maybe Gannick.'

'I've talked to them. I'll be talking to them again.' He waited. The FDA is responsible for more than food and drugs; Club Eden used a machine that affected people physically, hence it was under their jurisdiction. And hence, Winslow.

Resignedly, I said, 'Come on in.'

He was all questions. No accusations. And all the questions seemed routine. 'When you interview a returned vacationer for an endorsement, are they paid for the interview?' Things he already knew the answer to. Until he slung this one at me underhand: 'Are you aware of any sums paid by Mr Putchek or Mr Gannick or their representatives to agents or functionaries of the FDA?'

I thought: *No, they don't tell anyone but the guy they're bribing.* But all I said was, 'No.'

'Thanks very much.' He stood up and gave me a limp handshake. 'That'll do it for this time.' And he left.

This time?

I went out to a bar, found a pay phone, and called Gannick.

'It's nothing,' he told me. 'There's a little bureaucratic power struggle at the FDA. And this guy Winslow works for the guys trying to pull off the coup. They want to prove wrongdoing on the part of the FDA commissioners, take over their jobs. But they got nothing. Uh . . . did he ask about the Charred Pad effect? Corporeal side effects?'

'No. *What* side effects are those? Gannick, I'm supposed to get the straight scoop on this stuff when I – '

'Hey, we're not holding out on you. Nothing important. Don't worry about it; it's all bullshit. Hey, I got a steak burning; I gotta go – Listen, Barry: just head out to Connecticut and forget it.'

I knew Gannick's don't-ask-questions-if-you-love-your-paycheck tone. So I hung up, and tried to forget about Winslow.

God knows, it sounded good when people described it.

I was in my office, brainstorming a new fifteen-second spot for the Federal Broadcasting Agency's latest prime-time hit: *Yoshio Smith: Assassin for the CIA.* Club Eden was a major sponsor for the show.

I was watching a videotape of the writer Alejandro Buckner, talking about his first Club Eden vacation. He was beaming, still in afterglow. Buckner was round-faced, and normally he looked like a sadistic cupid; today he was positively cherubic. 'Heaven is not Christian, particularly; there is no biblical God in evidence, no angels, precisely, though the Prefects of Heaven perhaps fill the bill. But Heaven will satisfy the Christian, the Buddhist, or the Hindu. Anyone.

'Some people have claimed Heaven looks different for everybody – but it isn't really so. It's got a landscape, definite topographical features . . . It just depends on which part you tend to get projected to. And that's decided by your personality. Some people are projected into the pastoral Heaven, some of them into the urban one. Many into the one that's a sort of idealized suburb. Me, I'm an unabashed urban Heaven man – only, it was a series of rooftop gardens; a sort of Hanging Gardens of Babylon variation of the great penthouses of Manhattan. But of course, in Heaven there are no pigeon droppings; there is no smog, no acid rain; there are no thudding helicopters, screaming jets – though you might see some aerial gliders, impossibly graceful; everything has a sort of nimbus, like when you do certain drugs – but when you look close, you see it's just the shine off that thing's perfection, the natural glow of its excellence; you don't get tired in heaven, but sometimes you sleep, and it's somehow just when the people around you want to sleep; there are no mosquitoes, no venomous things, no maggots, no defecation, no halitosis; there *is* sex in Heaven, however you like it, but it's more like dancing – somehow it loses all its earthly clumsiness. And it never becomes excessive, even though the orgasms are slow, full, and not enervating. Food exudes from the tables as you need it, but you never fall into gluttony. You cannot break your bones; you cannot fall ill. Nothing dies. Everything is easy, but nothing is dull. There are no conversational dullards; no *faux pas*, or awkward silences. There are sharp smells, and soft smells, but no bad smells. I say again that Heaven is not in the least dull. There are storms, and there is snow – but only when everyone's in the mood. There is contention there, but never acrimony; all contention is glorious sport, in Heaven.'

It can't be that perfect, I thought. I didn't want it to be. Perfection is suspicious, is improbable, and I wanted Heaven to be real. So I was relieved when he said, 'You can't do just anything you want there. If you want to interrogate the other entities – they look like people, but then again, they don't; they're all sort of soft-edged and shimmery – anyway, if you want to ask awkward questions about the place, then you've brought a lot of "inappropriate psychodynamics" with you, as one of the Prefects said to me. You've brought "neurotic attachments". All inappropriate in Heaven. So the Prefects – they look like firefly glows, without the fireflies, and much larger – they swarm up to you and sort of smooth you out, and then you forget all your pushiness, your capacity for violence . . . and your questions. Your questions are answered only with a sort of impression: that the place is indeed something you're supposed to have earned. That it's a "higher state of communion with the universe". And that should be enough for you . . . But there's something else kind of funny about the place . . .'

I leaned forward, sharply attentive.

Buckner said abstractedly, 'The entities who are there all the time, who are native to it, well, they look at you like . . . um, they don't really *snub* you or anything; there's nothing unfriendly . . . but there's a sort of benevolent surprise. As if they sense that you don't belong there . . .'

The tape ended there. Gannick's interviewer hadn't liked the direction Buckner was taking, and we had enough 'good review' from him anyway. The tape ended, and the regular transmission on the TV monitor came on – I started to switch off, but found myself watching. It was a news bulletin.

Four tenements had collapsed an hour earlier, in the Bronx. About 270 people were feared injured or dead. 'Portions of the building just seemed to crumble into dust,' the housing commissioner was quoted as saying. 'Something similar happened about two weeks ago in Chicago – also a low-rent area – and we think it's a result of termite damage or acid rain damage to these old buildings.'

Insects or acid rain or both. Oh. An explanation. It felt good to have an explanation for something like that. Even one that felt *wrong* when you really thought about it. So don't think about it, I told myself.

The phone rang. It was Winslow. I didn't put him on-screen. I didn't want to see the white face and the black suit. 'Mr Thorpe,' he said, 'I just want you to know that if you want to tell me anything, anything at all, I will see to it that it'll be safe for you. With respect to prosecution.'

'You're with the FDA, not the FBI, Winslow. You seem to get them mixed up.'

'Let's just say that this investigation is a little special. If you can tell me about the Corporeal Side Effects report on the Club Eden phenomena – '

'I really don't know what you're talking about,' I said sincerely.

'If you want to play that game – fine. But we'll see who wins.'

'FDA, Winslow, FDA. The other one is the Federal Bureau of – '

He hung up.

I shrugged. But then I thought: *Either he's a loon, or we're in trouble and we don't know it.*

Don't think about it. It's Gannick's problem.

I went home.

* * *

I sat in my confoam chair, nestling into its artificial hug, with the windows opaqued and the lights dimmed, playing my hiding game, pretending it was nighttime and dark out; anyway, it was dark *in*. I sat there sipping Johnnie Walker and listened to the TV talk about vacationing in Heaven, and I thought: *I don't like this life. I don't like this world. So why don't I go?*

The Special Report anchormen talked about 'the Club Eden phenomenon'. Described the depression and ennui Club Eden returnees slipped into when the afterglow wore off. Noted that there was no actual physical addiction, but there *was* an indication of compulsiveness. 'After you get over the depression,' a returnee told the cameras, 'you get back into the groove of regular life. Everything seems kind of dingy and dirty and tired and stiff, for a while – but pretty soon you start to enjoy life again, and, you know, you stop yearning for Heaven all the time. But as soon as you've got the money again, man, you *sign up!*'

Certain psychiatrists, whom I knew to be in the pay of Club Eden, made great, soft-edged, rolling claims for the therapeutic benefits of a Club Eden vacation. A few Southern senators muttered darkly about the religious implications. Club Eden had stopped calling the projection plane 'Heaven', but that's what everyone thought it was. So the Moral Majority stamped their feet and pouted.

Senator Wexler called for an investigation into the risks, stating it was only a matter of time before the transport rigs went haywire and projected someone into a mountain, or the ocean – or maybe into Hell. And if that didn't happen, there was a danger someone might develop 'bootleg' transport rigs. Club Eden had resisted franchizing. It held onto the monopoly with all the legal strength; that the $400 million they'd made could give them. That was a lot of strength.

After the Special Report, I had my third scotch, and listened to the regular newscaster dolefully announce that, yes, the government had admitted that the country was sliding into a severe recession. Yes, there was a rather unexpected oil shortage, a general energy crunch, epidemic problems with power plant generators around the country; indeed, around the world . . . And the Shacktowns were growing.

I rewound the cassette, so I could listen to Buckner again, and take notes.

Club Eden was hot. Club Eden was The Buzz. There was suspicion, outrage, investigations. But Club Eden kept on through it all, and Gannick and I did our work.

Don't take Paradise for granted . . . until you've tried Club Eden. And: *So you think this* (a slick Kodachrome photo of a glorious South Pacific beach: deep blue sky, crystal waters, emblematically perfect palm trees) *is Paradise? You haven't tried Club Eden.* And: *Club Eden: Who needs drugs?*

I had my free pass, locked up in my desk at home. Gannick encouraged me to go. Putchek encouraged me. Putchek went himself sometimes. There was a limit to how often you could go, and how long you could stay, something to do with electromagnetic stress on the body, but Putchek went as often as the safety regimen would allow.

Gannick didn't go. He said poker at the club with a pretty girl bringing the dry martinis was heaven enough for him.

'But I want *you* to go,' he said. 'OK, Barry?'

So I sat in my apartment on a Saturday evening, a year after Buffy had vanished and came back, thinking about using my pass. Not worrying about Winslow – he'd come only once more, and it had been more of the same. I'd almost forgotten about him.

The Shacktowners couldn't afford a ticket to Heaven. But I had one. So why didn't I use it? I went to the safe I kept the pass in, and opened it. I looked at the pass. I couldn't quite –

That's when the doorbell rang, and somehow I knew it would be Winslow.

Guiltily, I locked the pass away and opened the door for him – and stared. He looked different now. The veneer was gone. So was the badge and the alumitech briefcase. He wore a cheap printout paper suit and dark glasses; and the left lens on the dark glasses was cracked. He smelled like beer, and he listed to the right.

I was seeing a different Winslow here, and I liked him better. 'Gotta talk to you,' Winslow said.

'Come on in and have a drink,' I said. 'As if you needed one.'

He reached into a pocket and took a gun from it. It was small, a .25, but it would put a hole right through me, at this range. 'No. You come out. We're going for a drive.'

We were walking along a pitted gravel road, under a lowering gray sky. The clouds at the horizon were reddening in sunset and beginning to shed rain; in the red tint it looked as if the clouds were bleeding. We walked between the shanties of Shacktown, through smells that would have stopped me like a brick wall if the gun hadn't been in Winslow's coat pocket. Winslow was talking, talking, talking, with a sort of excessive care that only underlined his drunkenness. 'Mr Danville – my supervisor – and I received a sort of anonymous tip, a transcription of a conversation between two lawyers, one for a certain Janet Rivera and the other working for Club Eden. Club

Eden was offering Janet Rivera a fat settlement, a million newbux, and she took the money and ran. It seems that with a very minor adjustment of the transport rig – or a power surge at the wrong time – the vacationer will arrive in something very like Hell. Perhaps it's like this . . .'

He gestured vaguely at the packed-in, mud-encrusted, sewage-reeking shanties; the drawn faces peering from beneath plastic sheets nailed over crooked doorways. He went on, 'Perhaps it's worse. Ms Rivera was sent to such a Hell. Apparently, Ms Rivera barely kept her sanity . . . Watch out, that dog wants a piece of your thigh. He's wild . . .' It was a bony yellow mongrel, its eyes cloudy, its muzzle ribbed with a snarl. Winslow took the gun from his pocket and said, 'This'll feed some'a these kids.' The gun cracked, making me jump, as he shot the dog in the head. Its legs buckled, and it fell twitching. An old woman, muttering to herself, scurried out and dragged the dead dog by the tail into her hut.

'The transcript got us interested,' Winslow went on as we continued down the road. (I glanced over a shoulder and saw a small crowd following us at a careful distance; a convention of scarecrows.) 'And we saw our chance to pull down the commissioners. They were corrupt, and we'd had enough. We probed, and probed, and came up with something we didn't expect. A correspondence between the increase in Club Eden vacationers and the statistical deterioration of the living conditions of people around them. Putchek knew about it: it was called "launchpad charring" because they likened the trips to Heaven to the launchings of rocket ships – and the launchpads are charred by rocket-ship engines, Thorpe. Club Eden's launchpad is our world; its charring is the side effects on the world: the worsening recession, the widening gap between rich and poor. And as it went on, the exchange became more . . . more literal. Look, Thorpe . . .' He gestured at something.

We had come to a pit in the earth. It was about four hundred yards across, and deeper than I could see, coated with fine gray-black dust. The shanties were built right up to its rim; those nearest it were half fallen, partly sunk in soft ashen ground.

Thick, oily drops of rain pattered down, freckling the gravel and drumming tin rooftops, drumrolling faster and faster as the downpour increased. Under its impact, three of the shacks around the rim of the crater collapsed at once, buckling like the shot dog, crumbling like sand castles under a wave; I heard human voices crying out from the shambles, a dissonant choir, wailing; glimpsed faces in the muddy ash, faces stamped with resignation. Swallowed up a moment later. 'There are lots more like these, Thorpe. All over the world. They sprang up after Club Eden got really big. Thousands of people have gone into these pits. They're all caught up in some kind of . . . of inertia. Despair. So they don't fight it. You can feel the pit pulling at you . . .' He was right: I felt the pit tugging at me, a sort of vacuum sucking at my sense of self-worth, my need to survive. Pulling me apart, making me want to take a step forward, to pitch myself in.

'There's a Federal coverup of all this – ' Winslow was saying.

'Shut up,' I said. I wrenched my gaze from the pit. The urge to throw myself in had almost overwhelmed me. I couldn't stand it there anymore. 'Shoot me or not,' I said. 'I'm leaving.' I turned and started walking back the way we'd come.

I waited for the gunshot. After a moment he was walking beside me, hunched against the rain. Once, he had to fire into the air to disperse the crowd. But in twenty minutes we were in his car.

*   *   *

'Perhaps what happened to me and Danville is part of the pattern of effects that hits anyone who doesn't visit Heaven,' Winslow said. 'Perhaps it'll hit *you*, eventually.' We sat in his car, listening to the rain hammer the roof. He took off his sunglasses and focused his pink eyes on nothing at all. 'We were fired. They said we'd gone beyond the confines of our job, which we had. That we'd made things up. We hadn't.' He tugged idly at a sleeve of his paper suit; the acid rain had worked on it, and the sleeve came away in his fingers. 'I've run out of money. My clothes are rotting on my back. But what matters – what should have mattered – ' he looked at me ' – are those people out there.'

I didn't say anything. I was choking on what I had seen.

He said. 'Why didn't you take the trip?'

'Just a feeling. That it was going too far into pretending that everything was all right. That it was going too far to wallow in our private Heaven when there are so many people in Hell. It was always wrong, but this way I couldn't look away, somehow . . . It was just a step too far . . . Guilt, I guess, is what it boils down to.'

'You had the right instincts, Thorpe. I knew it when I interviewed you – I could tell the whole thing bothered you. I did my homework on you. Read those pieces you wrote a few years back. I know you're not happy about what you do for Gannick; persuading people to squander millions on the pointless consumption of crap. It *bothers* you. But you were addicted to the money.'

'Mostly I was just scared. Of not having an income big enough to save up a safety margin. I was scared of ending up like those people . . . So I had to do it.'

'No, you didn't. You don't. You saw what it led to . . . So, Thorpe – what are you going to do about it?'

'I don't have any proof of bribery. Or anything else. And let me tell you something: the public doesn't want this thing to go sour. They don't want it questioned, or fought. They want Heaven, and damn the consequences, and they're paying into a lot of senatorial campaigns to see to it their chances for Heaven aren't disturbed. I can't do a goddamn thing.'

'You're wrong, Thorpe. What you can do is, precisely, a God Damned Thing.'

I knew what he wanted me to do. No reason I should do it. I could get away; I could escape this. I could begin going to Heaven myself. I could . . .

I couldn't. I saw the faces whose expressions had gone to dust. I felt the suction of the entropy pit. Having seen that, I was transformed by knowledge. I had lost my moral innocence. And knowing: I couldn't turn my back on it. 'What do you want me to do?'

'It starts with a trip to Heaven.'

It's going to be hard, Winslow had said. *Maybe the hardest thing you've ever done.*

It was. It was like someone who loves puppies being forced to throttle one; it was like seeing your mother for the first time in ten years, and then – though you love her – having to spit in her eye at the moment of reunion.

It was like being in Heaven and spurning it. The vista was sweet, soft, warm, like living in an Impressionist's landscape – and, like great Impressionism, never dull. I was nude but unashamed; for the first time I felt nudity without awkwardness. I was drifting weightless over the treetops, basking in just the right amount of sunshine, feeling the caress of the music they gave off, and reveling in the surge of joy that was arrival: the sight of Friends (Friends I had never known before) awaiting me in the garden, turning with a luminous gladness in their faces –

I wrenched myself away and began to Seek.

The act brought the Prefects of Heaven; they emanated

from the trees like a thought from a synapse, and spiraled gracefully round me: soft lights, living questions. They drew closer to assuage the misplaced Desire in me – but, with a crackle of lightning that was an expression of Will, I thrust them back. Refused to let them soothe me into Heaven.

What, then? they asked.

Without speaking, I asked them: How is it we're permitted here at all? For surely this place was something to be earned.

You are permitted here because you have come here. The Great Organizer has made this place; the Great Organizer is the living Principle, who creates all orderliness and harmony. You are here, in Absolute Harmony, so the Organizer must intend it.

I told them what had happened on our world, to the poor. How things had worsened. I asked them why it had happened.

There are Laws regarding the conservation of matter and energy. If you fill a cup from a bottle, the bottle will be that much emptier. Your world is the bottle. Your privileged are emptying it out: the others must suffer. There are machines of metaphysical truth that underlie physical things. You have tampered with the machines. Your wealthy surround themselves with stolen Grace, with unearned Grace: with the subatomic essence of orderliness, stolen from the exploited. This stolen Grace prevents them from paying the price: so others must.

This place, then, is no supernatural paradise?

It is a function of Law: all laws incorporating what you call Physics, all laws of what you call Science, and laws your people haven't learned. This place is a great device; just as in your world a church is a physical construct to represent the idea of holiness, here we used a physical construct to materialize holiness.

Heaven is created by a machine?

Yes. A machine birthed by the great Machine that is the universe.

Then tell me how I can make adjustments, to right the imbalance in the machine, to arrest the deterioration on our end of things.

The obvious, they said.

'For me, it began with a can opener. I saw a hand holding an old-fashioned can opener, the kind you have to stab into the can. But the hand was stabbing it into my belly, opening it like a lid, sawing toward my groin; through the pain I looked harder at the hand and saw it was my own. I could not say that I had no control over it. I controlled the hand, but I was making it cut me open. I was no masochist; I did not enjoy it. I screamed for it to stop, and I meant it. After a while the wound went away, but of course, by then I was making another. Not wanting to, but doing it voluntarily. The paradox sneered at me. At the same time I was watching the great screen where my humili-ations and stupidities replayed, and knew my mother watched on another screen as I bought the favors of a small boy in Spanish Harlem . . . My sensations of humiliation and suffering, in all their permutations, were not diminished in the least by time or familiarity. None of it brought me relief or a sense of expiation . . . Later I found gasoline and tools and grass with dog shit on it, and I used all these things to – '

> – From an interview with Frank Putchek,
>   in the security ward of Bellevue Hospital's
>   Mental Health facility.

It was imprinted in my mind when I came back from Heaven. The Prefects had imprinted the adjustments: the literal, electronic adjustments, the equations for the new guidance chips to go into the transport rig. We went from one Club Eden transport station to another, across the country, Winslow and I, wearing the Club Eden tech-nician's jumpsuits I'd stolen, pretending to be doing routine service checks. Making the adjustments.

We set it up so our readjustments applied exclusively to the new ten-minute vacations, which were available only to the wealthiest vacationers. The industrial barons, their spoiled children; the corporate vampires; the corrupt politicians.

And of course, there was Putchek. We saw to that. Because Winslow had spoken of Putchek, who had admitted he'd known early on about the side effects of granting First Class Tourist passage to Heaven. Putchek had known, and had not cared. Putchek was the first to go; the first of many.

By degrees, it began to work: the suffering of the exploited and the abandoned began to be reversed, and some of the garbage pits became gardens. The ashpits cleared up like the healing of geological chancres. The Shacktowners found strength: they organized, and built, and made demands. There was no Utopia there, and never will be. But there was dignity, and soon there was food and shelter.

We restored the balance. The adjustments worked. It worked because Club Eden had gotten sloppy about security. Which meant we were able to send a surprisingly large number of people to Hell.

But then again, maybe that shouldn't have surprised us.

Wolves of the Plateau

Nine A.M., and Jerome-X wanted a smoke. He didn't smoke, but he wanted one in here, and he could see how people went into prison non-smokers, came out doing two packs a day. Maybe had to get their brains rewired to get off it. Which was ugly, he'd been rewired once to get off *sink*, synthetic cocaine, and he'd felt like a processor with a glitch for a month after that.

He pictured his thoughts like a little train, zipping around the cigarette-burnt graffiti YOU FUCKED NOW and GASMAN WAS HERE and GASMAN IS AN IDIOT-MO. The words were stippled on the dull pink ceiling in umber burn-spots. Jerome wondered who Gasman was and what they'd put him in prison for.

He yawned. He hadn't slept much the night before. It took a long time to learn to sleep in prison. He wished he'd upgraded his chip so he could use it to activate his sleep endorphins. But that was a grade above what he'd been able to afford – and *way* above the kind of brain-chips he'd been dealing. He wished he could turn off the light-panel, but it was sealed in.

There was a toilet and a broken water fountain in the cell. There were also four bunks, but he was alone in this static place of watery blue light and faint pink distances. The walls were salmon-colored garbage blocks. The words singed into the ceiling were blurred and impotent.

Almost noon, his stomach rumbling, Jerome was still lying on his back on the top bunk when the trashcan said,

'Eric Wexler, re-ma-a-in on your bunk while the ne-ew prisoner ente-e-ers the cell!'

Wexler? Oh, yeah. They thought his name was Wexler. The fake ID program.

He heard the cell door slide open; he looked over, saw the trashcan ushering a stocky Chicano guy into lockup. The trashcan was a stumpy metal cylinder with four camera lenses, a retractable plastic arm, and a gun muzzle that could fire a Taser charge, rubber bullets, tear gas pellets, or .45 caliber rounds. It was supposed to use the .45 only in extreme situations, but the 'can was battered, it whined when it moved, its voice was warped. When they got like that you didn't fuck with them, they'd mix up the rubber bullets with the .45 caliber.

The door sucked itself shut, the trashcan whined away down the hall, its rubber wheels squeaking once with every revolution. Jerome heard a tinny cymbal crash as someone, maybe trying to get the trashcan to shoot at a guy in the next cell, threw a tray at it. Followed by some echoey shouting and a distorted admonishment from the trashcan. The Chicano guy laughed.

''Sappenin'?' Jerome said, sitting up on the bed. He was grateful for the break in the monotony.

'*Qué pasa, cabrône?* You like the top bunk, huh? Thas good.'

'I can read the ceiling better from up here. About ten seconds' worth of reading matter. It's all I got. You can have the lower bunk.'

'You fuckin'-*A* I can.' But there was no real aggression in his tone. Jerome thought about turning on his chip, checking the guy's subliminals, his somatic signals, going for a model of probable aggression index; or maybe project for deception. He could be an undercover cop: Jerome hadn't given them his dealer; hadn't bargained at all.

But he decided against it. Some jails had scanners for unauthorized chip output. Better not use it unless he had to. And his gut told him this guy was only a threat if he felt threatened. His gut was right almost as often as his brain-chip.

The Chicano was thick bodied, maybe five foot six, a good five inches shorter than Jerome but probably outweighed him by fifty pounds. His face had Indian angles and small jet eyes. He was wearing printout gray-blue prison jams, #6631; they'd let him keep his hairnet. Jerome had never understood the Chicano hairnet, never had the balls to ask about it. The Chicano was standing by the plexigate, hands shoved in his pockets, staring at Jerome, looking like he was trying to place him.

Jerome was pleased. He liked to be recognized, except by people who could arrest him.

'You put your hands in the pockets of those paper pants, they'll rip and in LA County they don't give you any more for three days,' Jerome advised him.

'Yeah? Shit.' The Chicano took his hands carefully out of his pockets. 'I don't want my *huevos* hanging out, people think I'm advertising some shit. You not a faggot, right?'

'Nope.'

'Good. How come I know you? When I *don't* know you.'

Jerome grinned. 'From television. You saw my tag. Jerome-X.'

'Ohhhh yeah. Jerome-X. You got one of those little transers? Chop into transmissions with your own shit?'

'Had. They confiscated it.'

'That why you here? Video graffiti?'

'I wish – then I'd be out in a couple months. No, man. Illegal augs.'

'Hey, man! Me too!'

'You?' Jerome couldn't conceal his surprise. You didn't see a lot of the brown brothers doing illegal augmentation. They generally didn't like people dicking with their brains.

'What, you think a guy from East LA can't use augmentation?'

'No, no. I know lots of Hispanic guys that use it,' Jerome lied.

'Ooooh, he says *Hispanic*, that gotta nice sound.' Overtones of danger.

Jerome hastily changed the direction of the conversation. 'You never been in the big lockups where they use paper jammies?'

'No, just the city jail once. They didn't have those fucking screw machines either. Hey, you Jerome, my name's Jessie. Actually it's Jesus – ' he pronounced it Hay-soo ' – but people they, you know . . . You got any smokes? No? Shit. Okay, I adjust.'

He sat on the edge of the bed, to one side of Jerome's dangling legs, and tilted his head forward. He reached under his hairnet, and under what turned out to be a hairplug, and pulled a chip from a jack unit set into the base of his skull.

Jerome stared. 'Goddamn, their probes really *are* busted.'

Jessie frowned over the chip. There was a little blood on it. The jack unit was leaking. Cheap installation. 'No, they ain't busted, there's a guy working the probe, he's paid off . . . letting everyone through for a couple of days 'cause some mob *vatos* are coming in and he don't know exactly which ones they are.'

'I thought sure they were going to find my unit,' Jerome said. 'The strip search didn't turn it but I figured the prison probes would and that'd be another year on my sentence. But they didn't.' Neither one of them thinking of throwing away the chips. It'd be like cutting out an eye.

'Same story here. We both lucky.'

Jessie put the microprocessing chip in his mouth, the way people did with their contact lenses, to clean it, lubricate it.

'Jack hurt?' Jerome asked.

Jessie took the chip out, looked at it a moment on his fingertip; it was smaller than a contact lens, a sliver of silicon and gallium arsenide with, probably, 1,500,000 nanotransistors of engineered protein molecules sunk into it, maybe more. 'No it don't hurt yet. But if it's leaking, it fuckin' *will* hurt, man.' He said something else in Spanish, shaking his head. He slipped it back into his jack-in unit, and tapped it with the thumbnail of his right hand. So that was where the activation mouse was: under the thumbnail. Jerome's was in a knuckle.

Jessie rocked slightly, just once, sitting up on his bunk, which meant the chip had engaged and he was getting a read-out. They tended to feed back into your nervous system a little at first, make you twitch once or twice; if they weren't properly insulated they could make you crap your pants.

'That's okay,' Jessie said, relaxing. 'That's better.' The chip inducing his brain to secrete some vasopressin, contract the veins, simulate the effect of nicotine. It worked for awhile, till you could get cigarettes. A high-grade chip could do some numbing, if you were hung up on *sim*, synthetic morphine, and couldn't score. But that was Big Scary. You could turn yourself off that way, permanently. You better be doing fine adjusting.

Jerome thought about the hypothetical chip scanners. Maybe he should object to the guy using his chip here. But what the Chicano was doing wouldn't make for much leakage.

'What you got?' Jerome asked.

'I got an Apple NanoMind II. Good megabytes. You?'

'You got the Mercedes, I got the Toyota. Usin' a *Sesó Picante* Mark I. One of those Argentine things.' (How had this guy scored an ANM II?)

'Yeah, what you got, they kinda *basto* but they do most what you need. Hey, your name's Jerome, mine's Jessie, they both start with J. And we both here for illegal augs. What else we got in common. What's your sign?'

'Uh – ' What was it anyway? He always forgot. 'Pisces.'

'No shit! I can relate to Pisces. I ran an astrology program, figures out who I should hang with, Pisces is okay. But Aquarius is – I'm a Scorpio, like – Aquarius, *qué bueno*.'

What did he mean exactly, *hang with*, Jerome wondered. Scoping me about am *I* a faggot, maybe that was something defensive.

But he meant something else. 'You know somethin', Jerome, you got your chip too, we could do a link and maybe get over on that trashcan.'

Break out? Jerome felt a chilled thrill go through him. 'Link with that thing? Control it. I don't think the two of us would be enough.'

'We need some more guys maybe, but I got news, Jerome, there's more comin'. Maybe their names all start with J.'

But they didn't. In quick succession, the trashcan brought them a fortyish beachbum named Eddie, a cadaverous black dude named Bones, a queen called Swish, whose real name, according to the trashcan, was Paul Torino.

'This place smells like it's comin' apart,' Eddie said. He had a surfer's greasy blond topknot and all the usual surf punk tattoos. Meaningless now, Jerome thought, the pollution-derived oxydation of the local offshore had pretty much ended ocean surfing. The anerobics had taken over the surf, thriving in the toxic waters like a gelatinous Sargasso. 'Smells in here like it died and didn't go to heaven. Stinks worse'n Malibu.'

'It's those landfill blocks,' Bones said. He was missing four front teeth (confiscated?) and his sunken face resembled something out of a zombie flick. But he was an energetic zombie. 'Compressed garbage,' he told Eddie. 'Organic stuff mixed with the polymers, the plastics, whatever was in the trash heap, make 'em into bricks 'cause they run outta landfill, but after a while, if the contractor didn't get 'em to set right, y'know, they start to rot. It's hot outside is why you're gettin' it now. Use garbage to cage garbage, they say. Fucking assholes.'

In the heat of the day the background smell of rancid garbage thickened. It turned Jerome's stomach more because of what it reminded him of than the actual smell. It made him think of garbage disposals, and Charlie Chesterton had once told him that prisons, in the year 2022, were the State's garbage disposal system . . . Get caught in the penal system and you could almost feel the dispose-all blades . . .

The trashcan pushed a rack of trays up to the plexiglass and *whirred* their lunch up to them, tray by tray. It gave them an extra one. It was screwing up.

They ate their chicken patties – the chicken was almost greaseless, gristleless, which meant it was vat chicken, genetically engineered stuff – and between bites they bitched about the food and indulged in the usual paranoid speculation about mind control chemicals in the coffee. Jerome looked around at the others, thinking: *At least they're not ass-kickers*. They were crammed here because of the illegal augs sweep, some political drive to clean up the clinics, maybe to see to it that the legal augmentation companies kept their pit-bull grip on the industry. So there wasn't anybody in for homicide, for gang torture, or anything. Not a bad cell to be in.

'You Jerome-X, really?' Swish fluted. A faint accent. She (Jerome always thought of a queen as *she* and *her*, out of respect for the tilt of her consciousness) was either Mexican or Filipino; hard to tell because she'd had her face 'girled' at a cheap clinic. Cheeks built up for a heart-shape, eyes rounded, lips filled out, glass tits looking like there was a couple of tinfunnels under her jammies. Some of the injected collagen in her lips had shifted so her lower lip was now lopsided. One cheekbone was a little higher than the other. A karmic revenge on malekind, Jerome thought, for forcing women into girdles and footbinding and anorexia. What did this creature use her chip for, besides getting high?

'Oooh, Jerome-X! I saw your tag before on the TV. The one when you kind of floated around the President's head and some printout words came out of your mouth and blocked her face out. God, she's such a *cunt*.'

'What words did he block her out with?' Eddie asked.

'"Would you know a liar if you heard one anymore?" That's what it was,' Swish said. 'It was *soo* perfect because that cunt wants another war, you *know* she does. And she lies about it, ooh *God* how she lies.'

'You just think she's a cunt because *you* want one,' Eddie said, dropping his pants to use the toilet. He talked loudly to cover up the noise of it. 'You want one and you can't afford it. I think the President's right, the fucking Mexican People's Republic is scummin' on our borders, sending commie agents in – '

Swish said, 'Oh God he's a Surf Nazi – but *God* yes I want one – I want *her* cunt. That prune doesn't know how to use it anyway. Honey, I know how *I'd* use that thing – ' Swish stopped abruptly and shivered, hugging

herself. With her long purple nails she reached up and
pried loose a flap of skin behind her ear and plucked out
her chip. She wet it, adjusted its feed-mode, put it back
in, tapping it with the activation mouse under a nail. She
pressed the flap shut. Her eyes glazed as she adjusted.
She could do that for maybe twenty-four hours and then
it'd ice her, sure. She'd have to go cold turkey or die. Or
get out. And maybe she'd been doing it for awhile now.

None of them would be allowed to post bail. They'd
each get the two years mandatory minimum sentence.
Illegal augs, the feds thought, were getting out of hand.
Black market chip implants were used for playing havoc
with the State database lottery; used by bookies of all
kinds; used to keep accounts where the IRS couldn't find
them; used to scam banking computers, and for spiking
cash machines; used to milk the body, prod the brain into
authorizing the secretion of beta-endorphins and ACTH
and adrenalin and testosterone and other biochemical
toys; used to figure the odds at casinos; used to compute
the specs for homemade designer drugs; used by the
mob's street dons to plot strategy and tactics; used by the
kid gangs for the same reasons; used for illegal congrega-
tions on the Plateau.

It was the Plateau, Jerome thought, that really scared
the shit out of the Feds. It had possibilities.

The trashcan dragged in a cot for the extra man, shoved
it folded under the door, and blared, 'Lights out, all
inmates are required to be i-i-in their bu-unks-s-s . . .' Its
voice was failing.

After the trashcan and the light had gone, they climbed
off their bunks and sat hunkered in a circle on the floor.

They were on chips, but not transmission-linked to one
another. Jacked-up on the chips, they communicated in a
spoken short-hand.

'Bull,' Bones was saying. 'Door.' He was a voice in the darkness.

'Time,' Jessie said.

'Compatibility? Know?' Eddie said.

Jerome said, 'No shit.' Snorts of laughter from the others.

'Link check,' Bones said.

'Models?' Jessie said.

Then they joined in an incantation of numbers.

It was a fifteen minute conversation in less than a minute.

'It's bullshit,' Bones was saying, translated. 'You get past the trashcan, there's human guards, you can't reprogram them.'

'But at certain hours,' Jessie told him, 'there's only one on duty. They're used to seeing the can bring people in and out. They won't question it till they try to confirm it. By then we'll be on their ass.'

'We might not be compatible,' Eddie pointed out. 'You understand, compatible?'

'Oh, hey man, I *think* we can comprehend that,' Jerome said, making the others snort with laughter. Eddie wasn't liked much.

Bones said, 'The only way to see if we're compatible is to do a systems link. We got the links, we got the thinks, like the man says. It's either the chain that holds us in or it's the chain that pulls us out.'

Jerome's scalp tightened. A systems link. A mini-Plateau. Sharing minds. Brutal intimacy. Maybe some fallout from the Plateau. He wasn't ready for it.

If it went sour he could get time tacked onto his sentence for attempted jailbreak. And somebody might get dusted. They might have to kill a human guard. Jerome had once punched a dealer in the nose, and the spurt of blood had made him sick. He couldn't kill

anyone. But . . . he had shit for alternatives. He knew he
wouldn't make it through two years anyway, when they
sent him up to the Big One. The Big One'd grind him up
for sure. They'd find his chip and it'd piss them off.
They'd let the bulls rape him and give him the New Virus;
he'd flip out from being locked in and chipless and they'd
put him in Aversion Rehab and burn him out totally.

Jerome savaged a thumbnail with his incisors. *Sent to the
Big One.* He'd been trying not to think about it. Making
himself take it one day at a time. But now he had to look
at the alternatives. His stomach twisted itself to punish
him for being so stupid. For getting into dealing augments
so he could finance a big transer. *Why?* A transer didn't
get him anything but his face pirated onto local TV for
maybe twenty seconds. He'd thrown himself away trying
to get it . . .

Why was it so fucking important? his stomach
demanded, wringing itself vindictively.

'Thing is,' Bones said, 'we could all be cruisin' into a
setup. Some kind of sting thing. Maybe it's a little too
weird how the police prober let us all through.'

(Someone listening would have heard him say, 'Sting,
funny luck.')

Jessie snorted. 'I tol' you, man. The prober is paid off.
They letting them all through because some of them are
mob. I know that, because I'm part of the thing. Okay?'

('Probe greased, fade me.')

'You with the mob?' Bones asked.

('You?')

'You got it. Just a dealer. But I know where half a
million newbux wortha the shit is, so they going to get me
out. The way the system is set up, the prober had to let
everyone through. His boss thinks we got our chips taken
out when they arraigned us, sometimes they do it that

way. This time it was supposed to be the jail surgeon.
Before they catch up with their own red tape we get outta
here. Now listen – we can't do the trashcan without we
all get into it, because we haven't got enough *K* otherwise. So who's in?'

He'd said, 'Low, half million, bluff surgeon, there here,
all-none, *who* yuh fucks?'

Something in his voice skittering behind smoked glass:
he was getting testy, irritable from the chip adjustments
for his nicotine habit, maybe other adjustments. The side
effects of liberal cerebral self-modulating burning through
a threadbare nervous system.

The rest of the meeting, translated . . .

'I dunno,' Eddie said. 'I thought I'd do my time 'cause
if it goes sour – '

'Hey man,' Jessie said, 'I can *take* your fuckin' chip.
And be out before they notice your ass don't move no
more.'

'The man's right,' Swish said. Her pain-suppression
system was unraveling, axon by axon, and she was
running out of adjust. 'Let's just do it, okay? Please?
Okay? I gotta get out. I feel like I wish I was dog shit so
I could be something better.'

'I can't handle two years in the Big, Eddie,' Jerome
heard himself say, realizing he was helping Jessie threaten
Eddie. Amazed at himself. Not his style.

'It's all of us or nobody, Eddie,' Bones said.

Eddie was quiet for a while.

Jerome had turned off his chip, because it was thinking
endlessly about Jessie's plan, and all it came up with was
an ugly model of the risks. You had to know when to go
with intuition.

Jerome was committed. And he was standing on the
brink of link. The time was now, starting with Jessie.

Jessie was the operator. He picked the order. First Eddie, to make sure about him. Then Jerome. Maybe because he had Jerome scoped for a refugee from the middle class, an anomaly here, and Jerome might try and raise the Man on his chip, cut a deal. Once they had him linked in, he was locked up.

After Jerome, it'd be Bones and then Swish.

They held hands, so that the link signal, transmitted from the chip using the electric field generated by the brain, would be carried with the optimum fidelity.

He heard them exchange frequency designates, numbers strung like beads in the darkness, and heard the hiss of suddenly indrawn breaths as Jessie and Eddie linked in. And he heard, 'Let's go, Jerome.'

Jerome's eyes had adjusted to the dark, the night giving up some of its buried light, and Jerome could just make out a crude outline of Jessie's features like a charcoal rubbing from an Aztec carving.

Jerome reached to the back of his own head, found the glue-tufted hairs that marked his flap, and pulled the skin away from the chip's jack unit. He tapped the chip. It didn't take. He tapped it again, and this time he felt the shift in his bio electricity; felt it hum between his teeth.

Jerome's chip communicating with his brain via an interface of rhodopsin protein; the ribosomes borrowing neurohumoral transmitters from the brain's blood supply, re-ordering the transmitters so that they carried a programmed pattern of ion releases for transmission across synaptic gaps to the brain's neuronal dendrites; the chip using magnetic resonance holography to collate with brain-stored memories and psychological trends. Declaiming to itself the mythology of the brain; re-enacting on its silicon stage the personal Legends of his subjective world history.

Jerome closed his eyes and looked into the back of his

eyelids. The digital read-out was printed in luminous green across the darkness. He focused on the cursor, concentrated so it moved up to ACCESS. He subverbalized, 'Open frequency.' The chip heard his practiced subverbalization, and numbers appeared on the back of his eyelids: 63391212.70. He read them out to the others and they picked up his frequency. Almost choking on the word, knowing what it would bring, he told the chip: 'Open.'

It opened to the link. He'd only done it once before. It was illegal and he was secretly glad it was illegal because it scared him. 'They're holding the Plateau back,' his brain-chip source had told him, 'because they're scared of what worldwide electronic telepathy might bring down on them. Like, everyone will collate information, use it to see through the bastards' game, throw the ass-bites out of office.'

Maybe that was one reason. It was something the power brokers couldn't control. But there were other reasons. Reasons like a strikingly legitimate fear of going batshit crazy.

All Jerome and the others wanted was a sharing of processing capabilities. Collaborative calculation. But the chips weren't designed to filter out the irrelevant input before it reached the user's cognition level. Before the chip had done its filtering the two poles of the link – Jerome and Jessie – would each see the swarming hive of the other's total consciousness. Would see the other as they perceived themselves to be, and then objectively, as they were.

He saw Jessie as a grid and as a holographic entity. He braced himself and the holograph came at him, an abstract tarantula of computer-generated color and line, scrambling down over him . . . and for an instant it crouched in the seat of his consciousness. Jessie. Jesus Chaco.

Jessie was a family man. He was a patriarch, a protector of his wife and six kids and his widowed sister's four kids and of the poor children of his barrio. He was a muddied painting of his father, who had fled the social forest fire of Mexico's communist revolution, spiriting his capital to Los Angeles where he'd sown it into the black market. Jessie's father had been killed defending territory from the mob; Jessie compromised with the mob to save his father's business, and loathed himself for it. Wanted to kill their *capos*; had instead to work side by side with them. Perceived his wife as a functional pet, an object of adoration who was the very apotheosis of her fixed role. To imagine her doing anything other than child-rearing and keeping house would be to imagine the sun become a snowball, the moon become a monkey.

And Jerome glimpsed Jessie's undersides: Jesus Chaco's self-image with its outsized penis and impossibly spreading shoulders, sitting in a perfect and shining cherry automobile, always the newest and most luxurious model, the automotive throne from which he surveyed his kingdom. Jerome saw guns emerging from the grill of the car to splash Jessie's enemies apart with his unceasing ammunition . . . It was a Robert Williams cartoon capering at the heart of Jessie's unconscious . . . Jessie saw himself as Jerome saw him; the electronic mirrors reflecting one another. Jessie cringed.

Jerome saw himself, then, reflected back from Jessie.

He saw Jerome-X on a video screen with lousy vertical hold; wobbling, trying to arrange its pixels firmly and losing them. A figure of mewling inconsequence; a brief flow of electrons that might diverge left or right like spray from a waterhose depressed with the thumb. Raised in a high-security condo village, protected by cameras and computer lines to private security thugs; raised in a media-windowed womb, with PCs and VCRs and thousand varieties of video game; shaped by cable-TV and fantasy rentals; sexuality distorted by sneaking looks at his parents' badly-hidden stash of Cassex videos. And always plugged into the Grid, the condo's satellite dish pulling in stations from around the nation, around the world, seeing the same StarFaces appear on channel after channel as the star's fame spread like a stain across the frequency bands. Seeing the Star's World Self crystallizing; the media figure coming into definition against the backdrop of media competition. Becoming real in this electronic collective unconscious.

Becoming real simply because he'd appeared on a few thousand TV screens. Growing up with a sense that media events were real, and personal events were not. Anything that didn't happen on television didn't happen. Even as he hated conventional programming, even as he regarded it as the cud of ruminants, still it defined his sense of personal unreality; and left him unfinished.

Jerome saw Jerome: perceiving himself unreal. Jerome: scamming a transer, creating a presence via video graffiti. Thinking he was doing it for reasons of radical statement. Seeing, now, that he was doing it to make himself feel substantial, to superimpose himself on the Media Grid . . .

And then Eddie's link was there, Eddie's computer model sliding down over Jerome like a mudslide. Eddie seeing himself as a Legendary Wanderer, a rebel, a homemade mystic; his fantasy parting to reveal an anal-expulsive sociopath; a whiner perpetually scanning for someone to blame for his sour luck.

Suddenly Bones tumbled into the link; a complex worldview that was a sort of streetside sociobiology, mitigated by a loyalty to friends, a mystical faith in brain-chips and amphetamines. His underside a masochistic dwarf, the troll of self-doubt, lacerating itself with guilt.

And then Swish, a woman with an unsightly growth, errant glands that were like tumors to her. Grown predatory for the means to dampen the pain of an infinite self-derision that mimicked her father's utter rejection of her. A mystical faith in synthetic morphine.

. . . Jerome mentally reeling with disorientation, seeing the others as a network of distorted self-images, caricatures of grotesque ambitions. Beyond them he glimpsed another realm through a break in the psychic clouds: the Plateau, the whispering plane of brain-chips linked on forbidden frequencies, an electronic haven for doing deals unseen by cops; a Plateau prowled only by the exquisitely ruthless; a vista of enormous challenges and inconceivable risks and always the potential for getting lost, for madness. A place roamed by the wolves of wetware.

There was a siren quiver from that place, a soundless howling, pulling at them . . . drawing them in . . .

'*Uh*-uh,' Bones said, maybe aloud or maybe through the chips. Translated from chip short-hand, those two syllables meant: 'Stay away from the Plateau, or we get sucked into it, we lose our focus. Concentrate on parallel processing function.'

Jerome looked behind his eyelids, sorted through the files. He moved the cursor down . . .

Suddenly it was there. The group-thinking capacity looming above them, a sentient skyscraper. A rush of megalomaniacal pleasure in identifying with it. A towering edifice of Mind. Five chips become One.

They were ready. Jessie transmitted the bait.

Alerted to an illegal use of implant-chips, the trashcan was squeaking down the hall, scanning to precisely locate the source. Stopping in front of their cell. Jessie reached through the bars and touched its input jack.

Midway through a turn the machine froze with a *clack*, humming as it processed what they fed it. Would it bite? Bones had a program for the IBM Cyberguard 14s, with all the protocol and a range of sample entry codes. Parallel processing from samples, it took them less than two seconds to decrypt the trashcan's access code. They were in. The hard part was reprogramming.

Jerome found the way. He told the trashcan that he wasn't Eric Wexler, because the DNA code was all wrong, if you looked close enough; what we have here is a case of mistaken identity.

Since this information, from the trashcan's viewpoint, was coming from authorized sources – the decrypted access code made them authorized – it fell for the gag and opened the cage.

The trashcan took the five Eric Wexlers down the hall – that was Jessie's doing, showing them how to make it think of five as one, something his people had learned for the Immigration computers. It escorted them through the plastiflex door, through the steel door, and into Receiving. The human guard was heaping sugar into his antique Ronald MacDonald coffee mug and watching *The Mutilated* on his wallet-TV. Bones and Jessie were in the room and moving in on him before he broke free of the television and went for the button. Bones's long left arm spiked out and his stiffened fingers hit a nerve cluster below the guy's left ear. The guard went down, the sugar dispenser in one hand swishing a white fan onto the floor.

Jerome's chip had cross-referenced Bones' attack style. *Commando training*, the chip said. *Military elite*. Was he a plant? Bones smiled at him and tilted his head, which Jerome's chip read as: *No. I'm trained by the Underground. Roots Radics*.

Jessie was at the console, deactivating the trashcan, killing the cameras, opening the outer doors. Jessie and Swish led the way out; Swish whining softly and biting her lip. There were two more guards at the gate, one of them asleep. Jessie had taken the gun from the screw Bones had put under, so the first guard at the gate was dead before he could hit an alarm. The cat-napping guy woke and yelled with hoarse terror, and then Jessie shot him in the throat.

Watching the guard fall, spinning, blood making its own slow-motion spiral in the air, Jerome felt sickness, fear, self disgust seeing this stranger die. The guard was young, wearing a cheap wedding ring, probably had a young family. So Jerome stepped over the dying man and made an adjustment; used his chip, chilled himself out with adrenalin. Had to. He was committed now. And he knew with a bland certainty that they had reached the Plateau after all.

He would stay on the Plateau. He belonged there, now that he was one of the wolves.